The Passion of
Mary–Margaret

Lisa Samson

THOMAS NELSON
Since 1798

NASHVILLE   DALLAS   MEXICO CITY   RIO DE JANEIRO   BEIJING

Published in Nashville, Tennessee, by Thomas Nelson. Thomas Nelson is a registered trademark of Thomas Nelson, Inc.

Thomas Nelson books may be purchased in bulk for educational, business, fund-raising, or sales promotional use. For information, please e-mail SpecialMarkets@ThomasNelson.com.

Scripture quotations are from the King James Version of the Bible.

Publisher's Note: This novel is a work of fiction. Names, characters, places, and incidents are either products of the author's imagination or used fictitiously. All characters are fictional, and any similarity to people living or dead is purely coincidental.

Library of Congress Cataloging-in-Publication Data

Samson, Lisa, 1964–
  The passion of Mary-Margaret / Lisa Samson.
    p. cm.
  ISBN 978-1-59554-211-3 (pbk.)
  I. Title.
  PS3569.A46673P37 2009
  813'.54—dc22   2008050890

Printed in the United States of America

09 10 11 12 RRD 6 5 4 3 2 1

For Deborah Leigh

With love and prayers and hope
as you enter this exciting new
stage of life. I'm so thrilled
to see the beautiful young woman
you've become.

I love you.
Aunt Bee

AUTHOR'S NOTES:

1. *The Passion of Mary-Margaret* is not a retelling of Hosea and was not written to be read as such.
2. The term *religious* is used in this work as a noun at times. A "religious" is a priest, a brother, a nun, or a religious sister who is bound by vows to an order or who has received the sacrament of Holy Orders.
3. A religious sister technically is not a nun. A nun is cloistered within the walls of a convent or monastery.

October 2000

Dear Angie,

All these years and it has come to this. You've outlived me. I knew it would happen and I knew you'd be the one to find this in my underwear drawer. Why Mary-Francis had to come up with the idea of writing down our lives for the benefit of those who'll follow us is understandable, but no less annoying. I think anonymity in serving God is crucial to the devout life, so I'm only going to let this be unearthed after my passing. However, I suppose Mary-Francis is right in the long run. We have a history here and it's part of the new sisters' story. We all belong to one another, but that doesn't mean they get to know everything about me while I'm still around. A girl has a right to keep some things to herself. But I do promise to tell this with as much love and grace as I can despite my attitude! (There's service in a nutshell for you.) So you can breathe a little easier, my friend.

I write for those who will follow us, so they'll know that sometimes God calls us to do things we may never understand, and that sometimes God calls us to do things we can grasp the reason of right away. Usually there's a little of both in the mix if you live long enough and develop the capability of recognizing the Divine fingerprint. Holy smudges abound indeed.

I've loved serving God with you. I am in good health as I write the following recollections at seventy years of age, and with Sister Pascal due to arrive in a few months, so young and full of the verve we could all use a little of these days, I thought maybe I should heed Mary-Francis's words. Perhaps we might impart a little of what we've learned even when we're gone. Although, indeed, I've never felt particularly wise, just willing. And even then, my brain sometimes protested like an argumentative Sophomore even though my body jumped in the car and took off. Jesus was always at the wheel, but he's not particularly cautious. In fact, he takes hairpin turns at seventy miles per hour if you want to know the truth of it. But as he is God, I've always figured he knows how to drive better than I do. Yes, I've left myself wide open for a smart-mouthed comment from you. Refrain yourself, missy. I'm not a slowpoke, I'm simply careful. And I'm not the one who had my license suspended when I was twenty, might I remind you. Oh, Angie, we've had fun, haven't we?

You've been my good friend, my companion, and my sister in the faith and in the Lord for so long. And we've eaten a lot of ice cream together too, made big messes in the kitchen, and laughed ourselves silly during the monologues on *The Tonight Show*. Selfishly, I hope you miss me. But you're not much younger than I am; I bet I'll be seeing you soon.

Love always,
Mary-Margaret Fischer, SSSM

P.S. You don't think this will offend anybody, do you? You'll notice I left out the time you, Jude, and I went down to Aruba. Nobody ever needs to know about that, I assure you!

This little collection of my scribblings is dedicated to the School Sisters
of St. Mary's who will follow me in this place. God be with you.
I'm praying for you and shall be until we meet face-to-face.

Mary-Margaret Fischer, SSSM,
Abbeyville, Locust Island, Maryland, October 2000

MY SISTERS, IF I BEGAN THIS TALE AT THE END, YOU WOULD know my heart is full of love even though nothing went as planned. I could tell you God's ways are not ours, but you probably know that already. And I could tell you that his mercy takes shape in forms we cannot begin to imagine, but unless you walked in my shoes for the past seventy years, you could not feel the mercy I have been given. The mercy God gives us is our own to receive, and while sometimes it overlaps with others' like the gentle waves of the bay on the banks of which I now sit, for the most part, the sum and substance of it, the combination of graces, is as unique as we are.

So I will begin this tale at the beginning, on the night my mother conceived me in a moment of evil, a moment not remotely in the will of God, although some might beg to differ on that particular point of theology. It's their right and I don't possess the doctrinal ardor to argue such things anymore. So be it. What you think or what I think on the matter doesn't necessarily make it true. God is as he is and our thoughts do not change him one way or the other. If you've an ounce of intellect, you'll take as much comfort in that as I do.

My mother, Mary Margaret the First, as my grandmother called her, began cradling my life inside of her when a young

seminarian took her against her will by the walls of Fort McHenry.
Most evenings after teaching second grade in South Baltimore,
she walked up Fort Avenue to the five-pointed star-shaped fort
from which the Battle of Baltimore was fought in 1814, rockets
red glare, bombs bursting in air, and so forth; and those British
frigates sailed up the Patapsco River with Francis Scott Key on
deck, penning what would become our national anthem.

The seminarian knew about what my Aunt Elfi called my
mother's "evening constitutional" and sometimes he would join
her in the gaslit, city twilight, hands clasped behind his back—at
least I picture him that way—bent a bit forward at the waist and
listening to her talk about her students perhaps, maybe the
other religious sisters, for she had just taken her final vows as a
School Sister of Notre Dame. Perhaps she talked about her
pupils' parents, or how she enjoyed listening to the radio shows
in the evenings in the cramped apartment she shared with her
friend, fellow sister, and coteacher Loreto; how their school
had been seeking ways to provide at least one good meal to the
children a day, considering how many of their parents were out
of a job after the crash on Wall Street.

I don't know what my father must have said in return, but
I've always wondered. She must have been caught by surprise,
surely, because Grandmom said my mother was sharp and quite
a good reader of people. He must have fooled her somehow.
Grandmom said he was the seminarian at nearby Holy Cross
Church. Perhaps he'd even heard her confessions. Not that
they'd have been shocking. Grandmom said my mother didn't
give her much trouble.

Perhaps as they walked, the sun slanted its rays against the
faces of the buildings, turning the stones and bricks from gold to
crimson, the sky blazing with magenta and violet as though sheer
scarves were waving behind the clouds. Maybe the cobalt night
soaked into their clothing during the chill months, deepening

the black of their coats, drawing the color out of their scarves and the character out of their features until they happened by a lamplight.

One evening something evil entered into him and he entered into her and I resulted. Did Grandmom tell me? If so, she certainly didn't employ that terminology. My age necessitated more delicate, obscure phrasing, perhaps something about the things only husbands and wives should do being forced on someone else. I can't recall exactly when I found out, but it feels like something I've always known and preternaturally understood. I might have overheard a conversation. I don't know. That my mother was a religious sister in an unwanted pregnancy threw fate completely out of balance. When I was thirteen, I figured I could put things aright somehow, maybe justify my existence by picking up the torch my own birth snuffed out.

It's bad enough to be born from the sin of two consenting adults. But I resulted from rage and control, from one person overpowering another in the assumption his right to take was more important than her right to give. That takes "man meaning it for evil but God meaning it for good" a giant step further. Yet blaming God for the lies of an Egyptian nobleman's wife who didn't succeed in getting Joseph to succumb to her hardly subtle sexual requests and that wine steward's selfish forgetfulness is somewhat different than giving him wholesale credit for rape. You have to draw the line somewhere or pretty soon Ted Bundy truly couldn't help himself and that terrorist they're talking about these days, Osama Bin Something or Other, really is on a holy mission, and who knows where that will end up? That sort of theology shouldn't sit well with anybody, whether you're from Geneva or Rome, so perhaps I have more doctrinal ardor than I realized ten minutes ago! Goodness me. I suppose I've grown slightly opinionated now that I've entered my eighth decade. So sisters, forgive an old woman a little rambling at times. Not that seventy is *that* old, mind you. Indeed not.

My mother came home to Locust Island to grow a healthy baby inside of her as she strolled by the shore and prayed in the chapel here at St. Mary's, feeling at home among the sisters. My grandmother's house was just down the street from the school. She prayed hours and hours on a kneeler, spending more time on her knees than at home. Aunt Elfi most likely joined her frequently because Aunt Elfi knew being present was the first way of helping anyone.

Grandmom said my mother would sit on Bethlehem Point every evening and stare out over the waters of the Chesapeake, her gaze pinned to the spider-legged lighthouse out on the shoals. And she'd cry. Grandmom didn't ask her to expound or emote. Grandmom was second-generation German. The chill had yet to dissipate completely.

I imagine Mary Margaret the First took hope in that whirling light of the lighthouse out on the shoals, as I always have. It makes me think that somehow there's somebody capable of warning you of danger, and if you find yourself in it, that person will climb into a lifeboat and come to get you. It's difficult to take your eyes off the piercing white beam when you sit here on a dark night.

We all want to be rescued and we'll look in the craziest places for that rescuer, won't we? We all want to be found.

Mary Margaret the First sat beneath the same tree under which I'm sitting now. It's one of the reasons I always end up here. The way the tangled roots protrude from the ground perfectly cradles my lawn chair, and on afternoons in late July or August, the canopy of leaves stifles some of the sun's heat. Only when my mother sat here, it was young, a tree with more hope than wisdom.

Conceived in sin, birthed in sorrow, I entered the world in

a flow of blood that failed to cease once I had been released into my grandmother's hands. After fifteen minutes or so, Grandmom knew the bleeding wouldn't stop on its own; my mother was dying. Aunt Elfi fetched Doctor Spanyer, who said with an aching stutter that by the time they'd deliver my mother to the h-h-hospital, having to procure a boat to the mainland and then ride two hours to Salisbury, she'd be d-d-dead. The poor doctor died a year later on the way to the very place my mother couldn't go, his wife refusing to believe he'd bleed out when his son Marlow ran over his foot with the lawn mower. He did. She moved away after the funeral.

The inhabitants of Locust Island formed a hardy, scrabbly sort of people back then because every person knew in their core that if something traumatic happened physically, the nearest hospital more than two hours away, there was nothing to be done but die. And if death was the only outcome, well, the sooner the better and heaven above let it be something massive and quick: a fall from a roof onto your head, a fatal heart attack or stroke, a smash on the skull with a sledgehammer. A lawn mower accident. Postpartum uterine hemorrhaging.

Aunt Elfi then slipped out into the rain and fetched Father Thomas, our parish priest. Tears in his eyes, for he was my mother's confessor, he anointed my mother's forehead, eyes, ears, nostrils, lips, hands, and feet and prayed the prayers of extreme unction, the first prayers my new ears ever heard. Aunt Elfi said he then picked me up and said, "The final puzzle piece in Mary Margaret's redemption."

I still don't know what that means. I can't say my life is completely explainable, that I don't have a lot of questions. God willing, the answers will be unearthed before I die.

My grandmother named me Mary-Margaret the moment my mother passed away. I've always liked the hyphen she gave, as if somehow it serves as a bridge between my mother and me, a gentle, silent "and so on and so forth." And it is my own hyphen.

Had my mother lived, I most likely would not be writing in this notebook. She planned on giving me up for adoption, wanting me to have both a mother and a father, and returning to her order, teaching, most likely farther away, leaving the entire ordeal behind her. And I wouldn't have blamed her. Of course Grandmom said she always planned to raise me there in the little apartment with one couch and too many straight chairs; that she would never have let me go to another family when ours was well and good and fully capable of raising a child. And I can only believe her as she never did pass me on to anybody else.

The main players in this morality tale have passed on: Jude, my mother, Grandmom and Aunt Elfi, Brister, Petra, Mr. Keller, and even LaBella. Except for John, Gerald, and Hattie, and myself. Actually, if you're reading this, *I* am dead too. I assume the raping seminarian passed away as well. I never knew what happened to him. Who among us would have the spirit to embark on such a search? I don't even know his name, if anyone discovered his crime, or if he slunk away into the arms of the Church.

And did he take refuge in the arms of Christ? Did he seek forgiveness? Did he, perhaps, turn into something more?

See? Questions. Never to be answered. Most likely I've waited too long. He'd be long in his grave by now. *I'm* old!

Well, my Aunt Elfi said my mother's soul passed into me as lightning trilled the air around us. Grandmom said she was crazy, we were all Catholic, we didn't believe in that sort of thing; surely the soul entered the baby well before she was born and would she please be quiet and help her wash her only daughter's body and clean up the blood?

The blood she gave for me. Yes, I'm painfully aware of the symbolism.

Aunt Elfi would have carefully rolled up her sleeves, donned an apron, and pulled back her long, white hair. She would have lovingly dabbed each rose-bloom of blood away, leaving a comet of iron-red across my mother's thighs as she wiped her clean. Aunt Elfi moved in a gentle, patting way, her voice never much above a whisper.

My mother, by the way, was the product of an indiscretion between my twenty-eight-yet-still-unmarried grandmother and an island tourist from Belgium. Though completely out of char-acter for my thick-jawed grandmother, even less understandable was that he found her horsey, Germanic face attractive. So sex seemed to be something unredeemed in and of itself in my family of females, but somehow taken up and looped around the fingers of the Almighty and put to rights in the aftermath.

Well, Aunt Elfi never misbehaved like her sister, but it only took one look at her to realize someone scrambled her brain with a fork before it was fully cooked.

Later on that September afternoon in 1930, the sky clear and the orange sun gilding the fallen rain, men and women walked home from the dock, from their fishing boats or the sea-food cannery at the western edge of our island. Cans and cans of oysters were shipped out from Locust Island every day. Abbey Oysters. The company used a monk as the logo even though many of the islanders were Methodists. As you can imagine, Friday was the best day for sales, a fact that did not escape even the most Methodist of Methodists. Sometimes I walked by the cement block building and looked through the grimy window, watching as the shuckers' hands darted like minnows extracting the smooth, precious meat from the rough, prehistoric exterior. Rounding the corner, the pile of shells grew with each day, only to be carted away and ground into lime.

Those men and women passed by, oblivious to the tragedy as they scuffled down Main Street in front of our building.

They didn't know the bell from St. Mary's Convent School that called the girls to dinner served as a death knell for Sister Mary Margaret Fischer as well as a ringing in of a new life, proof, some wise person once said, that God desires the human race to continue. They figured another day had passed, much like the one before and the one before that, back to the day one of their parents or siblings or children passed away or someone was born into this world. We always remember days when something begins or ends.

And as those two women washed the bloody legs and the pale, fragile arms of my mother—pictures of her display lovely, wavy, dark hair and dark eyes—I lay bundled on the bed, looking up at the ceiling. That's what Aunt Elfi told me. I didn't cry until Father Thomas returned to comfort us in our sorrow and he gathered me into his fragile arms, crying with me. He was a tender sort until the day he passed away.

I was two days old when Father Thomas, the older members of our parish, and our family, consisting of my grandmother, my aunt, and myself, committed my mother to the earth at St. Francis Church's graveyard. Afterward, they walked right inside the church, stood by the simple, stone baptismal font, and I was baptized in the name of the Father and the Son and the Holy Spirit. Sister Thaddeus, whom I'll tell you more about later, an older schoolgirl at the time, said she watched from the shadows, listening to the Holy Spirit telling her to pray for me every day. And she did.

Afterward, Aunt Elfi brought me to Bethlehem Point, this very piece of land on which I now sit, beneath the same tree, and she held me as the sun went down for good over my mother. She walked back home with me in her arms, fed me a bottle, and laid me in my bassinette, where I slept through the night. Exhausted, they both deserved that little ray of grace. I never gave them any trouble either.

So, my sisters, I figure I'll tell you what's going on these days while I jot down this little history, that way if something of note happens to me, this is all recorded and I won't have to scrape my brain to locate the information. I can tell you what happened forty years ago with little problem, but last week sits somewhere between the equation for finding the angles of an isosceles triangle and the name of the main character in *Breakfast at Tiffany's*. Am I killing two birds with one stone or robbing Peter to pay Paul by doing it this way? Feel free to be the judge of that.

Earlier today Sister Angie (given name Angelica) opened a blue and green webbed folding chair and set it beside mine. We've been together a long time. My mother's sugar maple tree blared that beautiful orange-red. Sugar maples get a bit braggy in the fall.

"What's in your lap?" She pointed to this notebook open to the passage you just read, my pen resting in the fold.

"Just writing down some memories."

She sat in her chair, stretched her legs straight out in front of her, and folded her hands atop her tummy. "Mary-Francis is on my case too. I need to get moving, I guess."

I agreed. During Angie's years as a school sister, she was

surrounded by a pack of wild dogs in a remote school in Alaska, was chased by revolutionaries in South America, and picnicked in France with rich schoolgirls. Angie was even arrested down at the School of the Americas, but that has nothing to do with our order. She's just an upstart when she finds the time. She taught in eight different schools and we ended up back here together at St. Mary's. She lived the life I thought I was going to. (Right, Angie? Yes, I can see you rolling your eyes.)

She adjusted the back of her chair, setting the teeth of the arms to recline a little. "I went to see Gerald and Hattie a few minutes ago," she said.

"How's Gerald doing?" I snapped shut this notebook and slid it into my tote bag.

"Not well. Hattie's so upset about his condition they had to give her a light sedative. But she told me that Gerald had something to tell you and to get on over there." Angie leaned forward and whispered, though no one else was around. "She said you wouldn't like it in the long run. She said it was about your mother when push came to shove."

My mother?

I stared at the old lighthouse out in the bay off the southern point of the island. Hattie and Gerald lived there for years, the last lightkeepers on the Chesapeake Bay. If you are reading this, I hope you've come, or will come, to love these waters as much as I always have. They are like a mother to me, the home to which I've always returned eventually. Jude would have gone crazy out on the waters had he lived there all those years like his older brother, Gerald; this island made him crazy enough.

Oh and by the way, this is Jude's story as well. You cannot hear mine without hearing his.

The light circled around inside the plastic lens. The great Fresnel lens, an artistic, graceful beehive of beveled glass, was smashed years earlier by a baseball bat held in Jude's hands.

Jude's soul frothed and foamed, stirred by an anger that began fermenting well before the day his mother left the light and took him with her. But I don't want to get ahead of myself. Jude and I had mother issues in common, indeed. Most likely, it drew us together. Unfortunately, back then, Jude was wont to concentrate on the mercies he thought he was *denied*.

"Poor Gerald. The last of the Keller men." I waved to Glen Keesey sailing by in his Sunfish. Glen waved back and held up his book, my copy of *Bluebeard*. Between March and November, Glen sails out to Hathaway Island, a small, uninhabited, marshy speck half a mile east of the light, so he can sunbathe in the buff. He joins us for a glass of wine every once in a while too, while we watch the sunset.

"Yep. All gone but Gerald." Angie nodded, removing a barrette from her hair and replacing it, retightening the entire arrangement. Her knuckles have become knobby, but she always keeps her nails so nice. She's prissy. Tough, but prissy. I've rarely seen her without some makeup, and her shoes, while comfortable, are never ever called sensible. "It's the end of an era, Mary."

The sisters all call me Mary. Mary-Margaret's a mouthful.

She looked upon the lighthouse too, a structure that seemed somehow less for all the automation going on inside. Aunt Elfi used to say that people dignify most structures, enliven them. Without us, what is the need? If you think I'm wrong, just imagine nobody ever going up and down the Eiffel Tower again. And why do ruins make us yearn to go live there?

I pointed to the lighthouse. "Mr. Keller saved many a life. Hard to believe the place is empty."

She harrumphed. "I'm sure the ghost of Mr. Keller got back there somehow. I think that lighthouse was the only thing he ever really loved."

Angie and I differ on what Mr. Keller should have done

when his wife, Jude's mother, contracted cabin fever. I say he couldn't have possibly known what was going on. She says any man worth his salt should have figured all was not right, that he had to have known somewhere deep in his soul something was horribly wrong with his wife.

"I'll see to Hattie." I stood and lifted the straps of my canvas tote up onto my shoulder, trying to shove those heavy thoughts aside.

"It would be a good idea. She needs you."

So I gathered my chair and traipsed through the tall brown grasses of early October toward St. Mary's Village Assisted Living. After Grandmom died of a heart attack, I went to live there at the age of eight. It was a convent school back then; Aunt Elfi moved to a monastery in Tibet hoping they'd be more amenable to her odd religious juxtapositions, hoping to find something resembling Shangri La, which she never stopped talking about after reading *Lost Horizon*. Although I knew how much she loved me, this didn't come as a surprise to me. Even I knew my grandmother cared for Aunt Elfi every bit as much as she cared for me.

I passed the entrance of the old drugstore—now a gamer café—where I first spent time with Jude, and I looked back at Bethlehem Point Light and, because I believed it only fitting and proper, prayed for those who once lived inside its walls.

It's late now and time for sleep.

IT'S EARLY MORNING AND I CAN'T SLEEP. MAYBE I DIDN'T want to start writing something like this because I know how much space it will take up in my mind.

So, sisters, let me tell you about where you've found yourself if you don't already know. Locust Island was put on the map by Captain John Smith back around 1608 when he explored the Chesapeake Bay. Its shape bears resemblance more to a chicken than a locust; however, when he happened upon it, a great population of insects inhabited the place. Maybe not much more than now, I don't know, but I'd wager to say even more waterfowl—diving ducks, dabbling ducks, geese, and swans—made their home here than we have today, what with the hotshots from DC buying up waterfront land for vacation homes so large you could house a whole plane full of refugees inside. One of them is bright turquoise! With yellow shutters. We are not in the Caribbean, might I remind them.

We're north of Tangier, the island where some folks still speak with an Elizabethan accent. I doubt the young people do now, what with television and videos. I've noticed a lot of the younger set have what Angie calls "the sitcom accent," slightly Valley Girl and mildly prepubescent, everything sounding like a question.

The town of Abbeyville, Maryland, was founded in the mid-
1600s by a relative of George Calvert, who received a Royal
Charter for Maryland from Charles the First. That relative was
a Benedictine abbot named Father Jerome Calvert, who founded
a monastery upon his arrival from Ireland, although he was
born an Englishman. Other settlers quickly followed and the
town was named Carringtown for reasons I don't know, but
Abbeyville, the nickname, ended up taking over sometime in
the early 1700s. After a century and a quarter, the monastery
followed the path of all earthly things and only two monks
remained and, rumor has it, they couldn't abide one another.
The legend goes that Brother Paul dug a pit and lived his life as
a hermit until the Carmelite nuns took over for another one
hundred and some odd years. They, too, went the way of the
Benedictines, only without digging themselves into pits or
becoming overly crotchety, and in 1887, the School Sisters of
St. Mary's took over and began St. Mary's Convent School for
Girls. The town had exploded during the oyster wars and the
sisters devoted themselves to educating children of watermen,
seafood canners, and the few farmers whose families had been
here for a couple of hundred years. The occasional child from
Baltimore City or Dover, Delaware, whose parents needed to
dispose safely of their child for reasons good and bad, sometimes spent their childhood days with the sisters as well.

During my nine years there, this happened to be Sister
Angie, my best friend. Her mother and father traveled in a
vaudeville show and sent her the most delightful cards and let-
ters from the road.

She's now threatening to write down her memories, but I'll
believe that when I see it. She was a science teacher. And by the
way, I taught art and English. I taught English so I could teach
art. I believe it's akin to having the football coach teach history.

A ferry service to the mainland began around 1900 or

thereabouts and the first car came onto the island in 1925. People still rarely use cars around the place; the island is only about a thousand acres. But some folk have them for traveling up to Salisbury to shop for items unavailable here. We sisters have a little white Honda Civic.

When I moved over to St. Mary's after Grandmom died, our dormitory window afforded me a view of the screwpile lighthouse, built in 1862. Its iron legs reached down into the muddy bottom of the bay, screws eleven feet long at their ends, holding up the white, octagonal house with four dormered windows on its second floor. Standing out in the water like the guardian it was, it really only needed giant arms crossed defiantly over its midsection to complete the picture.

Here is a picture from the old days. The shutters were crimson when I was a child, but Hattie painted them dark blue when she moved out there after she married Gerald. I believe this is from the late 1800s. The large rocks were dumped on either side to break up ice floes so they didn't damage the pilings. Can you see the little boat hung up on davits to the left there? Gerald used to hang his boat like that too. There was also a pulley system by which they'd raise heavier objects up into the house. Hattie bought a new refrigerator in 1965 and that turned out to be quite the job getting it up to her kitchen. But they did it. Nobody dared risk the wrath of Hattie Keller, let me tell you.

As Sister Mary-Francis always says, "What a broad!" And she's spot-on. Sister Mary-Francis has lived with Angie and me for ten years now.

I used to imagine what it must be like to live there, surrounded by the gray waters of the Chesapeake, standing on the decking that encircled the house. Did Jude look back to Bethlehem Point just west of our school and see me standing there upon the shore, a little dot of girl gazing over the waters? A little girl under a tree.

I first noticed Jude as he rowed out on the bay, his oars slicing through the water with smooth precision. He rowed almost every day, I'll warrant.

Jude Keller and his parents boated over to our town twice a month. The first time I ever saw him up close, around eight-thirty on a Sunday morning in May, Mass at St. Francis's had just ended. We proceeded out of the church in a double line, wearing our light blue Sunday dresses. The seniors, their majestic forms, tall and strung like a stretched rubber band from skull to spine, led the rest of us; the kindergarteners jumped along like grasshoppers at the end of the line. I was a fourth grader by that time.

Jude sat on the steps of the drugstore. Above his head, a calendar hung on the door, its picture displaying the Sacred Heart of Jesus, the swollen, robust heart crowned in glorious flames of passion for souls and wreathed with thorns that tell us he still feels our infirmities, and he does, sisters, he does.

But Jude wasn't much fond of religion. Not remotely. A picture like that would have been spooky to Jude, as it is to many others who don't know the story behind it. Many was the time he told me he thought us all a bunch of superstitious folk who believed in a lot of hokum. He believed in pleasure, plain and simple, and God, as far as he could tell, wanted people to feel nothing of the sort.

"Do you believe in God, though?" I asked him.

"Of course. You live in a house surrounded by water with storms and birds and all, you know there's some kinda power nobody can really explain away no matter how hard they try. I just think God likes that power a little too much." He told me that when I was fifteen and I had nothing to say in return. How does an innocent girl tell an already experienced boy that she was completely in love with Christ, the Son of the God Jude bristled against?

Even now it sounds a little odd, but there it sits. Hopefully, you who read this, having given your entire lives singularly to his service, feel the same. It does make it a bit easier in the long run, although there are plenty of other challenges to take its place.

And naturally, at that age, I wasn't able to talk about how God uses his power for love and goodness and for our benefit because, unfortunately, I've never been quick at defending my beliefs. Ten minutes after the conversation ends, oh yes, my goodness, I've got all the right answers. It's God's way of keeping me from being a real boob, I guess.

After calling me superstitious, he would proceed to remind me of the Crusades, the Spanish Inquisition, Bloody Mary, and, because he was smarter than he pretended and snuck over to the library when nobody was looking, every single pope who committed homosexual acts, had sexual relations of the hetero-sexual variety, sired children, or was otherwise a scoundrel. Don't even get started on the alcoholics.

Oh yes. If you find yourself in the Church, you find your-self with some of the *worst*. But thankfully, God calls sinners, not the righteous, and our tradition is chocked full of the former, as any parish priest could tell you.

From his perch on the step where Jude sat, his one leg fol-lowing the contour of the stairs, the other raised up next to him, bent knee providing a rest for his thin but muscled arm, he whistled at us—a juicy, leering sort of whistle that lifted up our skirts like an unwelcome wind off the bay, demanding a peek. He would have seen the standard issue white underpants we all wore in compliance with our uniform policy, which was as stiff as our dresses, but that wasn't the point. Even as a fourth grader I felt besmirched and yet a little bit excited at the same time.

I asked Sister Thaddeus about it that night as I handed her the mugs she lined up on a shelf in the kitchen. "Is that really the way it works?"

Sister Thaddeus, I figured, had her share of catcalls. "Yes. It is. For those of us mortals who feel those sorts of things." She wiped a brown curl away from her forehead. She tried not to be alluring, the Lord knows she tried, but even her habit did little to detract from her beauty and her curvaceous figure. We all felt sorry for her.

"Why is it like that?"

"Most of us are made to have babies. Boys like Jude realize that a little sooner than they're supposed to." She climbed down from the stepstool, holding up her light-gray habit to reveal, not surprisingly, a well-carved ankle, the beauty of which her black brogan failed to diminish. "Not that it's a big surprise in his case," she mumbled. Sister Thaddeus always mumbled her opinions, leaving it up to you if you wanted further clarification. I always did.

"What do you mean?"

She passed me a floor duster, its long handle smooth against my palm. I loved running it along the floor of the dining room, the great loopy strings snatching up crumbs and lint. Shaking it out over the lawn was even better, unless the wind blew right at you. "If he'd stayed at the lighthouse with his father, his life would be different. But"—she waved her hand—"but he's started living with his mother and that *oysterman*."

As if that said it all. And what it said, I had no idea. Nine-year-olds, unless you were Jude Keller, didn't know such things, not like children these days. But I realized it meant something regarding women and something regarding nice and something regarding how those two words never mixed together in the oysterman's abode, a little yellow-brick bungalow on the edge of town near the processing plant. I figured I'd know more of the details someday. Not that I didn't already have my share of maturation by then. It was just in other areas. I'd already learned about rape, being illegitimate, losing your mother and all the relatives that you've ever known and loved. But, sisters, I'd also talked with Christ face-to-face. Not that anybody knew. In fact, this is the first time I've written about it and I've *never* told a soul. Not even my dear friend Angie. Do forgive me, friend, as you read this. Some things you choose not to tell even your best friend.

~~~

From this point onward you will have to suspend your disbelief or do an in-depth study of Christian mystics who enjoyed an unusual relationship with Christ, and even then, the accounts I've read were nothing like my own. The mystics receive a great deal of flack from some of my protestant brothers and sisters who claim demons are responsible for their peeks into heaven, as if heaven is out beyond the stretches of our universe and the two plains never meet. Let's just say I disagree and leave it at that. Although the mystics' individual stories vary, this can be said of each one: they gave up everything for the Lord.

Most did this by choice, and that is why they are saints. Some, well, dare I say it? Oh, I'll go ahead; most likely I'm already dead anyway. Some seemed a bit mentally troubled. But God even meets his children there, doesn't he? How can he help himself? Doesn't love go to the end of the universe and back?

I am no saint. You'll read no story detailing holy anorexia or invisible wedding rings and stigmata. No self-inflicted wounds of penance and thankfully all that cutting and burning went out of fashion many, many years ago. Thankfully, we don't have to understand the saints to feel affection and gratitude for them. They preserved the faith we now know. They didn't drop the ball, so to speak. I do hope the generations ahead of us will at least recognize us for carrying on however much they might come to disagree with the way we did things. But perhaps they won't. Who can tell these things?

I was invited into this realm of the hidden holy and as I saw it, at the age of seven, I could either embrace it tenderly or kick it away like Jude's stepfather would kick their dog. I wish I was kidding or at the very least being cliché. The man actually and frequently kicked Spark, a mix of cocker spaniel and golden retriever who went rowing with Jude. The way his jowls would flap in the air like bunting still makes me laugh.

I chose to embrace the spiritual because already, by that age, I knew I needed something more. More than coming home to an empty apartment after school. More than my tired grandmother and my tired aunt who came home after shucking oysters or picking crabs all day at the cannery. More than shoes that pinched my feet. It seemed like less effort for me to bring God into the pitiful circumstances of my life than to demand a fancy, all-encompassing do-over. I thought perhaps that might be too hard for God. I confess, sometimes I still think some things are too hard for God. I mean, deep down I think that. But thankfully there's an even deeper down. Unfortunately, crawling down into *that* well hurts like the devil because we know God can do something and yet doesn't, and we don't have many choices after that realization, and none of them are one hundred percent easy breezy.

So. Talking to Christ face-to-face.

On Ash Wednesday, 1937, I walked over to St. Francis's for the seven p.m. Mass. I didn't have to go, we'd already been to Mass at school, and it wasn't a holy day of obligation. By that age, however, I'd already decided Lent was for me. My life was dark from the moment of my conception; why not take forty days to celebrate the fact? If I needed to do no real penance at that age, perhaps I could do so for my father, the raping seminarian, who surely must have ruined his life that evening by Fort McHenry.

I didn't voice these thoughts back then, but have merely put them together as I've aged, trying to figure out why Jesus came that night amid the ashes. I wasn't particularly sad or lonely as I sat in the sanctuary and heard I was made of dust and would return to the same. I pictured red blood turning to sand and grinding to a halt inside the tunnels of my veins.

We all come face-to-face with our mortality for the first time, and Ash Wednesday, 1937, was my scheduled appointment. Yes I was young, but I was steeped in death, formed in the womb of a dead woman.

I wanted to give up something for Lent but just couldn't come up with a firm idea. Sitting there on the wooden pew, weighted feet dangling downward from my bent knees, I thought about my favorite things. Candy, ice cream, toys, what most seven-year-olds would enjoy, weren't a regular part of my life anyway as my grandmother didn't have the money for the typical things from which a child might abstain. So giving them up would be silly, akin to giving up tiaras or rides on parade floats. Playing at the playground or running around with the other kids wasn't a good choice either. I had trouble in school, especially math. Each night I sat at the kitchen table, trying to figure out the problems in front of me, thankful for crazy Aunt Elfi who never minded going over and over my assignment. I didn't have time for much play, but Aunt Elfi was fun to be around, the way she'd make pudding at eight p.m. and let me eat half the bowl, or how she could snip out the most fanciful animals, flowers, and trees from a simple sheet of paper. Nobody had TV then and nobody ever went out to eat. I didn't drink coffee or beer or smoke cigarettes.

But I loved Jesus.

If you grasp nothing more about me, sisters, grasp this: I loved Jesus. I'm not embarrassed to admit it. If it makes me corny and predictable, I don't care. He alone, of all those who walk the earth, was my mother, my father, my husband, my comforter, my good and honest friend.

"But how can I give you up?" I whispered in my heart, feeling the sadness of a child who was supposed to get a bicycle and ended up with a pack of crayons.

Father Thomas, a younger man with the face of an angel and a puff of prematurely white hair, traced the ashy black cross on my forehead and said, "From dust you came and to dust you shall return." Then he reached forward, laid his fine, white hand atop my head, leaned toward me, and whispered in my ear, "May Almighty God bless you with all the gifts of the Holy Spirit, Mary-Margaret."

I looked up into his eyes and I saw love. Not just the love of Father Thomas, but the love of Jesus our Lord. Father Thomas faded away, the people faded away, the wooden pews, the stone walls and aisle, the glowing candles, and even the carved altar faded away, and I saw only those eyes, once blue, now a Jerusalem brown, and a voice said, "Do not give me up, Mary-Margaret. You are my daughter and I will always take care of you. You are my bride and I will always love you and keep you close to my heart. You are my friend and I will always walk beside you. I am yours."

I blinked and Father Thomas just smiled, removed his hand, and went on to the next parishioner. That moment shone like the North Star. My mother couldn't finish her calling, and Jesus made me his bride. There could be only one vocation. When a religious takes her final vow, she dons a wedding band, signifying that she is now married to Christ. That moment, when the cool gold would slide onto my finger, became what I looked forward to every day. As so many little girls look forward to becoming a wife and a mommy someday, I dreamed about becoming a religious sister. I decided that Ash Wednesday, alone in my bed, it was the only life for me.

If I tell you I had dark nights of the soul, it would be a lie. For most people, Jesus hides himself at times, like a lover who has been scorned just a touch and must remind his love what she has. But there was never any of that for me. He was true to his word, always taking care of this spindly, redheaded orphan, always keeping me close to his heart. I felt it beating every waking moment.

Not that he didn't ask anything of me. Oh no. There's where my walk with Jesus became an uphill climb.

YESTERDAY AFTER SUPPER, SISTER ANGIE AND I SAT BESIDE Hattie and Gerald's beds. St. Mary's Village provides everything from self-sufficient apartments to hospice. I hear that's big business these days what with the baby boomers nearing retirement age. As I said, it used to be the convent school, but enrollment kept dropping, so the order rents the facility to a company that runs such ventures. We're here to minister to them as chaplains, social workers, and "cruise directors." I conduct the arts and crafts classes. Angie advocates for patients' health care with Sister Mary-Francis who is actually a licensed social worker, and Sister Blanca serves as chaplain, spiritual director, and general person of prayer and supplication. In an official capacity, of course. We all do what we can on those fronts. Sometimes our duties mix and match.

Hattie and Gerald's room used to be the northern half of the science lab, which explains why Angie finds herself there so much. It was her old classroom.

I held Gerald's hand; she held Hattie's. The Mother Superior at school told us once that becoming a religious kept a woman from aging in the way married women do. And she raised one of her fine, winged eyebrows at us.

We laughed about it then, but I looked upon the hand of

Hattie tucked into Angie's and instead of the five years' difference by the calendar, there were at least fifteen by the scan of the
eye.

Much the same with Gerald and myself. Gerald, if you will
remember, was the last lightkeeper and Jude's eldest brother—
twelve years his senior. I squeezed his hands, compressing a few
of the brown age spots into a squiggled line along the tendons
stretched down the back of his slender, yellow-skinned hand.
Gerald was a ladies' man like his brother. But he took one look
at Hattie the day he returned from Japan to the island and every
other woman on earth might as well have either gotten married
or died.

"Gerald," I whispered. "Gerald?"

He opened eyes floating in puddles of sickness. I saw those
eyes, exactly the same, decades before, sitting in the eye sockets
of my grandmother. "Mary-Margaret."

"How do you feel?"

His smile bared false teeth hanging a bit low. His words
clicked a little. "Like trash."

"You don't have to wear those teeth now."

"Like heck I don't."

Well, perhaps a little of the Keller vanity remained. Both of
those boys should have been on the silver screen judging by
looks alone.

This spotty man with thinned hair scraped like silken floss
over his skull had once dated three women at the same time:
Miss Friday Night, Miss Saturday Night, and Miss Sunday Night.
And there he lay on his bed. Reduced. Spine curled at the top
like a fiddlehead.

"Good for you."

"My Hattie asleep?"

"Yes."

"Those drugs'll do that for you."

I laughed.

Jesus sat on the bed beside us. "Hattie will go first," he whispered. "Don't tell."

All right. That's a surprise.

"So what will you do when you come around, Gerald? Go on a safari? See the North Pole?"

"Oh no! Nothing wild or cold. I'd like to row over to the lighthouse once more, though."

"I'll take you."

Will you just let him go to the lighthouse one more time? I asked Jesus. *I'd like to go back myself.*

"Oh!" Hattie cried out in her drug-induced sleep.

I looked over at Jesus as he said, "In fact, Mary-Margaret, you will go before Gerald does too."

Soon?

"Let's just say, in the proper time. You're going to love what I've done with the place."

And I can't wait to go.

My heart was full of love and when he slipped away, the smell of lilies remained.

Gerald fell asleep, his dental plate slipping down and resting against his bottom teeth. A light snore trembled his lips.

I patted Angie's leg. "I've got a pottery class to teach in an hour."

"You go on, Mary-Margaret. I'll sit here with them. By the way, you got a letter from John in the mail this morning."

Hattie, who was once what Aunt Elfi called "a heroic figure of a woman," lay flat on the bed, her body deflating a little more each day. She will soon become even with the bed, only her small, shiny red face above the covers, its skin smooth by the weight of the excess flesh drooping beneath her jawline. Her hair, still the shocking red that Angie applied only three days ago as they laughed like schoolgirls, now fanned out against her pillow like a bloodstain. I leaned down and kissed her cheek with its liberal application of rouge. Oh Hattie. Good for you.

After peeking into several rooms down the hallway and saying hello or hearing a soft snore, I headed over to our cottage on the grounds and climbed the steps to my bedroom. And while it's true I can talk to Christ anywhere, that I see him in the eyes of each one he's given me to teach and to love, I love meeting him and the rest of the Godhead right here in my room. I lit some candles, knelt on the kneeler I fashioned out of driftwood, lifted up my rosary and my eyes toward the crucifix, and I pictured Hattie and Gerald and all those I looked in on, as well as the girls in our school who suffer with wounds nobody can see, and began to pray for divine mercy.

For the sake of his sorrowful passion, have mercy on us and on the whole world.

Jesus never met me at my private altar like he did elsewhere. There I was level with the rest of Christendom. And though for whatever reason he chose to accompany me to the nursing home, to the places where the sick reside—the lonely, the dying—at my altar it was different. And it is here I will die. I know this because I asked him if he would take me at this very spot. He said that would be fine.

I want to be on my knees when I die, I requested later when I sat in the dimness of Hattie and Gerald's room.

"Then that's where you shall be."

Lord have mercy.
Christ have mercy.
Lord have mercy.

THE DAY I FIRST ACTUALLY MET JUDE I WAS NINE; HE WAS eleven. Of course I'd watched him row on the bay for a couple of years by then, or stared at his kites when he flew them from the decking of the lighthouse. He could make them do such tricks, loops and dives and corkscrews! He'd come off the lighthouse for good by then, living with his mother, Petra, and his step-father, Brister Purnell, the infamous oysterman Sister Thaddeus clearly disapproved of.

Jude was the most beautiful human being I'd ever seen other than Sister Thaddeus. Because I began my life in ugliness, beauty speaks to me, and so Jude, as he stood there by our schoolyard, legs apart, arms crossed over his chest, drew me to him. His ivory skin had been tanned by hours in the sun that summer, the last summer he'd scramble around the decking of the lighthouse, his clear aquamarine eyes scanning the horizon. The sun had streaked his light brown curls with a generous brush. His muscles, already developed into sleek lines from all the rowing and swimming he did out in the bay, glistened with perspiration that only highlighted him like armor of light. He drew me to him, not as a lover is drawn, but as a rose bids the painter come closer. Beware the thorns, I must add. For if out-wardly Jude grew more beautiful as he approached manhood, inwardly, briars poked at the invisible flesh of his soul, shredding it, mangling it, and rearranging it. Satan likes doing it like that, leaving just enough there to fool you things are still the same, when in point of fact, nothing's like before. Well, almost nothing. He cannot take away the stamp of God's image. I don't know if God himself can even do that, or why he'd even want to if he could.

Jude's stance sizzled with challenge that morning as, finished with my kitchen chores, I hurried to my room to fetch my schoolbooks.

I walked over to him, flipping my red braid behind me, my heart feeling as if it were rolling around in my chest, throwing itself against the front of my rib cage.

"It's just as pretty up close," he said.

"What?" Not what I expected.

"Your hair. I seen it from the platform out at the light. You the girl that goes walking sometimes, right?"

I nodded.

"So it's pretty. You all need to not wear them stupid hats to church so I could see it better."

"Thanks. I like your kites that you fly."

"I make 'em."

"I've never flown a kite before."

"It's easy. What's your name?"

"Mary-Margaret."

"Two names in one."

"Uh-huh."

"Mine's Jude."

"I know."

He squinted. "How do you know that?"

"Sister Thaddeus. She says you don't live at the lighthouse anymore and that you have an older brother who went off to fight in the war."

He placed his hands on the fencing. "I'm the youngest."

"I'm an only child."

"So . . . you're the youngest too."

I nodded. "Did you go to the Labor Day parade yesterday?"

"Nah. Brister says who needs stuff like that. We sat around by the water and drank beer."

Oh. At his age?

"You row a lot. How come?"

He shrugged. "Can I come into the yard?"

"Nope. No boys allowed. At least that's what I think's the rule."

"I gotta get to school anyway. Bye."

He pushed off the fence and picked up a stack of books held together by a rubber strap.

I looked behind him toward the drugstore, wondering what it would be like to sit and have a soda with a beautiful rose like that.

"You wanna meet me there after school?" He scratched his side, the plaid of his shirt rubbing up and down against his soft skin, revealing the tanned flank above his belt.

"I have chores."

"After that?"

I couldn't figure out why someone so beautiful wanted to be with me. He was a Keller and I was a girl living on the charity of a convent school. I oozed chastity and dependence; he oozed carnality and freedom. Even at that age. Sister Thaddeus said some boys are just like that.

"Just for a minute. I could use some soap."

"Good."

He walked toward Locust Island Elementary School. Our bell rang and I ran into class. Sister Thaddeus touched my back before I sat down at my desk. "Can you come with me into the hallway?"

I followed her. She leaned forward behind the door. "Was that the young Keller boy you were speaking with?"

I nodded.

"What did he want?"

"He wants to meet me at the drugstore after school."

"Do you want to?"

"Yes, sister." I never could lie to Sister Thaddeus; she was that nice.

"Well, I need a new toothbrush if you'd like to walk over there with me."

"Yes, sister. Thank you."

~~

Jude waited, sprawled on the steps, leaning back on his elbows, the sun shining down on him like a spotlight he soaked in through the membranes of his cells. He scowled at Sister Thaddeus, who touched his light brown curls and swung into the store.

"D--- nuns," he said.

"She's not a nun, she's a religious sister. Nuns are cloistered."

"It's a convent school, idn't it?"

"Well, yes. Some of them are cloistered, but Sister Thaddeus isn't."

"She's a looker. Even in that penguin suit."

I rolled my eyes. And he laughed, baring his perfect teeth.

I laughed too. "She's gone in to get a toothbrush," I whispered.

He whispered back, "Is that . . . a secret thing? Nuns brush their teeth?"

"No. I . . . I don't know why I whispered."

"Don't go whispering around me, Mary-Margaret. I don't shock too easy."

"How old are you?"

"Eleven."

"I'm nine."

"I know. But you're older inside. Like I am."

"How do you know that?"

He shrugged. "I dunno. I just do."

He reached into his pocket and pulled out a peppermint. "Here. I got it inside. I had a feeling the penguin would show up."

"Thanks."

"I gotta go. Brister wants me on the boat this afternoon and if I don't get there on time, there'll be hell to pay."

"Does he beat you?" I remember the shock that spilled over the edges of my brain and into my heart.

"Yeah, the pansy. But I can take it." He jerked his head to the side. "There ain't nothing he can dish out I can't take."

Jesus sat down next to me. "Don't take his words at face value, my dear. Brister wounds his heart as well as his backside. There's more going on there than you can imagine right now."

Do you love Jude too?

"Oh yes."

"Well, it's been swell." Jude jumped off the step and ran down the street, his gait graceful and untamed. I didn't see him again until Christmastime. Jesus accompanied Sister Thaddeus and me back to the dining hall. I remember we had fried oysters that night for dinner.

They might not have been from Brister Purnell's boat, but I pretended they were.

Angie, Blanca, Mary-Francis, and I gathered around the table for dinner last night. We don't live at the school anymore now that it's a retirement village. We reside next door. For years Mr. Johnson Bray lived in this house along with his wife, Regina, and their eight children who were grown up and gone by the time I graduated from high school. Mr. Bray was the first person to show me the proper ratios for drawing the human form and he explained color theory based on nature. I was the only girl to live at the convent all year long. I miss him more than I could possibly say. He was a tailor by trade who cooked up fancy dinners on Sundays. The sisters let me go over there to eat during the summer.

The Brays' cottage now witnesses simple meals, beans and rice most days. Mary-Francis cooks up a large pot on Mondays and we eat off of it the entire week. She used to be a missionary in Mexico and likes to remember the people there, so we eat the same dinners they do. On Sundays Blanca cooks a roast and on Saturday I bake bread, five loaves for us, five to share. Angie shops. We banned her from the kitchen when she first moved into the cottage after arriving back to Locust Island from her transient life, aging but still going strong. It's a hard place to be when your bones grow brittle while the fire's left inside. But we're all in it together and we always will be until Angie, who we all bet will be the last to leave, goes on to our motherhouse in Baltimore. We have a nice assisted-living place for all the retired sisters. It's a fine order.

After lives of much excitement, the motherhouse won't be a bad place. Anybody who thinks being a religious sister is boring work must not know any of us. Between the four of us, we've been on every continent, even Antarctica. Blanca visited her brother stationed down there. She spent a good deal of her life in the Ukraine, China, and Hungary. I've mostly been here, although I went to Africa for a year a couple of years ago to visit and serve with my son, John. Mary-Francis served in Central America, Mexico, South America.

If Jesus comes to them like he comes to me, they're not saying any more than I do. For I know this, the day I tell is the day he stops appearing. He didn't have to tell me this; I just know it.

Angie covered my rice with a heaping spoonful of black beans. We gathered our napkins and placed them on our laps like the ladies we were taught to be all those years ago when St. Mary's was somewhat of a finishing school as well. The simple bands on the fingers of our left hands glimmered golden in the overhead light. Blanca, who's 4'11" and has always somehow managed to look fifteen even though her hair is white and her skin creased from her days teaching in the sun, calls us God's Harem. And rolls her eyes after she says it. Every single time.

We crossed ourselves and said grace. And my heart was full of love for my sisters. I gave everyone a scare back in 1958 when Jude showed back up. Angie thought she'd never get me back again. And at times, I thought she might be right. But some days it just didn't seem to matter. Others, I felt a longing so deep for life at St. Mary's I wondered if my heart was just a fickle fist of flesh. Sorry, Angie, I know you're cringing at the alliteration. But it just fits.

"Amen."

Jesus didn't need to show up right then, for he was smiling at me in the eyes of the women around me. My friends. My partners. Truly, my sisters.

~~~

I pulled on the chain of the lamp beside my bed in the room Angie and I share. She was already asleep, but she doesn't mind the light or the scritch of my pen as I write in this notebook. My goodness I've written so much today. These days Angie conks out right after *Jeopardy! The Tonight Show* is beyond us. Tomorrow is Saturday and we'll set this place to rights after the busy week. Blanca and Mary-Francis will give the house a deep clean. Angie will shop and run errands. I will bake bread, mow the lawn for the final time this season, and weed and mulch the flower beds for the winter. I'll finally get to planting those bulbs that have been sitting around in the toolshed for years.

Jude bought them for me back in 1964.

I wonder if they'll bloom. I doubt it, but I've been wondering about Jude a lot these days. Some people say our sins are purgated here on earth; others say there's a different plane. For Jude, I hope and pray the former is true. He deserves that, considering the way he died.

~~~

Angie mentioned John's letter. Here it is:

Dear Sr. Mom,

I wonder each day how you and the others are faring on the island. Did Sr. Blanca get over her bronchitis? How is Mary-Francis's father? What about Uncle Gerald and Aunt Hattie? It took quite awhile for your letter to reach me, unfortunately, which explains my tardy reply. I hope you weren't worried.

Everything is going well here in Big Bend. A church in the US recently built a structure at a carepoint where orphans are being fed daily. We've offered to teach two days a week those children who cannot afford the school fees and they've accepted our offer. I'll still run the clinic while Brothers Luke and Amos will teach school, the basics: math, science, English, reading in both siSwati and English. Religion, of course.

The medical needs grow here in Swaziland, as you can imagine. I ran into a Pentecostal missionary the other day who said that when he arrived fifteen years ago he was doing one funeral a week. Now, he's up to several a day due to HIV/AIDS. Not that anyone really dies of AIDS according to their relatives.

We need more antiretrovirals, but money is in short supply. We're doing what we can with what we've been given. Even for the little we do, the Swazi people are so thankful. But then, I'm sure this comes as no surprise to you.

I'm going to have to return to the US to keep up my hours. I'll be doing them at Hopkins so hopefully I can stay with you for a while. After all this time on the parched plain, I need your healing rains.

Much love,

Fr. Son

The other day I picked up a copy of *The Knowledge of the Holy*, by the protestant mystic Aiden Wilson Tozer. He'd don a coverall, slipping it over his suit and tie, and fall on his face before the Lord. He gave away most of his earthly gifts to feed the poor and help others. If it was up to me to decide sainthood, I'd go with the man. I came to know Tozer through the aforementioned Johnson Bray, a person I'll miss with a pinprick sadness until my dying day.

Mr. Bray also sewed ready-made suits before ready-made suits were the norm. He was a man ahead of his time. I would find him in his workshop, hunched over the machine, this giant, kingly black man with hands so large it astounded me they could do such fine work. His workshop looked as if a notions store had exploded. Buttons, trim, fabric, spools of yarn in no particular order covered every flat surface. He didn't allow his wife, his opposite, to step so much as a toe over the threshold. She was grateful for that.

Sometimes, when he did his handwork, hemming, and basting, usually late at night, I'd sit with him.

"Come on in, MM!"

And there he'd be, sitting in an old tapestry chair, his swollen feet pushing out the sides of his slippers resting on an ottoman. Holding that teeny needle in those big fingers, he usually was sweating underneath the lamp because when I talked most to Mr. Bray, I was on summer vacation and the nuns didn't always know what to do with me.

So we sweated together, him more than me, and as he sewed I sketched. Usually pictures of him or Jude. Or Jesus. But nobody's ever seen those. I keep them in their own portfolio.

"How you doin' tonight, Sister Mary-Margaret?" he'd always ask. He was the first person to ever call me that.

"Fine, Mr. Bray. Hot."

"Tell me about it."

"Whose suit is that?"

This was 1940 and I was ten years old.

"Mr. Clark Gable's."

"No!"

"Oh yes. Yes, yes."

"How did you get him?"

"Well now, it's a very interesting story."

Mr. Bray pronounced it in-ter-REST-ing.

Mrs. Regina Bray, a beautiful woman with the grace of a dove, always offered me a lemonade and I always accepted because she wasn't stingy on the sugar. She was every bit as lithe and willowy as her husband was thick and heavy. She wore yellow at least seventy-five percent of the time and her voice always sounded as if she were speaking in church.

"Oh, Johnson and his stories." She'd chuckle.

He'd nod. "But it's late and you should be in bed, shouldn't you?"

"No. Everybody's asleep. I'm free and clear at least until compline."

He'd laugh and laugh. And then he'd usher me into his workshop. That night he told me a grand tale of how Mr. Clark Gable himself came upon Mr. Bray right there in Abbeyville! My, that man could weave a story. Mermaids and miracles and just plain fancy. He was one of those people you suspected could be an angel. Mrs. Bray too.

"You tell a story better than Aunt Elfi," I said. "Unless she's not making all that up."

He laid a finger on the side of his nose. "She was a mystic for sure."

"That's what she told everyone."

"Oh no. I think she really was. Now, about her being the reincarnation of Catherine of Siena, well, that seemed a bit far-fetched, considering Catherine's a saint. What's the theology on that, MM?"

"Saints are people the Church is positive are experiencing the beatific vision."

"Heaven?"

"Yes, sir. Which makes it just seem plain silly that a saint could be reincarnated."

"Still, seems to me she found God in a way few have, I'll warrant. God meets people in the strangest places."

I found out a few years later that Aunt Elfi had been dropped on her head as a baby.

Back to Clark Gable. "So, is he really as good-looking in person?" I asked.

"Who?"

"Clark Gable."

"Better looking."

"I knew it!" I snapped my fingers. I was crazy about Mr. Gable.

~⌒

Sisters, here is one of my favorite portions from the book Mr. Bray gave me, *The Knowledge of the Holy*.

> *They that know Thee not may call upon Thee as other than Thou art, and so worship not Thee but a creature of their own fancy; therefore, enlighten our minds that we may know Thee as Thou art, so that we may perfectly love Thee and worthily praise Thee.*

An "amen" rings in my heart, and I remember Mr. Bray, long gone, and how he taught me not to tell God where he can and cannot go, who he can and cannot save, and why he can and cannot do so. "Love rules the day," Mr. Bray told me when I asked him years later why Jesus would have me reach out to Jude in the way he was asking. "If Jesus is asking you to do that, it's because he loves you both that much."

I miss Jude tonight. In truth, despite the tickle in the loins (which I thought a machination of the evil one), I initially viewed Jude as a call to obedience, a chance to understand what sacrificial love really means. But every once in a while, when we were teens and I walked with him at the edge of the point, and the light from Bethlehem Point Light swung around and around, I loved him a little. Or maybe it was just physical attraction back then. It doesn't matter now. And I was still a girl who loved Jesus more than some boy.

The third time Jesus came to me I was ten years old and sitting at Fort McHenry, the place of my conception. We'd come to Baltimore for a three-day field trip, the sisters traipsing us around the fort, the USS *Constellation*, the Washington Monument, Union Station, the Basilica of the Assumption, and to see the circus at the Armory. I'd detached myself from the group and sat on one of the star points of the old fort, my legs dangling down in front of the brick, my eyes tracking the ships sailing down the Patapsco River to the Baltimore Harbor and to the docks on the waterfront.

Naturally, I thought of my mother.

The circumstances surrounding my birth saddened me not so much because of what my mother went through, although clearly, that was something to mourn and at times I did. What saddened me the most was that I had such a bad man for a father. I often wondered if somehow his propensity for gross mortal sin was engraved like fine glass etching into my cell membranes. Was I lacking the ability to stop myself from placing my desires so forefront I'd force my will against another?

The noon sun lowered as I sat thinking about this, only not in such grandiose terms as written above. Did my father's transgressions leave some sort of mark on me? Something like the mark of Cain, only my sin was not my own? For certainly, the children at St. Mary's, other than Angie, tended to leave me alone. Was it more than the fact that I was deemed "odd" because of my orphan/charity status? Had some bubble formed around me, something toxic that mere contact with would render a person . . . what? Not popular? Stained? Damned?

"No. Not damned at all, T—."

I glanced to my left and there he stood, the grass, having wintered and grown too long before the first cutting, brushing against his bare ankles.

I remembered those eyes.

Oh my. He came back!

"Yes, it's me again. You think more deeply than you should for your age. And you must know there's nothing *you* can do that will damn another person."

"I hate how I was made. If that seminarian was doing the right thing, then I wouldn't be here."

"True."

He walked closer and rested his hand atop my head. Light and love flowed into me.

"But you still love me."

"You are very dear to me, T—."

It was then I found out what my real name meant.

"Because of the way I was made?"

"Yes." He sat down. "Listen to a story I will tell you."

He asked me to keep it between us. Jesus comes to many people, of this I'm convinced, but in many ways, and he always asks them not to brag about it.

So that was the day I fell in love with him.

That day Jesus took my hand and walked me to the water's edge. "I don't like that fort," he said. "Too much bloodshed. Too much plotting and planning of pain. Let's sit here instead."

We sat in the long grass together and he never let go of me.

"Let me know this is real somehow," I asked after the sun set and the sky turned a blazing lavender with shoots of golden cloud zooming across its breadth.

You see, the group had left without me. It was almost as if I had disappeared and nobody realized it.

He pressed his thumb into the soft spot of skin and muscle between my forefinger and thumb. Warmth surged in through his branding touch. I can't see the red spot it made anymore, but it still feels tender to the touch and reminds me of the day I was born anew, you know, when I became a little girl who really

and truly knew she was loved by God. That'll make anyone feel
brand new.

He told me a story that day, a story of how sin can lead to
God's mercy. My very existence was filled to overflowing with
God's mercy. "And that seminarian, though he didn't know it,
gave you to me to love, T—. Somehow, though it doesn't seem
to make any sense, we can at least be thankful for that."

THIS HAS BEEN ONE OF THE MOST EXHAUSTING DAYS OF MY life!

I was praying myself awake this morning when Jesus sat next to me on the bed. "I want you to do several things before I bring you home, T—."

T— is my true name and I don't feel comfortable writing it down. It's just for me. The name he gave me. We all have one, just not many of us know what it is. Indeed, do you think God knows you as the name your parents gave you or the one he gave you before the foundations of the world? Don't you ever wonder what that name might be?

All right, Jesus, I'll do what you ask.

"I want you to get Gerald out to that lighthouse as quickly as you can. Sneak him out of the facility if you have to. And you'll have to." He lifted my hand and squeezed it, and it was light and warmth and love. "Touch Gerald for me today, with this hand."

I will.

I went right over to Gerald's room, the hall lights low, the floor smelling freshly buffed, the aides' shoes seeming thicker and quieter, as though nighttime medical footwear had special requirements. The bulletin boards, so cheerful in sunlight, looked drained and depressed. I touched his arm as he slept, then slipped quietly back to Mercy House for Matins.

46

I returned later this morning after breakfast to find what seemed impossible.

Hattie was slipping away! I couldn't believe it. Before Jesus said what he did, we all thought Hattie was the stronger one while Gerald sat cross-legged in a pile of ashes on the doorstep of death.

Angie rushed into their room where I sat holding Hattie's hand. "What's going on?" She slipped off her jacket, sat down, and took Hattie's other hand.

"Her vitals are slipping. There's no reason for it. Her heart is strong, her arteries are in good shape. She's not having a heart attack or a stroke. It's medically unexplainable."

I want to tell you about Hattie before we proceed. Hattie lived for decades out on the light with Gerald. When Gerald came ashore, sometimes for several days to go into Baltimore for major supplies or to talk to his boss with the coast guard, she'd man the light.

Hattie saved the life of three watermen during Hurricane Agnes after their skipjack had slammed into the shoals. She got in her motorboat, ripped the cord of the outboard, and rescued them. I can picture her housedress clinging to her comfy exterior, her bottle-red hair sitting like a soaked octopus atop her head, the tensile muscles in her arms tightening as she reached forward, hand-over-handing the men to safety. Nobody would dare drown when Hattie was on duty.

They weathered out the storm aboard the light with her, the metal pilings creaking and groaning, the waves crashing almost up to the windows as Agnes grew angrier.

Gerald watched from the shore.

"Honest to Pete, when I got out there, Hattie was playing gin rummy with everybody, the place warm and cozy, and she looked up at me and said, 'Gere, did you remember the sugar?' And of course I forgot the sugar, so I took those men back to shore, picked up a sack of sugar, and made Hattie and me a tray of sugar cookies."

Hattie was fifty-five years old when she saved those men.

The lighthouse survived. They all did. Only minor repairs were necessary to Bethlehem Point. Other lighthouses weren't so lucky, but we all figured that light held together by Hattie's sheer, strong will. How it lasted the years before she got there, I couldn't begin to say.

And now, if she wants to die, she will. Most likely, she knows something we don't. Or perhaps it's just time. Who can know but God? And maybe Hattie Keller.

An hour later it was evident she was dying. Her heart rate slid down to twenty and her blood pressure barely registered.

"Why is this happening, MM?" Gerald, dressed in plaid pajamas and looking better than he had in a long time, sat in the lounge chair beside her bed. He looked a little lost among the pictures of flowers on every wall (not a lighthouse in sight!), and on every piece of furniture draped a multicolored, granny-square afghan. Little knickknacks—some crocheted with bits of silk flowers cascading from some orifice, some bearing words burned into wood—were evenly distributed around the room. I love Hattie—I hate her taste in decorating being the minimalist I am—but this brave, seaworthy soul can strew whatever she wants around her room as far as I'm concerned. At least there weren't any pictures of kittens or geese. Or far-fetched English villages.

"Did Hattie ever talk about dying?" I asked.

"Not much. She didn't like the subject. You know how some people—morbid people—talk about how they'd like to go? Well, Hattie would say, 'I'll go when I want to and that's that.'"

I pulled my knitting out of my tote bag. Sometimes, when a patient is sleeping, I'll sit and knit. Just being there does a world of good. My propensity was to start something for John and the other brothers, but summer is beginning in Swaziland. The yarn is a mustard gold. So I decided I'd just start on a scarf and see who ends up with it.

"Did Hattie leave you any instructions, Gerald?" I find it's best to be matter-of-fact about death issues. People appreciate it. It jerks them back from that unreal place where finality hovers in an iridescent hum you can almost see and somewhat hear. But not quite.

He ran a hand across the strings of his hair. "She left something out at the light years ago. And she brought that up two days ago, real wistful. Said she kept a sack under the floorboard near the refrigerator. Well, sort of important papers, she said. Said you'd appreciate it the most. Has something to do with Jude too, some letter to you or something he told her to give to you after he died."

"My goodness."

"She said he wrote it years ago, when he was planning on dying the first time. But then . . . well, it's easy to see how she forgot about it after all that time."

"Indeed."

"But she also said something about her mother's old recipe book too. I don't know, MM. She was babbling a little. I can't guarantee anything's there at all."

I set down my knitting. "I think it would mean the world to her if we got that book for her, don't you?" Inside, the thought of hearing from Jude again, across time, gave a greater sense of urgency. And yet, he might have removed it himself decades before. I knew better than to get my hopes up. I learned that lesson *long* ago.

"It could be a wild goose chase." He screwed up his brow. "Only the Coast Guard checks up on that place anymore. And it needs a fresh coat of paint in my opinion. They just don't care about the old gal like we did."

"They probably won't be there on a Saturday. We'll have to sneak by Janice, though, don't you think?"

"She's one cranky nurse."

No sense in delaying.

"Okay. We don't have much time." With the way Hattie was slipping. "Can you get yourself dressed?"

"Strangest thing. I'm feeling pretty darned good. Better than I have in a good five years or so."

Oh Jesus. Jesus, Jesus, Jesus. I should have known Gerald would rally.

Don't take my relationship with Christ the wrong way. I may be familiar with him, like a loving spouse is familiar with her husband, but I have the utmost respect. I realize he created all things and is the second person of the Godhead; that somehow he is one with the Father, though I don't feel the same closeness to Person One.

Now, the Holy Spirit and I have been getting to know each other for some time, but still this mysterious Person Three looks on from afar, the scout at the ridge, the captain in the wheelhouse. I know the Father has his eye on me and the time will come when he steps forward and demands equal billing, but I do feel that time will come when I say that final prayer on my knees and he pulls me in like a fish in a net.

God the Father knows I have father issues. And maybe he cares about that. Or maybe it's too late for any of that to be resolved here on earth. Who knows?

But still, I uttered a little prayer to him as I pulled my Wellies on over my gardening jeans. Today was typical October on the Eastern Shore—warm with a little nip sewn round the edges like tinfoil lace. I buttoned on a dark blue flannel shirt, figuring it would be best if I blended in with the water. Then I made a call.

"Cinquefoil's."

"Shrubby?"

"Yeah. That you, Mary?"

"Yes. I need to borrow your boat."

"You goin' fishin'?" He started in on our old joke.

"Yeah."

"You got worms?"

"Yeah, but I'm goin' anyway!"

We laughed.

"Just need the one with the outboard."

"Oh, okay. What you want to do with it?"

Shrubby's one of the last of the old-style watermen. Rugged but kind. Drinks too much, smokes too much, looks like an old leather portmanteau but with more expression and robin's-egg-blue eyes where the buttons should be. He needs a wife, but it would take a very unique brand of woman to marry old Shrubby.

"I want to run Gerald out to the light."

"You could get in trouble for that and you bein' a nun, well, I wouldn't recommend it."

"I'm a religious sister and we get in trouble all the time. People just don't know about it."

He paused. Shrubby's not exactly the king of comebacks. "I'll bring it around," he finally said. "Want me to bring it up to your dock?"

"I'd be grateful."

"Because that way, you'd be almost there before most of the town would spy you."

"Excellent thinking!"

"I ain't as dumb as I look, sister."

"You don't look dumb at all, Shrubby."

Amazing how life can beat down a man, isn't it?

As I waited for Shrubby, I couldn't help but stare out at the light and whenever I do that, I think about Jude.

One time when I was fourteen years old I stood out on Bethlehem Point, the spike of land jutting into the cool gray waters of the Chesapeake where I usually park my lawn chair, and I watched, as usual, the light swing round and round in the lantern of the lighthouse. Jude stole up behind me and poked his index fingers into my sides. I jumped. "Why do you always do that?"

He grinned, then threw himself on the ground. I lowered myself, first laying down a towel to keep my school uniform neat.

"Sneak out again?" he asked, pulling out two penny candies from his jacket pocket.

"You know I did. It's so hot in my room."

He held out a peppermint and as I moved to take it, he snatched it back. "I want to put it on your tongue."

There came that dirty thrill again.

But I really wanted the candy. So I held out my tongue. He just dropped it on there, the flesh of his fingertips failing to come in contact with my tongue.

"Thank you," I said.

"I just wanted to look at your tongue."

52

"Jude!"

He laughed. "One day, Mary-Margaret, you're going to get the real scoop on me. You won't just think of me as the youngest Keller boy."

"I've heard the real scoop." Boy, did I! He'd already done it with three girls. For certain. Probably more.

"Then why would you let me put candy on your tongue?"

I refused to answer.

He leaned back on his hands, crossing his legs at the ankles and jiggling them. "One day"—he pointed to the lighthouse— "I'm going to row you out there and I'm going to make mad, passionate love to you on the floor of what used to be my parents' living room."

"I'm going to be married to Jesus."

"Jesus may have other plans."

"Jesus never has other plans." At least not for me. I would make sure what happened to my mother didn't go unredeemed. Jesus said I was his bride. It all made so much sense.

"Mark my words. Someday. I know these things." He tapped his temple, leaned forward, and kissed me full on the lips.

"You sound like my Aunt Elfi. She knew things too."

"Yeah, but she was a nut."

I wiped my lips with the back of my hand and get behind me, Satan. I would not let the Deceiver steal me from my calling. However, I did wonder what a baby made by myself and Jude Keller would look like. But then, so did every other girl at school.

His eyes twinkled. "Yep."

You see, I told Jude all about my life and he told me about his. Every little thing. At least I thought so at the time. Some he didn't go into great detail over, and those items, I always followed up with Sister Thaddeus for corroboration. She seemed to know everything.

Apparently not as much as Jude, however.

"I'm going to be married to Jesus," I said again.

But my lips burned like I'd been kissed by an angel. And I wiped them off again.

"You can keep doing that, Mary-Margaret, and you'll still feel that way."

"Do all the girls feel that way when you kiss them?"

"No."

"Why?"

"Because I don't care a thing about *them*."

I took his hand in both of mine. "Jude, it's hopeless."

His eyes soaked up the autumn sky and he knew I was right. We both knew. "I'll take my chances," he whispered.

My heart broke for him.

We loved each other. In such different ways. And I would break his heart. Again and again. Until he finally left Locust Island. But in the meantime he kept coming back and I kept letting him. He did what he did because he loved me. I did what I did because I loved God. That, as any mom will tell her daughter, is not a combination that will lead to anything but disaster. The truth was, I loved the way Jude's lips felt pressed against mine. And I let him kiss me more than I should have. I loved the way he never bragged about me like he did other girls, that I was his sacred secret and he was my hidden carnality. It was a dance of sorts that neither of us quite understood or were capable of stopping. Looking back now, I know we both were looking for someone to love us, really love us, like the parents who couldn't because they were dead or dead to our hearts. I don't expect you to understand, sisters. (See what a can of worms you've opened up, Mary-Francis?)

That night as I helped sort canned goods to be taken to St. Vincent DePaul's in Salisbury, Jesus joined me.

"Leave Jude to me, T—."

Will he be all right?

"Eventually. He'll make terrible choices you won't."

But why will he have to go through that?

"Some do."

I don't understand that sort of thing. Why some are shielded and others aren't.

"You and I already love each other. Someone is standing between Jude and myself, and it will take many years and an ocean of love to dissolve that barrier. Do you remember when that beautiful woman broke the box of ointment on my feet?"

I love that story.

"She loved much because she was forgiven much."

So people like me won't love as much as those who've lived a rougher life?

"Of course not. You just learned to do so a little sooner."

Or we're frightened not to.

He smiled. "There are those. I prefer to be followed out of love, not fear, T—. But I'll take somebody's hand regardless of why they are reaching out to me. As we get to know each other, the heart grows full. That is always my desire."

And if it doesn't, if only the fear remains?

"My hand holds fast. But I grieve. I long to bring people to my Father, to know his love. I'm especially joyful when it happens here on earth. But it doesn't for everyone."

I'm not afraid of the Father, I just don't understand him.

"I'm with you as long as you need me, T—. But I can tell you this. You can trust him."

And Jude?

"Jude is in my view. I just want you to love him. And listen to my voice."

Am I supposed to go out with him, Jesus?

He chuckled. "No, my dear. Just do as I tell you. Although there will come a time when much is required of you."

You sure weren't kidding, Jesus, I thought as I headed over to spirit away Gerald to the lighthouse. He was dressed when I entered their suite.

I settled Sister Angie's windbreaker around Gerald, arranging the hood over his head like a monk's cowl.

"I feel a little silly in this thing." His gaze skittered down the floral fabric and so much for blending in with the bay.

"We're being clandestine. You're Angie right now."

"I'm much too old and out of shape to impersonate Angie."

Angie jogs three miles every day. At her age. And she's not a skinny-mini either!

"Hattie would get a kick out of it."

"Well, you're right about that."

I poked my head into the hallway and scanned each wing. Nobody. "Coast is clear. Let's go."

Gerald, who once stalked the decking of the lighthouse with giant, manly strides, who stood ringing the fog bell in the mists of great storms, waves crashing against him, who'd rescued a couple of overly eager sports fishermen who lost their craft and bobbed about in forty-degree water in their life vests, *that* Gerald hurried beside me in a reduced, scraping little gait, his slippers *whush-whush*ing along the linoleum tile. The plastic tips on the tie of the hood clicked against the tulips on the slick fabric of his jacket.

"Can you try and pick your feet up a little?" I asked. "We have to get there."

"I'm not so sure Hattie would think this is a good idea." He paused, then emitted a wheezy laugh. "Forget that. I bet she'll stay alive a bit longer just to see if we make it."

"Exactly."

Exactly, indeed.

You see, I've lived my life like the puzzle it is, pieces fitting in here and there, one at a time. Some portions are finished and I can look behind me and say, "Yes, there's the young bit.

There's the Jude bit. There's the John bit. And now finally, here I am as I thought I'd be." But some segments are tinier, made up of only one day, a week, or perhaps a month. And today was a major portion, one I'll not forget for a long time even though I don't know where it will lead.

Remember the father issues? Well, read on, sisters. Today was certainly a little crazy in that department.

We sidled through the kitchen and onto the patio where the residents diné during the mellow days of spring and autumn. Hurried as best we could down the brick pathway that leads to the water and from there we slipped behind the snowball bushes and rounded our way toward Bray's Cottage—our little home. We call it Mercy House these days because Blanca brings in at least one stray cat a month we have to fatten up and send on its way. Oh, the yowling some of those creatures do during the night!

Halfway to the dock, Gerald took hold of my arm with his other hand. "Stop just a minute, Mary-Margaret. I'm getting a little breathless."

We stood in front of a span of eelgrass, the ribbon leaves swirling in the gentle ebb of the water.

"I'm sorry."

He rested his hand atop his head, then rubbed. "Used to be I could drag you along."

"You still want to. Surely that counts for something."

Farther out, the last skipjack from our island sailed toward deeper waters for the day's catch. I sighed. I don't know why Elmore keeps trying. He's old and the crabs are low. Even Phillips Seafood is importing their crabmeat from the Philippines sometimes. And I don't think Mr. Phillips, when he started the restaurant all those years ago, meant there to be that obvious connection with his name. But the bay just isn't what it used to be.

"It's all changing, isn't it, Gerald?"

He unzipped his jacket, grimacing at either the heat or the tulips. I couldn't tell you which. "Every last darn thing. Remember how big those blue crabs used to be? The size they call larges these days we'd have thrown right back in."

He started forward and we continued toward the dock behind Mercy House. As promised, the boat awaited. Shrubby had probably gone home to his sorting shed where a bunch of hard crabs in large trays were losing their shells. Shrubby's always bringing us soft crabs. He's not Catholic, but he believes it can't hurt to bring food to nuns. That's what he says. "You gals seem nice enough," he says.

The tai chi class convened outside in the courtyard. Blanca, who teaches them before heading to St. Francis's where she heads up the CCD and the general doings of Christian education, waved as if I spirited away patients in rowboats every day. I waved back and helped Gerald into the boat.

The boat kept slipping away from the dock. In my exasperation I cried out, "Will somebody help us?" and looked up toward the heavens.

The boat stood still and I'm not sure who decided to lend a hand, a guardian angel perhaps? I do believe in those. Or Jesus himself? It didn't matter.

"How long do you think it'll be before they find the note?" I pictured the look on Angie's face when the nurse asked if she knew anything. Her perfected deer-in-the-headlights expression, along with her reputation for crying at dog stories, would aid her silence and keep her from telling falsehoods, direct or indirect. I don't have the same skill and I've been to confession many a time for many a lie. Never large, scheming, overblown ones. Just lies to keep me out of basic trouble.

After we settled on the wooden benches, Gerald in Spark's place near the front and facing out, me by the motor, I grabbed the handle of the pull cord and gave a fierce yank.

As if I thought it would fire up the first time.

Again, I tried. Again, I failed.

Gerald looked over his shoulder with a sly grin, and in that flash I saw Jude so clearly I felt as if my heart would stop.

"You want to give it a go?" I asked.

"You're doing just fine, MM."

We were both too old for this.

I pulled again, ready to demand heavenly help if it went amiss one more time, but the propeller stirred up the murky waters and I lifted the loop of rope off the piling. We puttered toward the light.

"No sense in hurrying unduly, Gerald. There's nothing they can do about us now."

"No. No, that's very true." He raised his chin and breathed in deeply. He turned and winked, his eyes jumping with a mellow joy. He surely did remind me of Jude's dog, Spark. "Here we go, MM. An adventure. Never thought I'd be having another adventure."

Indeed.

I pictured Jude and Spark on the waters. Rowing, rowing. Always rowing.

It took us about fifteen minutes, silence accompanying us because we never thought we'd ever do this again. I pulled up to the dock beneath the lighthouse and fixed the boat.

Climbing up the ladder to the decking, the green smell of the bay water and blue scent of the wind that made its way across oceans and grasses and trees enfolded me. It was the smell of Jude who spent much of his time on his stepfather's oyster boat. It was the smell that would touch me when he'd call to me from beneath my window in the middle of the night, and yes, I'd sneak out of the dormitory, my bare white feet glowing against the stone floor of the corridor, my breath scraping the holy stillness. It was the smell of lonesomeness and feeling trapped. It was the smell of trying to find your way.

Sometimes, however, when Jude wasn't thinking about it, it was the smell of contentment. But not often. And only when we were alone together and I forgot who I was, who he was, and we sat cross-legged facing each other and I held his hands as I told him about what happened that day. If it was something exciting, that is. We had our times. When the bishop would visit, when the seniors graduated, when I made breakthroughs with my art. Jude soaked in every word. Sometimes he'd lay a hand just above my knee and I'd let him. He had well-developed hands, strong and already like a man's at seventeen. It did something to me to see it there on my leg.

And somehow I saw a kite flying off the railing of a lighthouse, brightly colored and winging against the clouds.

~⌒

Gerald waited in the boat. "Do you think it's locked?" he asked.

"No."

Of course it could have been locked, but if it was, Jesus had provided another way. Jesus always provided what I needed to do what he sent me for. Even if it wasn't always apparent at first glance. Sometimes Jesus is sneaky that way. He doesn't always just hold it out there for us on a silver platter like tea sweets in front of the queen. He gave us brains for a reason.

My hand curved around the knob. "Yes, it's locked!"

"Look in the light next to the door. Always kept a spare there."

I opened the glass door of the brass light and felt inside. Metal moved beneath my fingertips. "I think I've found it." I pulled it toward the opening, tipped it up, and grasped it fully between finger and thumb. "Yes. It's a key."

He chuckled, shaking his head. "Hattie told me to leave it there."

"I'm telling you, Gerald. She knows a lot more than she's letting on." Oh boy, did she.

I slid the key into the lock and pushed in on the red door. Oh my. Oh my.

～◡◠

Quick note before I continue on:

I simply must remember to plant those bulbs tomorrow! It'll be a miracle if they grow, but I'm missing Jude and it would be nice to give God the chance to do something tiny and spectacular and maybe even a bit miraculous.

～◡◠

The lighthouse sitting room, empty now, brought back so many memories. The first time I came to the light I was fifteen; the walls were papered in a bluish floral print and Mr. Keller was reading a book in the comfortable chair near the kitchen door. Jude blew in, relieved in spirit yet despising his surroundings. I remember thinking, *Well, there are no girls out here.* He rowed me out himself and I admired his arms, his smile, the sun on his hair the entire time. He chattered away. Most people thought Jude a sullen youth. Not me. And it was summertime.

"Dad," he said. "I wanted you to meet Mary-Margaret."

Mr. Keller peeled off his wire-rimmed spectacles, stood up with a smile, and offered his hand. Men didn't shake the hands of young women much in those days. I felt grown up. I took it, we shook, and I realized why Jude left. This was a holy man of the sea, a man who enjoyed silence and contemplation, a man completely unlike his son. His blue uniform was perfectly pressed, his beard trimmed close to his jaw. In some ways I was right; in other ways I was completely wrong. But who could have known what Jude was really going through?

"Nice to meet you."

He made me a cup of tea and we chatted about his books and I told him I wanted to be a teacher, a School Sister of St. Mary, and he thought it a fine idea.

"So, I take it you're not one of J.G.'s paramours?"

Jude George Keller.

"No, sir. For some reason, Jude just likes to talk to me." Thankfully Jude didn't mention our kisses. And I didn't think I was truly lying. Not if he meant "paramour" like I did.

He sighed. "I'm relieved to hear he's talking to someone."

And the sadness of a father-son relationship that could never find that place where the similarities gather together like foam at the edges of the sea clung to us.

"Why do you stay here, Mr. Keller?" I asked.

"I don't know how to do anything else." He laid aside his book. "And I like the quiet."

His father before him had kept the light and he supposed he could go back to the fishing he did as a teen, but when the opportunity to succeed his father opened, he snatched it up. He already knew the job; there'd be little training on the part of the Coast Guard. "It was equally good for both parties. Only Petra didn't think so in the long run, I guess."

"Jude's mother?"

"Yes." And the matter of the ugly divorce predicated by Petra's hopping aboard her lover's skiff and puttering away permanently laid a hand at the back of Mr. Keller's head and pushed his chin to meet his chest.

And there he saw the floor. The pine flooring he'd run over as a lighthouse child, in a desert of water, removed but happy.

"She couldn't take the desolation. Kept begging me to take her to town all the time. But I couldn't leave the light. Finally, I got her a little boat of her own, little Elgin outboard, and she'd go every day, hair flying in the wind."

I pictured Petra in one of her bright floral dresses with loose angel wing sleeves of chiffon fluttering just above her slender elbow as she controlled that little motor, maybe the only thing she felt she could control. You might picture her a bleached blonde, but she wasn't. The same hair as Jude's grew out of her head in a heavy mass of curl that she clipped near the nape of her neck. And her lips, such sweet lips, she'd cover with pink. I thought her a free spirit, yet sweet. Not coarse or rough. Untamed, really, like periwinkle gone wild. The few times I saw her with Jude when we were young, she was just crazy about him.

He refreshed my tea with a shaking hand. "Of course people tried to warn me. She'd been hanging around the bar down near the shoe store."

"Broomhall's?"

"Yes. And then one day she met that man. But I suppose I lost her the day I bought her that boat."

Jude walked in from the decking, gold-brown hair mussed by the fingers of the breeze, cheeks pink, blue eyes still filled with the sun.

"Can I make myself some coffee?" he asked.

"That's fine, J.G."

And even at fifteen I saw their relationship in that inch-long snippet. Dad offers tea; son wants coffee.

Tea is good. Coffee is good.

Unfortunately, Jude and I left thirty minutes later. We skimmed over the bay, calm that day, and he said little and it didn't feel awkward.

I returned to school, to the prayer chapel where I said some prayers for my friend, Sister Thaddeus joining me silently. Jude went home and got the beating of his life from his stepfather.

He should have stayed at the lighthouse, but nobody knew enough to interfere in the situation.

~~

Gerald called up the steps, pulling me back to the here and now. "MM? Everything all right?"

I headed back outside and looked down to where my old friend stood on the dock beneath the lighthouse. Somehow he made it out of the boat on his own. His strength seemed to be returning, infusing a revived will in his muscle fibers, pumping blood to spots gone weak. In years gone by, the keepers kept their own live-stock down there on a platform just above the boat slip. It wasn't strange for cows and chickens to lose their lives to a squall, the waves of the bay reaching over the railing for the poor beasts and dragging them into the water. Of course, even back in the forties when I'd head out here with Jude, there was no longer a need for any livestock. They had installed a generator that ran their electric lights, and their stove and refrigerator ran on propane.

"It's fine, Gerald. Just a little spooky. I'm hearing the voices of years gone by. Do you think you can make it up the steps?"

He grabbed onto the railing. "If not, I'll die trying."

"I have to admit, it would be the perfect way for you to go!"

Gerald shook his head. "How you get away with being so car-ing and yet so unsentimental is beyond me."

I hurried down the steps and circled an arm around his waist as he climbed up to the only true home he ever knew.

"I'm not sure how you and Jude turned out so differently, Gerald. Could you be any less alike?"

"No." He grunted as he heaved his body up another step. "But Jude and I had different mothers."

"What?"

We paused. He nodded, his clear blue eyes picking up the light sliding in through the pilings. "He didn't know that. Only Hattie knows. I hate to talk about it. My father was first married to a fine woman. She didn't have those . . . urges that Petra had. Guess sometimes our paths are handed down to us in our genes."

"Oh, I hope not, friend. At least not completely. And I hope it's not ironclad."

.   "Well, that's where people like you come in, I suppose. Hopefully it makes a difference."

Oh dear Lord, yes. At least that's the hope, isn't it?

We continued the climb. A gull swooped in and out beneath the house, weaving her flight between the iron pilings; in the distance a couple of pleasure boats skimmed along the bay, their sails fully pregnant with the breeze. People on the water just know how to live, don't they?

"Do you think we'll get in trouble?" he asked, knowing the answer if his smirk was any indication.

"Would it be worth it if we did?"

"Oh, yes sirree."

It took us a full ten minutes, Gerald resting after each step, breathing like a runner after a mile, but, by golly, we reached the deck. And considering he was at death's door yesterday, I'd say we'd practically run a marathon. Gerald stood by the railing and looked out over his waters and I mean it literally when I say the lines of his face receded like the past back into which he slipped.

"So how did your mother die?" I asked.

"She was outside washing the windows to the lantern and fell down on the rocks. Broke both her legs and cracked her head open. She died three days later up in Salisbury."

How did I never hear this? Why would an entire town keep Mr. Keller's secret? Sisters, I still don't know the answer to that one. There were too many secrets out at that lighthouse. Jude's was the most dangerous.

We all grieve what happened to Jude, the massive repercussions he bore due not only to Petra's decisions but because of the woman herself. I believe it all goes back to this: none of them really believed God actually loved them.

It's hard to come to that point of realization. I know. Despite my calling, it took me years to see it myself. It actually took Jude for me to understand the tenacious love of God, and I told him that. He chuckled, but when I explained, he knew I was right. Oh, we'll get to that part of the story in due time.

The calmly committed love of Jude's father could have never filled the space left inside Petra by a clinging, suffocating mother who claimed she loved her daughter to pieces, but in truth, only used Petra to feel better, to complete her, to fill the gaping space left inside by parents who deserted her to her own grandmother's care. Petra had other matters to deal with, we've figured, perhaps her uncle or a man in the neighborhood. Nobody's left to tell us and we don't know for sure what or if anything abusive happened. But Jude and I couldn't imagine another scenario that would warp someone into what Petra became.

All those uneven links in a heavy chain holding up years of pain and the inability to cope—no wonder Petra snapped.

Unfortunately, she took Jude with her in the fall. Somehow he was handed down that maverick blood, or maybe he just heard her complaining too much when Mr. Keller was outside painting the lighthouse or up in the lantern polishing the brass and cleaning the 4th order Fresnel lens. He took his life practically in his hands every time he climbed outside the lantern and washed the windows. But Petra never saw it that way and she used Jude to make up for her husband's deficiencies.

So she scrubbed the inside of the house from top to bottom almost every day, the peace cords in her mind fraying with every swipe of the graying rag until one day, according to Jude, she threatened to jump off the lantern and onto the rocks supporting the structures.

The next day Mr. Keller bought her the skiff.

I never knew why that was the final straw for Mr. Keller. Now I do.

So Jude came by his restlessness honestly. I still blame myself for not seeing what was really going on with Petra Keller. But who could guess such a thing? We walk by people every day who are daily experiencing a horror, and we don't even know it.

That evening after we visited his father, Jude walked me back to school, made some smart remark softened by the look that came into his eyes at times like that, which told me yes, he understood the parameters of our relationship, but he didn't have to like it.

Brister Purnell, his stepfather, came off the boat in a "helluva mood." That's how Jude described it, and whenever I hear that word, I think of Helluva Good Cheese, which is actually pretty good cheese. Apparently some watermen from Virginia, real scallywags, were poaching from his crab pots, and kept Brister and his crew at bay by pointing their shotguns at them.

It was a poor catch that day to put it mildly.

"We gotta figure out how to keep that from happening again," Brister said as Petra placed a plate of crab cakes, homemade slaw, and home-fried potatoes in front of him. Say what you will about the woman, but she knew how to cook.

Jude slipped in just as his mother set his plate on the table, just under the gun, and they had a conversation that amounted to something like this: "Let me at them, Brister. Take me out of school tomorrow and onto the boat."

Brister, burned a reddish brown from his years on the water, set down his fork. "Brave words from the ladies' man."

Now, you must understand something about Jude Keller: he learned more from Brister Purnell than he ever did from Mr. Keller. Brister taught him the measure of a man was how many women he'd had, how many shots he could throw back and still walk a straight line, and how many fights he'd been in and had emerged the winner.

"Where's the harm in that?" Jude would say. "I don't take anything from anybody they're not willing to give. It works for Brister."

"Indeed?" I asked just before he left the island. "He doesn't seem to be so happy. Our bodies don't just house the *real* us, Jude. They're part of the complete whole."

Jude just scowled and told me to keep my theology to myself. He slept with the trampy girls and I suspect he didn't want to be reminded that they didn't make him happy either, just prone to be viewed as a man of sexual prowess. And in control.

That night Brister wasn't in the mood for the usual male bravado that stomped atop their table like gunfighters with spurs, only Jude didn't pick up on the new tempo.

"I can do more than love."

"Oh, you can fight?" Brister raised his eyebrows. "Well then, Mr. Big Shot, let's go!"

And despite Petra's cries, he dragged Jude by the collar outside the house.

"I didn't know what to do," Jude told me the next day as he pushed against the bruises around his eyes and on his face. "Do I hit my mother's husband? My stepfather? I mean, in general circumstances Brister's all right. What was I supposed to have done? Let me tell you, the guy can really pack a punch. I thought he was all mouth. Apparently not."

I didn't let him in on the fact that he'd turned the other cheek. Jude wouldn't have wanted the similarities between Jesus and his whupping to be highlighted.

Petra locked herself in her bedroom as Jude hauled himself down to Dr. Taylor to be stitched back together. When he came home, she asked Jude to watch over her that night.

The next day Brister did the same thing.

Jude took his own anger out on what he hated more than anything else. He drank some gin, grabbed a baseball bat, jumped in the motorboat, and headed toward the light. Mr. Keller knew better than to get in the way. He let his son rage and scream and curse him. He sat in his chair while Jude smashed the Fresnel lens, and he watched as Jude heaved the baseball bat like a gangling boomerang out into the charcoal waters of the Chesapeake.

He lied and said someone came and vandalized the light while he was ashore getting supplies.

Petra informed Brister she'd leave if he didn't stop treating her son that way, but Jude knew it was all talk. And he knew those boys from Virginia had stolen his stepfather's business right out from under him. If Brister couldn't beat them, he'd beat Jude.

At least that was Jude's take on it. I'd have to say the matter was far more complicated; I'd have to say Jude was just looking for an excuse to get away.

Jude returned to the light a few weeks later after school ended for the year, shook his father's hand good-bye, then returned to shore. He bought an old green Packard with the crabbing money he'd saved up and headed to Baltimore City. He never saw Mr. Keller again.

~~

And now here I was back at the light. Apparently as lost in thought as Gerald seemed to be as he stood outside, looking up the steps toward the lantern.

I didn't want to disturb him. We had at least an hour. I figured a good amount of time stretched before us until Hattie slipped away if things continued along the same track. But I knew I'd better make sure.

I slipped my cell phone out of my windbreaker pocket. I hate that thing, this bow to technology and the material, but the fact is, I always want to know when someone is passing away at St. Mary's Village. I like to be there for it. If they're Catholic, I call Father Brian who became the pastor of our parish a few months ago, and he meets me there to deliver the rite of the Anointing of the Sick.

Now, there's a sacrament that'll knock your socks off. You'd think I'd be used to it by now, but it never gets any less solemn, earthy, or ancient. I think of all the faithful whose sick bodies have been anointed for two millenia, the same bodies that will be healed, restored, and glorified someday. Gives me goose bumps.

And Father Brian is a sweetie. I swear that young man could shave three times a day and still fight with his beard in between. Sometimes I head over to the rectory and watch NASCAR with him. He loves that NASCAR.

Angie picked up on the first ring.

"Angie?" I gripped the phone.

"Yes," she whispered.

"Where are you?"

"In Hattie's bathroom. I don't want Janice to hear."

"How's our girl?"

"Holding relatively steady. She's still slipping, but not as quickly." She reported her vitals, which, naturally, I can't remember now as I sit here writing. I don't have a head for numbers.

"Okay. I think we'll be another couple hours. Just hold on."

"Nurse Ratched is furious you've stolen Gerald."

"How did she know it was me?"

"Security tapes."

"She didn't!"

"Yep. Dragged it all out like it was a big show. You'd have laughed your . . . behind off." Angie had a mouth on her when she was young and she's done quite well in curbing her once chosen verbiage. "Is Gerald holding up? I can't believe he can do this."

"It's supernatural, I think."

"Could be."

Angie's much more scientific and rational than I am, ready to find the natural explanation first. But her faith forces her to admit, "If there's always a natural explanation for everything, then billions of us are crazy as betsey bugs for having faith at all. Seems to me that's a *really* far-fetched explanation for religion."

"So anyway, Mary, I don't want to call more attention to myself than need be. I found Hattie's DNR by the way. In the drawer of her nightstand."

"That's a relief."

"If you don't mind my saying so, Mary-Margaret, it seems odd for you to be taking Gerald out to the light while we're pondering issues of resuscitation."

What could I say? I couldn't tell her Jesus told me to do it.

"You know me."

"Yes. You've always been a little nutty."

Indeed. Well, honestly, there are worse things someone can think about a person. Lazy, smelly, weak in the arches.

I hung up and patted Gerald's hand. "She's slowed down her descent."

"But still declining?"

"Yes. I'm sorry."

His eyes soaked up the gray of the bay and surprised me when they didn't tear up. "You know, Hattie's always done things her way. She's been dependable, loyal, but stubborn for all of that."

One year she took to wearing nothing but pink. Another year blue, and nobody could talk her into any other color.

"Who were you talking to in the room yesterday, MM?"

"Just praying, I guess." So he heard my conversation with Jesus. "Sorry, Gerald."

"I mean, different strokes for different folks, MM. If you need to pray out loud and sound like a crazy person, far be it from me to question that."

"Thanks, Gerald."

"Wish I could talk to God like he was right there with me." He gripped the railing. "I watched many a storm roll in from right here."

"I imagine."

"Agnes. Now, that was a crazy hurricane."

"I was in Ocean City at the time."

"Yes, you were. The bay was like one big pot of boiling water. You know, water is one of those things that seems all soft and nice until it gets angry and begins to scream and yell."

"I know some people like that," I quipped.

He raised a hand to visor his eyes. "Hattie was a real trouper during that dang storm. Saved those guys' lives. Those darned idiots."

"You know"—I picked up the trail—"people don't think when they're taking chances in dangerous storms, that maybe somebody will have to rescue them. That maybe they shouldn't make those kinds of choices for others."

Gerald chuckled. "You've been listening to me for too long, MM."

A houseboat puttered by, a woman knitting on deck as a man drove the boat. "Maybe. But just know I don't take everything you say as gospel truth, my friend. Would you like to go in?"

"Just give me another minute to drink this in. I never thought I'd ever get back here. You of all people should understand the thought of leaving something behind forever. At least *I* didn't lose my virtue here."

"No. You did that in the back row of the movie theater with Brenda Landruham."

He bapped me on the arm, frightening away the gull that had just landed on the railing nearby. "I had no idea you knew about that."

"I try to save things for the best time."

"Well, you picked a doozie. Still, hard to get riled with this breeze and"—he pointed to his left—"all those trees just blazing back on the island, isn't it?"

"Indeed."

We stood side by side, the wind collecting in our white hair, blowing it about our heads like pampas grass.

"We're old, Gerald."

"Yep. Old folks. And I'm even older than you are."

I didn't tell him, however, that he's destined to last longer. "I didn't lose my virtue here, Gerald. Did Jude tell you that?"

"Yep. When he was seventeen."

"And you *believed* him?"

Gerald grinned. "Been stupid before, and I guess I'll be stupid again sometime."

"Won't we all, my friend?"

From my perch at Bethlehem Point where I now write, the gray stone buildings of St. Mary's Village are illumined by a shard of light piercing the overhanging clouds. It gilds the stones laid by the School Sisters when they first took over and constructed a classroom building. The dormitory came next. They repaired the chapel and the monastery buildings as well. Those ladies were a thrifty and ambitious lot, let me tell you.

We're still here and expanding, but times have changed and expansion happens in different ways. Sister Pascal, soon to arrive, is a real whiz with computers. Even has her master's degree in information systems and whatnot. Times have certainly changed for our order as well. We need more young women like Pascal, I'll tell you that. She'll be teaching over at the elementary school and helping out at the assisted-living facilities.

I feel a certain affinity for this place that doesn't mind changing outfits to suit the times. After all, I'd thought my life was set once upon a time. And it did seem to move forward in the direction I'd mapped out for years; then Jesus upended my life and shook it like a box of cornflakes. But that didn't happen until much later.

I graduated from St. Mary's and went to the College of Notre Dame in Baltimore, a Catholic women's liberal arts college. I became a novice with the School Sisters of St. Mary's as I studied art and children's literature. As I continued through art school at the Maryland Institute, I went deeper and deeper into not only my initiation in the life of a religious but deeper into my relationship with Jesus.

He showed up quite frequently during my schooling, because, I know, he knew how much I needed him. By that time, Aunt Elfi had died. I had no one. Jude had disappeared. Neither Gerald nor Hattie nor I had heard from him for several years. I remembered my old friend though, lit a candle from time to time as a sweet offering of my faith to the One who could heal his heart and soul, and each night I prayed for him, not because I was holy, but because I'd tacked a picture of him up by the bathroom sink so I'd remember him when I brushed my teeth. I've always said the secret of the truly pious is a better memory than most of us.

The day I graduated from art school at Maryland Institute I returned to an empty one-room apartment on Howard Street and made myself a cup of tea. I made one for Jesus, although he always let his go cold. He liked that I did it anyway. "One day," he said, "we'll drink heavenly tea together." I'm not sure if he couldn't drink earthly tea in his glorified body.

He sat with me at the dinette that afternoon. "I'm proud of you. Second in your class, T—."

"Yes." I sighed.

"You are better than that fellow who was doing all that abstract expressionism—and it's not that I don't like abstract expressionism, for I see their hearts and know of their pain—but you're mine, you'll be doing my work, so second is a comfortable place. You might have become proud with being number one." He smiled so warmly. "I'm worried more about your soul than I am your standing anyway. I always have been."

"Yes, I know. But do you like my work, Lord?"

"Yes, I do. It's lovely, T—. So, you're twenty-five now, and before you go into the postulancy, I have some work for you to do in Kentucky for a little while. Contact Sister Sally at Our Lady of the Way Hospital in Martin. Look for a man named Nicholas. He'll be around fifty and will have been in an accident. He's been floundering in his faith for a long, long time. Since he was about your age. Can you show me to him?"

"As much as I am able."

"I'll be with you."

He reached out and caressed my cheek and I wanted to die at the beauty, the happiness of being in contact with him. Certainly he was made of flesh and bone, but it felt different, the skin softer even than that of a newborn. His white hair held such shine and was silkier to the touch than rabbit fur. But it was real and substantive. Real flesh, real hair. That makes his taking on human form two thousand years ago even more astounding. He took on flesh, human flesh just like ours, not just for thirty-three years, but for eternity. He didn't just rise from the dead, shed his skin, wipe his hands, and say, "Well, that's that." The thought never ceases to astound me.

I realize that not many mystics claim to have physically touched the Lord, and I've wondered if my times with Christ were hallucinations so strong I felt physical pressure and matter. But I always comfort myself with the story of Saint Thomas the Apostle. (He shouldn't be chained as the doubter forever, should he? The saint was run through with spears during his martyrdom. Surely he deserves a bit more respect.) I remember Jesus's invitation that Thomas put his fingers into the nail prints in his hands, that Thomas thrust his hand into the Lord's side. Christ cooked fish, having to lift up the physical: the wood, the flint, the fish. Oh dear, I do hope I'm not just a lunatic, but only faith, despite the tender spot between finger and thumb, keeps me clinging to the idea that I am not. And things always seem to work out the way Jesus says they will. Maybe that's just the rhythm of the universe, though, as some people believe. Ah, well.

So, after graduate school, my life changed completely. Angie moved in with me in Martin, Kentucky. She had married after high school, I was her maid of honor, but her husband was killed when the steering on his delivery truck went out and he careened into the Gunpowder River. So she joined me in a little apartment downtown. I taught English at the local parochial school and she got her teaching certificate. I taught art at the Buckhorn Orphanage, as well as following Jesus's instructions and making rounds at the local hospital, sketching silly little comics for the children, reading them wonderful stories, and ministering where I could, trying to take advantage of every opportunity because, to be honest, there wasn't much else to do in Martin anyway.

Jesus was right about Nicholas. The breeze blew him into the hospital on an autumn night, the balmy kind where the humid wind blows the leaves across your paths, crackled brown hands tumbling toward the storm drain.

I'd pictured a car accident would deliver the man Jesus told me to help, but it was an accident of a different sort.

"What happened to him?" I asked the older nurse who was tucking his covers around him. Thank goodness they'd sedated him.

"He was on the roof of the Coal Building, fixing something from that windstorm last night. A live wire ran a high-voltage current right through his hand and out his foot. They're amputating the foot and the hand first thing in the morning."

The next morning, after the surgery, I visited his room. Nicholas was sitting up in bed eating a bowl of Cream of Wheat and drinking a cup of black coffee.

"Good morning, Mr."—I glanced at his chart. I thought of

him only as Nicholas. I didn't remember his last name—
"O'Malley. How are you feeling?"

The voice that issued from him surprised me. Let me
describe Nicholas O'Malley.

Imagine a pear tree come to life. Thin, jointed arms and a
ribbed trunk. His face was white, almost delicate, but it was
twisted by, what I guessed then, years of disappointment, dejec-
tion, and even disillusionment. His weathered skin, just as thick
and hard as Brister Purnell's sea-roughened exterior, clung to
his armature like wet felt over a topiary frame, and his eyes had
soaked up a sadness that served to form a hardened gloss over
him. His hair, that dark, greenish blond, stood out from his
head by the roots.

But despite that, it was easy to tell he wasn't angered at the
whole world, really. Mostly, he didn't trust himself.

I suspected by the reddened end of his nose that he sought
solace in the bottle. Perhaps he lived alone.

You may wonder how I surmised all of that after seeing
him lift a spoonful of Cream of Wheat to his mouth. Well, I
can't tell you other than that the Spirit of God whispers these
things in feelings and knowings, and most times I peg people
for exactly who they are. Not always, mind you. My preju-
dices get in the way like everybody else's. It's hard to love the
unloving.

I try to look through the eyes of love too. It's the only way to
even remotely get a good read. And in my life, my service, getting a good read up front has been a true necessity.

Nicholas continued to improve. I discovered a wry humor,
judging by all of his stump jokes, as well as a will from which he
benefited every day of his recovery. Physical therapy wasn't
exactly a major player in healing back in those days, but I doubt
Nicholas would have needed that—even today. He learned how
to do what he needed before he was released. He did well walk-

ing with his prosthesis, even taking me in his arms one day and twirling me a little bit.

"I was quite the dancer in high school," he said.

I did the math. Back in the '20s. Must have cut a mean rug with the Charleston or the Black Bottom.

And so, that simple statement set the tone for the rest of my time in Martin. Well, at least as far as our relationship went. Every Saturday night I'd meet Nicholas at the VFW hall and we'd dance, my right hand resting in the hook of his new hand. My superiors in the order realized how good this would be for a multiple amputee and gave me their blessing.

"Is that what you meant, Jesus?" I asked him one evening after I returned from the hall to find him sitting at the kitchen table looking at that morning's issue of the local paper.

"Yes. When you get your foot blasted off, you need to know God still wants you to dance."

"All right. I'll make some tea."

Every once in a while Jesus would stay all night with me. Not bound by time like we are, I knew he could afford to remain as long as he wanted, as long as was good for me.

In truth, I would have stayed that way, on my sofa in the circle of his arms, until I was nothing but a skeleton weighted with the dust of decades.

～～

Oh, I've wandered off into the past again and left poor Gerald in the lighthouse! I wouldn't admit this to Angie or John, but I think I'm slipping a bit.

Gerald grasped the railing and pushed away. "Well, let's go in. We can always come stand out here before we leave."

"All right."

I led him into the main room, what he and his father always called "the parlor."

"What I wouldn't give for a chair." He looked around, his chest heaving not with exertion but homecoming. "What I wouldn't give . . ."

"Guess the Coast Guard won't let you move back out here for old time's sake?" I shoved my hands in my pocket, felt my Job's Tears Rosary, and said a quick Eternal Father for Gerald.

One side of his mouth lifted. "Don't think so."

Inch by inch, he turned a complete 360 degrees, eyes flickering from ceiling to floor, ceiling to floor. "Right there hung our school pictures, and remember my father's reading chair? Right over near the window?"

"How long did he have that thing?"

"Well, he brought it out here and died in it. I'd say a good long time."

We laughed.

"He was one of the last of the true gentlemen," I said.

Mr. Keller always wore a coat and tie and a hat when he came to town, a hat he'd tip at the ladies as he held the door open for them.

"Yes, he was, MM. Yes, he was."

"Why don't you just stand here for a bit and I'll see about the loose floorboard? Where did Hattie say it was?"

"In the kitchen. Not far from where the Frigidaire used to stand."

Hattie always filled her refrigerator with plenty of grape juice, and I could almost see it, standing on that bald spot of wooden floor. I pressed my foot into the planks. After several attempts, a board gave play beneath the ball of my foot.

Okay. Good. Okay. I took a deep breath.

Well then. I looked up at the ceiling, through the plaster, the second story, the roof and right up into the sky.

Jesus knelt beside me. "You're going to be fine."

"Should I be worried?"

"Who are you talking to in there?" Gerald called.

"Wouldn't you like to know?"

Jesus patted my knee, then left.

"You're a little screwy, MM."

"Indeed!"

Now. How to pry up the board? I searched the kitchen drawers and of course found nothing but some dead bugs. The cupboards extended as much help.

I dug into my khakis for my keys, knelt down on the floor, and gently inserted the key to our cottage in between the boards. I pressed, prying up the wood, then popped it free. It clattered on the boards next to it.

Several papers, rolled up and secured with a rubber band, rested between the supports. My fingers encircled the yellowed onionskin, and the band snapped halfheartedly. Dry rot. The papers fell from my grasp, separated, and glided fanlike at my knees. The small courier type from Jude's old Royal manual blared words I knew would change me.

Lord, how I need some changing. I guess I've just become stuck in a rut and for some reason ruts don't lead you down the wild pathways where you trust God in ways you don't on the beaten path.

~

All right, so now, if you who are reading this must know, I'm no longer writing this on the exact day I took Gerald to the light. In fact, it's several months later. I'm probably making up half the dialogue at this point, but the gist is there, let me assure you, and Angie told me to make sure it feels like a story. So I'm trying that now. She said she'd go back over it for typos too. I should never have told her about this! I don't know why I did. I can't have her learning about my conversations with the Lord either. I'm definitely going to hide this when I'm finished. I did tell her I'm trying to weave the past in with the present, and Angie, who's always reading prizewinning fiction, said, "How very postmodern of you, Mary."

She can be such a snot.

Anyway, Gerald called to me from the parlor of the lighthouse.

"What is it?" I yelled back.

"I'm coming into the kitchen now. Is that okay?"

"Of course!"

He peered in through the door, his color better than it had been in years. He pointed to the papers. "See you've found Hattie's stash. Any money in there perchance?"

"Not a dime that I can see." I dug in and removed the recipe book she talked about.

"Figures. Here's to hoping anyway."

"Exactly." Dust swirled in the air as I blew it off the book.

I could see why Gerald annoyed Jude. Gerald found hope close to home. It was never right around the corner or coming next year. Those kind of people can be annoying to the one born with a furnace for a belly and no vents whereby to dispel the heat.

Gerald, seeming a bit more limber, knelt down next to me, then sat on the kitchen floor with his legs out in front of him. He reached out for the bundle. "Can I see?"

"Sure." I turned to the first page. "It's Jude's typewriter. For me. But you look first if you don't mind. I'm a little nervous."

My nerves stood up straight, in fact.

He pulled off his glasses and held the paper close to his eyes. I watched the light blue irises, faded after so many years in the sun, skitter over the words and down the lines. Finally he turned the page and I saw,

I Will Always Love You,

Jude

written somewhere in the middle. Gerald looked up at me with
a whistle.

"I don't know if you want to see this, MM. You might get
upset with him for having Hattie hide this for so long. Here."
He handed me the papers. "Read for yourself."

I grasped the paper and set it beside me, then gathered up
the remaining sheets. Poems, at least thirty of them, and all of
them about me during the days he refused to see me.

"I'm going to read these first."

"All right. I'll go back outside."

I sat cross-legged in the empty room and realized afresh
how much Jude loved me.

"You done yet?" Gerald came back into the kitchen awhile
later and sat down next to me.

"I haven't read the letter yet."

The poems, even though they weren't very good, stirred up
such a storm in my heart, I knew I wanted to be alone when I
read the letter. Was it Jesus speaking into my ear? I think so. I
shoved the bundle of papers and the recipe book under my arm.
"Gerald, I don't want to read this right now, and we should
probably get you back to Hattie."

"Will you come by tonight and give me your reaction?"

Rarely did I see that much concern on Gerald's face. Oh
goodness. This was going to be upsetting.

"Can I promise you I'll be there tomorrow after classes?"

"Righto. That'll be okay."

We stood up with harmonizing groans, locked up the lighthouse, and placed the key back in the lamp by the front door. I
promised myself, knowing how easy it turned out to be, that I'd
be back.

An hour later I walked Gerald into their bedroom. Hattie
was sitting up eating a grape twin-pop. "Went out to the light?"
she asked.

"Yep." Gerald leaned down and untied his shoes. "I'm feeling pretty good, Hat. How about you?"

"Funny thing. I went to sleep last night, and woke up this afternoon and heard I was almost a goner. I'm not ready to go yet, though."

"Then don't." I squeezed her shoulder.

"In fact"—she sucked the drips from the bottom of the pop near the stick—"I think we should take a vacation, Gerry."

Gerald carefully folded the floral windbreaker and handed it back to me. "Sounds like a good idea. If you ever tell a soul I wore that thing, MM, I don't know what I'll do."

"Those aren't your colors, honey," Hattie said. "Shades of yellow would have suited you much better."

I handed her the recipe book and she thanked me in her terse, yet heartfelt manner. "You read his letter, MM?"

"Not yet."

"Many a time I was tempted to read it, but a trust is a trust."

When I left them, they were sitting on Hattie's bed, holding hands and watching Tom Brokaw. Hattie loves Tom Brokaw.

The roll of papers bulged out the waistband of my pants, the corners of the sheets poking inato my skin. Time to get on home.

WHEN I FINISHED THE FIRST TWO YEARS OF TEACHING, HAD gone off to our motherhouse near Baltimore for a discernment period, and formally entered the novitiate, Jude found me that year during a brief visit to the city. It had been almost eleven years since we'd seen each other. He glimmered with the light of society, and Mr. Bray told me he heard Jude had become quite popular with the well-heeled and was a man about the town right in Baltimore. Mr. Bray wasn't sure what Jude did to make a living but he'd heard it was shady, and I didn't want to ask Jude when he showed up just as I'd finished my shift. As a novice, one of my duties was to help care for our aged sisters in our care facility.

I ran into his arms with a scream, right there in the main lobby.

Jude was my friend and I loved him. I quickly ushered him onto the sidewalk outside.

He embraced me and I noticed he'd filled out to man-sized proportions, having left the island boy behind. The thought of him not rowing out on the bay anymore, little Spark in front of him, saddened me. And the sight of one of his kites sailing aloft would have done me a world of good.

"Mary-Margaret, it's like a shot in the arm to see you. You look great! Just the same."

"You're still pretty handsome yourself."

Now dusted with a mysterious glamour, his hands jammed in his pockets, he held himself with an indifference to his surroundings. He later told me it wasn't that he felt at home wherever he was, more that he figured he'd never feel at home anywhere and he'd accepted it. His clothing was well-cut from beautiful cloth and his hair was shorn close to the sides of his head, the curls up top spilling onto his brow.

We stared at each other for a while, the years piling up like a flash flood behind a dam, until I reached out and touched his arm. "I have a free evening. How about we get a piece of pie over at The White Coffee Pot?"

He held out his arm; I threaded mine through and we walked in the direction of the restaurant. Sometimes we walked down the Main Street in Abbeyville the same way, our arms zinging from the contact, him soaking it in and enjoying it for what it was, me cursing Satan but still enjoying it nonetheless. Sister Thaddeus told me it wasn't a sin letting Jude be a gentleman, that perhaps our walks, even our friendship, was the only time he got the chance to behave himself. "I trust you, Mary-Margaret," she whispered. "And it's summer, so the other girls won't see you."

I was much better behaved during the school year.

"I've missed you, Mary-Margaret," Jude said that day.

"Likewise."

I love Baltimore. And I remember walking from the motherhouse all the way to Highlandtown on Jude's arm. Up Eastern Avenue we sort of sidled, looking, I have to admit, quite the couple. Near Patterson Park, he reached in his pocket and pulled out a piece of candy.

I did not let him put it on my tongue this time.

He got a kick out of that. "So you're completely serious about this nun thing, aren't you?"

"Well, technically—"

"Yes, you'll be a religious sister. It's just easier to say nun, Mary-Margaret, and less confusing. Sister could mean two things and most people take it to mean something biological. Nun means a Catholic lady who foregoes marriage—"

"Gets married to Jesus."

"Semantics. And then goes on to hit kids on the backs of their hands with a ruler."

I howled with laughter. And he joined in.

Jude knew me. And he knew Sister Thaddeus and some of the others at my school.

Sure, there were people like Sister Antiochus, who we called Antiochus Ephiphanes after that lovely Roman ruler who destroyed the temple and liked a good massacre. She was just plain mean. Judgmental, austere, and prone to think if you weren't always in a posture of mourning, begging for God's mercy on your knees, you weren't being realistic about the state of your soul. None of us dared to mention we knew she snuck cigarettes around the back side of the garden shed. But people like the Ephiph were everywhere in life, always pointing fingers, looking around the beams in their eyes to stare at your splinter with dripping disapproval, so it stood to reason they'd enter religious orders too.

Jude knew he was overgeneralizing and he winked at me to let me know. "So what's happening after this phase of the nun business?"

Years later I finally learned to stopped correcting him.

"I'm heading to Georgia after I'm finished with my novitiate here."

"Gerald told me."

I stopped in front of the Patterson Theater. "You've contacted him?"

"Don't look so shocked."

"But don't you hate Gerald?"

"Not hate, Mary-Margaret. He annoys the heck outta me, the goody two-shoes."

We ordered hot turkey sandwiches at The White Coffee Pot. Here's an old matchbook cover from the place.

The white bread stuck to the roofs of our mouths and we laughed as, more than once, we actually had to dislodge the bread from behind our teeth with our fingertips. Schmidt's Bakery wasn't far away. I still buy Schmidt's Blue Ribbon Bread every once in a while, and when nobody's looking, I'll walk down Main Street to the small grocery store where Jude and I used to buy gum, and purchase two thick slices of Esskay Bologna (a Maryland favorite) and a slice of American cheese. I'll arrange that on a slice of bread and put some mayo smack on another slice of bread. Clap it together and you're ten again. Aunt Elfi taught me by example the proper way to eat a bologna sandwich. You simply have to smash the bread with your fingertips until it's one-quarter as thick and gets a little gummy.

Magnificent.

Jude ate them the same way.

The waitress at The White Coffee pot refilled our cups of coffee long into the evening, and soon he began to open up over slices of apple pie. I excused myself and called the motherhouse from the pay phone near the women's restroom, getting Angie to explain the situation for me. Like so many times on the island, she covered for me.

Apparently, Jude was already a widower, a father, and a man who had lost his child.

Jude went away from the light both literally and figuratively. It's hard to believe someone as smart and good-looking as he could have fallen down so utterly. As we sat in The White Coffee Pot, he told the tale. To be honest, when the story meandered farther down the path, I longed to take my hand from his, knowing where that hand had been. Several times I comforted myself with the remembrance that Jude, even as a boy, was a clean freak who washed his hands many times a day. Oh, not in the obsessive-compulsive way, but more in a mindful of germs manner, which made it even harder to believe he'd do such things with so many people. I assumed he took a lot of showers.

Jude arrived in Baltimore and proceeded to find a room down near the docks off Fort Avenue. The day job at Domino Sugar would have never been enough for Jude. And who could imagine him living the life I did? Coming home to a good book, a cup of tea, and Jesus Christ? Hardly.

He inevitably found himself accompanying some workmates down to The Block, Baltimore's red-light district. You'll rarely find a person in Baltimore that hasn't at least driven down the main strip of debauchery on Baltimore Street to get a look-see at the bouncers, the prostitutes, the destitute, and those who feed the beast with their money. I was no exception. But to understand what really goes on there, you have to inhabit such a place. Jude inhabited every aspect.

"It started out just selling some opium I'd get from one of the guys at the docks, Mary-Margaret. And I liked the money and started delving into prostitution."

I tried to pull my hand away, but he held on tight.

"Were you the pimp?" I asked, the word, not something you hear at the motherhouse every day, surprising me.

"No. Someone propositioned me and paid good money. Real good money."

If his skin had been peeled off his face, his expression couldn't have been any more naked.

"Are you a homosexual, Jude?"

He shook his head. "No. You know better than that, Mary-Margaret."

"So, who did you sleep with—rich, lonely ladies?"

He howled out a laugh. "On the Block? H--- no!"

"Men then?"

"Yes. And some women. Mostly men."

The wind went out of me. Pictures of Jude sitting on the step whistling up our skirts flew out with my breath. Who are you? I wanted to say, but I knew this was Jude. This had always been Jude. And my presence in his life was the odd bit.

"I had hoped . . ." I didn't know what else to add.

"That I'd come up here and end up a banker or a lawyer or something?" He laughed again, the sound brittle enough to blow away as powder. "I grew up on Locust Island. I never went to college like you did."

"You could have."

"With what money?"

"Did you say you made a lot selling drugs?"

"Yes. But I spent it all. We always spend it all. Cautious people don't sell drugs in the first place, Mary-Margaret."

"You're right. So you've got fine clothing. I assume you've upped the status of your clientele?"

"You could say that."

I wanted to ask him how many clients he'd had, but I knew he'd lost count. At least, in a way, I hoped so, because when you lose count of something, you stop holding on to each individual occurrence.

"You mentioned a wife." I held up my coffee cup to the waitress for a refill.

Jude did too. She left the table with a shake of her head. "I'll leave you a big tip, sweetheart," Jude said. And he would. Though obviously one of dubious morality, Jude was, and remained, a truthful man throughout his life. Figure that one out if you can.

Jude rarely exhibited a loss for words, but that night, as we sat in the diner, everything seemed to close in around us as I waited. He lifted his cup to his lips—the ceiling descended a few inches. He straightened his tie—the walls moved toward us. He cleared his throat—the waitresses grew large. Everything took on a close importance. "Remember us," the vinyl booths and the large plate glass window mouthed.

So I sat in silence, waiting for his story to emerge and I blinked my eyes, taking pictures with each shutter of my eyelids. The streetlight outside backlit little fingerprints at the bottom of the front window. The chrome coating on the push bar of the front door was worn to the left where folks laid their hands and gained entrance. The floor, green and white linoleum tile, was laid in a large checkerboard pattern, four squares of green, then four squares of white, and so on. And a middle-aged, blond man wearing navy blue coveralls ate a piece of lemon meringue pie at the counter that lined the left side of the room and drank his cup of coffee, holding the mug without using the handle. I remember thinking that he was carrying a great deal of heaviness, as if his coveralls weighed a thousand pounds, and when he got up to leave, he left all the spare change he had.

Finally Jude spoke at the same time as he looked into my face.

"I was bouncing at one of the clubs for a while, just taking a break from the other things."

"I imagine that chips at your soul."

"I have no soul."

You do, I thought. But theology had to take a back seat.

"I started seeing one of the dancers. She reminded me a little of you, Mary-Margaret."

Indeed?!

"Just in the way she was kind to me. She was hardened like a lot of the others, but there was something left untouched underneath."

"What was her name?"

"Bonnie."

"That's nice. Did she have a stage name?"

"Of course, but I won't say it in front of you."

The older he got, the fewer lines he would cross with me, the less he sought to shock me. Good thing, that. I would have grown tired of the comments had he kept it up. There's only so many ways a person can mutter lewdness before it just seems like a little boy making flatulence noises with his hand tucked under his armpit.

"Bonnie and I entered into a relationship. Of course most of the girls would have sex with a man for extra money, and she was no exception. She did have a taste for the finer things, so I stopped bouncing and went back to my old job so she wouldn't have to subject herself to prostitution."

"Job?" I laughed.

He shrugged. "I'm trying to say this all as delicately as I can, Mary-Margaret."

"Thank you."

"Don't mention it."

My heart felt pummeled, bruised, and more fists landed on the bruises until, like Jesus's face upon the cross, it became unrecognizable. The bit of pity I always felt for Jude due to his home life turned into something almost maternal.

"I'm going to make a long story short." He thrust his hands in his jacket pockets and slumped down in the booth. When he looked up at the ceiling, the heat rose to his neck. "She took sick. I moved in to help her. She got pregnant. I continued to bring in money; she continued to ask for more and more and more. It turned ugly, but she was carrying my kid. The pregnancy took it all out of her. She wouldn't go to the doctor no matter how much I tried to convince her."

"What do you think it was?"

"Cancer, maybe. I talked to one of my clients, a doctor, describing the symptoms and he said it was most likely colon cancer. The baby, a little boy, was stillborn eight months into the pregnancy and Bonnie died a few hours later."

"You said you were a widower."

"I married her when she was six months along."

"Despite the life you were living? Forced to turn tricks for her?"

"Nobody forces me to do anything, Mary-Margaret. She was pregnant with my child. That was that. By the time we got married, we weren't even sleeping together."

Such were the times, my sisters.

"This is terrible."

"Yeah."

"Does your father know anything about it?"

He shook his head. "I haven't seen him in years. Hardly anybody else knows."

"Not even Gerald or Hattie?"

"Hattie does."

"That makes sense. And she'll take it to her grave."

The waitress, scratching her scalp with the sharpened end of her pencil, approached with our tab. "We're about to close."

Jude paid for our food and we turned back out onto the avenue. We walked toward the center of town, passing by Pacey's Bridal and Formal. I stopped and, standing in front of the shop, squeezed his arm.

"Did you ever once in your life wish for this?" I cast a sweeping arm beside the display windows showing off white cupcake bridal gowns and foamy, pale pink bridesmaids' dresses.

"Honestly? Nope. This sort of thing has never entered my mind. At least not in this traditional way. What about you?"

I nodded. "I have to be honest with you, Jude. I do." I could hardly believe I was admitting it to myself. "But not for the wedding or the marriage even. You know I've never been one that needed male company."

He laughed. "An understatement."

"But I'd like to have a little baby. There's something inside of me that so desires a baby of my own."

"You were orphaned. It only makes sense to want someone all your own, someone you're related to, someone you have to put up with because they're family."

"You don't do that."

"But you would. That's the point." He touched the glass window. "I don't know what I want, Mary-Margaret. I may have a brother and parents, but there's where you're ahead of me."

He was right.

"So what's next for you?"

"I buried Bonnie and the baby about two weeks ago—"

"I didn't realize it was so fresh."

"Yeah." He tucked my arm in his and laid his free hand over mine and we continued down the street toward Haussner's Restaurant, the glass panes in its art deco doorway dark.

"Did you name him?"

"No. At least not out loud. But I think he'd have liked the lighthouse."

"Well, how about after your dad then?"

By this time, Mr. Keller had retired and Gerald was running the light.

He shook his head. "I just can't. Sometimes you just can't look back."

"Where is your dad, Jude?"

"Still over on Tangier, crabbing along the shore with his string and his bits of raw chicken. That's what Gerald says."

Disdain coated every word.

"Heard from your mom?" She'd left Brister not long after Jude ran away.

"Nothing. Probably for the best."

"Will you ever go back to Locust Island?"

We approached the motherhouse.

"Only to be buried."

"You hate it there that much?"

"I couldn't begin to find the words."

"So where to next?"

"I'm going away for a while. To Europe. With . . . well, who doesn't really matter, I just know I've got to get away from Baltimore for a while after all that's happened."

"Male or female?" I asked, instantly regretting it. "Never mind. Don't answer that."

"Don't worry. I wasn't going to. Where you headed after this stint?"

"I'll be leaving for Georgia to teach."

"Oh, they'll *love* you down there," he said, tone as dry as toast. "But you'll have your Jesus, right, Mary-Margaret?"

I laughed. "Right."

"Sometimes I don't know why I put up with your religious delusions."

What could I say? If Jude had known how close to the mark he'd come with that statement, I might never have seen him again. Then again, if I was delusional, Jude was obviously so lacking in perfection, he'd be in no position to judge.

"You put up with it because when we care about people, we make concessions."

I let him kiss me good-bye, praying nobody saw us.

Nobody did. Or if so, they never told me.

~~

After a year at the motherhouse, I packed up a trunk into which I placed all my belongings including nothing new other than an afghan Mrs. Bray crocheted me and the habit of our order, light gray, floor-length with a white veil. I began my mission novitiate, a two-year assignment with a group of our school sisters in Bainbridge, Georgia. Angie accompanied me. We felt like explorers in a way, heading into a clearly non-Catholic area and yet, I was a little frightened. I was finally going to be teaching. What if I loved the children too much? I'd have to leave them after all was said and done. It might tear my heart out. For an orphan these sorts of possibilities are a little larger than you might imagine if you've grown up with two parents and a sibling and a couple to spare.

I pressed my habit and a spare veil, packed the replacement pair of shoes I bought two years before, pajamas, slippers, bed linens, two towels, my prayer books, Thomas Merton's *Seven Story Mountain*, and my copy of the Scriptures. Had I left two years earlier I would have packed Aquinas, but a few months before I'd realized his total disregard for women and there went poor Tom. (Don't tell anybody I said that.) These days, however, I do like to read the bits I agree with. I still find some of Augustine's writings a little hard to stomach, so I stay away from him for the most part. We have two thousand years of people to choose from. Why get caught up on the same old, same old?

And yet, the Church is such a motley collection of pilgrims, which is why I fit in so well.

So off I headed to Georgia to teach at a parochial school, boarding school, and home for foundlings (read orphanage). Oh dear! I do hope Angie writes down some of her experiences at St. Teresa's too. I stepped off the train and was immediately blasted by south Georgia heat, in my woolen habit and my veil.

The stares felt just as oppressive, but I understood. It wasn't like Georgia was crawling with Catholics!

I looked at my directions, grabbed my suitcase, and walked down Shotwell Street toward the Flint River. Moss dripped from the trees. I'd seen that sight in pictures, but the real-life experience of it helped me to realize I'd entered another world.

As I unpacked my trunk in the small room, eight feet by ten feet, painted bright white, I hummed a tune. I always felt at home in institutions where children were present.

"I knew you'd like it here. You're going to have a good time."

I turned, crucifix in hand.

Jesus sat on the straight-backed chair near the small desk beneath the room's only window, a large enough window, granted, to take in the fields behind our dormitory on the second floor of what was once a plantation home. I was given the job of dormitory attendant. Unfortunately, I wasn't any good at keeping order. I simply outlasted them. Cards? You want to play cards? Chinese checkers? Popcorn, you say? I was always the last one standing. Not one girl ever spilled word of our nighttime escapades to the director.

"Will there be some excitement?"

He nodded. "Some good, some bad. You know how it usually works by now, T—."

"How's Jude?"

"Off-limits to ask, my dear."

"Okay. Grandmom?"

"Good. She'll never be beatified by the pope, but she's with me." He laughed.

I sighed and fell on my knees by his chair. He put his arms around me as I lay my head on his lap.

After hours—days? years?—I lifted my head and looked into

his eyes. He cupped my chin in his hand. "You'll suffer in my name here. Are you ready for this?"

I nodded. "If you'll be with me."

"I'm always with you." A shaft of sunlight illumined the golden brown of his eyes. "You know, I was in a tattoo parlor the other day disguised as a prostitute when I heard the artist say something I liked. 'If Jesus takes me to it, he'll take me through it.' The things my children come up with. It's delightful though, isn't it?"

"It pleases you?"

"If it's from the heart. And in that man's case, yes, it was. He and I have been through a lot together."

"Does he know you're the prostitute?"

"In a way, yes. He always gives me a cup of coffee and lets me warm myself before I head back out onto the street."

I sighed and put my arms back around him. "I love you."

And I laid my head against his chest this time, heard his sacred heart, real flesh and blood, beating in time with the universe, and I heard how much he loved me too.

~~~

All righty. It's been long enough. Let's find out what was in Jude's letter.

Angie, who always locks up Mercy House around ten, had gone to bed at least an hour before I unrolled the papers. My bed light cast a yellow hum down on the aging sheets, and in my head I heard the words to the *Agnus Dei.*

Agnus Dei, qui tollis peccata mundi. Miserare nobis.

Agnus Dei, qui tollis peccata mundi. Miserare nobis.

Agnus Dei, qui tollis peccata amundi. Dona nobis pacem.

Lamb of God. Oh Lamb of God, have mercy on me. I smoothed out the papers. Lamb of God. Grant us peace. Grant me peace.

I half expected Jesus to show up. But he didn't. The Spirit surrounded me with a warm breath. Still I shook, from the skipping of my heart, outward to the tips of my fingers as they skated across the smooth, onionskin paper.

And there was his signature. Just his given name.

Jude. The boy who had always loved me.

"All right," I whispered into the gloom surrounding the circle of light. "Let's get this over with."

The quiet of the room—my plain white room like so many others before it—grew dense, thickening like foam in my eardrums. I pictured the blazing trees of autumn in the darkness outside and their steady beauty gave me courage.

November 1960

Dear Mary-Margaret,

I'll just cut right to the chase. I think someday you might need to get to know your dad. I figured out who he was a few weeks ago but don't feel the time is right to tell you. If you find him and learn the truth about your mother, I don't know if you could handle it. At least right now. There's a lot to adjust to as it is these days. And you don't seem to be yearning for your dad or anything and this could screw you up.

We all mess up. Obviously he did. But you're here reading this letter and I think you need to know that somehow it's all in the bigger plan of things. Maybe you already do know that. Heck, maybe you're a realist like me. Bad things happen. But still, we both know somebody's up there looking down on us. You've given me the proof of that. But I'm rambling. I don't feel too good right now. And I'm not sure how long it's going to take for this disease to progress.

His Christian name is Brendan Connelly. I knew you knew he was a seminarian at the time of the rape. I think he's from an old Baltimore

family. He went to Mount St. Mary's Seminary in Emmitsburg. You can
find him from there, if you want to. I could say more, but that info should
be enough to get you started.

I quickly counted up the years. He would be ninety-five
now. Most likely a dead man. Although I'm getting old and feel
great, so maybe I'm taking after him. Perhaps he's privy to those
yogurt-consuming, mountain-spring-water-drinking genetics.
No, I doubted he was alive.

"So why this? Why now?" I whispered aloud.

Jesus doesn't appear at my whims, you see. And he didn't
that night either. I was left with the same wonderings everyone
has: wondering if this was truly important, wondering if this was
just some sort of crazy plot of Satan to trip me up and keep me
from my true mission, wondering if God was in this or it was
merely a crazy coincidence.

And now. Wondering about my mother? Mother? Jude
knew how much everybody had loved her here on the island.
Her picture hung at St. Mary's School all during my growing-up
years, in memoriam. We put flowers on her grave once a month.
What could possibly be so bad?

But no. Jesus told me to take Gerald out to that light. So I
clung to that. Lately I'd been wanting to know if my father felt
bad about what he did, if he'd turned around, if he tried to find
me. My mother would be okay if I did a little digging.

I'm telling Hattie to hide this here at the light so you won't find it at the
apartment. If you don't get this information while I'm alive, I've told her
to give it to you after I've died, but only when you're over what happened
to me. And she has no idea what's inside this letter, in case you want to
shoot the messenger.

For now, I don't think you're ready. You're still pretty angry with
the guy and I doubt he'll be able to take it if you meet him now. I've got

your number even if you don't, Mary-Margaret. That red hair of yours tells the true tale even if you try to keep things under wraps.

I guess I'll just have to trust it'll fall into your hands when it's supposed to.

His signature made me cry.

I'm writing again out at the point. It's chilly, but I just needed to get out of the cottage. Angie tried to make crème brûlée and burnt it but good. The whole house stinks. We've banned her from the kitchen yet again. Blanca ate it like it was the best thing she'd ever tasted, but that's Blanca for you.

I believe the last time I wrote I was talking about my time in Georgia. My fellow sisters welcomed me that evening, prepared a simple meal, and we prayed the evening office. School wouldn't begin for a month, so in between prayers and planning for my classes, I walked through the wooded areas alongside the river. It inspired me. My art had primarily been achieved with paint, ink, charcoal, or graphite up to that point. My mattress and box spring anchored a secret collection of portraits of the only two men I ever loved: Jesus and Jude. But what about wood? Sculpture? It was there I discovered the joys of bending wood.

I often wondered whether I captured what Jesus really looked like, or simply what he looked like to me. We all see Jesus in such different ways. Some as conquering king, others as Jewish carpenter. The gentle shepherd; the defender of children. The friend that sticks closer than a brother; the rebuker of the Pharisees. The cleanser of the temple; the defender of the adulteress. The eater of grain and healer on the Sabbath;

the speaker in the synagogue who came not to abolish the law but to fulfill it.

The face of Jude often flowed from my pencils and brushes, his many expressions: surliness, delight, mischief, anger, and love. That Jude loved me I never doubted; that Jude felt he deserved to, he never believed. What a subject, however. I wondered if his face would one day become famous, certainly more than the artist that drew it, again and again and again, her fascination of its even planes, its sensual curves and hard places never waning. I'm most likely the most unfamous artist there is!

However, that November, having escaped the humidity and the mosquitoes for several months, I began sculpting, chopping down small saplings in the woods behind the school and setting up pulleys and ropes in my art studio to bend them into shapes unnatural yet somehow organic. The branches seemed to bow down their heads, imploring their Creator on behalf of those in the walls of the school. And so began the series called To Pray.

Sr. Mary-Margaret's sculptures were installed at the Hirshhorn Museum in Washington DC in July of 2015.

My favorite student quickly showed himself to be a fourteen-year-old black orphan named Morpheus Sloan. (Actually all of our orphans were black.) Morpheus was the son of a woman from Detroit. Beatrice married his father and they moved back to his family homeplace near Bainbridge only to find he simply wanted her to take care of his sick mama. Which she did, despite the fact that her husband left only two months into their marriage and was neither seen nor heard from again. Six months after Mr. Sloan deserted his new bride, she gave birth to Morpheus. Her mother-in-law, Dorothea, lived for three more years and was a sweet old lady, grateful for everything. When she died, Beatrice did her best to try and raise Morpheus, but it was difficult. Finally, sick and not able to feed and care for her son like she wished, alone and without family, she dropped four-year-old Morpheus off one summer night with a note pinned to his blouse. She went home and put a gun in her mouth.

Morpheus didn't know that. He thought both of his parents were killed in a train wreck. He still doesn't know the truth, and I doubt he'll ever get his hands on this notebook to find out.

Morpheus was a powerful boy, the oldest boy, and my obvious choice to help cut down saplings. The first time I asked, he rubbed his hands together. "Why, sure, sister. What kind do you want? Because I know where everything grows around here."

He took me into the woods and together we cut down young softwoods: larch and cedar, pine and oak, willow if we could find it. Beside the school, he helped me strip them of their small branches and anchor them to the ground with stakes. We tied ropes around their middles, hoisted the hemp up over the branches of the oak trees in the yard, and pulled down on the ends of those saplings, bending them into graceful arcs and securing them to stakes Morpheus drove deep into the red clay of the Georgia earth.

We didn't talk much. We didn't have to. He took to the work so naturally I invited him into the studio to experiment with other bits of wood and metal parts we'd collected. Amazing what people throw away, isn't it? What fun we had with a couple of blowtorches and some hardware.

When the priest from the nearby parish would come on Thursdays to say Mass, Morpheus would serve at the altar in our chapel, his black skin gleaming like onyx against the marble white of the vestments.

Jesus told me he had special plans for Morpheus and it proved to be the case.

Teaching at St. Teresa's was a happy experience that first year. The day students would arrive each morning. Some Protestants' children tried to peek under my habit.

"What do you think you're going to find there?" I asked.

"A tail," one little boy named Homer said. "My sister says you all are devils in disguise."

Louise piped up. "My cousin says you all have horns under your veils."

I laughed. "Really?"

We were in the art room making hand turkeys for Thanksgiving cards. I handed out brown paper bags to each student. "Now, do you really think there are horns under here?"

Several of them nodded and I realized the conversation was so metaphorical, especially in these parts, as to the misconceptions of the faith I'd come to love so much. Catholicism was of the devil to so many of these dear people, people who thought we loved Mary more than Jesus, and the Church more than God himself.

"Would you like to see under my veil?" I asked.

Another little girl with tiny, clear-blue cat glasses gasped. "No! I'd be scared."

I knelt down beside her and took her hand. "Elaine, we've been in this class for almost three months now. Do you really think I'd hurt you?"

She shrugged. "Granddaddy says he wouldn't trust you all more than he would a ni—negro."

I got so tired of hearing what they call the N-word these days. So tired!

We had two different schools going on. One for the paying students and another for the orphans, primarily black children.

I did, however, show the children my head.

"What beautiful red hair you have!" Louise crooned, reaching out, then snatching back her hand.

"See? No horns."

I let each of them pat me on the head.

～✕～

Morpheus laughed so hard when I told him, I thought he'd cease to breathe. "Oh, Sister Mary-Margaret. Horns? Why, that's the funniest thing I heard in a long, long time."

We tromped through the woods looking for a dying tree to strip bark from for a wood mosaic Morpheus dreamed up the week before. The saplings we'd bent were ready to be taken into the studio to finish drying and curing. What I didn't know at the time was that somebody didn't like me poking through the woods with Morpheus, who, quite honestly didn't look a day under eighteen.

We set down our sacks and rested our feet before returning to the school. I pulled an apple out of my pocket and set it between us on the log. "Do you have your pocketknife?"

"Yes I do."

"Let's split it then."

Morpheus, last time I saw him, still has the same type of hands he did then. Much like Mr. Bray's, they are meek and move with an economical grace, yet powerful, their strength under humble control. That day he placed forefinger and thumb on one side of the scarlet skin stretched over the apple. He sliced it with the pocketknife he'd already cleaned on the outside hem of his shirt. When the free side of the fruit toppled back, wobbling on the crusty bark of the log, he stabbed it with the point of the knife and held it out to me, completely untouched by his hands.

Without a word, I took the other side and bit exactly where his artistic, dexterous, creative, made-by-God fingertips had been, their prints invisible nonetheless.

He lifted one side of his mouth in a smile and shook his head. "Horns. On you." And then he *tsked*.

Listen to me, sisters. If you don't know it already, you will be hated at times for who you are, at the very least misunderstood, by those who claim to love the same Jesus you do. You will be named with the Whore of Babylon, and you will be called "unsaved," "not born again," even an "idolater." Love them anyway. Without Love, as the apostle Paul says, all we say, all we do, even our faith, is nothing.

We can shed our faith no more than Morpheus could shed his skin. And if we love completely, it should be just as obvious as the color of our skin. Don't be hated just because you took a stand; be hated because you laid down your life.

~⌣~

Now. What I did about that letter from Jude.

I was just finishing up my string art class the day after the lighthouse trip when Angie caught me in my supply closet scribbling *plant bulbs* on the palm of my hand.

"You're acting strange." She ran her hand along the stacks of plastic tubs holding paints, brushes, markers, pencils, scissors, glue, foam shapes, pompons, pipe cleaners, tape, wire, and, well, check the inventory sheet if you want the complete list. "Gerald told me about the letter, so you might as well spill the beans."

I led her out of the closet and grasped the long-handled hook used to open and shut the clerestory windows that flooded the activity room (used to be my art classroom) with light. "It was a beautiful fall day today, wasn't it? I thought I'd let the breeze come in."

"I did the same thing in my room. The trick-or-treaters should be coming by tonight. I bought Hershey Bars this year."

I pulled shut the final window. "You buy Hershey Bars every year, Angie."

"I'd hate to disappoint them. So, the letter." She sat down at one of the tables with a sigh, then pulled up her knee-high pantyhose and kicked off her shoes, those black, cloth Mary-Janes people wear in China. "Remember when Jude tried to get you an exhibit in Salisbury?"

I nodded and sat down on the corner of the desk. "He was always trying."

"I hated Jude until then. And then I knew. I saw it all."

"I didn't realize how much that mattered to you then."

"Oh but it did."

Filling a bucket with soap and water at the sink . . .

"So. About the hidden papers."

"Gerald was asking whether or not you planned to do anything about it."

I turned off the spigot. "I haven't quite decided."

"He wouldn't tell me what the letter said even though I asked."

I grabbed the large sponge. Time to wipe down the work surfaces.

"So anyway, Mary?"

"Well, it's about my father."

"The raping seminarian?"

"Angie . . ." I wrung out the sponge and began circling it atop the tables, the pristine aroma of the lemon detergent released into the air, the sponge leaving a shining wake.

"I know. Why would you want to know anything about *him*?"

"Apparently Jude thought I might someday. Although he didn't put down a whole lot of information about him, just his

name and when he was a seminary student. He said something
about my mother, not wanting me to get upset."

"What else could have happened to Saint Mary Margaret the
First we already don't know? Sister Thaddeus sings her praises
to this day. So what's your next step? That is, if you've decided
to explore the matter more." She leaned back in the chair, the
two front feet off the floor. I swear every time she does that my
heart jumps in my throat. And she's been doing it for years.
And has never once fallen. Perhaps I should trust her more.
Her table came next.

"Angie? What good can possibly come of this?" I rubbed
the sponge back and forth over an ornery spot of dried paste.

She steadied the chair, leaned forward, and clasped my
wrist. "We all have a need to know about our father."

"Really? I don't think I do." Yes, I was lying. I mean I did *want*
to know. Maybe. But I didn't *need* to. Indeed. I'm old. Wouldn't
it be fine to just die someday and figure it all out quickly on the
other side? I think so.

"You need to, Mary. Trust me." She let go.

"You really think so?"

"I know so."

"But how can you be so sure?"

"We've been together a long time. I'd like to think I know
you pretty well."

I continued scrubbing. "How about an ice-cream cone?
They've still got pumpkin flavored across the street."

"Let's go."

She grabbed a sponge and we made short order of the work.

~⁓~

When we'd situated ourselves at the back table in Clare's A Sweet
Thing, I pulled out the letter from my pocket and handed it to
Angie. "Take a look."

Clare sidled up, hands in the pocket of her apron. Her bright red hair sprang from either side of her thin face in two long ponytails. Her lips matched. "Hey, little sissies. Pumpkin? The last of it too, so you just made it."

Sissies. You just have to love that.

"Sign us up!" Angie rapped the table.

"You two doing okay? I heard you kidnapped Gerald and took him to the lighthouse yesterday, Sister Mary."

I whistled. "Word sure gets around, doesn't it?"

"Yep. Good for you. I'd have done the same thing. Heard he had a miraculous turnaround too." She crossed herself even though, as far as I know, Clare is one of those new emergent Christian young people who worship down at the old bowling alley. It seems like it's about the furthest thing you can get from Catholicism, I think, in their lack of hierarchy; I don't quite understand it, but they love Jesus and who am I to tell the Holy Spirit when and where to show up? "We started lighting candles for people down at The Alley. Want me to light one for him?" she asked.

"Please do. I'll do the same up here at our end of the spectrum."

She pulled on one of her ponytails and gave me a smirk. "We could learn a lot from you guys. You should come down sometime."

"Maybe we will. And we'll learn from you too."

"Lord knows us old gals could use a shot in the arm," Angie said.

"I'll get your ice cream."

She whisked back behind the counter, her mid-thigh-length plaid skirt brushing jauntily against her striped tights.

I settled my chin in my hand. "Do you ever miss the fact that we didn't get to be funky, crazy girls in wild tights and bright red hairdos?"

"All the time," said Angie. "Oh, I guess I could have been crazy when I was a young married, but I was swooning so much over the whole deal, I just wanted to make sure Mack came home to a clean place and a good supper and some crazy love-making."

"Angie! Spare me, please."

"Oh, come on. Don't look so shocked. It's not like you never—"

"Hey!" But I held up my hand to my mouth and stifled the laugh.

"You know it's true." She whispered, "You slept with the best-looking guy I'd ever seen. And built too."

"Angie!"

"Jude looked like an angel, Mary. A rough-and-tumble, hard-edged angel."

I couldn't help but picture his ice blue eyes and the way he'd lift his hand to cup my jaw. "He was the prettiest boy I'd ever seen."

"Okay." She set her hands flat on the table. "Tell me about the papers."

~~

Let's see, I need to tell you about what happened in Georgia because that's really part of my religious sister journey and many of you might relate to the teaching aspect.

For half a year, I taught art as well as literature to the orphans. In fact, it was in the spring of my first school year that we decided, after seeing how competitive their testing was, to blend the two schools. Only Angie and myself and two other sisters, Magdalene and Joan, taught at the school anyhow, and we were all on board. Separation of church and state was on our side.

We worked hard that summer, expanding the curriculum, whipping the classrooms into the best shape they'd been in years. Yes, the facilities, an old plantation house and stables, seemed to be in need of constant repair, but by the beginning of our second year at St. Teresa's, everything gleamed with a fresh coat of white paint.

"It's a little slice of heaven," Morpheus said about two weeks before Labor Day as we bent some more saplings out in the backyard.

"Sister Angie says it looks like an asylum."

"Oh no. They's love in there, Sister Mary-Margaret."

We lost a lot of the day students when we announced our plans, but a few of the more forward-looking families stuck with us, and a large Catholic family moved in that year with eight school-aged children (of fourteen!). One Baptist woman named Minnie (for Minerva) sent her son and became one of our most ardent supporters. You simply can't tell where the Spirit of God will work, can you? Minnie even sewed uniforms for us and taught deportment, throwing a high tea that next year. Some of the social mavens tried to shun her by refusing to attend her Thursday afternoon card club; she immediately filled the spots with younger women on the waiting list. She ended up adding four more tables for the deserters after they came back with their tails between their legs.

The fact that we even had a school year was a miracle.

What happened the night before school began, the day we were set to throw open our doors to the brave and the bold, turned out to be, quite possibly, the worst night of my life. And it had been such a nice Labor Day. But let me tell you a little bit about Bainbridge, Georgia, first.

~~

When General Sherman marched to the sea leaving a wake of sorrow and destruction, he missed Bainbridge, Georgia. Along Shotwell Street, mansions sit shoulder to shoulder, their intricate woodwork harboring some inhabitants who'd thank Jesus for his cross one minute and burn it the next. If I could have understood it, I'd have foregone the opportunity. Blanca, from Lexington, Kentucky, told me not to be so judgmental. "Why, Mary, in my own home city the Church began St. Peter Claver so the black folk wouldn't go to St. Paul's. And the Episcopalians did the same thing with St. Andrews."

Sad, but true.

But there were a lot of wonderful people in Bainbridge too: the man who helped us with repairs, Jack Dryden, and his wife, Sue-Ellen; Pastor Lundquist at the Presbyterian Church. Bitty Ann Shea, who ran the grocery store, always gave us a big smile and some conversation whenever we went in. Oh, and lots more.

If you walked down to the end of Shotwell Street, you arrived at the Flint River and the edge of town. Two hundred yards from the riverbank sat our school where, on that Labor Day in 1958, we tacked up the final maps and washed the chalkboards with warm, soapy water. Angie lifted new dictionaries from a cardboard box, raising each book to her nose and breathing in the fresh, pulpy scent of paper with more than its fair share of citrusy-smelling ink inside, before sliding it onto the bookshelf.

I sat at one of the student desks, drawing pictures of mathematicians and scientists for her to tape up over her doorway and windows. "We might not get away with this."

"Somebody's got to be the first. We'll say we didn't have the money to continue with two separate schools."

The orphan school was a one-room school in a small trapper's cabin right on the river. The four of us each took one day a week. The day school met on the bottom floor of the big house, the upper floors housed the orphans, and the attic housed the sisters. Hot as blazes in the summer, and thankfully, south Georgia didn't get so horribly cold in the winter.

"Well, I guess that's true enough." I gave Blaise Pascal a jaunty feather in his hat. "But God always seems to provide."

"You and I both know that, but why *should* he provide for something so obviously misguided? These poor children forced into that little building, so chilly in the winter, so hot all the other times. It's shameful. It's time something was done and I'm glad we're the ones."

The orphans helped as much as they were able. Helping us all summer as we sanded and painted, patched plaster and painted, washed and painted. "I'll never live anywhere so fine as here," a girl named Birdie said when we washed out the last round of paintbrushes. Father Cook came through and blessed the building, the children all dressed up in their church clothes, prouder than a new sofa. I soaked in their expressions hoping that maybe, for the first time, they really knew what it felt like to move forward because you worked so hard and believed it was possible. And all the praying we did didn't hurt either.

That evening we sat out on the porch drinking iced tea, pressing the perspiring glasses on our cheeks, our foreheads, the sides of our necks above our collars (my, how hot those habits got), fanning ourselves with paper fans someone had taken from the funeral home years before, and judging by the looks of them, perhaps the original owners of the plantation. The cicadas buzzed in an almost deafening profusion and a great, green grasshopper landed on my knee.

"That's good luck right there." Angie pointed to it.

But it flew away. Almost as soon as it landed.

I drew quite a bit that night, I seem to remember. Several pictures of Jude, what I imagined he looked like more settled into his man-face and man-body.

I began drawing Jude when I was twelve and he was fourteen. Well, I should say I began drawing Jude from life at that time.

I'd drawn him before from memory, but it was never quite right. Jude seemed amused at the whole thing.

"Well," he said when I'd turned sixteen, "if I can't get in your pants, at least I can get on your paper."

"You're so crude."

"I know."

And that tickle arrived again. To be honest, many a night the tickle erupted down there because of thoughts of Jude. Satan was doing a number. I told Sister Thaddeus, who said don't be sure about that. "You need to wait until you absolutely know for sure whether you say something is of the devil, Mary-Margaret. Don't rush to judgment, because if it's from God and you give credit to his enemy—well, it's just something you want to steer clear from."

Steer clear from.

Sister Thaddeus used that term quite a bit.

So I asked Jesus about it and he remained mum. "T—, you know I'm not at your whim as your personal seer."

I sighed that night in the kitchen where Jesus and I sat together, sorting canned goods for a drive St. Francis had the week before. "I don't love him, Lord, but I like him, you know, in *that* way."

"Yes. I know."

"Is that wrong?"

"Not if you don't dwell on it. We made bodies to react that way. It's all right."

"I'd hate to think . . ."

He reached out and laid a hand on my shoulder. "Nothing goes to waste, T—. I wouldn't dream of it."

"But what does the future hold for Jude and me?"

"Nothing at times. Everything at others. You'll see."

A tear slipped from my eye. "I just want to be with you," I whispered.

He set down a can of creamed corn and drew me to himself,

so tender and loving. "I told you a long time ago, I'll always be near."

Truth is, I yearned for my mother. She'd tell me more about being a woman and how it feels when we awaken to all our senses. I knew she was a chaste woman, and yet somehow I also knew she'd understand and guide me in a way that meant more than anyone else could have. She was pretty. I was sure she'd had her fair share of interested boys. During those teens years, I think I missed her the most, imagining her, and yes, making her a saint. At least that's what Jude told me when I'd go dreamy-eyed in my maternal imaginings. I never mentioned my father, however, and neither did he. Even crass Jude knew where the boundaries lay buried like one of those electric dog fences.

And now I know my father's name. Connelly. It could have been my last name. Mary-Margaret Connelly.

Mary-Margaret Fischer.

Mary-Margaret Connelly.

Well, at least the Fischer doesn't seem so utter Irish-cliché.

~⌒~

Given possession of my father's name from Jude's letter has done something to me, as if tiny roots have sprung from the bottoms of my feet and fixed me to the earth, making me a real human being, not some halfling with no right to walk the face of an orderly creation where two lives begat one and most children at the very least knew the identity of both parties.

Suddenly, I am part of the world in a way I've never been before. Seventy years old and I finally feel, for the first time in my life, just a little like everyone else. I had a father and his name was Brendan Connelly.

The next morning after I read the letter from Jude, I threw my covers aside, dressed, ate a quick bowl of oatmeal, went to

Mass at St. Francis for the Holy Day of All Saints, sent up a
"Hello there!" to St. John Almond, my patron saint. I let Jude
pick out my patron saint when I was confirmed at thirteen and
he decided on the obscure Englishman who was hanged, drawn,
and quartered in his homeland when being a Catholic priest was
illegal. At least there's a bit of dignity to the choice, which is
more than I can say for Angie's twin nephews Richard and
George, who picked John and Paul as their confirmation names
so they'd have the Beatles complete between the two of them. (I
can't help it. It *is* funny.)

I headed across the grass to St. Mary's Village. On the way
to the activities room, I stopped at the main office and made a
phone call to Bainbridge, Georgia.

"Sloane residence."

"Morpheus?"

"Sister Mary-Margaret?"

"Morpheus, you're a fifty-seven-year-old man with five
children and two grandchildren, please call me Mary."

"Now, you know I can't do that."

"Oh, all right, you stubborn old man. I have a question for
you."

"All right. I'm fixing a cup of tea. Can you hold on for a
minute while I put in some honey?"

Morpheus keeps bees now as well as a firm foothold in the
art world. We were tried in the fire all those years ago and as I'd
followed in his footsteps one night long ago, he'd followed in
mine. He took what I did with young trees and went a step further, bending pieces of wood I wouldn't have dreamed of. One
of his pieces is on permanent display near the Calder room at
the National Gallery East Wing in Washington DC, and he's had
shows all over the world. He's a rich man now, but he stays on
in Bainbridge and supports St. Teresa's and is even a deacon at
the parish in town. And let me tell you, becoming a deacon in

the Catholic Church takes years of study. I'm as proud of him as I could be. He always gives me credit for the original idea behind his work, however, even though I've told him again and again I saw it in a book myself.

"Okay, I'm back. Sitting on the back porch and that elm tree in the neighbor's yard is lit up with so much gold," he said. "What's on your mind, sister?"

"Fathers."

"And how can I help you with that?"

"You grew up without a father too. Do you feel some great need to know him? Or at the very least to find out more about him?"

"No."

"See? That's what I thought! I can't wait to tell Angie."

"Whoa, whoa, whoa! What are you talking about?"

I settled in the secretary's desk chair and fiddled with a paperweight that said:

Confession Is Good for the Soul but Bad for Your Career.

Indeed.

"I have the opportunity to find out more about my father."

"The raping seminarian?"

"Lord have mercy, that's just what Angie said."

"You called him that for years. That's how I think of him."

"I did? To *you*?"

He chuckled. "Not until I was much older. Don't worry."

"I did. Yes, I did call him that, didn't I?"

"So then maybe you better find him, Sister Mary. Sounds like you've never made peace with the idea."

I rolled the chair back a little and rested my calves across the corner of her desk as Mrs. Cunard hurried by on her way to the shuttle to Salisbury and her weekly trip to the beauty parlor and a nice lunch afterward. We both lifted hands of greeting.

"What good would it do to find him anyway? He's most likely dead."

"Well, it's like this"—he slurped his tea—"hmm. Okay, tell me where you heard the story about your father in the first place."

"My grandmother told me."

"Could she have been wrong?"

Did his great brown hands come out of the phone and give me a little smack on the side of the head? Indeed they did!

"I never thought maybe there was a different story to it all."

"I'm not saying there is. And most of us don't question the family lore without good reason. We just trust the stories, take them as gospel truth. It could be just as your grandmother said. But then again, parents tell themselves things about their children all the time if it takes away blame, because if something goes wrong with the child, well, they're partly responsible. And nobody wants to admit to that."

I sucked in my breath. "You're right! What if I'm . . . a *love* child?!"

And Morpheus laughed his great laugh, smoother than gesso and warmer than the leaves on the elm tree in his neighbor's yard and I wished I sat there with him, drinking tea with the best honey in the entire state of Georgia, maybe even the world.

We hung up and for the rest of the day I tried to think of different scenarios, but all I could come up with were the words, "Maybe they really and truly loved each other?"

But then, why did she leave him?

Part of me longed to let it all be, but part of me knew Angie was right, darn her. The woman usually is. Maybe I did need to know my father.

I looked up at the ceiling. "I'm too old for this."

~⌒

That next Friday, two days into November, our stash of full-sized Hershey Bars taken by little hands and gobbled by chocolate-coated mouths, I slid into the driver's seat of Mercy House's compact car and headed for Mount St. Mary's Seminary in Emmitsburg, where Jude located Brendan Connelly. No sense in wasting time.

I settled into the car on that fall morning, the kind where every inhale feels like you're biting into a cold, crisp apple and you delight in the heater vent down at the floorboard. "Well, let's hope they've kept good records," I said to Angie.

Angie leaned her forearms on the ledge of the car window. "It's the Catholic Church, Mary. That's one of the things we're extra good at."

I clicked the gearshift into drive.

"Why you couldn't just call them, I don't know."

"I need to get away. And this way, they won't be able to turn me away so easily. Thanks for taking my sessions."

"Sure thing. I'll have them make hand turkeys." She hugged me through the open window.

"Who doesn't love a good hand turkey?" I hugged her neck. "At any age?"

"And then I've planned a little nature hike around the island."

"Good girl."

She huffed. "Oh yeah. That's me. I never get in any trouble."

Oh, there I go again, telling you about what just happened while you've been left hanging about that awful night in Bainbridge. I can't keep things going in a straight line anymore. Let me finish this part of the tale now, then. Back to that night after the Labor Day celebration.

~⌒

Glass shattering in bright notes as torches were thrown through three of the windows on the lower floor awakened me. Earlier, we'd all fallen into our beds there in the plantation house, Labor Day hot dogs and snow cones in our bellies. The smell of fabric eaten by flame propelled me from my bedroom just off the girls' dorm room.

"Wake up!" I screamed, wrapping my robe around me. "Fire!"

I ran into the dorm room. "Hurry! Angie, Joan!" I yelled up the steps to the attic rooms. "Fire!"

"We hear you!" Joan yelled.

I could smell the growing burning and now I heard it too, the roar of boiling flame raising the volume of our shouts to one another.

Thank goodness some wise soul thought to put a fire escape at the end of the hallway. We didn't have to go downstairs to the main floor. At the other end of the house, our houseparents, an elderly couple named Mr. and Mrs. De Cecco, who took care of the boys, did likewise. I heard their soft Italian accents, calm yet urgent, prodding the boys forward.

Angie and the other sisters joined me to corral the girls.

"Take them down to the carriage house!" I ordered. "If it's not already burned down," I said to Angie.

They filed down the hall, then the fire escape, their white night gowns and nightshirts all that was visible as the children made their way into the darkness near the carriage house. Poor babies. As if they hadn't been through enough in their little lives.

We were the last people out of the building, our freshly repaired and painted school building (all those hours we spent for nothing!), our tidy little bastion of hopeful, though obviously shortsighted, defiance. Morpheus stood next to me and I reached out and held his hand in mine.

"It's the only home I've ever known, Sister Mary-Margaret."

"I'm sorry, Morpheus."

"It's the Klan." He wiped the sweat from his brow with his shirttail. "I can tell you that right now."

"I don't know who else it could be."

Angie hurried up beside us, the youngest orphan, a little tot named Babe, on her hip calmly sucking her thumb. "Sister Magdalene has headed into town to get the fire department."

Before us now, the old plantation home was engulfed in a hungry flame that defied our progress and sought to destroy the vestiges of human love and sacrifice the old building might have come to represent. I hadn't been there long, so I didn't cry; I just let anger land on me like the sparks shooting up into the midnight sky, and I let it burn through my skin and down to the bone. Unable to understand the evil in the hearts of men, I whispered, "Jesus, oh, Jesus."

I see, he said back as if he stood right next to me. *I see and I know. Someday, Mary-Margaret, all will be well, and all manner of things will be well.*

"I can't imagine it," I whispered back.

"What?" Morpheus said.

"All will be well. Someday."

He squeezed my hand. "If I didn't believe that, Sister Mary-Margaret, I think I'd just jump on in that blaze right now and put myself out of my misery."

"How could they do such a thing?"

"Simple, Sister Mary-Margaret. They hate us is all. You should know. You're a Catholic."

"But there's got to be a good reason for this kind of hate."

"No disrespect, Sister Mary-Margaret, but there's where you're dead wrong. Take heart, though. You could be Catholic *and* black!"

I threaded my arm through his and we watched our dreams crumble in the blazing glory of stupidity, some of it, considering the times, most likely our own.

～～

The next morning we picked our way among the ashes, just Morpheus and myself. The rest of the staff and students slept in the old carriage house, mouths and noses still blackened with soot. But I'd been rising at five a.m. for years and years, and that morning was no exception.

Morpheus, sleeping on hay, heard me and joined me on the short walk to the smoking ruins.

We stood in silence, watching the final embers die. The fire department never did show up, so the blaze raged through everything.

"Good thing you moved your studio to the loft over there." Morpheus jerked his head toward the carriage house.

I nodded. "So much gone. What are we going to do?"

"Call the bishop?" He raised an eyebrow.

I laughed. "Yes. I guess that would be a good place to start. Do they do this sort of thing much around here?"

"Depends. You sure struck a nerve. I'm sorry, Sister Mary-Margaret."

"Me too. And I'm sorry for you, Morpheus."

"It wasn't like we weren't warned."

We'd received threats, yes. But we sisters were too naïve to believe they'd carry them out. And that, my sisters to whom I write, is a good thing to remember. Evil doesn't have many boundaries, and if you live long enough and try hard enough, someday it will do what it promises if you ignore its ultimatums. So use the brain God gave you.

That morning, a breeze, soft and filled with the scent of a

waning summer, that blend of late flowers blooming and leaves just beginning to decay, caught my hair and fluttered our nightclothes. I thought of Jude who would have been furious over the happenings of the night and I wondered what fires he was quenching, or rather whose.

"Look! There's that negro boy with that papist!"

He didn't say negro, sisters. I simply can't bring myself to write the word he did say.

The words barely registered before a rope banded my arms to my sides and lifted me onto a horse.

A horse! In 1958! Yes, sisters. The whole thing felt a bit medieval. And not in the fairy princess, knight-in-shining-armor fashion either.

～～

Those Klansmen sure went nuts that morning after the fire.

The rider threw me down from the horse and into a patch of muddied ground back in the woods, the earth itself reaching into the fibers of my nightgown. And it was so hot and humid, that summer thickness rendering difficult my breathing.

The kicking began, their hard shoes slamming against my ribs, my buttocks, my thighs. I tried to cover my head with my hands and arms; I curled myself into the smallest ball I could. I suppose it didn't last long, but time slowed and each kick took minutes.

Finally someone lifted me to my feet and in a red flash, something hard made contact with my face. I still don't know whether it was a fist or a bat or a pipe. I crumbled completely, the rage of agony filling my face in a crimson flash.

Two men, mocking me for all I held dear, dragged me to a tree and secured me to its trunk, the rope biting into my arms as mosquitoes bit into my legs. Each insult I endured because, you see, what they didn't know was that Jesus held me while they cursed me, and he wept and moaned with me, tenderly kissing my brow and whispering, "I'm sorry, T—. I'm so sorry. Would I could keep you from this."

Why can't you?

"Their sin hasn't yet reached its fulfillment. But it will. My Father and your Father will not let this go on forever. Their days are dwindling."

One is the pastor down the street.

"Yes. He does this in my name if you can believe that. He believes himself one of mine because he prayed a prayer when he was ten. He believes he can do whatever he wants because of that, and that whatever he wants is what I want."

Many shall say unto me, Lord, Lord . . .

"Yes, my dear. That's exactly what I was talking about." He talked with me, keeping my mind off what was happening.

Please don't let them . . . rape me. Please, Lord.

And I saw a man coming toward me, good-looking in that raw-boned way, the left side of his face glowing in the torch-light, the right side barely lit from the as-yet-unrisen sun. He reached for his belt, flipped the tail through the buckle, and went for the button at the top of his pants.

"Oh, please, Jesus, no."

I felt the Lord's arms go around me, and I cried and cried as the chief of police approached. There would be no recourse. He would force himself upon me and would walk away with no punishment. Who would believe me?

He unbuttoned his pants and pulled them down past his hips as someone began loosening my ropes behind the tree, and he laughed and stroked my cheek. "The little sister finally gets what she's always wanted but thought she'd never have."

Physically ready and exposed, he snapped at whoever was behind the tree. "Hurry up!"

I shut my eyes and turned my face into Jesus's shoulder.

"Watch now, T—."

He breathed in, then blew out and that quickly the sky filled with clouds, thunder barreled down the heavy air, fire filled the heavens, and a driving hail pelted the scene, hail so large and thick the men ran, holding their arms over their heads, shrieking and hollering like children, leaving me tied to the tree, the great icy stones pelting me on my head, my shoulders, my feet.

The chief of police yanked up his trousers as he ran, and I couldn't help hoping his zipper did a number on him.

I feel nothing. Each hailstone just bounced off me like a piece of fluff. Maybe I was numb from the beating, but I began to laugh with joy.

"You won't even have so much as a bruise in the morning, my dear. At least not by my hail. Your face, I'm sorry to say, will need a great deal of attention. Get to the hospital in Valdosta as quickly as you can. Ask for Doctor Flowers."

By the time the sun rose over Bainbridge that same morning, by the time Morpheus found me tied to a tree downriver, by the time he cut me loose with his pocketknife and carried me through the woods to an old home overgrown with vines that he'd found on one of his treks to cut down saplings, I was almost unrecognizable, my right cheekbone was smashed in and my eyes were swollen shut. "Shh, shh," he kept saying, his whisper tortured and melancholy. "Oh, Lord. Oh, Lord, have mercy. Let's get you away from here, Sister Mary-Margaret. You just hang on."

"I need to get to Valdosta. My face." To this day I don't know how he understood me.

"Don't you worry, Sister Mary-Margaret. I'll run for help."

Did I tell you I loved Morpheus? Really and truly? My heart filled with the love of Christ and the love of a human. And my sisters, you will find, if you seek to own such a heart, God will be more than happy to give you one. Of course, don't expect it won't get you into trouble.

After the plastic surgery and the general recuperation time in the hospital, I was sent by train back to the motherhouse in Baltimore to heal completely. I couldn't draw; I couldn't sculpt. All I could do was look at art books, go to Mass, and work in the garden. Every once in a while a musician would come and give a concert, and I'd attend, sitting in the back row, letting the sound that bounced off the plastered walls of the stone chapel seep its way into my soul, cleanse me a little more of the fear that had soaked into my psyche during the attack. I kept seeing those men, knowing they were still down there with my sisters, with Angie, and with Morpheus and all the children.

My sisters gathered around me. Young and old and all those blessed in-betweens. They blessed me with care and loved me just as I was, so broken and frightened, and they told me that I would be fine one day, and what was more, I believed them. Not because I simply wanted to or needed to, but because Jesus told me exactly the same thing, and his word was true, at one with his utter faithfulness. How can his faithfulness include that attack? A question for the ages if there ever was one. All I know is, he is found amid suffering in a way like no place else. Why that is, I can't say. Perhaps we'll know one day. In the meantime, accepting it will give you one less thing to worry about because as Jesus said, "The day has enough troubles of its own."

WELL, IT'S A NEW DAY OF WRITING, AND I NEED TO TELL YOU more about the saga of my father while it's fresh in my mind. As you can imagine, the times of the past are a bit more cemented than these days. And I feel more at ease filling in the missing bits, what people actually said and whatnot, when writing about the past, than I do when writing about the present. So I headed up to Mount St. Mary's Seminary on that beautiful fall morning. I stopped and purchased a cup of coffee to sip and a pack of chocolate Donettes to nibble as I made my way east.

Mount St. Mary's Seminary's main building, McSweeney, spreads its stony arms like a giant lady dressed in gray with white lace trim. She must be German because she's as boxy as my grandmother was. I ascended the steps and located the Office of Records on the directory board near the door. Second floor.

Okay, Jesus, if you say so.

Not that he's spoken a peep on this, but I figured since he wanted me out at the lighthouse, this must be tucked in his pocket of plans somewhere.

I approached the desk and the sound of a real keyboard pounder. "Excuse me?"

A young woman in a burgundy blouse and gray pants,

brunette hair pulled back in a ponytail, looked up from her computer and ceased her clacking. "Yes?"

A charm bracelet dangled from her slender wrist.

Time to pull out the Catholic credentials. "I'm Sister Mary-Margaret Fischer. I'm looking to find the whereabouts of a family member I lost track of years and years ago. He was a seminarian here back around 1930."

"Oh. That's so long ago." She tapped her pen on the desk, the charms jingling. A cup of cold coffee rested forgotten on her blotter, the cream coagulated into an island on the beige surface. "Anything past twenty years is down in the basement." So be a nice lady and leave me alone. Got it?

I'm really not what anybody would call a "sweet old lady," but I decided that's the direction I needed to go. "I've driven all the way from the Eastern Shore."

"Oh." She tapped her pen again, then glanced at her wristwatch. "Hmm. Well, let's see. It's almost noon."

"I could come back around three, perhaps?"

Leaving time for lunch and a look-see down in that basement, dearie.

"Oh. Well . . ."

Work with me, young lady. Hop to!

"I'd so hate to have to go back empty-handed, Miss . . ."

"Porter."

"Miss Porter. Poor Sister Angie, you know." Indeed, she was probably nursing a gigantic headache after a nature walk with three people with canes, two walkers, and a wheelchair. Not that it had anything to do with my father.

"Well, I guess I could go down there myself."

"Oh, would you?" I sucked in a little breath like I'd just been told I won the lottery. I even allowed my voice to crackle, like people do when they're imitating someone older. I must say, my voice has held up better than I'd hoped.

"You said you could come back at three?" She actually took a sip of that coffee.

"Yes."

She sighed. "Well, all right. I'll have it at three." She picked up her pen. "Now what's the name of the seminarian?"

"Brendan Connelly."

"Nineteen thirty you say?"

"Yes."

She wrote the information in a tight scrawl. "That should be helpful. Do you know where he was from originally?"

I shook my head. "No. But I think Baltimore."

"You said you were related?"

"Yes. A very long story."

"Because we can't pull records for just—"

"He was my father."

Her eyebrow raised. "Oh?"

Thank you, Lord! Here was the angle I needed!

I nodded and leaned forward, whispering dramatically, drawing her into my conspiracy. "And he still became a priest!"

"Oh!"

Standing up straight, I gathered my purse higher on my shoulder. "Is there a good place to eat around here?"

"Main Street Grill is pretty good."

"That sounds like just the ticket."

She rubbed her chin. "This is interesting. I don't get a request like this every day."

I walked out of the room hoping that little bit of intrigue would send her down to the file room in time for me to grab the info and get back to the motel before rush hour. I decided to spend the night as I hate to drive in the dark.

The thrifty side of me won out and I ended up with a Big Mac on my plaid blanket by the playing field in front the seminary building. We don't have a McDonald's on Locust Island. I sipped on a Coke and read some Julian of Norwich. The sunshine heavied my eyelids, so I set my watch for 2:55, reclined back in the gilded light, and fell into a delicious sleep. I dreamed of Jesus. Only a dream, not a visit, and it was like one of those dreams after a loved one passes on in which you're sitting with them, eating a bowl of cereal, talking, or maybe watching some television, and suddenly you look at them and say, "Well, this is nice, but you're dead, aren't you?" And as the realization dawns, they fade away as if only allowed to be with you as long as you don't realize the real nature of the visit. I kept trying to bring him back as I dozed there, and sometimes he came and sometimes he didn't. But as I said, it was just a dream.

When my watch beeped, I gathered my bag and blanket and deposited them in the car.

Miss Porter was ready for me with a file and she was wearing her happy face! She was all chummy, her interest clearly piqued. "Well"—she tapped the edge of the file on the palm of her hand—"we actually had a Brendan Connelly from back then, and, I have to say, Sister Mary-Margaret, you have his eyes and mouth."

Those words scraped through me like barbed wire being pulled through the long channel of my spine. That I had a father had always been abstract. No talk of eyes and noses, or hair, or attributes of any kind.

"May I?" I reached out my hand.

"Here, take the file. I made copies for you. It's all there. You're going to be surprised."

The manila paperboard felt smooth and cool, and the racing pulse in my red fingertips heated the surface right away. "Thank you, Miss Porter."

She shook my hand, her bracelet sounding its music. "I hope you find what you're looking for. Most likely he's already passed away. I mean"—she chuckled nervously—"who lives to the age of ninety-five?"

I shrugged. "I'm actually counting on that, truth be known. I'm too old for that sort of upheaval."

She sat back down in her desk chair. "Did he know about you?"

"I don't know. I have my doubts, though."

"Wow. I've got to admit, I'm curious."

"Me too. I thank you for your kind service, Miss Porter."

"I hope it all works out."

She truly did. I could see it in her eyes.

Back in the car I rifled through the pages. Brendan Connelly, born 1905 in Towson, Maryland. Parents: Etta and Niall. My grandparents.

And there was his picture. The raping seminarian.

He was thin-faced and handsome in a fragile way, his light eyes kind. His hair, most likely red and coarse like my own, waved back from his forehead in that Danny Kaye manner.

I ran my fingers down his face and tried to feel something akin to affection.

"Nothing," I muttered.

I had a Father in heaven already, and despite the distance I felt between us, I felt I really didn't need one more.

My eyes skated over the papers, grades and such—he was intelligent judging by his marks, room assignments, mostly administrative details, until I came upon an interesting little scrap—a letter to a teacher who obviously felt it worthy of putting in his file. In June of 1940.

"You'll most likely be surprised to learn I have become a Franciscan brother. I've taken on my confirmation name: Joseph."

The *Franciscans*?! The raping seminarian? A *Franciscan*? Well, I supposed he must have felt bad about what he did, at least. And a brother too. So he didn't enter the priesthood after all. Or maybe he did eventually. Oh, all still such a mystery.

"I'm now at a mission in downtown Baltimore situated just off our red-light district known as The Block. We call it Heart of the City. The folks call me Brother Joe."

Brother Joe? Brother *Joe*?

Oh, Jesus. I could hardly believe what I was reading.

You haven't met Brother Joe yet, sisters, but you will. And you'll be shocked I didn't actually faint when I realized he was my father. Some folks would call it a great coincidence. But I stopped believing in coincidences long ago.

He looked so different as a young man from when I met him in 1959. The kind redheaded man whom Jude adored. Jude knew this much, but he didn't tell me it in his papers, I was sure of it. But if he had been sitting there in the car with me, I wouldn't have had to look to see the expression on his face.

"See, Mary-Margaret?" Jude would have said. "You just can never tell. You needed to know. And now you know why. I think somebody was lying. Either your grandmother or your mom. Can you imagine Brother Joe raping anybody? But people go nuts sometimes, right? I'll give you that."

I knew how people went nuts, that was for sure.

Brother Joe. I owed him more than I could say.

I'M SITTING IN THE KITCHEN NOW WHILE MY BREAD RISES. I missed the time to plant those bulbs and now I'm going to have to wait until spring. So I'll get back to what happened after receiving the file that day at the seminary.

I decided to head down to The Block, where Brother Joe worked at the mission. At first I couldn't bring myself to get out of the car; I just drove up and down the street, staring at the bouncers and the hookers and pictured Jude, overcoat wrapped around him on a cold night, collar upturned against the angle of his jaw, gold-brown curls brushing the wool. Most times I couldn't think about what he did all those years to earn money, so much potential so thoroughly wasted in backseats and fleabag motel rooms, or high-rise office suites. It didn't matter the location when it was someone you cared about. It wasn't like I thought, *Well, hopefully he's servicing someone well-mannered and with good hygiene tonight.* The vice wasn't less if the venue and the players were disinfected.

I slowed to a stop by Blaze Starr's Two O'Clock Club and watched a variety of men trickle in and out. Men in respectable suits, young guys in jeans and polo shirts, the requisite hairy-chested, slick-shirted men who flaunted their sleezeball status unlike the respectable-looking people who fooled themselves. I wanted to pray for them, but all I could do was stare in wonderment at so many lives gone so sour and putrid they failed to smell their own stink any longer. At least Jude never fooled himself. I had to give that to him. He didn't make excuses, didn't act like sex-for-sale was okay if it was between consenting adults. "It's sickening, Mary-Margaret. It's nothing but people using each other, not one bit of romance. Don't you think I know that? Why you still want to be my friend is a mystery to me."

But what Jude didn't know then was that in comparison to God's love and holiness, our own goodness is but a tiny shell in a sea. My shell in comparison wasn't much bigger than Jude's. I tried to explain it, and I think he got it eventually, but it was a long time coming, and a very long road to navigate.

I sat there in the little white car and wept. Then I drove around to Heart of the City Mission, parked, stepped inside, and had a cup of coffee. Mary-Francis, the secular Franciscan running the place, sat with me and told me about their ministry, going on for fifty-five years now.

"Did the famous Brother Joe start it?" I asked her.

She fiddled with a baby dreadlock. "No, but he gave the place its heart. What a saint. Lord have mercy, the stories he would tell. That man knew how to give life."

You said it, I thought.

A woman, most likely a prostitute, most likely in last night's getup, stumbled through the door, a gash in her forehead bleeding down onto the hot pink sequins of her minidress. She tottered on a pair of silver stiletto, thigh-high boots.

"Gotta run." Mary-Francis hurried toward the woman. "Lindelle! Did he hit you *again*?"

The woman nodded and broke down in tears. Mary-Francis put her arms are her. "Come back sometime and see us," she said to me, her milky brown skin creasing around her light brown eyes. "We're always open!" she said. "Right, Lindelle?"

Lindelle nodded and looked up at me, blue eyes shattered into too many pieces for a human to count.

I couldn't pummel Mary-Francis with questions. They would have to wait.

Perhaps I would be back soon.

Perhaps? I knew I'd return as soon as I could get the time off. Fire spread beneath my scalp and I needed to leave. I hurried back to the car and sat for another hour, watching the foot traffic thicken as the night descended, the slack conditions of the buildings receded, and the carnival lights glowed to attract and feed the soul-starved denizens of Baltimore Street.

I drove right to the motherhouse and proceeded to Sister Thaddeus's room. She's in her eighties and is doing well. She dresses simply but somehow manages to look stylish. In other words, she hasn't lost it!

As always, she hugged me tightly and made me a cup of tea. She wears her hair bobbed and got her ears pierced ten years ago. The little gold balls look positively Parisian on her. I don't know what her secret is.

We sat on her sofa.

"You look wonderful, Mary. How's the artwork?"

"Fine."

She nodded to a picture I painted years before, a wild dervish of color telling only the tale of my heart at the time. "Still holding up, don't you think, the old gal?"

"Yes. I'm happy you love it still."

I told her what brought me to Baltimore and come to find out, she realized Brother Joe was my father too. "You two look a great deal alike. I wondered about it when I saw him, but figured you all had that certain redheaded way about you."

"So, should I follow the trail?"

"Indeed, Mary-Margaret."

Now you know where that "indeed" comes from.

She invited me to stay the night there instead of spending money on a motel and we stayed up until one a.m. remembering and chatting, me giving her news on the women who once went to school with me, relaying the jaunt to the lighthouse and . . .

"Oh, Mary-Margaret, you've always been quite the woman, haven't you?"

She waved me off in the parking lot the next day, then headed downtown to help out at the sour beef and dumpling dinner at her home parish. I prayed the silly prayer that she'd live for another fifty years or so.

WELL, THE BREAD IS NOW IN THE OVEN AND I'VE GOT THE gardens mulched for the coming winter. And as I finished up I became filled with the minute beauty of nature, thinking about those beautiful, tender little shoots that would come up in the spring, remembering my time in the woods all those years ago, having healed as much as I was going to initially, and ready, finally, to move forward into the order.

I was about to enter my tertianship—a thirty-day period of intense reflection before saying my finals vows. Before it officially began at our retreat house in western Maryland, I decided a visit to Locust Island was crucial, to see the people I cared so much about: Gerald and Hattie, Sister Thaddeus, and the Brays.

And I hoped to get a little time with Jesus. But of course, that was entirely up to him. Checking out one of the school's canoes, I paddled around the island, not venturing too far out from the grasses. I even spent some time on Glen's reading island, though Glen didn't live on Locust Island yet. He was still acting on Broadway during those days. Locust Island provided an escape for him back in 1995. He comes to Mass with me sometimes. I think he used to be Catholic. I think he lost his way and wonders if he'll ever find it again.

As I expected would happen, a few days into the stay in that sad 1959, I ended up paddling out to Bethlehem Point Light. Hattie saw me from far off, waved her arms in the pale spring sunlight there on the surrounding deck, and hollered, "I was wondering when you'd finally make it out!" She wore pink pedal pushers, a pink work shirt, and had tied her hair back in a pink scarf.

"And here I am," I said as I pulled up to the dock ten minutes later. "It's only April, Hattie, I'm cold, and I'd sure appreciate a cup of your spearmint tea."

"Sure thing, hon."

We tied up the canoe and she thrust out one of her strong, square hands and almost hoisted me out of the boat by her own steam. We climbed the iron steps. "Let me put the kettle on. You just go ahead and make yourself comfortable in Gerald's chair."

"Where is Gerald?"

"In town. I forgot the baking powder on my trip yesterday, and you know that man can't go a day without homemade biscuits—"

"Yours are the best." I followed her into the kitchen where the radio burbled "High Hopes" sung by Frank Sinatra. I loved Frank. Hattie was partial to Bobby Darrin, but I always thought he attacked every single song.

To be honest, Gerald's chair was Mr. Keller's chair, and I always felt like I shouldn't sit there. Something sad and sacred went on there for years as he sat in his loneliness, and honestly, I had enough crazy sacredness in my life. If people knew about Jesus's visits, they would have sent me to Crownsville and committed me for life. And the loneliness? Well, that had never really been much of a problem, but I didn't want to tempt fate and allow it to ooze into me from the chair, freshly reupholstered notwithstanding, through my backside.

"I'll just sit right here." I pulled out one of the wooden chairs and sat down at the table. A straw mat to one side held a napkin holder, salt and pepper shakers, and a sugar bowl. All in a lighthouse theme.

I picked up the pepper shaker. "Isn't this a little overkill? Out here and all?"

Hattie filled the kettle at the kitchen sink. The rainwater collected in a large cistern at the side of the building. "People keep giving lighthouse items to me. Can you imagine doing the same thing for a person living in a two-story colonial or a rancher?"

"No." I folded my hands. "So. How's everything been out here?"

She rested a surprisingly well-manicured hand on her broad hip. You just never knew with Hattie. "A calm year. Mild winter. Not much ice damage. No rescues. Good, I'd say."

"And Gerald?"

"He's been sick over Jude, quite honestly."

I think I imagined a bit of accusation in her tone; perhaps she felt that, as his friend, I should have been able to talk him off the streets.

"Has he seen him?"

She nodded, turned on the burner, and settled the kettle on the gas flame. "He went to Baltimore a few weeks ago. Found him at a mission down there. You heard of Brother Joe?"

I shook my head. "I'm afraid I haven't."

"Runs a place for prostitutes and the like."

"Jude being one of the like."

She sighed. "I don't know, MM. He really won't give us any information, but what are we supposed to think?"

"You're probably right." I didn't want to let on what I knew.

"So anyway, it breaks Gerald's heart. That woman."

She was speaking of Jude's mother, Petra.

"I know, Hattie. How she could take him in with that man . . ."

"Well, at least that's all over with now. He'll never have to go back there. Not even to visit. We figure she's dead. People like that don't stay gone. The things they do they do for show just as much as for change. You know what I mean?"

I nodded.

"So how long are you here for?" She scraped down a China plate of cookies from the cupboard.

"Just a few weeks, I think. I'm about to say my final vows."

She set the plate on the table. "You know, it's funny. I said to Gerald when I first met you that you were destined to be a wife and mother and the sooner you got those ideas about being a nun out of your head, the better. With hips like that, MM, well, it's a shame to let that kind of baby-making body go to waste."

"Thanks. I guess."

She waved a hand. "Oh, you know what I mean. But I guess I was wrong about that. Are you sure you're ready for this, hon? I mean, don't you want a man? A nice man and a family? Maybe some kids? I know I got the man, and the good Lord hasn't seen fit to give me the children, but I'd sure welcome them if he did. You're so good with the kids, MM. Gerald'll laugh because I was just so sure about it. I guess you never can tell, can you?"

I smoothed my skirt. "Well, to be honest, there's a part of me that's always wanted to have a baby, Hattie."

"I knew it!"

"But I want Jesus more."

"Can't you have both?"

"I don't know. I've never even thought of that as a possibility."

Wouldn't she have flipped at my visions? Dependable, earthbound Hattie? She'd have thought I was a complete loon.

"It is for a lot of women, hon. Hasn't there ever been a boy you've been interested in?"

"Well, not really."

"Not *really*? So who was the *maybe* interest then?"

You had to be so careful about what you said around Hattie because she didn't just read between the lines, she read between each word.

I looked down at my hands and whispered one word.

Her fingertips flew to her mouth as she gasped. "No! *Jude*?!"

"Yes. He's always made me feel a little . . . excited. But of course, now that he's . . ."

"Oh that. I mean, why couldn't you look the other way, a few little indiscretions?" She laughed, but her eyes saddened. "Did he ever know?"

I shook my head vehemently. "No! We'd kiss and all, but that was the extent of it. I *never* gave him any hope we had a future! Because we don't." After all, my mother had given her life for me. It was the least I could do.

"I believe you!" She held up her hands, the palms red and callused from scrubbing the decks surrounding the lighthouse. "But I sure am sorry for it." She poured the boiling water into a teapot and settled a few tea bags inside, leaving the strings to drape over the neck. "You might have been his savior."

I dropped my forehead into my hands and whispered, "Please don't say that, Hattie. I can't bear that kind of weight."

She sat down. "I'm sorry. You're right. Jude wasn't your responsibility. If he was anybody's, he was ours. Gerald tried." She dunked the tea bags up and down. "I tried too. But there was just no getting inside of him. He was so closed up. Except for you. Do you think you could have loved him, even a little?"

"I did. Just not enough to . . . set my dreams aside. And now that he's taken to this life . . . well, I just can't imagine . . . Does that make sense?"

"It does. I wish it didn't. I wish sometimes people could make all the mistakes in the world and go back to square one with everyone they left in their wake."

"Only God gives us a square one when we don't deserve it, Hattie. Only God can afford that sort of luxury."

"Still . . ." She looked out the window. "There's Gerald! Oh good. He can have tea with us."

The heavy conversation out of the way, we sat around the table and talked about the old days. Sometimes you just need to talk about the old days.

IT'S BEEN AWHILE SINCE I'VE WRITTEN. THERE ARE ALWAYS a million things to do, it seems.

After visiting the mission in November, I went back to Locust Island and taught for the rest of the autumn and the winter. Angie and I went to Florida for Christmas and remembered the Y2K New Year's Eve of last year with some Sisters of Providence, one of whom has a sister who owns a condo near St. Augustine, a name quite fitting for vacationing religious!

So back to the story. I was still visiting St. Mary's before entering my tertianship when, walking down the cloister after supper in Sister Thaddeus's quarters that night, I saw him across the yard, standing by the gateway where we first spoke.

"Jude?" I called. "Is that you?"

He cupped his hand to the side of his mouth. "Gerald told me you were here!"

I ran across the newly sprung lawn, breathless by the time I reached him.

He looked like he'd just been pushed out of hell.

"Jude! What's happened to you?" I reached up and touched his cheek.

He leaned his face into my hand and smiled, a phantom of the old charm still hovering around the corners of his mouth, but his eyes were old and tired, their blue faded and shelfworn, their whites pink and weary. He'd lost weight, his collarbones pressing out the broadcloth of his shirt, his cheekbones traceable beneath the skin of his face. At least his hair was still as it used to be. I don't think I could have stood it if it had changed.

"I just came to see Gerald and Hattie for a few days. I'm finally headed over to Europe."

"Are you in trouble?"

He looked down, then turned his head to the side, squeezing the top of the iron gate, whitening his already protruding knuckles. "Yeah."

"What is it?"

"Drugs, Mary-Margaret."

"Are you selling them?"

"I was."

"And the prostitution?"

"A guy's gotta make ends meet."

I felt like I was going to throw up. I could feel the blood pooling in my cheeks and my pulse pounded in my temples. "Are you using drugs? You look so thin." Now, after that description you might think I'm an idiot. I knew he had to be using, but I wanted him to say it.

"I was using. I'm not now."

I didn't believe him. "How long are you on the island, did you say?"

"A few days. Gerald's going to meet me with the boat in just a minute or two, but I saw your hair through the ironwork, or, well, what I'd hoped was your hair. What are you doing back from Georgia already?"

"It's a long story. Can we meet tomorrow?"

"Say when and where."

"At Bethlehem Point. By my mother's tree. Is eleven a.m. too early?"

"I'll be there."

And there was no leering stare, no saucy comment. He reached out and touched my hair and before I could say anything, he turned from the gate, shoved his hands in his pockets, and slipped away.

That night I lay in my bed in one of the guest rooms at the school, and I stared up at the ceiling, praying without words for Jude. I had no idea what to say, what to even hope for. I only wished I could do a little something to help him, but he was beyond my aid, wasn't he?

Wasn't he?

I mouthed the words and they remained in a mist over my head and I realized the answer just might not be, "No."

I could barely breathe.

Oh, Jesus, I prayed. *Please. Tell me this isn't what you want for me. Hattie was wrong when she said I could help Jude.*

I heard nothing in response.

～⌣

I got a letter from my son, John, today. He's taken to sewing clothes in the evenings for some of the orphans who live near his mission. It's a family tradition, I suppose. One of my favorite memories of my grandmother was watching her sew my clothes. Grandmom didn't emote much, being the German type. I rarely received more than a brusque hug and fond swat on the behind as I rushed out the door to school in the mornings. But Grandmom showed her affection in her sewing. In my keepsake trunk I still have three of the dresses she fashioned for me when I was a little girl. The intricate smocking bespoke hours of love oozing from her fingertips, the piping sewed around the waists, the collars, and the sashes told me how much she cared, how glad she was I was around. I still have one she made for my mother, as well as the christening dress we both wore.

Aunt Elfi, on the other hand, was the cook and the love bug. She always made me rice pudding. That was her way. And a lot of hugs and kisses. She'd hold me on her lap, read books, and after the final page was read, rock us so raucously it was a pure wonder neither of us ended up with cracked skulls.

Grandmom showed me what prayer looked like. She'd gather her prayer book, purse, gloves, and a head covering some mornings and we'd let ourselves early into the church. St. Francis was left unlocked because those were the days people sought out God on his turf and didn't feel silly doing so, and nobody would dream of stealing from a church.

We'd enter the hushed quiet and kneel before the altar in the second pew after lighting several candles. Grandmom would pray for an hour every Tuesday morning. She'd bring paper and crayons for me and she said, "Mary-Margaret, just draw your prayers to God."

I've been doing that ever since, I guess. Each week brought improvement as I figured it out by trial and error. There was no great moment when I knew I loved to create art. I guess, like faith for a lot of people, I learned it in church until one day I realized I was an artist.

Aunt Elfi showed me how to minister mercy. Honestly, she *was* a little touched in the head. She never did well in school and was probably riddled with learning disabilities nobody knew of back then. But she knew everybody on our street, and when someone was sick, Aunt Elfi was making bean or chicken soup, hoping the chicken was nobody she once knew. We'd deliver her ministrations together and she'd never just drop off the dish; she'd do laundry, mop the kitchen floor, vacuum, or just sit and let the person babble on about their troubles. Aunt Elfi could listen to people complain and moan for hours on end. That, my sisters, is sainthood.

Aunt Elfi would also pack up my pencils and papers and

she'd say, "Draw a pretty picture for our friend today. Maybe it will help ease his suffering." So I'd draw pretty trees, flowers, animals, mountains with a sunset in between, and she'd tack it up where they could see it.

I've been trying to do that with my art ever since too, I suppose. And I don't know if that's why I've never really made it in the art world. Maybe there's just too much motive behind my work. Art for art's sake and all that. I don't have the type of brain that can figure that out. I just like to do what I like to do. Angie, I believe, sports a bit of a grudge against fate on my behalf because I've never been recognized as any sort of artist of merit. But I can't be bogged down by that sort of yearning for other people's approval. The art world doesn't seem to be filled with people I'd want to drink a cup of tea with anyway. At least that's the way it seems in the movies.

And I've gone off on a rabbit trail again, but at least you know more about Grandmom and Aunt Elfi.

~~

Jude and I were supposed to meet that next morning, but he didn't show up. I suppose his sin had not yet come to completion . . . like those KKK boys. He'd spent the night at Brister's house according to Hattie and the two got drunker than Friar Tuck after a raid. He stumbled onto the ferry the next morning and headed, I supposed, to Europe with, hopefully, somebody clean at the very least.

So I spent a few more days cloistered at the school. I prayed the divine offices, helped with chores, ate with some of the sisters in the silent dining room, rested in the garden, and read and prayed.

Angie called me from Bainbridge. "Why are you doing all that now? You're going to be doing that for a month during your tertianship."

"I figured I'd practice up a little. How's it going down there?"

They did what they could from the carriage house, then moved the school to downtown Bainbridge. They were renting an old hotel scheduled for demolition the coming summer. "By that time, a new building will be built and guess who's the chief donor?" Angie said.

"I have no idea."

"The police chief's father. That old coot!"

"Oh my goodness!" (I never told her I was almost raped by his son.) "And Sister Magdalene's going to take it?"

"You bet!"

"Wonderful! Listen, those boys'll never get caught. The least we can do is take their money."

I arranged my habit, set my feet on the secretary's desk, and rapped a pen repeatedly against my knee.

"How's Morpheus?"

"Fine. Turned fifteen last week. We had a little party. Everybody likes it at the hotel just fine. So we're doing well. I'll be back in the summer then, and I'll start my tertianship as well. By September we'll be back on track, Mary. Just don't do anything crazy in the meantime." She laughed herself silly at that.

After I hung up the phone, I realized I'd always taken the obvious path. They hadn't always been easy, as my time in Bainbridge proved, but they were most certainly, at the time of decision, the paths of least resistance.

I settled my feet on the floor, stood up, and looked out the window onto the quad. I rushed over to the art room, dragged out a canvas I'd prepared the day before, and painted with all the force inside of me, my veil swinging in an arc almost parallel to the floor as I swiveled back and forth from palette to canvas. Black and yellow and cream slammed against the canvas in great swaths and arcs. Next came a deep black-red and my brain forgot to whom it belonged and that small dot of a portion deeply buried took over.

When I was finished, spent, sweaty, and leaning against the desk like it was the railing at a roller rink, Sister Thaddeus stood in the doorway and applauded. "Wonderful! Just as good as any of that Long Island set."

She was speaking of the Abstract Expressionists.

"Yes!" I breathed in heavily. "Except I'm late to the party as usual."

"It's beautiful." She practically floated across the room in her habit, still a stunning woman whose hair, I expected, was probably starting to gray at the temples. "I just wanted you to know how much I've been praying for you lately. The Holy Spirit keeps bringing you to mind, Mary-Margaret, urging me to pray, pray. Are you sure about saying your final vows?"

I was, I wanted to say. But I couldn't. I couldn't say yes. I couldn't say no. I just remembered Jude standing at the fence a few days earlier, and all I wanted to do was run away from the memory of his shrunken cheeks and shaded eyes.

Jesus went after that one lost sheep.

"Well, I just wanted to let you know that we could use you here next year, Mary-Margaret, to teach art and, if you don't mind, some English courses. It would be wonderful to have you back in the routine of St. Mary's once you've taken your final vows."

Yes. And of course, it would seem like the perfect path for me. Just right. The obvious next step.

～～

A few days later, Hattie and Sister Thaddeus waved me off at the bus station in Salisbury and I journeyed first to Baltimore and the motherhouse, then to our retreat center in Luray, Virginia.

Something about the mountains feeds the spirit. The high

spines of the Blue Ridge sprouting the massive growth of oak and pine, the brooks with their large, smooth stones on which you can rest your bottom and your soul. And if you're in the mood for something a tad more extravagant, the Shenandoah River with its graceful loops and soft flow provide a nourishing place for soul rumination.

Of course, the practice run at St. Mary's did little to help me at first. I walked the leafy pathways in the woods, hiked the trails, and strolled by the Shenandoah for a week with the world whispering in my ears and buzzing about my head like flies around trash. I argued with an imaginary Hattie at least every hour about Jude, about how her brother-in-law was not my problem, that he needed a bigger fix than I could provide. Indeed, if Jude had been the type of sinner who justifies, sanctifies, and glorifies what they do, I might have had something to work with. Instead, he fully admitted his transgressions and failed to react positively against them. Most of us are under the delusion if we can simply convince somebody they're wrong, they'll turn away from their error. But arguments cost nothing. Only love and faith are up for such a task. Faith I had, at least a little. But love—who did I really love in such a manner? Nobody. Jesus didn't count—who wouldn't love him if he visited them like he visited me? Did I really even know how to love at all? Did I know how to love as Jesus loved? Giving myself completely to one who didn't deserve a bit of it, not just because it was the right thing to do but because I was so filled with love and grace I couldn't help myself? Can anybody love like that?

Well, Hattie did, leaving the world behind for Gerald's sake. My grandmother. Even Sister Thaddeus, who, I would find out years later, gave her portion of her inheritance to the order to finance my education all the way through graduate school. It was a good thing I didn't know that then, or I might not have followed the Lord down the path he was going. And surely he would have found a replacement to bring Jude to himself. I'd like to think so.

I thought of a dozen conversations I wanted to have with Angie about the school and how they should set up the art room. I tucked a copy of the New Testament in my pocket and even reading I Corinthians 13 and I John, my favorite standbys, did nothing to settle my soul into the rut of peaceful cohabitation with silence.

I thought of Thomas Merton and almost cursed him a time or two with his talk of silence. Easy for him. He was a contemplative. I was just a young woman who visited with Jesus through no doing of her own, a person with a very noisy brain who looked at her splitting fingernails during the Eucharistic prayers. He came to me not because I deserved it but because of his great mercy. He knew I was alone in some way, that blood ties are important, that someone without a mother, like the mother he so loved and adored, needed something extra.

He knew my heart. How much I loved him.

Was I a mystic? Well, I seriously doubt it. I'd read Julian of Norwich and Jeanne Guyon and the like; Jesus seemed to have very different conversations with them than he did with me. They didn't make him a cup of tea and he didn't talk about how the one pair of sandals he owned gave him a callous on his big toe like you wouldn't believe.

Jesus joined me there in the woods at times and he said little, just took my hand as I walked along. "It's all right to wrestle, my dear," he said several times.

Finally, the silence came and I heard the music of God around me, a strain from heaven is the only way I can explain it, for the birds' music formed into something rhythmic and melodious. It was as if I'd been given jazz ears. I soaked in it, rolled in it, glorified God and felt like the Trinity let me in on Their little secret, an age-old secret suddenly real.

You love, T—, because we first loved you.

On my last day, as I packed my suitcase, Jesus sat on the end of the bed.

"You need to find Jude," he said.

I turned. I hadn't realized he'd come. "What?" And then I flew to my knees beside him. "I'm so sorry!" I gasped, slamming my hand over my mouth. I'd never questioned him before.

"Shhh, my dear."

He swept an arm around the plain room, over the desk with my copy of the Scriptures and prayer books, over the white wall with the crucifix, over the simple bed with a rather flat pillow and a wool blanket. "Mary-Margaret, do you love me more than these?"

Horror filled my chest cavity. "Of course, Lord. You know I do."

"Feed my lamb."

"But, Lord—"

In his one hand, he picked up the veil I'd laid out to be folded and packed; in the other he hung my rosary from his fingers. Oh, how many times I'd prayed the Divine Mercy Chaplet on it, I couldn't have said. "Mary-Margaret, do you love me more than these?"

"Oh, my Jesus. Yes, I do. You know I do."

"Feed my lamb."

He picked up my sensible shoes and laughed. "Mary-Margaret, T—, do you love me more than these?"

I joined in with his laughter. "Lord, you know all things. You know I love you more!"

"Feed my lamb."

I rested my head on his lap. "What are you telling me, Jesus? What do you want me to do once I find Jude?"

He ran a gentle hand across my hair, smoothing it back from my brow. "We've been together for so long, T—, and we always will be. You know how much I love you, don't you?"

"Yes, Lord."

He continued to caress my head. "I remember the day you were born. Such sadness in that room. Your mother's time had come for many reasons. The chief reason she was brought home was to save her from herself. But you'll find out more about that on your own someday. But *you* came into the world. You realize I had been forming you, watching you grow for all those weeks. I gave you that fiery red hair to match your zest for life, to reflect the passion I knew you would develop and, quite frankly, my dear, will need for this leg of the journey ahead." He lifted my head, drew me to my feet, and set me beside him. He took my hand. "T—, the next few months are going to be the most difficult of your life, but I've got a plan for you. It's the Father's plan and the Spirit will guide you. Do you trust us? Do you know that nothing we do will be for your detriment, but ultimately for your good, for your own perfection? Do you know that we will not harm you, that not a hair on your head will be touched that we don't will? Do you love us enough to seek the lost lamb with us? It's what we want of you. Of course, we won't force you, my dear."

I looked into those brown eyes, so soft and winsome, yet deep inside the fire of holiness and Deity and an all-consuming love that no human will ever duplicate no matter how long we've been in heaven with him. He smiled and raised an eyebrow. I placed my hand in his and he squeezed it. "Well, T—?"

"All right." I touched his cheek with my other hand. "All right."

To be honest, despite the Holy tenderness, my stomach rose in my throat and I wanted to throw up. The sun streamed through the window I'd opened a few inches with the morning breeze. I pictured the scene outside my window at St. Mary's. The fishing boats would be long gone from the dock, and in the distance the light at Bethlehem Point would be spiraling around and around.

"I've always loved it there, Jesus," I said, knowing I didn't have to explain my thoughts. "I hope I can return there, live there, teach there, be there. It's all I've ever wanted. Other than you."

"Yes, I know. It's up to you whether or not you'll go back to the Island in the long run. But for now . . . will you follow me?"

"Yes, Lord. I'll follow you where you want me to go."

He placed his arms around me and drew my head to his chest. I felt the softness of the heavenly garment of white and heard his heart again, beating with love for all the world.

"I want you to marry Jude Keller."

IT'S AMAZING HOW YOU CAN PUT A PROJECT DOWN THAT means so much to you and end up walking away for months. It is now December of 2001 and I'm in Florida once again for the Christmas holidays. I still haven't looked into Brother Joe's whereabouts after his time at the mission on The Block. And I still haven't planted Jude's bulbs either. You know, I knew what kind of flowers they would produce years ago, and now I simply cannot remember.

This past summer I tried, and failed, once again to get a showing at a gallery in Ocean City and I vowed to never try again. That owner has something out for me because he hangs all manner of seascapes with waves that are about as luminescent as a pot roast and even sculpture that's crafted from old lawn mower parts, but my sculptures are, in his words, "Pedestrian, Mary. Utterly pedestrian." If I go down in obscurity, so be it.

I visited with Morpheus for two weeks in June, stayed at the retreat house in Virginia for a week in July, then, amid flower-arranging classes and beading sessions, had to get my plans ready for the coming year to submit for the budget. I needed to develop a more advanced painting class for two women who were going great guns, as well as a few of the men decided they wanted to learn how to carve decoys. Researching, finding a teacher and inexpensive supplies, not to mention a field trip in early August to the Waterfowl Museum in Havre de Grace, took up the rest of my summer.

All wonderful, happy reasons to forgo a search.

Unfortunately, however, after a vacation to Niagara Falls with Gerald and Hattie that included a ride on Maid of the Mist and dinner at a Tyrolean restaurant, as well as a visit to several wax museums, Hattie took a turn for the worse. They'd stepped down their care level and moved into a lovely little unit with a kitchenette, a bed and bath, and a sitting room. On September 11th, she had a stroke just after watching the second plane slam into the World Trade Center. She's been in a vegetative state ever since. We can't figure out if the attack caused the stroke or it was just a coincidence. I figure the latter; Angie, of course, says Hattie was probably more frightened of the changes in the world than she ever let on. The woman who rescued people in hurricanes single-handedly? I just don't think so. "She lived in a lighthouse most of her adult life, Mary. That's quite a sheltered existence."

Whatever the reason, Gerald can't cope, simply put, so I haven't felt the freedom to just go traipsing off to find my father. Aunt Elfi trained me too well. However, Hattie's youngest sister finally convinced Gerald to visit her in Hagerstown for the Christmas holidays and I begged him to go.

"Hattie might linger for many more months. But if she does wake up, and it would take a miracle, Gerald, I think she would be glad you took a trip to see Adele. Don't you? Honestly?" We were sitting in the facility dining room eating tapioca pudding with vanilla wafers ringed around the inside of the pedestaled, glass dessert cup.

"I think you're probably right. But what if she dies while I'm gone?"

"You'll come home from Hagerstown and I'll return from

Florida and you and I will walk through that valley together. I'll be with you every step of the way. I promise, Gerald. Do you understand?"

After what Jesus told me about our death order, I felt fully confident saying that. Jesus doesn't lie.

He whipped a white handkerchief out of his back pocket and dabbed at his eyes. Hattie's illness aged him a good five years. "You've been a good friend all of these years, MM."

"I've tried. And you've always made it easy, Gerald." I lightly pinched his bony forearm. "So don't start making it difficult for me now."

"Aye, aye."

Later I took him in my arms as we sat at the edge of Hattie's bed, just like Jesus always took me into his. Gerald said, "All right, MM. I'll go."

I've got to get back to the mission. Maybe I will after vacation. But for now, I've got my toes in the sand, a very large hat on my head, and this notebook. And so I will continue my tale.

My latest letter from my son John in Africa bore good news. Unfortunately, he wasn't able to come back to the United States for classes last summer and ended up completing his hours in Johannesburg.

Dear Mom,

I miss you as always and am craving a plate of your crab cakes as usual. Please tell me you eat them at least once a month. I've been hankering for some good old Maryland seafood lately.

December is always the worst time here in Swaziland as all the rituals with the king are in full swing. I'm staying put here in Big Bend and putting off my trip to Mbabane until after the New Year.

The church from Colorado finished their building out at the nearby carepoint and we were able to start classes for the older children who cannot afford school. We have thirty students ranging from ages 14–18. You'd love them so much. I think a few of them will actually make it in this world. At least a third of them are already HIV positive.

I'm so very sorry to hear about Aunt Hattie. Poor dear. I know you two have always been good friends as well as sisters-in-law. Tell Uncle Gerald the brothers and I are praying for them.

I don't have time to write a detailed letter as the drought has been terrible this summer and a steady stream of patients rolls through the clinic. I did want to tell you to pray for a girl named Tengetile. She is fourteen, head of household, and her uncle is raping her regularly. We're doing all we can for her, but this culture fails to protect these girls. Pray for her safety and that we can show her a little kindness in the name of the Lord. I'm sure she has AIDS and if she isn't pregnant already, she soon will be. At times like these, as you might well guess, I feel utterly inadequate.

You are always beside me in my thoughts and prayers. I hope you'll come next summer. We sure could use the help, and I'd love to see you.

Much love,
John

If John is still alive as you read this, sisters, please offer up a prayer for him.

Well then. Let's pick up where we left off with Jesus dropping that whopper of a request on me! Marry Jude? Lord have mercy!

I called Angie first after I landed back on the island, still shell-shocked at the marching orders Jesus had given me. She still lived in Bainbridge though the school year had ended, helping to set up the new school.

"You don't do stuff like this, Mary," she said. "Not even close. What's gotten into you?"

"God told me to do it."

"How?"

"He has his ways." I rested my feet up on the secretary's desk again. It was amazing the woman didn't kick me out of her office. But Patty was a nice enough lady who, I can tell you right now, almost always eavesdropped on the conversations anyway, and the fact that she found them so interesting just proved how boring life at St. Mary's could be.

"Care to tell me?"

"I can't. Just suffice it to say I know it for sure. Do you really think I'd be doing this of my own accord, Angie? Jude Keller? Captain VD as you've so taken to calling him?"

She chuckled. "That wasn't very nice of me, was it? But I swear, Mary, I didn't think he'd end up as your darned husband."

"Don't jump ahead of it all. He may refuse."

"Are you nuts? The guy's been cuckoo over you for years."

The bulbous black receiver began to feel heavy in my hand. I sighed. "You're right. I was just clinging to the hope he'd think I was too good for him."

"Well, he'd be right about that!" she snapped.

"You don't sound happy."

"Why should I be? We had plans, Mary! Big plans and now you're telling me God's told you to give up everything you've ever wanted to be, all your entire life, from practically the cradle—"

"Not the womb?"

"Have it your way. The womb. And you're going to find one of the most . . . disgusting men ever to walk the face of the earth and marry him? Did God say anything about having sex with the man?"

"No."

"Well, at least there's that."

"Angie!" Boy, would Patty get an earful now. "The Church encourages sex within marriage and you know as well as I do they deem it a sin not to procreate if it's possible."

She blew a big breath into the phone. "Yeah, yeah. I know, I know."

"I'm sorry. I don't really want to do this. I mean . . ."

"You do love him, though, don't you?"

"Yes, but not like a wife should."

"But, okay—how to say this delicately—you feel *excited* by him, don't you?"

"Well, yeah, but that was—"

"The devil? You've said that before, but I'm not so sure. So he excites you and you feel love in your heart for him."

I had to say it. "It's a pity love, Angie! What kind of a marriage is founded upon pity?"

"Apparently yours."

Apparently so.

"And probably more marriages than we realize," she snickered. She paused. "Okay, cut the crap, Mary. It isn't pity and you know it. I don't know what it is. I don't even think you know. Heaven knows it's confused and convoluted. But is it enough?"

"Will you pray for me?" I couldn't think of anything else to ask.

"Of course. Probably more than I have time for now, so thanks for that. Have you told the higher-ups?"

"No. I called you first."

. . .

"Angie?"

. . .

"That's all I needed to hear, Mary. You say the word, you need anything, I'll drop everything. Okay?"

"Okay."

I hung up and walked to the graveyard of St. Francis. I had no flower to lay upon my mother's grave, no white rose to express the sorrow I felt at not fulfilling her dream and my own. My loyalty felt shattered and spread like pulverized glass upon the grass over where she lay, but I had a greater loyalty. And surely she would understand that. I tried to picture her, reaching forward and comforting me. But I could not.

I sat cross-legged next to her as the day waned, until Sister Thaddeus found me and sat beside me as the night set in.

～～

After withdrawing from the order of the School Sisters of St. Mary, a day that still hurts my back teeth so much I hate to think about it, I cried in the arms of Sister Thaddeus. I had visions of my mother, whose dreams were shattered by that seminarian, and now, mine were shattered by Jesus. The irony was inescapable. I thought I knew what Jesus meant when he told me I was his bride.

Apparently I jumped to the wrong conclusion. But I could share none of this with Sister Thaddeus.

She sat me down and made me a cup of tea. She appeared so fresh in her gray habit and white veil, her long skirt and shirt pressed perfectly, a far cry from my habit that always ended up wrinkled, underarms circled with perspiration.

"Let me tell you what I left behind to follow God's path for me, Mary-Margaret." She eased down onto a hard chair, her back pin-straight, sitting ladylike yet at ease. Still, there was always a bit of a nervous twitter to her fingers. "My father was a very rich man. Very busy too. He owned one of the shipbuilding companies in Baltimore."

"My goodness."

"Yes. He gave me this good education here at St. Mary's and planned on enrolling me into university and handing the company over to me someday." She picked up her teacup and stared into the reddish brew. "He was very forward thinking."

"You gave up the life of wealth and privilege?"

"Oh no! More than that. All that wasn't what I was looking forward to. I was looking forward to working alongside my father for a couple of decades, learning what he loved, and what I loved too, and giving him peace of mind in his old age. But mostly, just being with him. You'd had to have known him to know what I mean. I had no other siblings and my mother was always ill. She was delightful but highly delicate."

"Do you ever have moments of regret?"

"Not regret." Her eyes softened. "But sadness at what never could have been. It's sad to leave behind what we love, what we thought we were going to do, even for the best of reasons."

"Do you understand, Sister Thaddeus?" I leaned forward, feeling the edge of the table knife into my belly.

"I believe you when you say this is from God. If you really know that, then I believe you."

"I'm so sorry." I shook my head, heart in two pieces.

~~~

After that, I looked at myself in the mirror for at least thirty minutes so I could examine my own head. Then I packed my suitcase once again, took the ferry to the mainland, hopped the bus to Salisbury, got on the Greyhound, and made the pilgrimage of my life. I was finding God's lamb, and hopefully he was still on The Block and not in Europe. Talk about going from one world into another! Our Mother Superior thought I was as crazy as Angie did because why would God call someone out from a religious vocation to a marriage with the scum of the earth?

Only she said it much nicer than that. And I knew she just wanted the best from me.

Marriage to the scum of the earth.

Isn't that what God called Jesus to do? I wanted to ask her. But I held my tongue. Still, she hugged me to her and I sniffled and teared up and she rested her olive-skinned hand atop my head in blessing. She told me she'd pray for me, and she held true to that promise.

Once in Baltimore, I hopped onto a streetcar outside the bus station, wishing I could be doing anything else at that moment other than heading into red lights and sordid lives. But there was no use in putting off the inevitable. Perhaps somebody there could give me some information about Jude's whereabouts in Europe. I remembered a woman he mentioned, a friend who billed herself as LaBella. So, arm in arm with the Spirit of God, I stepped onto Baltimore Street in plain street clothes I bought at Epstein's. A calf-length black skirt and a yellow blouse. I kept the sensible shoes for good measure. I guess I didn't realize then I was ahead of the times in general "nun-wear" as Jude would have called it. The thought makes me smile as I write.

I liked the old habits, if you want to know the truth. Angie, on the other hand, wanted to have a habit-burning bonfire after Vatican II. I told you she was an upstart.

Hoping against hope I wouldn't have to walk by too many clubs and peep show parlors with the notorious leering doormen, I strode up to the first doorman/bouncer I saw, hugging my purse against my breasts. I suppose now's a good time to tell you that they're ample. Not overly ample, but enough to be classified as "full." I never really thought too much about them until that moment in front of the Gayety. The doorman handed me a flyer. I still have it. It reads:

· G A Y E T Y ·
Coolest Place in Baltimore
PEPPY BURLESK
MATINEE DAILY

FRENCH FROLICS
With
FRITZI WHITE
TOMMY MILLER, Your Favorite Funster

EXTRA! EXTRA!
PARISIAN ART MODELS

My first thought? French! LaBella! Glory be to God, my prayers were answered!

"I'm looking for a . . . dancer. She goes by LaBella?"

"Do she or don't she?" the doorman, obviously a hunk of muscle overlaid with the fat of too much drink, too much sitting around, and too much all-you-can-eat prime rib, said, his voice low but strung with a nasal twang.

"Let me take that back and make it a statement then. I'm looking for a dancer named LaBella. Have you heard of her?"

He nodded appreciatively and tipped his cap back a little. "Yeah, sure. She works down at the Two O'Clock Club. Blaze's place."

Blaze Starr. I hadn't heard of her then. She'd yet to have her famous affair with the governor of Louisiana, or was just beginning it. I don't know the exact dates of that. As if that's a big surprise.

"Thank you."

"Uh, if you don't mind my askin', what's a gal like you doin' down here? You need to be careful."

I stepped back into the middle of the sidewalk and began strolling toward the club. "I'm not alone!" I called over my shoulder.

"Suit yourself!"

There's not too many sadder locales than places that are supposed to be all lit up and fancy-looking just sitting there like every other building during the day. All the cracks are exposed, the dirt, the smears, the graffiti. Nobody cares enough to make them presentable by sunlight like the lawyers' offices do, the banks, the clothing stores, the grocers. Those establishments operate with God and everybody looking on and not thinking a thing. But right now, these places aren't allowed to be hidden by the dark night, or obscured by the neon lights and flashing bulbs. You see it truly naked. I do believe that's why so much sin happens in the dark. You can't really get a good view on it for what it is.

Blaze Starr was out getting her hair done when I walked into her club, thank goodness, and wouldn't be back for at least another hour. I'm sure religious sisters and strippers have some things in common. Chiefly, doing something that is and always will be a mystery to most other women. I asked the doorman, a skinny guy with zinging black eyes and bark brown hair that skimmed the edge of his collar, if LaBella was in. He said she didn't get there usually until around nine p.m.

"Could you give her a call?" I asked. "I'd like to see if I could come around and ask her a few questions about a mutual friend of ours."

He got a "knowing" look on his face. But he couldn't have known.

"I'll be right back."

"His name is Jude."

"Jude!" He snapped his fingers. "I remember him. Nice enough kid when he first got here. But—man, he toughened up but quick."

"I'll wait outside."

Honestly, I just didn't want to know what it was like in there.

"What's your name, kid?"

"Mary-Margaret."

"Figures."

While I stood outside, I was actually propositioned by two men. "In these shoes?" I hollered at them where they sat in their car. "You've got to be joking!"

"What's your angle then?" the passenger, a man in a yellow sport coat, said.

"I'm a nun! God loves you!"

They sped off. I laughed.

Did I lie? Nope. In my heart, I was a religious sister. And somehow I always would be. It didn't make any logical sense. It was just the way it was. Jesus, he would always be the one I was really married to. I couldn't have even considered doing as he asked with Jude if that hadn't been the case.

The doorman returned with a slip of paper. He held it out.

"Highland Avenue?" I asked. "What kind of stripper lives on Highland Avenue? In Highlandtown, for heaven's sake?"

"She's not like you'd imagine. You're going to be surprised."

And why not? It wasn't like I wasn't already overwhelmed by the unexpected.

"Her real name is Rosalie."

"Thanks."

He scootched back up on his stool. "Be careful out there. This isn't the place for a gal like you."

"I know. Why are you being so nice?"

"My sister has red hair. What can I say?"

I asked him if he knew which bus would get me there and he said the number eight. He pointed me to the closest corner. "It'll come by near the top of the hour. I'll keep an eye on you."

So I waited there, glued to the pavement, and I looked up at the heavens and I thought, *Jesus, what have you done?*

I felt silly entering Jude's world like that and my heart was shrouded in a cloud of doubt. Of course Jesus knew what he was asking. But I didn't know what I was doing. Because I had no doubt I would find Jude. The problem was in picturing myself asking him to marry me. How in the world was that going to go?

But I wouldn't need him. I would be married to him. I would love him as a Christian loves the lost lamb. I might even be excited by him if I could get past the fact that he'd slept with multiple men and women (and I doubted I'd ever really get past that), but I would never need him. I would only be there because I wanted to save him, and I only wanted to save him because Jesus told me to.

That, to be perfectly honest, stank to high heaven.

Maybe I was really crazy, a stark-raving lunatic, Jesus just a figment of my imagination, and I was listening to my deep-down craziness, or worse—there it was again—the devil. In fact, maybe the whole religion business was just a worldwide delusion, that the moving of the Holy Spirit wasn't anything but events and coincidences and happenings we knit together on our own as having some kind of cohesion to make it seem like Divine intervention.

And yet, I got on the number eight bus.

～

Rosalie answered the door to her row house, a two-story, narrow affair covered with postwar Formstone in the block between Eastern Avenue and Fleet Street.

I imagine she puttied on a fair amount of makeup for her act, but standing there behind the screen door, she looked sixteen, her brown hair feathering around her shoulders, her pale skin a perfect ivory expanse but for the pink blush of her cheeks. Her greenish grey eyes, hit from the side by the sunlight, glowed with gold flecks. An older baby sat on her hip.

"Mary-Margaret!" she said, her smile broad and baring pleasingly crooked teeth that reminded me of Audrey Hepburn's. "The club called and let me know you were coming. Come in!"

"Thank you." I felt large and oafish when I stepped into her home. I'm not a large woman by any means, but Rosalie wouldn't have surprised me if she'd taken off her pink sweater and shown me a pair of shimmering wings. Ethereal didn't begin to describe her.

And yet, her home was quite the opposite. A heavy old wood-framed couch upholstered in gold and white damask, once likely her grandmother's or, well, somebody's grandmother's, was set against the green sidewall. Dime-store prints hung on the walls, mostly depicting opaque flowers in bulbous vases against dark backgrounds, what Morpheus calls "Almost Flemish."

"Come keep me company while I make dinner."

I skirted the television—she must have done pretty well to have afforded one back then—and followed her back to the kitchen as she chattered about Jude.

"I've known him for almost ten years now and he's told me so much about you, Mary-Margaret! I feel like I know you already!"

We could have been women meeting at the park, or at church.

She set the baby, dressed in a light blue dress, white tights, and black patent leather Mary-Janes, into a mahogany Jenny Lind high chair. "Just a minute, Alice, and I'll get you some din-din."

Alice was almost bald with bright blue eyes—the picture of vulnerable innocence, naturally. I wondered if she'd ever find out what her mother did for a living or if Rosalie would quit by the time Alice could figure out something wasn't quite normal around their home. People have kept secrets far longer, I suppose, and double lives aren't so uncommon that nobody's ever heard of one before.

Rosalie motioned to a chrome chair upholstered in off-white vinyl with silver flecks. "Have a seat if you'd like. We're about to eat dinner. I eat early so I can have time with Alice before I leave for the club."

"Who watches her when you're working?"

"Oh, my husband, Jack. He'll be home soon too. You're welcome to join us for a bite if you have the time."

I shook my head, the wonderment obvious on my face.

She laughed. "It would take all night to explain it and neither of us have that kind of time, I'll warrant." She rubbed her hands down the sides of her black skinny pants, then pushed back her bangs. Even a little harried and worn by the day, she was beautiful and glamorous in a carefree, natural way, as if her costumes and makeup colored in some of the missing bits. Her

body, thin and lithe, didn't seem to be that of a stripper, her
breasts small. She didn't ooze sex appeal. She did look French
though, very classy and continental. Maybe that provided its own
sort of fantasy for those oafish men who would never get the
opportunity to bed a woman with such seeming style and grace.

I became painfully aware of my shoes because it's one thing
to wear such sensible shoes when you're a religious sister, but as
a person on the street, well, it says more about you than you'd
like someone else to know. Perhaps. Or it might just say you
have corns and bunions. Which I didn't.

Oh dear.

"So you must have met Jude when he first made it to town?"
I asked.

"Oh yes! Young and angry with everything to prove but
nothing to show for it and very little to concretely offer in the
long run. Especially coming from a place as remote as Abbeyville.
We see those types all the time down there on Baltimore Street.
But I liked Jude. We took him in for a few weeks until he found
his feet. I tried to guide him a little, to not take it all so seriously, that it would kill him if he didn't view it as a job and
nothing more."

"Jude could never do that."

"You're exactly right." She leaned down and extracted a can
of peas from the bottom cupboard, then slid open a drawer and
plucked out a can opener. "Peas!" She jiggled the can at Alice.
"Your favorite, sweet girl!"

I could barely take all of it in. Rosalie—LaBella. Housewife
by day, stripper by night. How in heaven's name did she find
herself at home in both worlds? Leering men, feathers, bumps
and grinds on the one hand, canned peas, diapers, bibs, and sea
foam green cabinets on the other? A dinette, for goodness
sake!

I couldn't help it. "I just can't add up what I'm seeing here."

She ground the blades into the top of the can. "It's like this. They're just breasts. That's all I bare."

"But they're your breasts."

"I know it's not the best of choices for a job, but I landed it years and years ago. I'd run away from home. Can we talk about Jude, Mary-Margaret? I don't know how you will possibly understand me."

She was right. "If you'd like. I'm sorry."

"No offense taken. So anyway, Jude and I have remained close friends over the years. Never intimate in any way. I never found him all that attractive."

"Really?!" I blurted out.

"Well, your reaction is most women's when it comes to him, I'll tell you that."

My cheeks burned and she laughed.

"When was the last time you saw him?" I asked.

"About a week ago. He was planning on heading to Europe, he'd said, but came home to do one more piece of business. I don't know what it was. Said he'd been out to the island and saw you, but just couldn't bear to drag you any further into his life. Then he went to the doctor for a fever, headache, and a rash on his abdomen. I told him it might be scarlatina and he shouldn't mess with that. Well, he ended up with a diagnosis of syphilis."

"Oh no!"

She turned on the burner beneath the pan of peas, reached into the refrigerator, and pulled out a pound of ground beef. "Hamburgers," she said. "Mashed potatoes and gravy too. Sure you can't stay?"

I shook my head almost wildly. She just told me someone had syphilis and then, another dinner invite. What a wacky world.

I didn't know much about syphilis. I'd have to get to the library.

"Yes, thank you, I'm sure. So after the diagnosis, what did he say?"

"He changed his plans. Said he didn't feel like going overseas after all." She handed the baby some zwieback. Alice smashed it against her gums and grinned.

"What about the trouble he was in due to drugs?"

"He had a windfall. Probably bribed somebody important after he did his business with him."

"That doesn't sound like Jude."

"No. You're right. He's always been straightforward. Anyway, I didn't ask where the money came from. Jude doesn't confide in anybody, anyway."

He always did with me, I thought.

Rosalie began to form the ground beef into patties. "The truth is, Mary-Margaret, the light had gone out of him. I don't know how to describe it, but something happens there on The Block. If you make it your entire life, pieces of you die. At least that's what I've noticed. I don't know if it's possible to see it when it's happening to you. I doubt many of the folks down there would say they weren't all they used to be. But it's true. And when enough dies, you either slink away or end up down at the mission."

"What mission?"

"Brother Joe's. The Catholic priest down there. Heart of the City Mission. Does some good work with the alkies and the streetwalkers. Started up sometime after the war. Good man. Anyway, Jude found himself there and it scared him. Then the diagnosis came"—she sighed and laid a patty on top of the other two she'd formed while speaking—"and that was it for him."

"So where did he go?"

"I'm not sure. All he said was that he was going to the place he should have never left in the first place. As I said, about a week ago."

"Did he ever talk about his childhood, growing up out at the lighthouse?"

"Only once. And then in passing. When I'd ask him about it, he said he didn't like to talk about it."

I nodded, giving her the one-minute version of Jude's childhood. "I don't know who he would have been had he stayed."

"There's a wild streak in Jude, always one to do whatever he wants. Location wouldn't have changed that, Mary-Margaret. It's like he was born to go against the grain."

Aren't we all? I wanted to say.

I stood up. "Well, I'd better go, I guess. Thank you for your time, Rosalie. Thank you for being Jude's friend."

She set a cast-iron pan on a burner and turned on the gas flame. "Oh, you know Jude. Despite the edges, he's not bad to be around. There's something inside there you just feel sorry for."

~~

Jesus didn't have to tell me where Jude was. How he got out to Bethlehem Point Light without anybody knowing was beyond me, though. Maybe he hired somebody to take him across and paid them a little extra to keep quiet about it. Most likely that was the case. It being May by this point, the waters still would have been too cold to swim and in his weakened state, a fever and all, he couldn't have made the half-mile swim anyway.

What did Hattie think when he showed up?

Thoughts like those milled about my brain as I sat on the bus back to the island. The large tires vibrated against the tar joints of the Bay Bridge, and the sight of the water that next morning, the sun throwing a healthy smattering of glitter over the waves, comforted me. Water always does. Cleansing water. Holy water.

God likes water. Of that I'm sure. We baptize with it and the people of Israel would purify themselves ritually with it. And something holy happened. I don't pretend to understand why God uses the stuff of this earth to commit holy acts for his people, why he allows the ordinary to become sacred, but I read the Old Testament rituals he designed himself for Israel, and I can't escape the fact that he uses his creation, makes it holy, to bless his people.

So that morning, the expanse of water flowing from either side of that miles-long bridge, I drank in the power of the Spirit. I remembered the circumstances of my baptism long ago. I remembered the love of God for me. I remembered my response in kind on a Pentecost Sunday in 1941 when I felt the Holy Spirit's power flood my soul and I said, "Yes, yes," to a life of following Jesus. I thought about the expanse of water I sat in front of for more hours than I could count, staring out at the lighthouse, the same expanse of water that now separated Jude from his bride.

His bride. Me.

I felt sick again. I'd been feeling sick a lot.

The whole syphilis revelation didn't help any either. Was he getting treatment? Was I supposed to sleep with him if he refused to get help? Was there treatment? I didn't even know. I'd get to the library later. The first order of that day was find Jude. Hopefully, that little house on the water, the light swinging round and round, had not, or would not, become his tomb.

~~~

I stepped off the Greyhound around eleven a.m. and found a ride on a produce truck to the ferry. I knew the driver slightly, a quiet sixteen-year-old named Patrick whose family owned the supermarket on the island. I sat beside him as he drove without saying much. I said little as well. It was awkward when I offered to help with the gas, but Patrick wouldn't take so much as a dime. Patrick ended up in the military, dying in Viet Nam in 1968. His wife teaches second grade on the island and is very helpful with the altar society at church. She remarried and had six children, but she keeps a picture of Patrick in her Sunday missal.

Wondering for the first time where I was going to stay, I realized I couldn't ask the sisters at St. Mary to provide a room. I'd just, in all practicality, turned my back on them, on all the years and hours they'd invested in me, loved me, rebuked me, and encouraged me. Oh, how glad I am I didn't know Sister Thaddeus was my benefactress. And when I think how she supported my decision, how she trusted me implicitly, it amazes me further.

Mr. and Mrs. Bray. I knew they'd take me in. And maybe they'd understand what had been happening, because the Lord knew nobody else really did, least of all myself.

Suitcase in my grip, I clipped down Main Street, past the school, the drugstore, and negotiated the tree-lined gravel lane that led to the Brays' cottage. As I write this, Mercy House is painted the palest, creamiest of yellows, but back then the Brays' chose an eager blue that reflected the emotions of the sky and the Bay. The lacy trim has always been painted white as far as I can remember. It's always a relief when what to do with something is that evident.

Regina Bray opened the door, her eyes widening at the sight of me with a suitcase. "Mary-Margaret? What are you doing here, child?"

"I'm on a mission of mercy."

"With that suitcase? Come on in."

I followed her yellow-chiffon-clad form, so thin and lithe and golden brown despite bearing all those children, into their parlor. Mr. Bray made his wife the most beautiful clothing. She was by far the smartest dresser on the island. And she had her hair done every week at the beauty parlor for black women. Its soft waves flowed into a turned-under curl around her shoulders that bounced with each footstep. She'd slid her feet into matching, kitten-heeled pumps. Perfect.

I made a mental note to ask Mr. Bray if he'd give me a few sewing lessons, something to keep me occupied.

And then it hit me. How were Jude and I going to support ourselves? He was a drug-dealing prostitute and I a former religious school sister. Perhaps the local elementary school needed an art teacher. But I doubted it.

I mentally pictured myself crossing my fingers in blind hope. And, after being in the shadow of the Church's wings all my life, the thought of "getting out into the world" like everybody else scared me silly. Is that what my faith had become, a place to hide from society, from possible pain, from vulnerability?

Nah.

Even if I was doing that, who could blame me? I was handed a raw deal from the get-go.

"Don't beat yourself up for that," Jesus whispered in my ear. "You were right where I wanted you, my dear."

Thank you, Friend.

Mrs. Bray gestured toward her brown, crushed velvet sofa that had clearly just been vacuumed judging by the satiny, then suedelike streaks. Regina Bray's house was perfect all the time— pillows placed just so, the fringe on her area rug combed, the walls washed and nary a cobweb (even in the attic, I suspected)—I do believe she cleaned it every day. And in such beautiful clothing too. Truly a modern housewife, such as they were at the time. At least in the advertisements.

Somehow Regina achieved what most women only hoped for.

I had to stifle a laugh at the thought of the house I was going to keep. Art supplies everywhere, sandwiches for dinner, ironing-

on-demand, laundry only when the undergarments ran out, an
overgrown lawn.

This whole thing is destined to be a nightmare, Lord, an absolute nightmare.

He didn't answer back, but I did get a quick vision of colorful flower gardens.

"Would you like some iced tea or lemonade?" she asked.
"Maybe a cup of coffee?"

"Are you thirsty?" I asked.

"Not really. I just had a cup of tea."

"I'm fine then." I set down my suitcase, then sat on the
couch.

"You look like you've got a story to tell." Mrs. Bray sat on a
mustard-gold occasional chair with a rattan back. She crossed
one leg delicately over the other, the top leg dangling down
close to the other, the top foot not so very far off the floor. I've
noticed that thin people's legs always do this and it looks so
elegant. Her spine supported the entire effect like a pillar.

I sat with my left foot crossed behind my right ankle, like the
nuns taught us to sit, so proper, and I folded my hands in my
lap. "I left the order."

Her hand slapped against her heart. "Mary-Margaret, no!
That was the last thing I expected to hear! Are you sure about
this?"

"Unfortunately, yes."

"Is this God's doing?"

"Fortunately, yes."

"Oh dear. Oh, my my my. You need to tell me about this.
But first of all, do you need a place to stay?"

I nodded. "I'm sorry."

"You came to the right house. Now, our spare bedroom is
tiny, but I think you religious are used to small rooms, aren't
you?"

"Indeed we are."

"Of course. So then this might actually seem downright spacious!" She chuckled, a warm breeze of a chuckle, the final "hmph" upswept in the same curl as her lips.

"Thank you."

She stood up. "So tell me the rest of your story and I'll help you unpack."

I've always found the Methodists to be good listeners.

~~~

Two hours later, a cup of tea and some fresh-baked cookies down the hatch, Mrs. Bray wiped her eyes, then neatly folded her hankie and placed it in a hidden pocket in her dress. "Oh, sweet pea, I don't know how you know God wants you to do this, but I know you wouldn't be doing it for any other reason. It's too crazy to consider something like this all on your own." She reached out where we were sitting next to one another on the sofa and grabbed my hand.

"I just have no idea where we'll live. I realized that on the bus here."

"Let me just tell you about my sister's little place over near the wharf. It's a cute little two-room apartment above the bait and tackle shop, you know, that touristy place?"

I nodded. "Ron Purnell's?"

"She owns the building. Her renter's due to be moving out next month. I can talk her into giving you all a good price."

"I'm going to need to find a job too. I was hoping the elementary school might hire me."

"Art?" She tapped her finger against the spot between her mouth and nose. "I don't know. Now, at the Negro school, we could use an English teacher in the fall. You think you might be interested in that?"

A dream fulfilled? "Of course! You know I would be."

I quickly filled her in on what happened in Bainbridge.

"Lord have mercy!" she cried. "God restoring what the locusts have eaten. We can go by and talk to the principal tomorrow."

~~

Mr. Bray was full of love and encouragement, mystified, truly, like most people, but trusting. "Mary-Margaret, I never known you to do anything stupid or rash. I believe you mean what you say. But I do wonder this. What if Jude turns you down?"

"What?" I set my fork on my plate and reached for my water glass. "I guess I haven't imagined that."

"Oh, you should! The man has been around the block a time or ten, so he's obviously feeling worthless and ready to pack it all in if he's back at the light. He may not want to drag you into his sorry life. I imagine it feels pretty complicated to him. If he truly loves you like you say he does, he'll turn you down flat."

"My goodness," I breathed. "I hadn't even considered it. But, well, you may be right."

"Oh, I'm sure he is." Regina handed her husband the platter of fried soft crabs. "Johnson has a sixth sense about people. He really does."

That night I walked to Bethlehem Point and sat beneath my mother's tree. I prayed—well, talked to God would describe it better even though, yes, that's technically prayer. I whispered words of fear, of trust, of anguish, of anger too, and finally Jesus came and stood in front of me, blocking my view of the light.

"I am the light of the world, T—."

"Yes, Lord, you are."

"The way will be clearly marked for you. We don't do that for everyone, as you well know. But this is something you can count on. You'll know what you need to know *when* you need to know it. Don't be afraid."

And then he spread wide his hands and showed me a portion of his glory, his skin glowing like molten steel, his eyes like
white-hot coals. He pulled aside his robe and revealed his flaming heart and I gasped at the beauty and fell on my face before
him, reveling that One so full of majesty and power and love
loved me so completely. I worshipped his holiness, feeling small,
but altogether safe in the light of his grace.

~⁓~

I must have fallen asleep, or Jesus himself ushered me to a state
of unconsciousness, because I awakened around eleven p.m. and
headed back to the Brays' with my chair tucked under my arm
and Jesus tucked even more firmly in my heart than before. A
light glowed in the window and a note on the dining room table
said, "Feel free to warm up some milk. We're glad you're here."

~⁓~

The next morning Mr. Cinquefoil (the father of Shrubby—the
man whose boat I used to spirit Gerald out to the lighthouse)
said upon my request, "Well, now, Mary, I don't have time to be
takin' you out to the lighthouse today. I got oysters to catch." He
pronounced it *ersters*.

"Please! I'll pay you."

I thought about all I had in the world. Fifty dollars.

"I don't need yer money. I just don't have much time." Mr.
Cinquefoil's wiry hair stood up on end and blew in the island
breeze like sea grass. His hands were as calloused as the shells of
the oysters from which he made his living. He was a loner, but
would say hello if you spoke first. In the evenings, he sat on his
porch and smoked a pipe while his wife chatted inside on her
telephone.

"How about if you take me out on your way to the oyster
beds?"

I pulled my sweater around me. Five a.m. in May can still be a little cool on the Chesapeake.

He ran a hand over his head. "I can't pick you back up until I'm on my way back in."

"I'll just have Gerald bring me back."

"All right. Hop aboard. Hattie know you're comin'?"

"No, unfortunately."

I looked at the light swinging round and round in the darkness and wondered if I was doing the wrong thing.

No. I just had to get it over with.

"It's a mite early to be visiting folk, ain't it?"

"A little."

"Well, it's your funeral."

If I could be so lucky.

~~

Of course Gerald heard the burbling putter of Mr. Cinquefoil's engine as he pulled up near the lighthouse. He hurried onto the deck in his robe and slippers. "Who's that?!" he shouted and I saw the silhouette of his shotgun in the porch light.

"Put that peashooter down, Gerald!" Mr. Cinquefoil shouted back. "It's me. Randy. And I got Mary-Margaret here. She wants to see you folks so bad she practically commandeered my boat!"

I stifled a laugh.

Gerald shielded his eyes, trying to peer into the darkness, his form a fuzzy silhouette in front of the white siding of the lighthouse. "MM? What's the matter?"

"I've come to see Jude. This was the only ride I could get. I wish you all had a phone."

"He's real sick."

"That's why I've come."

"Well, suit yourself. Although I don't know how you found

out about it." He leaned the shotgun against the house. "Want me to row out and get you?"

"I'd be thankful if you did," said Mr. Cinquefoil. "I wasn't much keen on losing my lifeboat today. I mean, you just never know with this bay."

"Give me five minutes."

Mr. Cinquefoil's boat was much too big to pull up to the dock beneath the lighthouse, so I waited while Gerald dressed, then climbed into his small boat, pulled on the starting cord of the outboard motor, and came to collect me. With each minute, my nervousness seemed to increase exponentially until I hoped and prayed I'd be able to make it from the fishing boat down into the motorboat.

What a dope! I thought. People disobeyed God all the time and God was merciful despite it. In fact, they were the ones who ended up with the best stories. Wouldn't he be merciful to me as well?

Gerald's face lit up in the lights of Mr. Cinquefoil's boat and it brightened further with a smile.

Oh, but I wanted the good stuff from God. Not the second best or the mercy despite the disobedience. I wanted fresh-picked grace from the top of the heap, ripe and burgeoning with refreshment. I had to believe that obedience right away made a difference; that those who honored God without wandering received something special, that it mattered. If I didn't believe that, my sisters, I would have told Mr. Cinquefoil to turn that boat around and take me back to the Brays'. The next morning I would have returned to Baltimore and the mother-house and I would have dedicated my life to God through my order and the holy Catholic Church.

And I would have been turning my back on the wild, seemingly insane plan that Jesus cooked up for me that made about as much sense as high-heeled tennis shoes.

~⌇

By eight thirty I'd yet to see Jude. After I'd dozed some on the couch, ate a breakfast of Hattie's biscuits, fried ham, and scrambled eggs, and read a searing chapter from one of Hattie's dime-store romances—well, as searing as they got back then, anyway—Gerald took me into the kitchen and sat me at the table over which Hattie had laid a yellow cloth covered in embroidered daisies. Over that—a sheet of clear vinyl, corners of which could draw blood on your thigh if you weren't careful.

Gerald occupied the chair catty-corner from me, folded his hands, then smoothed back his hair, which, I'd noticed, was going quite gray at the temples. He was a looker too, like his brother. Just more contained.

"You look weary, Gerald."

"I'm more than weary, MM. I feel like punching Jude right now." He had rolled up the sleeves on his blue shirt and began applying some sort of creamy ointment to his arms. Poor Gerald had eczema so badly on his appendages and his job didn't help the matter. "He said he won't see you."

"Really?" The response sat on my tongue like a stamp I'd moistened but forgotten to remove. My chest tried to support the weight of his words, but it couldn't. I sank into myself. "I didn't expect this. At the very least—"

"Neither of us did." He shook his head. "Darn it, MM! I don't know what's gotten into him. He asked if we'd take care of him while he recuperated, but he's been laying in there for a week now and he doesn't seem to be getting any better."

"Has he taken any penicillin?"

"For the flu?"

Oh dear.

"Hattie can't even convince him?"

"She's trying." He stood up. "I'm hungry. I know. I know

we just ate breakfast, but I always eat when I'm nervous." Opening
the fridge door, he peered inside and grabbed a plate of sliced
salami and something wrapped in brown paper.

He set them on the counter, unwrapped the paper to reveal
several slices of Swiss cheese.

"Can I have a slice to nibble on?" I asked.

"Yep. Here you go." He peeled off a slice and handed it to
me.

I don't really like Swiss cheese all by itself, but I'm with
Gerald when it comes to nervous eating. You hope the momen-
tum of feeding your mouth will continue out into the universe
and bring about resolution regarding whatever's eating at you.

I bit into the musty slice, the fumes gently filling my nostrils, the tang spreading from my tongue into the back of my
jaw.

Gerald spread some yellow mustard on a piece of rye bread.
"He said he'd see you until I told him you came out here at five
thirty in the morning. Then he got suspicious. How did you
know he was here?"

I told him about my visit to Rosalie LaBella. Minus the
syphilis information, of course. Jude's shame was his own to
deliver to others, not mine.

Hattie entered the kitchen and picked up a piece of salami.
She rolled it up and bit it in half. Anyone could have told you
she was a nervous eater. "I don't understand it. It's a mystery
why he doesn't want to see you."

"How does he look?" I ask.

"Not well. He's lost a lot of weight since I've last seen him."
She popped the other half into her mouth, leaned against the
counter, and chewed, crossing her arms across her bosom.
"The saddest thing, which leads me to believe it might be more
than the flu, is that his hair—"

"His hair?" I leaned forward.

"There are some patches where it's gone. And so much thinner. He looks—"

"Like a Halloween skeleton," Gerald said, still disgusted. "But with a rash."

"What kind of rash?"

Hattie grabbed another piece of lunchmeat. "All over his abdomen. And the bottoms of his hands and feet."

I had to get to the library and research the disease.

She rolled up the salami like before. "I think he's sick from going down in the water like he did. It's still cold enough to take your breath away."

"What happened?" I asked.

"He rowed out here and the boat—I think he stole it from one of the older folks's homes. You know how there always seems to be a boat rotting somewhere on people's properties."

"Indeed."

"So it sprung a leak and he had to swim the last hundred yards or so, sick as he was. I told him when I pulled him out of the water, 'That was a baptism of stupidity, Jude Keller.'"

"What'd he say?"

"Laughed and said, 'Well, I had to be dunked sometime. Might as well be now.'"

"Maybe you can talk him into seeing me tomorrow."

"You got binoculars?" Hattie asked.

"Yes." You don't grow up on the bay without a pair.

"I'll hang a sheet over the railing when he says it's okay for you to come out. No sense in making poor Randy bring you out every day like that. Not that he wouldn't do it."

"All right. Gerald, would you mind taking me back to the island then?"

"Not at all, MM."

Hattie said, "Let me see if Jude wants you to pick up anything while you're there."

Gerald rolled his eyes as his wife disappeared from the kitchen. "She's spoiling him! I'm telling you. The good Lord didn't give us a child, so I think she's figuring he gave us Jude instead. Which, to my mind, isn't a very equitable trade."

I laughed and finished my piece of cheese.

Hattie returned a few minutes later. "He wouldn't budge. But here's the thing, Mary-Margaret. If he doesn't agree to it, what's he going to do if you go in anyway? Throw you off the lighthouse?" She winced and laid a hand on Gerald's arm. "Oh, baby-doll, I'm sorry."

"It's okay, Hattie. That was all a long time ago. Don't worry about it." He looked at me. "Ready to head back to shore?"

I nodded.

Time to go learn about venereal disease.

I find myself doing the oddest things sometimes.

～✺～

What did Jude think when I left that day? I never asked him, but I think something inside him softened a bit, maybe broke in two, or just twisted a little. It might have been the start of the next leg of his journey or the ending of his present track. Sometimes they're one and the same.

Even so, I spent two days in the library reading all I could about syphilis and looking at pictures in medical journals. Thank goodness a heavy dose of penicillin would clear things up. Most likely Jude had already received the treatment at the doctor's office and he was waiting for it to take effect. Gone were the days of having to die from the disease, going blind when it attacked your eyes, or demented when it attacked your brain. And, indeed, let's not discuss the liver. Syphilis progresses to the tertiary stage in about one-third of those who contract the virus. Perhaps Jude would escape it altogether.

Here are the stages:

Primary stage: lasts four to eight weeks after infection
Secondary stage: one to two years
Latent stage: one to twenty-five years
Tertiary stage: until patient receives treatment or dies

The primary stage begins with a chancre, a disklike sore, normally painless, and sometimes hidden. It can be on the penis, near the anus, the mouth, or any place the virus entered the body. I saw one picture of a woman with one on her thumb.

I know. I know. As a former religious sister, I was dealing with sex in a way I'd never dealt with before. These are simply the medical facts, sisters. I'm not trying to shock you purposely, or make you feel sick; I just want you to understand even a little bit what I was facing. Quite honestly, this information wasn't making me at all excited about marrying Jude.

With syphilis, Jesus? Really? Did you know about that when you told me?

Of course he did. I just felt miffed sitting there in the library. Now, I loved that small library down Talbot Street, tucked between the hardware store and the print shop. I spent many hours there as a child, looking at picture books in the U where two parallel shelves met the wall. The same display case of birds, stuffed by a local man who dabbled in taxidermy, still sat near the restrooms. The water fountain still tried to clean out your nose before its stream got to your mouth. The same tables rested around the place, chunky wooden legs and tops polished yet bearing the gouged-out names of people I never met and people I still knew. Of course, on the first table, right smack in the middle of a pool of sunlight for a good portion of the day, Jude had emblazoned his name. Mine, on the other hand, was carved on the underside of the very back corner table, the table near the auto mechanic manuals.

It was at that table I sat, pictures of private parts with sores and lesions staring up at me, affirming the decision I made years ago to remain chaste. Who would take a chance if this might be the outcome? I simply didn't have the psychological makeup to understand it. It couldn't have simply been people are stupid. I've known smart people who can't control themselves sexually. I could only assume it filled a place I didn't possess. Lord have mercy, I wanted to throw up.

You probably think I have a problem with nausea. But here's the thing, I rarely actually regurgitate. I get that sick feeling in my stomach and so I yearn for a slice of Aunt Elfi's homemade bread and a glass of cold Coca-Cola. That always made me feel better.

The photos were glorious indeed. I wondered where Jude's chancre had been deposited on his body by whoever passed it on. Any spot was bad and all for different reasons. And the people I pictured who might have given the disease to Jude! Oh dear! For the sake of myself and all who will read this, and I may just decide to burn it after all is said and done, I'll just leave that to your imagination. Some things I'd rather not relive, thank you very much.

I realized I'd have to find a way to put his past behind him entirely, and I hoped and I prayed he'd do the same. If he kept bringing it up, over and over again, after I've said it's all gone as far as I'm concerned, it was going to be a very sad state of affairs indeed.

If I could convince him to marry me at all.

Marry me?

Seeing me at all would be a good first start.

I kept on reading. Yes, he was obviously in the secondary stage. Rash all over his torso, the soles of his hands and feet, and there could be another kind of rash, a grayish, raised area around the delicate parts. And oh my! This was too much!

Jesus! My heart cried out. *Please tell me this is too much! Do you hear me sitting here at the library? Do you smell this musty journal? Do you see these pictures? Can you possibly understand how I feel right now?*

~~

Other symptoms of secondary syphilis include sore throat, swollen joints, fever, aching muscles, and hair loss. Other than the hair loss, is it any wonder he thought he had some sort of flu? LaBella, being the conscientious mother she is, went to a medical book for kids and saw strep right away. I remember having it myself once when I was six, that little pinprickly rash all over my chest and belly and, oh, my poor throat, barely able to swallow anything but cracked ice and cold soda. I sat on either Grandmom's or Aunt Elfi's lap for three days. It wouldn't be hard to guess who it was that let me have as much soda as I wanted.

The next morning would tell me whether or not he wanted me to come out. I knew Jude. He was smart. He would have read up, at least a little, on what was going on. And he would have seen that the symptoms come and go and then bury into latency in some people. Maybe he was waiting until it seemed like he was better. I decided I'd give him that out.

Each day for the next two weeks, standing on Bethlehem Point, the summer warming up but good, I raised my binoculars at least three times a day. But no sheet waved over the railing of the lighthouse.

Mr. Bray taught me how to sew some simple garments. A straight skirt with a zipper, some easy, belted dresses for day wear. I asked Mrs. Bray if she'd pick out the fabric. She chose soft floral patterns, and silky, feminine greens and yellows and pinks. For my birthday, they bought me a pair of buff-colored pumps with a bit of a heel. Very pretty shoes.

I figured by the time Hattie hung the sheet, I might even have an entire wardrobe ready for married life.

What to do about a wedding gown was yet another matter. That could wait until the future looked a bit less foggy.

Jesus, if Jude doesn't fall in line with your plan, does that mean I failed?

He didn't answer. I didn't think he would. A part of me wanted Jude to be obstinately opposed to a life with me—a large part, in fact. But I couldn't pray for it. That would have been like praying for a Mercedes when you know children are starving not only in Africa or China or where have you, but in your own hometown.

I tried to remember all of Jude's sterling qualities during those days of waiting. He was honest, handsome, hardworking (yes, that takes on a different slant depending on the line of work, but he worked the crab boat for years), loyal (in an odd way), and consistent. Certainly I could have forced the issue and had Mr. Cinquefoil take me back out to the lighthouse, but it wasn't as if I wanted to hasten the whole affair. If we needed a white sheet to proceed, by golly, a white sheet would have to be hung! The surrender aspect to it seemed like a tidy metaphor as well.

I had as much time as it would take, and as far as I was concerned, the longer the better.

The Brays procured me the job at the Consolidated School for Negro Children. I'd be teaching English to all the grades and art to the seventh and eight graders. The salary come September would be pitifully small. However, Regina Bray's cousin offered to let me, and someday Jude, stay in the apartment above the tackle shop rent free, utility free, and I doubted we'd need a phone, so that bill wouldn't need to be paid.

What if Jude didn't want to live on the island?

Well, of course, that might have been a possibility, but I'd wait and see how the path before us unrolled. It could be straightforward, or maybe crook off to the side and take us someplace else. But until Jesus gave me word otherwise, I'd stay close to the lighthouse, close to home.

I did ask Jesus to tell my mother I was sorry not to have fulfilled her dream for her. He said not to worry; Mary Margaret
the First was just fine with his plans for me.

~~

Finally, in mid-July, while I was helping with the yearly carnival
at St. Francis, not to mention planning my curriculum for the
next year, the white sheet flapped in the swift air of a briskly windy
day. Whitecaps danced on the waters of the bay, and I decided
Jesus wouldn't mind if I waited until the waters settled down.

"I don't," he whispered, leading me to believe he was looking for steadfast obedience, not utter recklessness. A comfort,
to be sure. It's the difference between ministering in a war zone
and walking down the middle of the street during sniper fire.
There is a place where faith and prudence can meet even in
danger zones.

I spent that day sitting at the point, reading books on art
history from the library. Oh, we'd do fun projects, but these
children wouldn't escape without a working vocabulary of art-
ists, schools, movements, and techniques. We'd start back with
the Egyptians and the Phoenicians. A project with hieroglyphics
would be a big hit. They could write their names on parchment
to mimic papyrus.

Of course, I could do a long unit on African art. We could
make masks and bowls, baskets, and try our hands at textiles.

Oh dear! It would cost so much money. I needed to keep
praying.

"Yes, T—, you do."

I looked beside me where I sat out on the point. "You
came!"

"It's been a little while."

"I've missed seeing you."

"The time is coming soon for you to woo Jude. Have you

thought of how to do it, my dear?" He stared out over the waters toward the light.

"I have no idea." I sighed so deeply I know it went straight into his heart. "I don't have any experience in this sort of thing."

"Which is perfect. Jude doesn't want experience, do you think?"

"No." That made me feel a little better. "Can I tell him about you, us?"

"No, my dear."

"But how am I going to convince him to marry me without letting him know this is your idea?"

Jesus threw back his head and laughed, long and full and with great gusto. I looked around me. Surely the whole island could hear. "Oh, T—. That's the last thing in the world that would convince Jude."

"True." I smiled and put my hand on his shoulder. He placed his hand over mine.

"Lord, what's Jude's name in heaven?"

"Well, normally that's for him and me to know, but you've been trustworthy so far with the secret things, so I'll tell you. His name in heaven is Jude too."

"My goodness!"

"Yes. Sometimes people get it right. Isn't that interesting?"

I nodded.

We sat while the sun set, looking out over the water, the light swinging around like it always did.

"I love lighthouses," he said.

"Me too."

My goodness me, time has once again rolled along and here I am with this notebook again. It was a busy winter. Hattie passed away on Valentine's Day. We buried her over by the Presbyterian Church. After everyone had left, Gerald and I stood together by the grave and held hands, saying little. Just sighing. Sigh after sigh. Until the sun set and the light revolved from the lantern of Bethlehem Point Light.

"Look how it whisks across her tombstone, Gerald."

"That's nice."

Finally, after the chill of the dark began to settle deep into my bones, or so it felt, his voice bled through the intermittent darkness. "I guess I could just give up, but truth is, MM, I've been without her a good while now."

"Yes, you have."

"And I survived."

"You did."

"And I hate that assisted-living place. All those old people around all the time. It's downright beginning to bug me."

"We'll spring you out of that place tomorrow and find you somewhere to live."

"Good. The sooner the better." He knelt down. "Well, Hattie,

194

my sweet, I'll see you tomorrow." He swiveled his spine and neck to face me. "Lucky for me, Abbeyville's a little town."

He kissed his fingertips and patted her grave.

Oh, Hattie.

∿

The next day during a morning walk with Blanca—we both decided we needed to start walking after New Year's—at the marina where people keep their sailboats and motorboats, I noticed a sailboat for sale. Thirty-five footer, rather new.

"Gerald!" I rushed into his room. "How would you like to live on the water again?"

By the end of the month, that's just what he was doing.

∿

I'm sitting out on Bethlehem Point and it's hot as blazes and not much breeze either. But Mercy House is even warmer. My back is coated in sweat.

I got another letter from John two days ago.

June 6, 2002
Big Bend, Swaziland

Dear Mom,

    Since there's that summer intern doing your job, I thought it would be a good idea for you to come to Africa and visit me and the brothers here at the mission. There's a little boy here, Samkela, who's exhibiting extraordinary artistic talent. Of course, since I didn't inherit anything artistic, I'm of no help, and the others aren't much better if you'd like the truth of the matter.

    Not only that, we're tired of beans and pap. We could all benefit from your vegetable stew, especially me. I miss you more than I can

express. We've lost so many wonderful people this past month our grave-
yard has little room left. Please pray for us. We'll have to clear out more
of the bush on our property soon. My only consolation is that I believe
them to be with Christ now.

Love always,
John

P.S. Plant those bulbs!

Well, in the interest of not getting too far behind on what's been happening here in "modern times," I simply must tell you about my follow-up visit to the mission just off The Block. I was able to head over there a couple of weeks ago and Angie went with me as I knew she would because she's nosy and likes to be in on things. She liked Brother Joe too.

We started out before dark because I wanted to stop in Pasadena for breakfast at Tall Oaks Restaurant, which is quite the blast from the past, as they say.

Sheltered, as the restaurant's name suggests, in a glade of tall oaks, it looks as if someone sprinkled growth powder on it and rooms were magically added on like a root system. Great plate glass windows look out over the drive and flood light over the long, glossy wooden tables that seat at least eight. At the head of each table, next to the wall, a table lamp casts a warm, homey glow on the polished surface.

Tall Oaks takes its status as a family restaurant seriously and if the size of the tables was any indication, there must be a lot of Catholics in the area indeed!

I ordered the breakfast special: two eggs, hash browns, and toast. Rye is my favorite.

Angie's a pancake type of gal. She splurged and ordered

sausage because she likes to swirl the link around in maple syrup before she bites off a piece and we don't eat much meat at Mercy House, so it's a treat.

Had we been there for lunch, you can believe I would have ordered a crab cake.

The waitress refilled our coffee cups as we sat back to let the food settle.

"I can't believe we're doing this," she said. "It's so exciting. Did you ever once think, all those years ago, you might find out who your father really is?"

"No. I guess I thought I knew all I needed to know."

Angie shook her head. "Something doesn't add up, Mary-Margaret. If he did rape your mother, why didn't she blow the whistle on him? It would have been the right thing to do considering he was studying for the priesthood and she had taken her final vows."

"What people should do and what they end up doing are sometimes two radically different things, Ange."

"I know. What do you think?"

"I think he might have raped her. But I will concede to the fact that there might be at least a little more to the story."

The waitress presented us with the tab, a sure sign to get a move on and see what we could find out.

Angie arose and smoothed her khaki stretch pants. I yanked my navy pants from behind into a more comfortable position. Our shirts were askew and we laughed. "We're just a couple of old wrecks, Angie."

"Tell me something I don't know. But here we are, just like we thought we'd be all those years ago."

"I think we actually look pretty good."

Angie always wore her hair long, the sides pulled up in two barrettes, one over each ear. Her small, wire-rimmed glasses had come back into fashion again, and her propensity for compulsive knitting, which she succumbed to during the entire drive to the city that day, produced wonderful sweaters. We all looked slightly hip in an old-country granola way. In the summer, we wore shirts I made from the fabric I wove myself, all sewn very simply, like tunics. I, however, couldn't stand to fiddle with my hair, so in May, unable to cope any longer with the feeling of it down my neck and over my ears, I had it cut extremely short at the barber shop. Arty tried to talk me out if it. Even offered me a free haircut. Unfortunately, I'm a woman of many cowlicks and it sticks out all over my head these days. I look slightly crazy, which, upon rereading all I've written about Jesus, I just might be indeed.

Fine by me.

I'm sure you'll have your own opinion on all of this, and that's fine too. I'm dead now, so it doesn't make any difference one way or the other. And now I know whether or not it was all real. You, however, will have to find that out on your own.

It's interesting to think what gave me so much comfort might, if it really wasn't what it seemed, have been my greatest flaw.

∽

When we walked into the Heart of the City Mission, it was clear the building had enjoyed a paint job inside since my last visit. A mossy green covered the walls. Mary-Francis still manned the battered front desk where guests were invited to use the phone when they needed. Her dreads had grown longer and she wore loose black pants and a long black T-shirt. On a leather cord around her neck hung the Third Order Franciscan Habit in what looked like pewter.

"Sister Mary-Margaret!" She stood up and gave me a hug. "I was wondering if you'd ever come back."

"How did you remember my name?" I couldn't believe it.

"Oh, I make it a point to remember everyone who walks in this door. I've been here ten years and you know, just the other day, in walks James DeLillo. Came in about five years ago on a cold night in January. I sure was glad to see him. That man sure could use some Jesus along with some warmth. But anyways, he came in this time to pick up a prayer book. Isn't that something? He looked pretty good too!"

I was an old friend to her. I could tell that right away and it pleased me as much as a letter from a friend. I introduced her right away to Angie, who asked for a tour Mary-Francis was only too happy to conduct.

I listened and heard about my father. His vision for the place. "Now, he didn't want much more than a safe, warm spot for folk. Those who need more care we send down to The

Hotel. You heard of The Hotel? Sister Jerusha runs it. She's a Sister of Charity."

"I've heard of her," I said.

Sister Jerusha was a local celebrity of sorts, the way she was always taking on City Hall with the ordinances regarding the homeless. I saw her on the news when students from Loyola were forbidden to give out homemade sandwiches to the street people because the street people had no place to wash their hands. I remember she kept saying it was all "hogwash." And I wondered why she chose to use that word over and over again.

Apparently Brother Joe ministered to folks at Heart of the City until 1962, about two years after I'd met him. (You'll get to that part of the story in a bit.)

"What happened to him after he left?"

"Well, he finally became a physician, then a Jesuit priest. That took awhile. They don't mess around."

So . . . the mission was penance, then.

"Really?"

"Uh-huh. You see, the entire time he was here, he was also studying to be a doctor. He ended up in Africa in 1967, I think. Sixty-two years old. The man had a long road, but he remained faithful."

I felt my scalp heat up like a hot skillet. "Do you know which country?"

"Swaziland, I think." She crossed her arms, looked up at the ceiling tiles, then nodded. "Yes, definitely. It was Swaziland."

Angie laid a hand on my arm, obviously noting I was upset. "When was the last you heard from him?"

"About five years ago."

So he must be dead. I'd be lying if I told you I wasn't relieved. And something inside me was happy he'd kept the faith and ended up doing good things even though he didn't deserve to. I knew Jesus better than to think he'd make Brother Joe be an ineffectual member of the flock for the rest of his life. We hugged Mary-Francis and thanked her for the tour.

"I'm hungry," I said as we climbed into the car, the only parking space we could find near the Gayety. Still there, still having Parisian Art Night, I suppose. Or maybe not. These places don't even pretend to be classy anymore.

And why oh why oh why do they call these nightclubs "gentlemen's clubs"? Would somebody explain to me how watching a naked, or near-naked woman, expose herself, objectify herself for you, would automatically categorize you as a gentleman? I have never understood that. All right, I'll shut up now.

"Well, let's not eat around here." Angie pointed to the sleazy bouncer sitting on a stool by the front door of the club. He wore low-slung jeans and tennis shoes like marshmallows with laces and soles.

"All right. I don't want to anyway."

"You're upset."

"Yes. And I know I always eat at times like this."

"That's okay. Let's go get a crab cake down at the Inner Harbor. We can sit outside and watch the paddleboats and the water taxis."

Bless her heart; she was trying.

"Whoop-dee-doo," I said.

Swaziland. Oh goodness me.

The first thing I'd do when I got home was write a letter to John.

～～

After some time of deliberation and prayer not only from myself but my sisters, not to mention permission from the order, I actually e-mailed John *after* I ordered the plane tickets. He goes into Manzini once a week to say a daily Mass at the cathedral and checks his e-mail. He should be heading in tomorrow.

Dear John,

> *I do believe I'm going to take you up on your invitation to come to Swaziland. I can come next week for the rest of the summer. I'll be land-ing in Johannesburg around 7:30 a.m. on Tuesday, July 3. The only flights I could get routed me through Heathrow. An eight-hour layover. I think I may take the express train into London and have tea with the Queen since I'll be there for so long! Or I may just bring a good book and sit in one of the restaurants and drink espresso until they kick me out. Yes, that's surely what I'll do.*

> *I hope you'll be the one to come get me. It would be nice to have several hours together on the drive to Swaziland. I love you.*

Yours,
Mom

P.S. Remind me to plant those bulbs again right before I leave to come back to the States. Maybe I'll actually get them in this autumn.

Oh, those blasted flower bulbs! How can one thing just prick at you and you feel powerless to do something about it? I just despise that. Well, anyway.

Back to the story, sisters. Back to the lighthouse. Back to quite possibly the worst case of wooing a man that has ever been recorded on pages of mashed-together wood pulp.

So, the waving white sheet still hung the next day, barely flickering over a serene expanse like a calm hand waving me in, saying, "Come. Come."

And then I thought of "Church in the Wildwood," a song Mr. Bray loved to sing.

There's a church in the valley by the wildwood
No lovelier spot in the vale.
No spot is so dear to my childhood
As the little brown church in the vale.

Sometimes Regina Bray would breathe in deeply, push back her shoulders, and thrum the "come, come, come, come" rhythm as he sang. After about three lines, they'd break out in laughter.

That's what I want, I thought as I rowed out to the light in Mr. Bray's rowboat that day after the sheet flew off the balcony, the Brays' song providing a cadence for my oars. I wanted a marriage where you could be a little crazy, have private jokes, be comfortable. I just couldn't imagine that happening with Jude. He'd been through too much; I'd been through too little of his much. And frankly, I'd had a wider range of experience with my teaching. Had he almost been killed by the KKK? I think not! How could he possibly understand me either? Really? The real me?

I doubted he could.

But be that as it may, my doubts piled one by one into the boat with each "come" that ricocheted around the song mill in my head, and I rowed and rowed, thinking I'd never rowed so fast, so economically with each pull of the oar. How did I make it to Bethlehem Point Light so quickly? The breath of heaven blowing behind me, most likely, darn it. Of course, Jude would have bested my pace handily back in the old days.

They didn't see me coming. I don't know how that happened. Well, I didn't until Hattie ushered me inside and there sat Gerald taking a nap, snoring like an old hound dog right there on Mr. Keller's chair. He'd had a long night trying to keep the windows of the lantern clean during the storm. More than one lightkeeper died trying to do that sort of thing.

Hattie had roped Jude into helping her with her photo albums. When she showed me into the kitchen, he was cursing as he tried to insert a picture into some paper corners he'd stuck onto the page of the scrapbook.

"D--- it, Hattie! Why did I let you—" Then he saw me. He stood and all I can say is, when love and fear and remorse mix together in a person's eyes, it's a fierce sight to behold. My heart broke for the second time in my life.

I simply moved forward into his arms.

He tightened them around me and he put his lips so lightly against my hair, I knew he was hoping I didn't feel them. But I did, featherweight caressings of a heart so shattered, a life so worn through with holes, it couldn't stop the wind and the rain. It couldn't hold back the hailstones and sparks from the fire. It could only allow it all to pass through, hopefully unnoticed, but normally, not so.

I allowed my arms to creep up his back and then my hands to curl around and grasp his shoulders from behind. His clavicles protruded so profoundly I could almost hook my fingers underneath them, and his scapulae grated against my palms, moving beneath his movement forward as he pulled me closer, his back becoming a C around my head and shoulders.

Hattie left the room; I could tell by the sudden lessening of the decibels of Gerald's snore as she closed the door.

"Jude," I whispered, his name like sweet glass in my mouth.

"Why are you here?"

"I wish I knew," I said, meaning every word. "Why are *you* here might be the better question." I breathed in the scent of his shirt. Hattie was, as you might guess, very thorough in the laundry department. The light blue cloth smelled like Tide and the faintest hint of cigarette smoke. "Hattie's making you smoke outside?"

He chuckled. "What do you think?"

I pulled back and examined his face, reaching up to re-arrange a limp curl above his left eyebrow. His eyes were still as blue as the sea. A sea of sorrow, surrounded by a withered life.

What was gone?

I searched his eyes further, curling my hands around his shoulders and squeezing. "Jude?"

He closed his eyes.

"Jude, what happened?"

"I was just a little sick." He opened his eyes again and tried to smile.

Anger.

The anger was gone.

Oh no. No wonder he looked deflated.

"No. You're different."

I didn't want to say defeated. But that was it exactly. He looked the picture of that verse in Ephesians. He looked "dead in his trespasses and sins."

"Your pride is gone," I said.

He let go of me, shrugged, and stuffed his hands in the pockets of his pants. "Mary-Margaret . . ." Then he cleared his throat. "Never mind. Would you like some coffee? Hattie just made some."

"That would be nice." I figured it was time to act normal. Just be Mary-Margaret from over at that strange Catholic school. "Did she happen to bake cookies?"

"No. But there are a few biscuits left over from breakfast."

I was nervous. "I'd love one."

"I'll get it for you."

My first thought was, with *syphilis*? And I realized it would be a long, long time before I'd ever feel comfortable with this man, if I ever would. I might even contract it, become just like Jude. But that didn't mean that the Sister Mary-Margaretness of me would ever go away.

He buttered the biscuit, then set it under the broiler for about a minute. It was the best biscuit I ever ate. To this day.

I realized I, the orphan who'd learned this many times in the twenty-nine years of her life thus far, would take what I could get.

Jude was frayed and shopworn, having been sold again and again only to be returned for another round in the marketplace. And I was buying this thing for keeps.

He started to butter one for himself and another one for me.

"Would you like some grape juice?" he asked, opening the freezer. "I'd like some, I think. I'll make some up."

"Okay."

He squeezed the foil-lined, cardboard tube of frozen concentrate, dropping the icy juice cylinder into a hard plastic pitcher, then covered it with water from the rain barrel. He smashed it up against the sides of the pitcher with a wooden spoon, and the ice crystals scraped against the sides. Lightly. A breathy clicking as if he were crushing the grapes into the water.

Finally, he pulled down two glasses. After he poured it into one, I took a deep breath. "Let's just share. No sense in dirtying up another glass."

"Oh, but that's okay. I know Hattie won't mind—"

"No, Jude. I want to. Remember when we were younger and we'd split a milkshake at the drugstore because that's usually all the money we had? Come on, for old time's sake. It's not going to kill us or anything."

I remembered how he'd always say, "Well, if I can't kiss you, at least I can get your germs off the straw." Until I let him kiss me, of course.

Oh, Jude. His name always winged through my head like a sigh. Sometimes pleasurable, sometimes weary, sometimes both.

"I won't be talked out of it."

"I heard you quit the order." He set down the glass.

"Who told you?" I took a sip and handed it to him.

He took a sip, I believe, without thinking about it. "News gets around. One of the visitors from town."

"Who?"

"I'm not sayin', Mary-Margaret. You know me better than that."

"Yes, I do." I made sure he knew what I meant by taking his hand. "I want you to come live in town. There's a place near the docks that's available."

"I don't have any money."

"It's for free."

"What's the catch?"

"You have to marry me, Jude."

He froze. In fact, I think the bay froze, the island froze, the world froze in wonder. Not at my severe mercy, but at, what seemed on its face, my sheer stupidity.

"I think you'd better go now," he whispered.

Well, at least we shared the cup.

I reached forward, took his biscuit, and bit down. I handed it to him. He bit down too.

"All right, I'll go."

At least we shared the bread.

So here I sit now in Heathrow Airport, the slick, polished floors, lights, skylights, and chrome not exactly conducive to napping.

I'm generally convinced Brother Joe wasn't serving with John. Certainly he would have mentioned him. And whether or not he was still in Swaziland—he was ninety-seven after all—remained a mystery. My first stop would be the Cathedral of the Swaziland diocese in Manzini. Perhaps I could talk John into taking me there right away.

I bought an interesting memoir that's supposed to be funny and heartwarming, not tragic, but I suppose I'm more in the mood to tell my own story, which, while not tragic, certainly isn't heartwarming in the usual sense. So I write.

Religious Sister Marries Syphilitic Male Prostitute.

Dandy. Just utterly dandy. Who wants to read a story about that?

Sounds like an idea that only Jesus would come up with, doesn't it?

"Well, yes it does."

You're back!

He came and sat beside me.

"I figured you'd need the moral support. This is quite a journey you're on."

What is it I'm supposed to find out? I already know who my father is. Is he alive? Must I meet him face-to-face?

"Now, my dear, do you really think I'm going to answer that?" He smiled.

Jesus just put his arm around my shoulders. Had I not been at Heathrow, I would have nestled into him like a child. I always still feel like little Mary-Margaret when he's with me.

So this will be a mystery then?

"It's usually my way, T—, to be a little mysterious about the details. You're just not used to it like most people. I told you earlier you'll get exactly what you need when the time comes."

Will it be dangerous?

"No. That I can tell you. You won't find yourself in physical danger."

Spiritual?

"That, of course, is always up to you." He shrugged. "Of course, we do what we can . . ."

I laughed. *I love you so much. But you know that. You know everything.*

"Nevertheless, I never get tired of hearing you say it, my dear."

He sat with me for a while and asked me to pray for several people who walked by, giving me tiny peeps of their stories. And I felt afresh the collective pain of humanity, the weight he must bear being so in love with his creation, and seeing us destroy each other.

I'm sad. I know you've overcome the world, but sometimes, Lord, it just doesn't feel like it.

"I know, T—. But all will be redeemed."

It better be, I thought, not toward him, but well, it just popped into my head. Oh my!

He laughed. "No, my dear. You're exactly right. Or my word isn't true." And then he was gone.

So, now I think I will read that book and perhaps head on over to the duty-free shop and buy a Cadbury Dairy Milk chocolate bar the size of a place mat. With any luck I'll have some left by the time the plane lands in Johannesburg.

~~

Finally, when my plane was called, he whispered a final "I will be with you always" into my brain. At the gate, the airline employee looked down at my ticket "Why, you could have boarded sooner, ma'am, you're in first class."

"What?"

She pointed to the words *First Class* on the paperboard ticket.

It's happenings like these that tell me I'm not crazy. Then again, computers always make mistakes.

So now I'm settled in my seat and it's time to keep going on this tale while I'm still awake.

I'm not good at communicating on a romantic level, which is what I figured was expected of me if Jude was to be convinced. Then again, Jesus knew my capabilities. But one day in mid-July, I finally got Jude to come off that lighthouse. I had rowed out every day previous trying to wear him down. If he didn't break soon, I'd end up looking like a bodybuilder from my neck to my waist. I pretended I never asked him to marry me and he never brought it up.

We rowed around the bay, drifting at times. We even flew kites from the lighthouse. We held hands and he let me read to him. I read *Of Human Bondage*.

"It's a great book, Mary-Margaret, but that guy should have thrown her overboard the first time she dumped him."

And so in mid-July I moved into the apartment over the

tackle shop, settling in with some used furniture from the parish-
ioners at St. Francis who were desperately trying to understand
my decision and failing miserably. They still loved me, though.
And Sister Thaddeus still had tea with me on Thursdays, happy
about my teaching position at the Consolidated School. Jude
and I set out to Baltimore to buy supplies for my art classes. I
knew exactly where I was going to go, my favorite art store,
Towson Art, and my favorite art store owner, Carl.

Jude accompanied me with one request. "Let's not go down
to The Block, Mary."

We were just climbing into Gerald's motorboat. After landing we'd get into the car of Regina Bray's sister. She was only too
willing to let us take it if it would bring art supplies to the
school.

My mouth dropped open. "Jude, why in the world would I
go down there?"

And I think, for the first time, Jude really, I mean truly and
actually, realized that most of the people in the world don't find
themselves in the red-light district; that those on the margins,
and those who like to fancy themselves so, if only for a few
hours, find themselves in places like the Gayety or the Two
O'Clock Club.

Road trips provide wonderful space for talking. Give people
a couple of hours or more in a car and you never know what's
going to be said side by side and not face-to-face. This time,
however, I had a lot to say, and Jude wouldn't be able to plead a
relapse and head into his bedroom. He'd been doing that out at
the lighthouse during my visits, particularly when I began pressing him for information about his illness. Thank goodness his
hair was growing back again.

We'd been driving for a while in a white, wood-paneled station wagon. I had just cleared Salisbury when I figured now was
as good a time as any to say what needed to be said.

I gripped the steering wheel and glanced over. He was looking out the window at the farm that happened to be whizzing by, sitting with a bone-straight back as though the white vinyl seats were made of oak. The Eastern Shore of Maryland is flat and highly suitable for farming. It's lovely, not breathtaking, but gentle and fruitful. But then, sisters, you live here too, and I suppose you'd know that. I'm tending to think, as I write this, that some of you are on unfamiliar territory, and yet I would think you noticed the landscape on your way over from Washington DC or Baltimore. In the summer, as on that day with Jude, you'll pass stand after stand selling fresh produce.

Now, I don't mean to be proud, but white Maryland sweet corn, the kind we call Silver Queen, is quite possibly the best corn on the cob you'll ever eat. Uniform kernels, so sweet that the sugar juice bursts from the kernel, mixes with the butter and salt, and if you weren't holding the steaming cob, you'd clap. You might even give it a standing ovation if it's your first bite of the stuff. Unfortunately, it ruins you for corn anywhere else. Other strains become mere vehicles for melted butter.

Our beefsteak tomatoes are nothing to sneeze at either. As a child, before I came to live with the sisters, Grandmom and Aunt Elfi would let me eat as many as I wanted. And I did, slicing up the meaty red flesh, salting them, and sitting out on the back stairs that led up to our apartment, the late-July sun beating down on the back of my neck as I forked up mouthful after mouthful, the juice collecting in the plate and dripping down my chin to mingle with the sweat on my neck.

Of course I ended up with canker sores lining my mouth from all that acid. But I didn't care.

You'll also see a seafood stand or two. The thought of steamed crabs, too expensive for Mercy House and her inhabitants, makes you want to cry you want some so badly. And the smell of the spicy steam as it escapes the vats, along with the sight of those hard crabs, red and encrusted with spices, will send you running for a pitcher of beer, some mallets, and a stack of old newspapers to lay out on the table.

Enough ruminating about produce and food. I guess it's hard for me to tell the next part of the tale and I'd like to put it off, but I should move on.

"Jude, I know you have syphilis."

He turned his face toward me. "You've got to be kidding me. You've known all this time?"

"I heard about it from LaBella before I found you at the lighthouse."

"What have you been doing then, Mary-Margaret? And why would you ask me to marry you knowing this?"

"I . . ." I tried to think of a response that wouldn't be a lie. "I think you need somebody, Jude. And it might as well be me."

That was pretty darned close to the truth anyway.

"So . . . you see me as a mission or something. That's just great."

"No. I do"—and could I have hesitated just a few seconds more to make it even less convincing—"love you—"

"Oh yeah, right! You can barely get the words out of your mouth. Mary-Margaret, I'm not a dope. The disease hasn't climbed into my brain yet."

"So you've read about it?"

"All that I can."

"Me too."

"That doesn't surprise me. How did you end up talking to LaBella?"

"I went to her house."

"I gotta hear this."

I told him the story as we zipped up Route 50 toward Easton, marshlands and estuaries glimmering in the summer heat, the waning rainfall pulling the green from the long grasses growing closer to the road.

"You're a busybody, you know that, Mary-Margaret?"

"Yes, I do. But tell me. All those comments you've been making for years about wanting to . . . well—"

"Get in your pants?"

"Well, I was trying to put it a little more delicately, but, yes. That. Well, now I'm giving you invitation—". Pictures of the chancre came to my mind and turned my stomach, but I smiled anyway.

"At quite a hefty price."

I scoffed. "Oh goodness, Jude. As if you have so many other offers."

He looked back out the window, hand gripping the door handle.

"Don't make a jump for it. I swear I'll run you down," I said.

To my relief, he laughed. "I was just thinking how ironic life is. If this had happened when we were much younger, it might have made all the difference in the world. But now—well, I don't know—it seems impossible."

"Why? I mean, you've taken penicillin, haven't you?"

"Mary-Margaret, next chance you get, pull off the road, will you? I've got something to tell you. You're not going to understand it, and you're really not going to like it."

I figured that maybe some conversations truly needed to happen face-to-face, not side by side. So I pulled off into an Esso station and came to a stop under a large maple tree toward the back of the station's lot. I turned off the engine and we opened our windows, the smell of tar mixed with freshly cut hay borne in on the breeze rolling off the fields to our left. A mother yanking on the hand of a small boy disappeared into the restroom.

I faced him. "Okay, what is it, Jude?"

He placed his hands on his thighs, just above his knees, and squeezed. Of course, with the weight he'd lost, his legs looked almost like old man legs, hard bone knees from which the gabardine of his slacks draped. I wanted to cry at such reduction. "I'm not getting treatment for the syphilis. It's why I can't marry you."

"Lord have mercy," I whispered.

If hearts stopped at bad news, I guess we'd all be dead. However, it felt as if mine did. For just a few seconds. I reached forward and clutched at the dashboard with my left hand. "But you know you can't do that, don't you?"

"I can, Mary-Margaret. I'm going to."

"But why?"

"I'm tired." His words held three decades' worth of baggage, three decades moving forward on hands, knees, and sometimes his belly, three decades of hunger and thirst never satisfied during the long journey.

"But this . . . this death. Do you realize how horrible it will be? Not only for you, but for those taking care of you? Most likely Hattie and Gerald, I guess."

His eyes flashed and I was glad to see it. "What makes you think I'm going to ask anybody to take care of me, Mary-Margaret? No, I'll be gone long before it comes to that."

"No! You can't do such a thing. It's a mortal—"

"I'm not a crazy papist like you are."

"It doesn't matter whether you are or not. It's still—"

"Shut up, Mary-Margaret! Just shut up!" He yanked on the door handle and sprang out of the car. "You think you know so much when the truth is, you're just a parrot for that pope of yours." Slamming the door, he walked toward the trunk of the shade tree. He jarred his back against it, then bent double, grabbing his hair, once so thick and beautiful, with both hands, clenching the lackluster strands into his fists. And he let forth a feral moan that lasted, or so it seemed, until the sun set and the fields went black, the darkness settling on the drying hay, the heat receding just a little, the crickets grating their legs together in a scraping chorus that gave no comfort. Only the sight of boats out on the bay, their lights reflecting on the surface of the inky water soothed me at all as, by this time, we sat together on the hood of the car, and he held me as I cried.

Not you too, I sang in my brain. *Not Jude.*

The thought of his death brought with it a desolation and a loneliness at the realization that nobody else would love me, truly, ever again. At least not in a way that went into the marrow of their bones. Angie loved me like a close friend does, even one almost as close as a sister. To Sister Thaddeus I was still a little girl—not that I usually minded.

But no one needed to love me, save for Jude.

"I won't let you commit suicide," I said, looking up at the stars. "Just don't do that."

"There isn't any other way."

"Marry me, Jude. Let me take care of you. I want to."

"I don't want to be your mission."

I grabbed his arm, feeling now the dissipation of his form. "I need you to be. My life hasn't turned out to be even close to what I expected. Jude, please. Would you do it for me? I need you to love me. Nobody on earth loves me like you do. And I need to love you too. I don't know what it means to love like that."

And I found I meant every word of what I was saying. Without the school sisters, I was nothing. I needed him. I needed Jude Keller.

I could hardly believe it myself.

~⁓~

Of course, he didn't commit to anything that day, or even that week. But we had a nice time together at the art store. I strolled among the paints, wondering if I should buy watercolor sets or tubes of paint I could divvy out on plastic pallets.

"Well, the pallets can be reused every year, Mary-Margaret." Jude picked up a paintbrush and twirled it between finger and thumb. Jude had beautiful hands, his fingers extended and refined, his nail beds square and long. "I'd try to accumulate as many lasting things as you can."

"That's good advice."

The significance seemed to just pass by him and I thought about Jesus's words. "He who has ears to hear, let him hear."

Then give Jude those ears too, Jesus. Because he's going to die soon and nobody should die without knowing, really knowing, you love them. That would be the biggest shame of all.

So I prayed that prayer over and over for the next couple of months. *Give Jude ears. Give Jude ears. Give Jude ears.*

It sounded as silly then as it does now, but then, my whole life had become a joke to the people on the island. Mary-Margaret left the order to chase that reckless Keller boy? Is she crazy? What kind of a person would do something so thoughtless, so ridiculous? She's always had her head on straight before this. Doesn't she realize what she's doing?

Honestly, I don't think I really did. Definitely a point in my favor.

I'VE BEEN SITTING OUTSIDE OF CUSTOMS, AT THE BAGGAGE claim of the Johannesburg airport. They're sure not worried about snazziness here. I normally try to pack lightly, but, figuring I'll be gone for almost six weeks, I shoved as many blouses and pairs of underpants as I could into my duffel, as well as some art supplies for my time working with Samkela. So here I sit with my little notebook, jotting things down while I wait for John. He said he'd be a little late due to the day's appointments at the clinic. You see, John's specialty is birth deformities; he's quite the plastic surgeon. So once a month, he devotes his day to those sorts of surgeries. He's also a general surgeon as well and that skill, I'm sure you'll agree, is more necessary to his work at the clinic. Some of the things he does there at the clinic at Big Bend astonish me because there's not a chance they'd let such procedures be carried out in such rudimentary circumstances in the US. But as John says, "I'm a Jesuit. We'd rather ask forgiveness than permission."

And so I write. I'm tired, by the way. I never sleep well on planes and I sat next to quite the snorer. I try to be upbeat, but it's hard to think of anything nice to say after six hours of that rattling racket. On with the story. I really just want to get this thing done now.

~~

Jude didn't agree to marry me all that summer, but at least he purposed to be helpful. He painted my apartment, polished the floors, then roped Brister Purnell into building me a rudimentary art studio on the grounds of the school. Together they hammered and sawed and raised a wooden building twenty feet by fifteen. A tin roof covered it and for heat they placed two old woodstoves in opposite corners. Jude said he'd keep the woodpile stocked once the winter set in.

"I feel kind of like Laura Ingalls Wilder when she went and taught on the prairie. Woodstoves and wood and teaching in a new building. It's exciting. I may just have to bring a lunch pail with me each day." I scooped out some vanilla ice cream for the both of us. One bowl, one spoon. I figured he'd get acclimated to me sharing his germs. After a while, he stopped asking for his own portion.

"Who's Laura Ingalls Wilder?"

I explained, much to my sadness. "Didn't you read when you were little?"

"Not much."

"Not even *Farmer Boy*? I loved that book. They were always eating pie and sausages."

He spooned the ice cream in his mouth. "I don't know, Mary-Margaret. Sounds kinda boring to me. Anybody ever get killed in those books?"

"Not really. Jack the dog died. I remember that. And I cried so much I thought I would throw up."

"Dead dogs. Hmm."

Jude liked to read true crime.

"So school starts day after tomorrow," he said. "You excited? Nervous at all?"

"Of course. What if they don't like me? What if they think

I'm just some do-gooder who's doing this to make herself feel better?"

"Are you?"

"No! I need this job!" I took the spoon from him and dug up my own bite of ice cream.

"There you go, then. Most kids can see the truth. You'll be fine."

By this time, Jude's syphilis symptoms had disappeared. He was out of the first stage and the second. We both wondered when the tertiary stage would begin. Truth was, he could remain in the latent stage for as long as twenty-five years. It could take him years and years to die. Then again, he could be dead in relatively few. I know that's what he prayed for. I'd talked him out of committing suicide for the time being and I prayed to love him and to love him and to love him.

~

The next evening I put together packets of supplies for each child. I'd purchased used men's shirts at the thrift store for smocks. With a smock, I gave each child a watercolor palette, two paintbrushes, a stick of charcoal, an eraser, two pencils, a bottle of ink, and a nibbed pen. These I placed in shoeboxes. Their first assignment would be to decorate their shoebox. That would give me a good idea as to each child's imagination, manual dexterity, and natural style.

My kitchen window allowed the sounds of the island settling down for the night to filter through. Murmurs from the house next door rose from their living room window, sometimes the television, sometimes the commentary of the elderly man who chattered to his wheelchair-bound wife about nearly everything he was doing. "Now, Myra, I think I'll go get myself some milk." Or, "That pothole down the street still hasn't been fixed." And she, with a softer voice, would reply. But I could never hear her words, just the soothing timbre of her high, smooth tones. He always set her in their car so gently and they ate fried Spam a lot, if the aromas from their kitchen were any indication. Cabbage as well.

The revolving light from Bethlehem Point Light would snag its beams on the frills of the curtain and when the breeze would blow just right, it was almost as if the ray itself pushed the gauzy fabric forward.

I decided, despite the heat, to make a cup of tea. I put just enough water for one cup into the kettle and turned off the spigot.

"Make one for me too."

"Jesus!" I laughed at the sound of his voice, my back toward him as I filled the kettle higher.

"Gee, Mary-Margaret. I've never heard you take the Lord's name in vain before."

I wheeled around. "Jude!"

He walked forward. "Who'd you think it was?"

"Well, nobody."

He stopped and crossed his arms. "Surely not Jesus."

"Of course not! He would have asked politely." I laughed in an effort to distract him. "What are you doing here?"

"I've been thinking. Can I sit down?"

He'd gained some of his weight back and his hair looked almost normal. I remember thinking maybe our physical union wouldn't be as appalling as I feared. Even the pustules on his arms and legs were healing nicely, leaving only faint scars that would, hopefully in time, fade completely. Inside of him, however . . . Lord have mercy.

"Of course. Have a seat." I turned on the burner and set the kettle to boil. "What have you been thinking about?"

"This stage I'm at, the latent stage, could last for years."

"This is true." I sat down and began securing each student's collection of pens, pencils, and brushes with a rubber band.

Jude caught on to the process and began to help. "So, anyway. Maybe this is a chance to get a fresh start, even for just a little while. Until the final stage settles in."

"What are you thinking?"

I wasn't going to suggest that this bit of hope he was feeling might be put to good use by taking some antibiotics. He'd have to come to that conclusion on his own. Jude simply had to come to his own conclusions.

"I'm thinking I'd like to take you up on your offer. Would you still marry me, Mary-Margaret?"

"Are you asking?" I set down the bundle I'd just secured.

The teakettle screamed. I jumped.

I turned down the flame and grabbed a pot holder, circling it around the iron handle of the kettle.

Pouring the tea, I felt his hands descend on my shoulders. "Yes," he whispered into my ear. "That's what I'm doing."

All those quivery feelings from when we were young went sliding from that ear right down into my private parts. I'm so sorry to have to write it like that, but that's exactly what happened and I wasn't prepared for it any more than you just were to hear it.

He turned me to face him. "If I don't have a good reason to stay here, I'll go back to my old life. I can't do that. I've always loved you, Mary-Margaret. You know that."

"Yes, I do."

"I'm sorry about that. I guess, what I'm saying is, I'm sorry I didn't know what to do with that. I just didn't know."

"It's okay. I didn't either." I laid my head against his chest. And we listened to the murmur of the old folks, and through the window the light circled on us again and again.

"So what's your answer?"

"It's yes, of course."

"But there's one thing. We can't have sex. I'm not going to give this disease to you."

"All right."

Jesus only told me to marry him. He didn't tell me we had to have children together. I mean, I doubt even the pope would insist on my procreating with a syphilitic man.

Jude wasn't the romantic type. He let me go with a squeeze and I poured the tea. When I sat down at the table with him, he said, "Let's always have a cup of tea together. Every night. Let's make it the last thing we do."

I always drink tea with Jesus, I wanted to tell him, and then I realized something. Jude was Jesus.

～～

I walked with him to the dock where he'd tied up Gerald's boat and we held hands. "This is as far as it's going to go," he made sure to tell me. "Other than hugs. And no kissing either. I don't even want to sleep in the same bed with you, Mary-Margaret."

We stood on the dock, the water lapping against the pilings. "You'll get the couch then," I said.

"Okay."

"I mean, I'll need a good night's sleep if I'm going to teach all day. And I get grumpy without my sleep."

He stepped down into the motorboat. "I'm going to go back out on the water with Brister."

"But, Jude, he—"

"Is calmer than he used to be. He's settled into his life. My mother didn't help that process any. He said it's fine. I'm a thirty-one-year-old man, Mary-Margaret. I'll beat the sh-- out of him if he tries to throw a punch."

"I'm sure you will."

I watched as he rowed cleanly back to the lighthouse. His boat cutting through the reflection of the moon.

Oh my. These memories tumble down the inside of my body so easily, yet every so often a barbed bit scrapes along. I'd quite forgotten I was in Africa! It's been so long since Jude died, the rawness of our beginnings as man and wife, and the pain of losing him that day, have bowed this old white head down so that my chin almost meets my chest.

And I have a cramp in my neck now.

Oh, John, where are you?

I check my watch. Just another three hours, Mary-Margaret, and he'll be here.

～✓

There are some days an orphan misses her mother more than other days. But the biggest, most keenly felt of those days is surely her wedding day.

Jude wanted to get married as soon as possible, while he was still in good health. I did too. So we set the date for September 30th. The leaves would be starting to turn and the blue of the sky would deepen from the heat-addled expanse of summer. We'd get married right at Bethlehem Point, under the maple tree, Bethlehem Point Light looking on.

At least that's what I thought. Until I voiced the idea to Jude over our nightly cup of tea. I'd made it through my first week of school. It felt like the old days actually.

"No!" he said, his jaw muscles clenched so tightly I thought his lower face might fold in upon itself.

"Why?"

"No, Mary-Margaret. I won't get married to you with that lighthouse looking on. I can't."

That was the first inkling I had that something went on at that lighthouse none of us knew about. Not Hattie, nor Gerald.

Not myself. And it affirmed what Angie said about me for years
that I always denied—I was a lousy judge of character.

"Can you tell me why?"

"I don't like to speak ill of people. You can say a lot about
me, Mary-Margaret, but I don't backstab."

"You're right. Are you speaking of your dad?"

"Yes. Among others."

"All right." I slid the plate of cookies toward him.

"I'm not hungry."

"Me either."

"What would be a good second choice for you?" he asked.

"St. Francis's, I suppose."

He screwed up his face. "A church?"

"Yes." I said it with a finality that must have got through to
him because he only nodded in reply and said, "Okay."

~⌒~

I loved teaching at the consolidated school. My little art barn
was, I hate to say it, the envy of all the other teachers. But I put
in a hot plate and a percolator, and soon we were meeting after
school for a cup of coffee. If you've got something everybody
else wants, I find that sharing it actually takes away the resent-
ment. After the first week, the other members of the faculty
were bringing in sweets to go with the coffee.

I felt so white.

I don't know if it's all right to say that, but I did. And I often
wondered what they said about me behind their backs. Did they
call me a do-gooder, the great white hope? I hope not. I hope
Regina Bray told them I was in dire straits. Thankfully they probably heard about Jude and thought I was as crazy as a betsey bug.
Believe me when I say they were the ones doing me the favor.

In quiet moments I wished Jude had been the type who had
hidden who he was, but no, everybody in Abbeyville knew what

he'd been doing with his time for the past decade or so. I never did find out how that leaked into seemingly everyone's basement.

Jude ate dinner with me most nights as well. Our time together during the days lengthened from one cup of tea at seven thirty to him walking me home from school after a day on the boat and staying until nine or so. As promised, he wouldn't so much as kiss me. And when he emerged from my bathroom, all washed up, still smelling of water and wind, his skin now browned and his eyes glowing the blue of the periwinkle blooms in the Bray's yard, I wanted him to kiss me. I missed all those kisses in our teens and wanted to kick myself for not relishing them. They'd just felt like something to enjoy and then regret back then.

"Mary-Margaret," he said about two weeks before our wedding. "Sit down and I'll make the tea tonight."

I rested my chin in my palms, my elbows perched on the edge of the table. My arms pressed my breasts together and a stunned feeling washed through me as I realized how easily sexuality was coming to me.

Jude laid a hand over mine. "I know all the signs, Mary-Margaret. I know you want me."

I sat up straight. "You're crazy."

"You look nice when you blush." He sat down and sighed. "You're the sweetest thing I've ever seen. You always have been. It's almost hard to see you acting like a woman. I guess I always wanted you to, but now, the way you're brushing up against me when you really don't have to, and letting me know you have breasts . . ."

I couldn't help it. I burst into laughter. He joined me.

"This is awkward," I said half a minute later after the teakettle had screamed and he was pouring the water into the pot. "You're right. It's like the tables have turned in a way."

"A very small way. Your overtures are sweet, Mary-Margaret.

Much better than what you see down on The Block. Honest and natural. It's hard to believe how contrived sexuality can become in the name of doing what comes naturally. Honestly, if they had just two naked bodies and nothing else, they'd be bored to tears in thirty seconds."

"Oh. You're not going to go on and extrapolate further, are you?"

"Nah. I've already said too much. But here's the thing. Being on the other end of the sex business, the supplying end, I've seen a lot."

"I know," I whispered. *I don't want to know*, my heart wailed.

"People keep thinking if they have one more thrill, one experience further down the road, take even greater chances, they'll find it."

"What's *it*?"

He shrugged. "I guess it's different things for different people." He set the pot in the middle of the table.

"You know what I have to say to that, Jude."

"I'd agree with you if I didn't see the Church as providing the same service as I did."

"How can you say that?!"

He took the sugar bowl off the counter. "People going in and out of church don't look any happier than the people going in and out of the clubs."

"But the Church is nothing without Jesus. Do you see him like someone plying the sex trade?"

"No. I wouldn't go that far."

"You can't confuse Christ with his institution on earth. The Church is temporary, you know."

"Then why are you so devoted to it?"

"Because, as imperfect as it is, it's all we've got. I've always been content there. Yes, it's had its share of scoundrels to be sure, but the Holy Spirit always seems to correct things."

"Like the Crusades?"

For some reason, I never flinched at those accusations.
"Exactly! Christ loved his Church too much to let it keep doing
those things!"

Like the sex scandals nowadays.

"You're a weird bird, Mary-Margaret. A weird bird with
very beautiful breasts. I like the way you're sitting."

I sat back against the rungs of the chair. "You're a pill."

"I'm more than flattered. I've always wanted you, you know
that. I'm wishing I could take you up on your offer."

"I didn't offer anything," I whispered, thinking of the disease quietly attaching itself, mostly likely, to his liver and
internal organs, and even his brain. *Dear Jesus, help me not to want
him. It just wouldn't be good.*

"You're right." He spooned some sugar into my cup and
stirred it for me, his breath brushing my cheek. "I've been
trained to act on the signs. Assigned some sort of motive on
your part."

"I'm sorry."

"Don't be."

He fixed his own tea, which basically meant pouring it into
his cup. "I want to tell you what's happened to me over the
years, Mary-Margaret. Everything that I can remember."

"Are you sure?" My mouth dropped open so far, I was surprised my lower lip didn't end up in my teacup. Was *I* sure was
the better question. Certainly it was better just guessing how
he'd lived, wasn't it? Certainly I knew the basics. Wasn't that
enough?

I remembered something I read in a Church history class in
college about the early Church. Confession, at the beginning,
was done before the entire congregation. Imagine! That would
keep you from doing a lot, wouldn't it? (At least if you had the
fear of God in you, it would.) Right then, in that little kitchen,

with tea and blowing curtains, and the old folks still murmuring next door, with plans for an unpredictable future stemming from an impossible request for obedience, I knew Jude Keller needed to confess his sins.

We all do. It's like cauterizing a wound. It hurts like the devil but feels like you emerged from his pit of despair afterwards.

As he began, I saw Jesus sitting in a chair in the living room, his face toward me, nodding. The High Priest came to hear it firsthand and he would offer absolution. I'd lived twenty-two years with Christ visiting me from time to time, but this time was different, this time his grace glowed with such clarity I wondered if somehow he'd taken our little place to the gates of heaven itself. If I turned to the window, would I see deep space and not the light whirling around at Bethlehem Point Light?

Then Mr. Plumber next door (I'd found out their names) said, "Myra, I've got a terrible case of gas tonight!"

And Jude, Jesus, and I laughed.

"Perfect timing," I said. "Go ahead, Jude. Do you want to go sit where it's comfortable?"

"Okay." We picked up our teacups and sat on the couch. Jesus stayed in his chair.

"Would you like me to close my eyes?"

"Okay. Actually, that might make it a little easier. Where do I begin?"

"Wherever you'd like."

The words that came out of his mouth I never expected. "My mother began fondling me when I was four. At least that's the earliest I can remember it."

"Oh, Jude!"

"Close your eyes, Mary-Margaret. Please. I've never told a soul that." He paused and took my hand. I felt the warmth of his skin in the darkness of my closed eyes and I tried to relay my feelings through the contact. "Hate killed my heart except for one place, the place I saw a little redheaded girl on shore from the time I was five years old and she was three, sitting with her aunt under that tree."

Jesus pulled up a chair beside me, one I couldn't see, and I felt his hand on my shoulder, and I felt it shake as he cried. If only Jude could have seen who had been weeping with him all along.

"Why did you move with her from the lighthouse?"

"Because my father made me. He said it wasn't right for her to go there alone. I was her son. She was my mother. Children needed to be with their mother."

"Did he know?" I opened my eyes again.

"I'd hinted, but he never took the bait. He wanted to pretend we were okay, that nothing bad infested our life there on that lighthouse."

"No wonder you hated him," I whispered.

"Now you know."

"It's so awful. I always thought she was so nice. Wild, surely, but a good person deep down. I'm sorry I didn't see it, Jude."

"Oh, Mary-Margaret." He squeezed my hand, making me a conduit between him and Jesus. "I'm surprised you know what fondling is!" He laughed. I didn't. "Well, anyway, so there were those things I did with her. I thought I was partly to blame because I could . . . perform. Because my body . . ."

The picture of them pushed its way into my brain and I pinched my eyes shut against the image. "I'm so sorry," I whispered.

"My mom relied on me emotionally too. Called me the 'man of the house' and treated me like a husband and like a slave too. And this d--- island . . . I felt so powerless. So when I got older, I was already well versed and I realized I finally felt in control when I was with those girls. In high school and all. And then later, on The Block, it was completely on my own terms."

"You don't have to go on."

"Yes, I do. Brister's ideas about what makes a man a man, along with my mom, made sex a little less valuable than you've always made it out to be."

He moistened his mouth with a sip of tea and continued, so much of his sexual precociousness making terrible sense now.

"I truly lost my virginity, my intercourse virginity, I guess you could say, when I was thirteen."

"With your mother?"

He nodded. "If I had wanted revenge, I wouldn't have had to lift a finger once we moved in with Brister. The anger at my mother went so deep, when Brister started hitting her, I didn't do anything to stop it.

"One slap and she'd snap to," Jude said, shaking his head. "I've always felt guilty about not stepping in."

"Really?" I found I couldn't feel an ounce of sympathy all of a sudden. At least Jesus was there to do that for the both of us.

Yes, T—, I am. You see, Petra has a story too. And it breaks my heart as much as Jude's. She was the sweetest little girl long ago. Her uncle, you see . . .

Jude blew through his junior high and high school foibles, all, as far as I was concerned, understandable considering what had been going on at home.

He stood up and rinsed out his teacup. "I think getting through my high school years is enough. Maybe we can continue the rest tomorrow."

I had to agree with him on that one. Already we were up to seven partners.

"Mary-Margaret, are you sure you can handle this?"

Jesus squeezed my shoulder again and whispered. "Yes, you can."

"Yes."

He leaned over, kissed my cheek, a quick, brotherly peck, grabbed his jacket, and headed out the door. "'Night."

I walked into the arms of my Friend and cried as if I could fill the bay to overflowing. He cried with me, his tears soaking into my skin, holy water, blessing what I was about to do.

"You must love him, T—. Completely."

"Physically?"

"Yes."

"But why?"

"You are his bride, he is your bridegroom. You must be infused with him to be in true union."

I looked up into his eyes. They were kind and filled with more love than I can possibly tell you. Oh, we mortals try to describe the infinite, but we can't.

"There is nothing to fear," he said. Then he kissed the top of my head and left.

I just checked my watch. John should be here in about an hour or so, so there's plenty more time to write. Jotting this down has brought back such a flood of feeling I'm surprised it's not sweeping all the luggage away here in baggage claim. Nowadays, we're well aware of sexual abuse, but back then we didn't even have a name for it, other than incest, which almost sounds consensual. And then as now, male victims were more likely not to tell a soul. But my sisters, what I want you to know is that Jesus truly means it when he says not to fear. The syphilis was just one of many of Jude's ills, and yet he stood with me the entire time.

There's so much I'd like to convey to you with this story, but perhaps it would be best to simply let you draw your own conclusions, to let God speak as he will. Feel free to be the judge of me when you've turned the last page.

The next day, as Jude collected me from the art barn, figuring we'd be in for more confession, I suggested we do something different. "Let's go by the Tastee Freeze and get a couple of hamburgers and have a picnic."

So we sauntered together down Main Street toward the burger joint. I threaded my arm through his, held my head high because the most handsome man the island had ever produced escorted me down the sidewalk, and even though nobody understood why I cast my lot with his, it didn't matter. He loved me and I loved him in return. I didn't understand why or how, but as we sat out on the docks eating hamburgers near Brister's boat, our feet dangling over the water, each word of confession he spoke I took into myself, covering it with my own innocence, drowning it in my own inexperience, until all he had done, or at least could remember he had done, had gasped its last breath inside my heart.

"It's over," I told him.

He sighed, his breath mingling with wind and winging out over the water latticed with moonlight. I laid my head on his shoulder. "I love you, Jude."

He pulled me close, cradling my head against his chest, rubbing my cheek with his hand. "And for the life of me, I can't believe it, or figure out why. But I'd be a fool not to grab hold of it with both hands."

"You've always been good at that."

"Yeah, yeah I have."

~~

For the sake of Jude's privacy and out of respect for the dead, I'll just leave the details of Jude's life on The Block up to your imagination. I suppose what you dream up will depend upon your own past experiences, but suffice it to say, you probably haven't a clue unless you walked in the type of shoes Jude walked in. But please don't judge him. He was beautiful to me.

~~

Surprisingly, there was an element on the island that thought Jude was crazy for marrying *me*! It's easy to suppose the pure virginal person is half-cocked for marrying the boy who squandered himself, body and soul, on strangers. Indeed. What woman in her right mind marries a former male prostitute drug addict? The drug addict, well, that's not quite so sensational. But certainly, there's something beyond the pale about the prostitution aspect. As well, there are some who would look down on Jude for his past, even though they did the same thing for all practical purposes. They just didn't get paid for it. For the life of me, I can't understand that sort of splitting of hairs. At least with Jude there was no pretense the liaisons were anything less than transactional and any less devoid of meaning.

However, a couple of Jude's wilder buddies from high school days were more than happy to fill him in on the fact they thought his "marrying a nun" (even though he wasn't) was the most hilarious thing they'd ever heard. I knew Jude wanted to punch their lights out.

"Well, at least you're getting a redhead!" one friend called after us about a week before our wedding. "I hear they're wild in the sack."

Jude just raised a hand as we walked on. That was a tame comment compared to most. But then he turned on his heel and headed over to his old friend from high school, a guy named Ben Cropper.

"Ben, can I talk to you for a minute?"

"You bet. This'll be good." Everybody laughed.

They walked down to the corner and I stood near the bar where the group gathered. No use pretending to be otherwise engaged, I just planted my feet and watched the conversation I couldn't hear. Some of the women, dressed in tight shirts and skirts, stared at me, and I tried to smile, but I knew they didn't trust me. I couldn't blame them one bit as I stood there in a skirt covered with old roses and a pink blouse, an "almost nun" to boot. There's something so otherworldly about the Church, something that causes outsiders to distrust us. And when you are devout, well, so much more of which to be suspicious. It's a little creepy to the uninitiated.

The conversation seemed civil enough, little body movement until Ben ran a hand through his hair and shook his head. I heard his words. "Aw, man, Jude."

They shook hands a minute later and Jude joined me. He threaded my arm through his and we continued down the street.

"What did you say to him?"

"I told him the truth. I told him I have syphilis and you're marrying me so you can take care of me as I die."

"Why did you tell him that?"

"Because that's what you're signing up for. People should know. You deserve that, Mary-Margaret."

"But your privacy! Jude, they didn't have to become aware of this."

"It doesn't matter. I'll be gone soon enough."

"That's not what I want to hear."

He kissed the top of my head and we walked toward the dock, and the tackle shop, and my apartment that was soon to be his.

~~

The next day, Sunday, he showed up at my door fifteen minutes before Mass over at St. Francis's. He wore a suit and tie and stood there looking over my shoulder as I said, "You're going to church with me?"

"Can I come in?"

"Yes, of course. I was just gathering my scarf and purse. Would you like a cup of coffee or something?"

"No thanks."

Discomfort seemed to mill like ants between his skin and his clothing. I whisked a pink headscarf off the counter and grabbed my purse. Regina Bray had made me a pink dress for church and with a pink cardigan, buff pumps, and purse, I felt like I looked quite smart, but not having any fashion sense, I have no idea whether I ended up looking smart or like Ethel Merman in an Audrey Hepburn getup. I didn't have many new clothes, but she made sure everything worked together.

"Ready?"

"You look pretty, Mary-Margaret. Pretty and fresh-looking."

"Thank you. I'm still a little shocked to see you."

"There's still a lot you don't know about me. It's not all bad."

He took my hand as we walked up the street toward the church. The aromas of bacon and coffee settled around us and I thought of the breakfast I'd make after we returned to the apartment.

We sat through the liturgy of the Word, listened to Father Thomas's homily, after which began the liturgy of the Eucharist. Jude knew the Creed, the Gloria, when to sit, stand, kneel. Everything. And when it came time to file to the front to receive Communion, he followed me. He crossed his hands over his chest, bowed his head, and received a blessing from Father Thomas, the same words the priest said to me all those years ago when his eyes turned into the eyes of Christ. He laid his hand on his head. "May almighty God bless you with all the gifts of the Holy Spirit." He removed his hand.

Jude said, "Amen," then followed me back to our seats.

I just looked skyward and said to Jesus, *You've got some explaining to do, my Friend.*

~⌣~

I honestly never pictured that day in my mind. As a little girl, I didn't dream of my wedding, plan a menu, figure out who, at that time, would be my maid of honor and who would be my bridesmaids. I didn't have but one baby doll so I never dressed a doll up in bride clothes. Mint green, soft pink, or sky blue bridesmaids' dresses? Who cared? In fact, I'd only been to one wedding in my life and that was Angie's. It was a beaut! She was such a snappy, sassy, and cute bride.

We figured the least fanfare the better in regard to the actual ceremony. Some of the best things happen quietly. Johnson Bray made my dress, a tea-length silk satin with rosettes scattered on the skirt. The simple bodice was covered by a short jacket with three-quarter sleeves. I wore my grandmother's mantilla, the webbing of the lace almost snapping beneath the pressure of my fingers. Regina Bray curled my hair and applied makeup, something I wasn't used to doing myself.

"You look lovely, Mary-Margaret," she said, turning me to face the mirror over her bedroom bureau.

I did. Fancy? No. But a little shinier than usual? Yes.

Angie entered the room wearing Regina's yellow chiffon dress and carrying a bouquet of yellow roses. "You look beautiful!"

"Really?"

Do you see? I'd never really been told that by anybody other than Jude. And honestly, at the time I thought, what did he know? He was just trying to sleep with me.

I looked at myself in the mirror, really looked at myself, and I realized I looked nothing like my mother. The hair was most likely the raping seminarian's, but I always liked it.

"Really. You ready? Your groom is waiting."

Mrs. Bray smiled and handed me my bouquet, a full, side-arm bouquet of calla lilies.

No. I never saw that day coming. I pushed each sadness aside. I'd only have one wedding day whether I wanted it or not! With the amount of Divine maneuvering this took, I knew I wouldn't go through it again after the syphilis took Jude.

"Can I just spend a few minutes alone?" I asked the ladies, and they understood, filing down the steps for a quick cup of coffee before the ceremony.

I sat on the edge of the bed picturing him there with me and I felt certain the sweetness of his breath whispered upon my cheek as I finally arose and walked toward what was probably one of the strangest marriages ever arranged.

"Only you, Jesus."

I placed my hand on the doorknob and slowly separated the door from its frame. My future wasn't secure. I was joining myself to this man, but I had no idea what was going to happen after I did. And how was I going to convince him to sleep with me?

First things first. Marry the man, Mary-Margaret. I could hear the words in my grandmother's voice and I couldn't help it—I laughed out loud.

God help me, I prayed. So this is what cold feet feel like.

Perhaps it wasn't too late to run back into the arms of Sister Thaddeus.

But would I really have run? It's a question I can only guess at, and thankfully, I don't feel the need to figure that out all these years later.

OH DEAR. I PUT THIS THING DOWN AGAIN. I'LL GET BACK to the wedding, but I have to tell you about my first day in Swaziland.

Fr. John Keller, my son, is forty-one years old now, a fact that astonishes me. He doesn't look much like me, other than the pale complexion and the red hair, and John's isn't the color of carrots my father's and mine was, but darker and richer like rust in the rain. His red hair is now going a little white at the temples and, unfortunately, he has my grandmother's propensity to gain weight around the middle even on rice and beans. He did inherit his father's eyes and nose, so when the sun catches him from the side and he smiles, the corners of his eyes pushed up by his cheeks, I see his father in him. And then there's the beard. A great red beard!

When he came toward me in the Johannesburg airport, I was a little surprised to see him in surgical scrubs. It's not like the Jesuits wear a habit or such, but I don't know, you expect to at least see the priestly collar and a black shirt.

"Mom!" he rushed toward me, face lit up like a blowtorch. I haven't seen my son in three years. The lines on his face are deeper from time in the African sun, and I suppose he has his worries as well. He's seen so much misery and death.

Oh, he felt so good in my arms. Now, with his height I suppose it would be more accurate to say I was in his arms. Brother Joe's height came in play on that one, I suppose. John is a bear of a man to put it mildly. Six foot four and a half inches from that little twenty-inch baby that only cried for thirty seconds after he was born.

And his laugh! It rings. I'm not sure where he got that. He says at seminary. It was either laugh or cry, he always said.

He laughed as he embraced me. "I can't believe you're here, Sister Mary-Margaret."

"Me either, Father John." When I at last took my final vows, we started calling each other by our titles as a joke. "Your Uncle Gerald was beside himself when he drove me to the airport."

"He can barely see!" And that laugh rang out so much so that half the people in baggage claim looked over. Half of those smiled. And half of those laughed too.

"It was a nightmare!" I picked up my backpack as he grabbed my duffel. "My life flashed before my eyes at least five times. I prayed five Divine Mercy Chaplets for him to make it back to the island alive!"

I'm the most me I ever am around my son.

Right now I'm sitting in front of John's clinic at Big Bend. It's winter here in mid-July. Luckily I remembered and brought a jacket. Even so, the sun shines now near high noon, and the earth is dusty under my feet. It's about sixty-five degrees today. Tonight it will most likely go down into the low forties.

Theft is high here. A lot of the stick and mud homes are broken into and the blankets stolen. I've already e-mailed Angie on a trip to Manzini and told her to collect some funds from the School Sisters so I can buy blankets for distribution.

So after John picked me up at the airport, we headed right to the Nazarene Hospital in Manzini where he does surgery. But first we had to get through Johannesburg, which claims the dubious honor of one of the highest murder rates in the world. Razor wire tops fences and the concrete feels harder against the soles of your feet, more likely to bruise and batter you if you fell upon it. Black and white still keep separate, even more so than in the US. I remember a few years ago, during my last visit, I met up with another School Sister of St. Mary's, a woman from Nigeria. We had lunch in a little restaurant and I was given a glass of water. She wasn't. Until she asked. My order was solicited. She had to push in and say what she wanted to eat. The man seemed so put out, his head set in an angle of defiance, his eyes saying, "The law is the law, unfortunately."

I felt such outrage I began to speak until my friend laid her hand atop mine and said, "Jesus was despised and rejected of men."

Well, I suppose so.

And so, driving along the highway, it feels like the city almost spits you out into the African countryside. The flat land widens and sprouts shrubs and grasses, tufts of life springing from the earth. The deep coal mines, their ziggurats of leftovers looking like miniature Babels, fuel the various power plants that crown the horizon. And then the land buckles, undulating as we head away from South Africa, stretching its muscles and rolling over. Mountains form, green and tall, and Swaziland steals your breath.

It does this to me every time.

At the hospital, we locked the ancient brown Land Rover up tightly and John took my arm. The hospital is decrepit, several buildings held together by a labyrinth of breezeways and courtyards. The cement-faced buildings were painted a dull goldenrod, the concrete walks worn smooth and shiny by the many feet that scuffled along its path since a Scottish couple opened the hospital fifty years before.

"Why don't you go into the women's ward?" John said. "I'll

probably be a couple of hours. I have a friend there in the corner on the far right side. She has no one. Her name is Precious. I try to feed her when I'm here, but I'm only here once a week." No laugh now. "I honestly don't know if she eats any other time, Mom. I hope she's still alive."

"I'll find her if she's still there."

"She's unmistakable. She looks like a famine victim. I'll come get you when I'm finished."

I watched him as he walked away, his large form just a little hunched up at the top of his spine. Probably from the hours spent looking down over patients. Or as he calls them, "My friends."

John calls everyone "friend." Like Jesus did.

I gave up so much to bear that child. Instead of a life teaching children in exotic, or at the very least, remote places, perhaps putting my life in peril, I made countless tuna sandwiches, read numberless books, took walks on the beach, flew kites, and loved him like he was wine and I was the imbiber with no control.

Can I tell you it was worth it? Because it was. Every day I missed my sisters was worth loving him. And I did miss the life I forwent. It wasn't as if Jesus took away those yearnings. I missed stealing into the chapel at odd hours to pray. I missed the daily offices. I missed the serenity of being only with my own gender. That surely does remove a certain kind of pressure, indeed?

Anyway, I digress. Again. And I'm getting ahead of the story. Again. Forgive me, but I'm just getting old, I suppose.

The women's ward is like nothing you've ever seen in the US. One long room, divided up into three sections, the ward houses around thirty women. Many of them are dying from AIDS, although to hear their families tell it, none of them are. For a country with one of the highest HIV rates in the world, it's amazing how nobody has AIDS, how people disappear in back rooms of homes and are never seen again. Not really.

I passed through several sections, feeling quite pale. It's good to feel pale after feeling so "regular" all the time at home. Making eye contact was difficult, for truly, I am an imposter; as well-meaning as I am, I don't belong. But sometimes you have to go where you don't belong if that's where Jesus tells you to be. I don't understand it, but I do know in my own life, the times I was most on edge were the times Jesus was seen most clearly; the times I was pulled from my element into a place of uncertainty were the times I was carried in his arms.

I spotted Precious right away.

There's a photo from the Sudanese famine that everybody in America should be required to view the next time they complain about the fact their dinner is an hour late and they say, "I'm starving." Honestly.

The man looks like this:

His heels look three times the size they should be, don't they? How can he be alive?

My squiggles can't possibly do the image justice, or extend that man the right of truth. The truth. I hear people talk about the truth all the time, people terribly underexposed to the real truth of the world they live in. As long as their truths, what they believe, are all lined up in a neat little row, they believe they know the truth. But the truth is that they shove food into their mouths at potlucks and banquets while God's other children go hungry, their skins stretched like dried leather over the armature of their pitted bones.

And me? How many meals have I eaten without regard? Did I really need that extra skirt or pair of shoes? God help me when I have turned my back on The Truth and what he taught. God help me when I have failed to love my neighbor as myself. In that ward, I was reminded of my own selfishness and failure to live every moment for the Lord.

Does God love me anyway? Oh yes. Did I feel there in the ward that I still had a ways to go in loving God more? Yes to that too.

Precious lay in her bed looking at the ceiling, her lips pulled back from her teeth, the flesh clinging so tightly to her skull, the ridges of bone beneath sparse hair sprouting from her head in tufts. The seams of the bony plates knit together in the womb were visible like fault lines.

There was loss and death come too soon, and in her suffering, for the beating I'd given myself only moments before, Jesus drew me to himself as he lay in the bed inside the skin of Precious. My heart joined with hers because I had lost my family too: my mother, Grandmom, Aunt Elfi, and countless others I wasn't ever introduced to or told about. I felt the emptiness and the loneliness of desertion in a time of need, of anguish. And then when Jude died—

I closed my eyes, opened them, and reached out my hand. "Precious."

She turned her face toward me. "Yes," she whispered in English.

I laid my hand on her shoulder. Hard bone. "I'm Father John's mother."

The smile appeared gruesome. But it was beautiful to me.

"How is my friend, Father John?"

Her voice, though raspy, was high and musical.

"He's in surgery. He told me to come visit you. I'm Mary."
I realized I was Precious's Mother Mary and her John and Mary
Magdalene, the one come to comfort her on her cross.

"Sister Mary-Margaret." Her eyes provided the exclamation
point.

"He's told you about me?"

She closed her eyes. "Tells me stories."

On the bedside table I noticed a cup of orange juice and a
slice of toast. I checked my watch. Four o'clock. "Breakfast?"

Precious raised a hand.

"Nobody comes to feed you?"

"My family, they all gone."

Her strength was so taxed, I decided to ask John about her
background instead of getting it from her.

I picked up the cup of juice. Ants swam around the lip of
the cup, and it was much the same with the toast. This woman
literally starved while the bugs ate well.

It's so different there, sisters. Family must come and feed
their relatives and give care. No nurses tend the sick carefully as
in our hospitals. I have nothing with which to compare it so
you'll understand.

As I picked the ants from the stale bread and broke off a
piece, a group entered the ward. They were singing an old
hymn. "What can wash away my sins . . ."

Oh good, I thought, *maybe they'll help some of these poor people eat.*

I scraped the ants from the cup of juice and skimmed the
drowned ones off the surface with my thumbnail as the group
gathered in the middle of the ward. The patients stared at them.
Some of the family members sat up in their chairs as the group
quieted down.

I slid an arm under Precious's back, her shoulder blades protruding against my forearm, and lifted her to a sitting position. Precious's head fell back and I leaned in to support it with my shoulder.

The group went right into "Leaning on the Everlasting Arms." And music always makes a person feel a little better, doesn't it?

Precious moaned as I raised her, fully sitting, her legs, knees turned out, thin-line *Vs* on the mattress.

The group, women in colorful dresses that contrasted with their dark brown skin and covered their knees, and the men, in slacks, shirts, and ties, sang in such rich harmony, goose bumps rose like miniature mountains on my arms.

"It's pretty, isn't it?" I said, hoping Precious was paying attention. She nodded and opened her mouth as I held the cup to her lips. A bit dribbled out the side of her mouth and I wiped it with the hem of my shirt. After all those hours of traveling, the orange juice was almost an improvement!

A man in the group, in his thirties, I'd say, his white shirt glowing against his skin and the shabbiness of the ward, lifted up his Bible and waved it a little as he spoke in siSwati.

Several of the nearby women lowered themselves down into their blankets, all the covers different from bed to bed, some brought from home. Many pairs of eyes went glassy as his words tumbled out faster and faster and his pitch rose in a stunning crescendo. What was he saying?

I could only hope they were words of mercy and hope, not condemnation. These people were dying. Was he telling them of a God of mercy and love, who enfleshed himself in our fragile dimensions? Oh yes, I hoped.

By the time he'd finished, Precious had eaten half the piece of bread and drank half the juice. She shook her head when I offered another piece.

The group dispersed, following the pastor, walking to each

bed, shaking the hand of the patient and moving on. He squeezed Precious's shoulder and quickly turned.

I don't blame him. Perhaps his theology tells him things mine doesn't. That God doesn't ever want his children to suffer, and if they do, there are two reasons. The first is that somebody did something wrong. The second by default, then, is, he cannot comport his will on earth. There might be many nuances in between I've never thought of simply because I've been spared that.

I laid Precious back and opened her drawer to find a brush. She had little hair left, but perhaps it would be soothing. Inside the drawer lay a copy of *The Imitation of Christ* and a little prayer book.

Oh, Jesus! This is far better than a brush.

I leaned forward and whispered in her ear. "Offer it up, Precious. Offer up your suffering."

Now, my theology tells me suffering can be for a purpose if we make it so. Perhaps she was giving God her suffering as a prayer for a wayward son or a fragile nation. Precious could barely speak. So I will never know.

But again she nodded, and as she fell asleep to my gentle brushing, her lips moved silently. In prayer? I hoped so. I believe so.

The church group finished shaking hands and left.

I prayed for them too. Who knew the suffering in their homes? Maybe a song and a sermon was all they had left to give. It wasn't my job to judge.

~~

John stayed in surgery until ten that night. I gave Precious her dinner, a small portion of it anyway, and fed three other people as well. Many had family to tend them. Family ties are as strong as anchor chains inside some of these Swazi women; you can imagine how beautiful I, as an orphan, think that is.

I began to think about my father and what I would find. My first step was to ask John about him. It just wasn't something I wanted to do in a letter. I pulled my father's pictures out of my backpack, one from the file at the seminary, so young and smooth, and then a snapshot from our wedding. Sitting next to Jude, both of them in lawn chairs, leaning forward, head to head in a deep conversation.

It was then I realized, sitting among the death, the AIDS, the senseless starvation, the ants, and the home-provided blankets, that I owed my father two of the three greatest happinesses of my life: my marriage and my son. Of course, the third I'm living out now.

Sister Mary-Margaret indeed!

I wanted him to be alive.

~⁓

So I think it's important I tell you about the wedding.

I stood near the front doors of the church, peeping into the sanctuary around which Mrs. Bray had strewn some bows and flowers. The Brays sat next to Sister Thaddeus, and my friends from the consolidated school dotted the pews, as well as the ancient set at St. Francis who always showed up for daily Mass and the altar society. Perhaps thirty of us in all. A nice, circumspect little gaggle to be sure, people I knew wouldn't make a fuss. So when Rosalie LaBella walked in with a man in a brown habit, nerves overcame me as two worlds crashed in the middle of the narthex, and I hoped that Jude would be all right.

LaBella sallied right up to me, concern etched on her face. "Jude called and invited us. I hope you don't mind," she apologized.

I sighed in relief. "No! That's fine."

"And he asked me to sing a song a song at the reception. I hope you don't mind."

I hesitated.

"Don't worry. It's appropriate. I'll talk to the priest if you'd like."

She certainly had dressed herself appropriately, more the lady in the row house on Highland Avenue than the stripper down on Baltimore Street and thanks be to God for small favors. She'd chosen a cranberry suit with a black belt, a small black hat, and mid-heeled pumps. Her heavy, dark hair was curled sweetly around her face and she'd applied her makeup sensibly.

"I believe you," I said, reaching out and bestowing a quick lady hug upon her.

"This is Brother Joe," she said.

Brother Joe stuck out his hand, his voice soft-spoken but intense and so kind. "It's good to meet you, Mary-Margaret. I always knew somebody would tame that young man. Leave it to the Lord to make it someone going into the religious life."

I know. It was my father. I didn't know it then. His hair blazed like mine; his eyes squinted like mine. He was angular like me. But I didn't see the resemblance that I saw when I looked at his picture from seminary.

He was a fifty-four-year-old man by this point, the coarse cloth of his brown, Franciscan habit falling down from sharp collarbones. Even as I remember him, I can't quite get my mind around the fact that he was the raping seminarian.

Oh yes, I suppose I could talk myself into remembering some haunted guilt rummaging through the goodwill in his expression, but at that time, all I could think was, *This man loves the prostitutes and the sinners.* And I would have been foolish not to believe that his love for Jude, his open doors, weren't instrumental in bringing Jude back from the dead.

Brother Joe was a smiling redheaded Franciscan who ran a rescue mission. Nothing about him hinted at anything different.

No Mass was said, since Jude wasn't Catholic and it wouldn't be appropriate if we couldn't share Communion together. But Father Thomas, still with the face of an angel, but not looking as young as when he buried my mother, lent his overall air of holy joy to the sacrament, and we knelt, and were blessed, and we said our vows, Jude gently taking my hand between his own.

And in the name of the Father and Son and Holy Spirit, we were united in the eyes of God, the Church, our friends, our family, and each other. I looked at him, love spilling out from my heart. His eyes smiled into mine and I ran my hand along his jaw.

I never wanted to be here and yet, the joy inside of me swelled. Joy at what was, and yet, pain at what would never be.

Fear not. Fear not.

He pulled me to himself and held me so tightly I wondered if I'd keep breathing.

"You love me, Mary-Margaret," he whispered against my neck.

"Yes. I do."

I don't think Jude believed it until right then.

~~~

Even now, I'm trying to remember Brother Joe better. After the ceremony, we went out onto the lawn for the reception, a down-home potluck. Mr. Bray had roasted a pig all the night before, digging a pit and keeping vigil until the meat was falling off the bones. With his sauce, Mrs. Bray's baked beans, and bowls of greens and potatoes, sweet potatoes, potato salad, coleslaw, corn on the cob, and, much to our surprise, a whole bushel of steamed crabs compliments of Brister, who came over after the ceremony, we feasted until we all thought we'd pop.

Jude ate about half as much as I did, but he sat and watched me pick crab upon crab. "We didn't get these much at the convent school," I explained, shoving bite after bite of the glorious meat into my mouth.

"We ate them all the time. I'd rather have a crab cake."

He still hadn't kicked the cigarette habit, and when Brother Joe came over to chat, he excused himself for a minute to go smoke.

"I prayed I'd see this day and always wondered why I felt the urge. Now I know why." Brother Joe smiled as the soft-spoken words came forth. "You know, we do what we can at the mission, and we see some success, more with the women than the men unfortunately. But this beats all."

"Have a crab." I laid out some newspaper beside me on the picnic table, three pages thick, and plopped down a small wooden mallet.

"I believe I will, thank you."

Of course, you know and I know that I'm filling in these conversations with what I hoped happened. I remember the gist of things, but the exact words? Well, as I sit here and think about my father, Brother Joe, I wish to goodness I could recall it all exactly.

But the truth is, I just remember a quiet, happy person eating crabs with me, enjoying every bite and sipping on a mug of beer. I remember how soft his brown robe was, obviously washed dozens and dozens of times. I remember thinking those people down at The Block were extremely fortunate someone was giving his life for them and asking nothing in return. I remember thinking how grateful I was he was there when Jude needed someone to keep him alive.

I haven't gone into Jude's drug use much. He hated that part of himself even more than what he did and I'm still not sure why. Maybe it had to do with him being out of control. He took the story of that bit of him to his grave and I let him. Of course, so much of his selling his body had to do with feeding it heroin. Brother Joe found him on the street one night in the dead of winter, passed out, needle in his arm.

He brought him inside the mission.

Jude never told me what happened after that other than this: "I was there for two weeks, Mary-Margaret, and when I emerged, I never shot up again."

I still don't know how Brother Joe got Jude to kick his addiction to such a powerful drug, but he did. And maybe, if I can find him here in Africa, he'll tell me. And maybe he'll tell me how Jude knew all the prayers and creeds as if he were a cradle Catholic. He wouldn't tell me about that either.

La Bella stood to her feet and sang, a cappella:

The bells of St. Mary's
Ah, hear, they are calling
The young loves, the true loves
Who come from the sea
And so my beloved
When red leaves are falling
The love bells shall ring out, ring out
For you and me.

Jude saved up some money from working on Brister's boat for a two-day honeymoon in Ocean City. We drove Brister's car two hours across the lower portion of the Eastern Shore the day after the wedding. Sunday. We stopped for Mass in Salisbury at St. Francis de Sales Church, Jude sitting in the pew as I went forward to receive the Eucharist. When I returned to the pew and knelt down to pray, he joined me on the kneeler and took my hand.

We made it to the Plim Plaza Hotel by lunchtime, a grand old hotel that had seen its better days come and go. We wiled away the rest of the afternoon on the rocking chairs lined up along the front porch, facing the ocean. The town had basically closed up for the season. A few people pedaled their way down the boardwalk on brightly colored cruisers; some walked hand in hand or jogged; others just seemed to wander along, the stretch of wood an invitation for the mindless rambling of those who have no place else to go or be.

Jude heard the stories of my life I'd forgotten, laughing at Angie's antics, listening intently as I described my favorite pupils including my friend Morpheus from Georgia. When I told him about the night I was almost killed, his skin blanched to a shade that echoed the cirrus clouds shredded overhead by the stiff breeze.

"See?" I said. "You weren't the only one living an exciting life."

"Well, at least I know you know what it feels like to think you're about to die."

"I was so frightened. Not so much about death, but about the pain involved."

"You were never one that could handle physical pain well."

He was right. I was always at the infirmary for something. But Jude, his motto had been since he was a young teen, "If you don't need to sop up the blood, you don't need a doctor."

We ate dinner in the hotel dining room where a tuxedoed old man played a tinkling piano, caught some more live music, jazz, over at The Commodore, and, as planned, Jude slept on the sofa in the sitting room of our suite.

I don't know why I thought he'd change his mind about climbing into bed with me. But disappointment flowered inside of me, a bloom much larger than I expected.

All the next day I took his hand, held on to his arm, did all I could to display affection. He responded in kind, but with no one-upmanship. I realized that any progression in our relationship would be up to me. He'd handed over the keys of the car to a woman who knew only the bare facts of driving and from a book at that.

Our second and final night there, I felt that responsibility flow down onto me, coupled with the newness of this life with Jude, the leaving of my sisters, and the lack of a family; I quietly cried in the darkness. I tried not to make much noise, but, sisters, I don't cry delicately. My nose fills up and you could collect my tears in a bottle. I lay there sniffing and sniffing.

The bed dipped at the right side and he lay down. He pulled me close to him in the bed, and we fell asleep that way, snuggled together, our breath skimming one another's shoulders. When I awoke in the middle of the night, he was back on the couch.

I grabbed the bedspread, laid it down on the floor next to the sofa, and covered myself with a blanket. The next morning I was awakened as Jude lifted me in his arms and placed me back in the bed. His lips rested on my temple and his hand rested on my head. I pretended I was asleep.

"Oh, Mary-Margaret. You're a silly, silly girl." Tenderness tempered the words he didn't think I heard.

He gathered together his clothing for the day, then undressed. I watched him through slitted eyes as he stripped to nothing, his muscles close beneath his skin, his legs long and lean, his hips slender. His arms and neck were so much darker than the rest of him, I wanted to laugh. But those legs also were lightly pocked by the scars from the pustules of the secondary stage of syphilis he'd come out of several months before. And beneath that skin and hair and muscle and bone, the disease might well be attaching itself to his organs as I watched him.

"It wouldn't take much," I said.

He turned, standing without a stitch on, completely comfortable, forgetting, I suppose, he was supposed to feel naked. "I didn't know you were awake. I'm sorry. Maybe I should have just left you on the floor."

"I'm fine."

"Why did you sleep over there anyway?"

"To be with you. It's why I married you."

He ran his fingers through his curly hair. "What were you talking about when you said, 'It wouldn't take much'?"

"Penicillin."

"Oh." He lifted a pair of boxer shorts from atop the dresser and slid them on. I wanted to tell him to stop. I know this may sound strange, but he was mine. He was given to me and I liked seeing him.

When he walked over to yank his shirt off the hanger, I said, "Stop."

"What? I just thought I'd go down and bring us up some coffee from the restaurant."

"I know you don't want to . . . do anything. But I just like looking at you."

"You and a thousand other people."

He might as well have slapped me. And it wouldn't have been undeserved. What was I thinking? I'll bet I sounded just like those awful women and men who'd hired him.

"Oh, Jude! I'm so sorry!"

It was then, sisters, that I really and truly realized Jude wasn't some pervert who lusted and used and to hell with the world. He was one of the broken ones, the severely broken ones upon whom sin settled down and stayed, screwing its bolts into him, body and soul, piercing the muscles, grinding the bones to bits and stirring the marrow. His complicity in it didn't make it any less so, didn't make his own choices any less wounding.

"I'm sorry," I said again. "Get dressed. I will too. And we can just go have breakfast in the dining room."

I took my clothes into the bathroom and changed where he couldn't see me.

"Thank you," he said, when I emerged. "I'm sorry I snapped at you. You couldn't have known."

At least there was that.

He twined his fingers amid mine and we headed down to eat.

～⌒

We lived above the tackle shop, Jude sleeping on the couch as promised, me in the bed. Every so often I'd sleep next to him on the floor, and he'd lift me up and put me back in the bed.

"You pulled a Plim Plaza on me last night again, huh?" he'd say the next morning. But the truth was, I wanted to be near him. I was, at twenty-nine, turning into a woman. I loved being with him, near him, touching him, but he wouldn't go beyond holding me in his arms, kissing me softly, caressing my face.

"I just want to lay in your arms, Jude."

"I can't. I don't know what will happen if I stay with you."

"Would it be so bad?"

"Mary-Margaret! I'll give you syphilis. Why in the world do you want to take a chance like that?"

And since I couldn't say Jesus told me to do that, I just said nothing.

I've been in Swaziland for two weeks now. There's so much to do I forget about writing in this thing. But I feel like I'm with Jude again in the penning of the tale and that is wonderful. And there's so much to tell about my stay here as well.

John fetched me that first night from the women's ward at the hospital around ten fifteen, leaning down to hug Precious and speak soothingly to the other patients. The ones he knew personally he touched, rubbing their arms or blessing their heads. Calling them friend. Many of the women sat up, bare breasted. It didn't bother my son. I was proud of him.

It took us almost two hours to arrive in Big Bend. We stopped at a Spar (a grocery store) in Manzini before we really set out on the road and bought Cokes, the sweetest Coke you've ever tasted. I felt nervous, so the calories were welcomed. John bought me a candy bar as well, a Nestlé Aero bar, the perfect candy bar for smashing against the roof of your mouth with your tongue when you're feeling at all apprehensive.

Driving at night in Swaziland isn't such a good idea. Cows wander the roads, people walk alongside, some of them having imbibed too much; a person could find themselves hitting just about anything.

Once the city dissipated into the countryside, it was hard to see, but I knew that homesteads dotted the darkened landscape. I could sometimes see a kraal against the night sky. Kraals are where cattle are kept and where village meetings take place between, normally, the chiefs and the men. They are interesting corrals, large sticks driven into the ground and secured with wire or strapping of some sort. You cannot take pictures of a kraal, because it is an official building. Taking pictures of official state buildings is illegal in Swaziland.

But here is a drawing. They're beautiful, like a modern, organic sculpture or a giant crown, the sticks bending in lovely curves and angles.

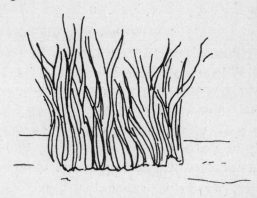

Of course, some dark decisions can take place in a kraal, but this is not that story. I didn't stay in Swaziland long enough to get in that kind of trouble! Now, if Angie had come, there's no telling what would have happened. Oh, I do hope, for your sakes, sisters, she wrote down her adventures.

By God's grace we made it to Big Bend.

John's clinic lay beneath one bare light on a pole, its anemic rays illumining a corrugated tin roof that protected the cement block building. Behind the clinic a smaller building consisting of only four rooms sat darkened. And then there was the church, a little chapel whitewashed near the road. Only two percent of Swaziland is Catholic.

He unlocked the door to the living quarters. "The others have gone to bed. We'll just make our way quietly back to my room, Mom. I've got a cot set up for you. We'll have to bunk together this time."

"Has another doctor joined you?" I asked.

"Not yet. He will. One of our medical priests from Mbabane."

Mbabane is the capital city to the northwest. It's pronounced Buh-bahn.

"You remember me talking about Father Ignatius all these years, right?"

"Yes."

"I just set up his room this morning. He's old and sick and he doesn't want to go back to the States. He wants to die in Africa, so we're going to take care of him. I mean, I'm here because of him. It's the least I can do."

"Tell me a little more about Father Ignatius," I requested as I put fresh linens and a blanket on the cot. "He's been over here a long time, hasn't he?"

Father Ignatius recruited John.

"Yes."

"Where did he go to school again?"

"He graduated from Mount St. Mary's way back in the thirties."

"Where was he before he came to Africa?"

"He ran a ministry to street people in Baltimore. Down at The Block."

"Was he called Brother Joe then?"

"Yes! Do you know him?"

I felt like I'd been shocked on a pasture fence as John handed me a pillow. I sat down on the edge of my cot. "Father Ignatius used to be a friend of your dad's. He was at our wedding. We lost track of him." Obviously he hadn't lost track of us.

I pulled out my snapshot from my backpack. "Look. Is that him?"

John examined it by the lamp. "He's so old now, Mom, I can't tell if that's really him or not. But when I arrived eleven years ago . . . well, I guess, yeah, that could be him. Of course, he was already well past eighty by then and pretty ancient. No offense."

"Hey, I'm only seventy-two!"

If the laughing tones of Jesus had met my inner ear, I wouldn't have been surprised. But honestly, I just felt loved. Jesus was bringing my father to me. Still, my nerves seemed to rise to the surface of my skin.

I yanked my duffel bag up onto the bed and pulled out my pajamas. My inner clock was so befuddled. It was only 5:30 p.m. at home, and yet, not being much of an in-flight snoozer, exhaustion had begun to seep from the core of my bones into my muscles and skin. "You'll have to tell me all about him tomorrow." I just wasn't ready to hear more.

"You can come with me to pick him up."

He gathered together his pajamas and headed to the small bathroom. The water to the house was stored in a large, green plastic cistern on the roof. A water truck kept it filled on a regular basis. They used it very sparingly, using a smidge when only a smidge was necessary.

I quickly changed into my pajamas, afterward securing a robe around me. We brushed our teeth together. He leaned in close, his arm touching mine as we moved those toothbrushes in much the same manner, owing to the fact I was the one who taught him how to brush.

Did I tell you how much those little rituals meant to me?

I felt so at home in John's room, the icons hanging on the cement block, the crucifix of rough-hewn wood and a pewter corpus cast in an artistic fashion hanging on the wall at the head of his bed. The carpet at his bedside was worn in two spots where his knees had rested countless times.

John prayed for his friends. He told me once, "I can give all the medicine in the world, do all the surgery I can, and it doesn't hardly matter if prayer doesn't accompany it. Prayer is more important than the medicine. It is the real medicine, I guess."

I tapped my toothbrush on the sink. "He's coming tomorrow, you say? How did that happen?" I tried to sound breezy.

"He's been looking out for me for years, Mom. I owe more to him than I can say, so, well, I guess now it's time for me to pay him back a little. He's an amazing man."

The raping seminarian. An amazing man.

Father Ignatius. Yes, the Father Ignatius John talked about for years. The raping seminarian.

Well, yes he was, so it seemed.

I BEGAN ART INSTRUCTION WITH SAMKELA TODAY! WE can't understand each other's language, but lines are lines and colors are colors and shapes are shapes. John was right. He's something! He's latched onto the poppy red Prismacolor pencil and I don't blame him one bit. It was my mother's favorite color too, according to Aunt Elfi. One of the few items I owned from her belongings was a scarf in that color.

One Saturday, not long after our honeymoon, I went through my old trunk. In between Grandmom's one fine tablecloth and my Aunt Elfi's drawing, that red scarf pierced my vision.

I felt a sense of loss so profound I smashed the fabric against me, and a soft moan escaped from my mouth. I missed my mother so badly. I missed that I couldn't be her daughter and that, if Jude prevailed, I'd never have a daughter of my own.

"Mary-Margaret!" Jude rushed in and knelt just behind me. He rested a hand on my back. "Are you all right? Are you sick?"

I just shook my head. "I just found this. It's been so long since I've seen it. It was my mother's."

I told him the few stories about Mary Margaret the First that I remembered, not that he hadn't heard them before. He was patient. "She would have been such a wonderful mother."

He said nothing, just held me close and kissed my face, over and over, then my mouth, and with a moan, he deepened the kiss for the first time since we were teenagers and I pressed myself into him. It was as if he said, I'm all you have, and I'll try to be enough.

After that day, he continued to kiss me and I felt like the teenager I never had been. Maybe he did too. A teenager that found someone safe to love early on, who didn't have to waste himself on acquiring women, collecting experiences, and then drugging himself out to cope. Maybe it was the first time he'd ever really kissed the woman he loved and who loved him in return.

That thought was like fresh water to me. In a way, Jude was as innocent, as untried in the building of a loving relationship, a life, as I was.

I kept that scarf around though, setting it on the windowsill in the bedroom. I told you how someone who is orphaned feels the need to be connected to someone else, to know your blood flows in someone else's veins too. I'm sure people look at their parents and take that sort of thing for granted, their brothers and sisters, maybe even their own children. But when you're all you've really got in the world, relationally speaking, the old saying "Blood is thicker than water" lands on you with a thud, bruising your chest right down through your ribs and into your heart.

Maybe if I had a little baby of my own, I reasoned, some of the loneliness would go away.

But that, of course, would be up to Jude.

~~

The first year of our marriage progressed, turning into a new decade filled with new possibilities. We had our first Catholic president and even more of a miracle, Jude joined the Church at Easter with little fanfare and almost no discussion with me about it other than "I'm ready to take that plunge, I guess. Maybe it's not the hocus-pocus I thought. And it's important to you, so . . ."

"It needs to be important to you too, Jude," I said as we puttered out to the lighthouse to visit with Gerald and Hattie.

"It is."

"Well, that's good, then." And I left it at that. I knew better than to make a big deal out of it with him. He'd been meeting with Father Thomas every week since Thanksgiving, even though he didn't think I knew about it.

I stood by his side when the waters of baptism were poured over his head. I stood by his side when the chrism oil, fragrant with the scents of crushed olives and myrrh, was placed on his forehead in the shape of a cross, its perfume vining through the air and all around us. *Cum Sanctu Spiritu*, I prayed over and over again, and the Spirit joined us, its presence strong as it hovered over us in the little church. I watched as the hair on Jude's neck stood on end. He felt it too. I prayed as he took the Eucharist for the first time and I prayed next to him on the kneeler when it was all over and the church had emptied out, people hurrying over to their Easter dinners and family celebrations.

Jude knelt there endlessly it seemed, eyes closed, his lips moving silently.

"Stay as long as you need," I whispered after an hour. "I'm heading home to rest."

I tiptoed toward the front doors, crossed myself with holy water, and burst into the April sunshine as joy spilled from my soul, a joy that had not ceased in the hearts of believers for almost two thousand years. The day was chilly, one of those Easters nobody really feels like wearing her white shoes and straw hats. The breeze from off the water picked at my dress and hair while I walked across the street and down to the tackle shop.

When I let myself in, Jesus sat there.

"You are risen!" I cried.

"Indeed."

And he held open his arms. It had been so long.

I stayed there for a good while, knowing I could trust his timing in regard to Jude's return.

"You brought him in," Jesus said. "It's a grand day, Mary-Margaret. Your faithfulness is being talked about in heaven, let me tell you."

I hugged him more tightly. "I'm so happy."

I burrowed into him for a good while as his love washed over me, feeling somewhat the joy he felt as the lost lamb came home.

And yet. Jude still said nothing about taking the penicillin.

Finally, I lifted my head. "I'm trying so hard, Lord. There's just no convincing him there's something to live for."

"He's still basically a self-centered individual."

"Why does he want to die, now that there's me and so much life?"

"I'm not going to tell you that. One step at a time. But be patient, T—, I'm working on him. Little by little. He'll break down one night. And he'll need you like he's never needed anyone before. I doubt he'll even remember his disease. Will you accept him?"

"Of course."

"Good. I knew I could trust you with him. Jude's very special to me."

"I'm glad."

"In essence, he's an orphan too. And you know how I feel about orphans."

"Widows too."

"Yes."

"I don't want to be one of those either, Lord," I said dryly.

He laughed. "Just wait and see, T—."

～

When Jude shoved his key in the lock and swung open the door, I was just lifting a pan of ham slices out of the oven. The brown sugar bubbled on top.

"Smells good." He set his hat on the telephone table near the door.

"Wait'll you see the potatoes." I slid out the scalloped potatoes next, browned on top. Sister Thaddeus's mother's recipe.

"I'll set the table."

Jude was helpful. When he was a younger boy, catcalling and making lewd gestures at us girls, I couldn't have foreseen this side of him.

I waited for him to speak about the day's events, but he said nothing about them. After the meal he suggested we take a blanket and a book and go to Bethlehem Point.

"Are you sure, Jude? You hate sitting there looking at that lighthouse."

"It's time to leave it behind me, Mary-Margaret. Or at least to give it a try. I'll lay my head on your lap and you can read to me."

"Then you pick the book."

He walked over to the shelf and pulled down a copy of *An Introduction to the Devout Life,* by St. Francis de Sales. "I think I need this one."

"A wise choice."

We finished up the dishes, folded up a quilt and a blanket, bundled up in sweaters, and walked to the point.

"You read." Jude flapped the blanket and settled it on the ground. I lay on my back, Jude lay down too, and rested his head on my stomach.

I began the words of Francis de Sales, the Gentleman Preacher, as he was known, a man whose desire was to bring spirituality and a close relationship with God to the men and

women who live normal lives, not like those in monasteries or
hermitages. In short, I realized with a shock, people like I had
become. The last time I had read the book, I read it from the
other side. Jude didn't realize the importance of his choice.

"'Dear reader, I request you to read this Preface for your
own satisfaction as well as mine.

"'The flower-girl Glycera was so skilled in varying the
arrangement and combination of her flowers, that out of the
same kinds she produced a great variety of bouquets; so that
the painter Pausias, who sought to rival the diversity of her art,
was brought to a standstill, for he could not vary his painting so
endlessly as Glycera varied her bouquets. Even so the Holy
Spirit of God disposes and arranges the devout teaching which
he imparts through the lips and pen of His servants with such
endless variety, that, although the doctrine is ever one and the
same, their treatment of it is different, according to the varying
minds whence that treatment flows. Assuredly I neither desire,
nor ought to write in this book anything but what has been
already said by others before me. I offer you the same flowers,
dear reader, but the bouquet will be somewhat different from
theirs, because it is differently made up.'"

"He sounds humble," Jude said.

"Yes."

"I need some of that."

"We all do."

I read until the sun set so low I could no longer make out
the words. "Ready?" I closed the book.

He sat up and reconfigured himself, lying parallel beside
me, arranging the second blanket over us, wrapping me in the
circle of his arms. And he kissed me softly over my face and my
lips, my hair and my shoulders as the light from Bethlehem
Point flickered over us, again and again.

ANOTHER DAY IN AFRICA HAS COME AND GONE. I VISITED Precious and fed her and read to her. She's slipping away. She sleeps most of the time now.

A couple of weeks ago, that night before we went to pick up Father Ignatius, I'd have given anything for a good sleep. Even though my body ached for repose, and my eyes, so dry from two days without much sleep, begged my brain to follow their lead and close up shop, my brain was busy walking down the aisle of memory, picking up a can of conversation here, a package of observation there. Maybe Morpheus was right. Maybe he wasn't the raping seminarian at all. Maybe my grandmother lied to me.

Or maybe my grandmother didn't know the truth. And why did Jude never tell me? He'd mentioned the truth about my mother. I don't know what that could have been, though. Finally I got out of bed and went outside. What I did know, as I sat under the African moon, the flat, dry land around me quiet for the night, was that God kept that poor man alive all these years for this moment. He sounded like a saint, a person most likely ready for the beatific vision upon death closing his eyes. And yet he was still lingering at the age of ninety-seven or thereabouts. Indeed! The poor man.

Huts stood around me and lined the road, simple, one- or two-room structures made of sticks and rocks and mud. Pulling the blanket around me more tightly, feeling the chill of the mild winter, I wondered how I'd broach the subject with my father.

Jesus sat beside me. "T—."

I leaned into him. "Friend. You've taken me on some crazy journeys in this life, but this one, well, you've certainly made it easy."

"Sometimes I do that. You're not getting any younger, you know."

We laughed.

"I just wanted to come be with you," he said. "Tomorrow's a big day for you. For John. For Jude. For your family."

"Most of them are gone."

"Oh no, my dear. They're all thrilled at what's happening. But don't ask me to say any more."

"Yes," I sighed. He put his arm around me.

"Just be, T—. Lean on me. Let me love you here on this plain. I have work for you to do as well while you're here. You'll need my strength. Don't you adore Samkela?"

"Oh yes. His skin is almost charcoal, it soaks up the sun and is still soft despite that. And his eyes look on the world as one big art project, don't they? We have such a good time together, laughing, drawing, building, sculpting, unable to communicate any other way and feeling just fine about it."

"Indeed you do. This is going to make all the difference in the world to that little boy, my dear."

I had no doubts about that.

～

We left the mission early, around six a.m. to pick up Father Ignatius, or Brother Joe, or Brendan Connelly, and stopped in

Manzini for breakfast for fried dough balls. The bakers sprinkle
them with powdered sugar and sell them for basically ten
American cents. With some espresso, we sat in the Land Rover
and ate three each.

"What made you put two and two together with Father
Ignatius being Brother Joe?" John sipped his coffee.

"It was the seminary he went to. Add to that his mission on
The Block."

"Why was he at your wedding?"

We never told John about Jude's past. We didn't think it was
information any child, no matter how mature and caring, could
handle knowing about his father, the one he looked up to,
emulated, and, in John's case, adored. Jude wanted to leave it
behind. He wanted that guy crucified for good.

I didn't feel the Spirit telling me to do anything different as
I sat there with John.

"Oh, you know how us Catholics find one another. I
thought he was actually a Franciscan priest at the time, but now
I realize he must not have taken final vows then."

"He said something about becoming a priest a little later on
in life."

"Was he a good doctor?"

"Yeah. Just great. A wonderful diagnostician. Did a lot to
bring good medicines over here. In fact, before he got sick,
Mom, he was trying to work on a better mental health situation.
We have only one psychologist in all of Swaziland."

"My goodness!"

He pulled the Rover away from the curb. "I know. But his
groundwork will most likely go undisturbed from here on out.
There's just nobody to take his place that we know of. The rest
of us can't add another item to our task lists. We're swamped."

"I imagine."

John went on to tell me how many children were traumatized, how much molestation went on with the girls. "There's a man who runs a home for children near Piggs Peak who has his girls there wearing pants."

"Isn't that against the culture?"

He nodded. "Sure is. But as he says, he's more worried about providing a physical barrier against rape."

"Lord have mercy."

"I know. Can you imagine having to make decisions like that in America?"

"No indeed."

"So, with all the sexual abuse going on, can you imagine how much we need psychiatric help?"

"It's hard to even picture."

He turned onto the main road heading toward Mbabane. The mountains stretched along each side, glorious and green, craggy humps of something ancient and maybe even a little unforgiving. Nothing like the flat landscape at Big Bend. "Women here mean nothing."

He was right about that, sisters. When I took him and my father to lunch after we picked him up, they were served first, and I had to make sure I got out of the way on the sidewalks.

Funny how much we can take for granted. My faith tells me women are valuable, we religious sisters have a bona fide vocation, and let's face it, our tradition tells us the greatest Christian who ever lived was a woman.

My father sat on an old black trunk in front of the house he lived in, apparently, with three other Jesuit priests who taught at Mater Dolorosa School in town.

I wouldn't have known he was Brother Joe except when he stood, straightening almost to his full height (his back had buckled a bit near the top), he held himself much the same. His white hair glimmered with that peculiar pinkishness redheads get as they age.

Oh. Like mine.

I forgot that the years had stolen away my youth as well. But I was old, not ancient. Nevertheless, he looked eighty, not ninety-seven.

"This is Father Ignatius," John said.

"Mary-Margaret," he said immediately. "It's been so many years. I was Brother Joe then."

And, Lord help me, I couldn't hide it. I wanted to get to know him, wanted to ease us into the truth of the matter, but then I realized, he knew. This wasn't all a big coincidence. He knew exactly who I was, who John was. It was why he'd taken such an interest in John, had overseen his vocation as priest and physician. In fact, every year half of the expensive tuition at Mount St. Mary's, then at Johns Hopkins, was always paid by "a donor who wished to remain anonymous."

We thought it might have been someone from our parish on Locust Island, or even Gerald and Hattie, who, remaining childless, spoiled John just a bit when he went for several weeks each summer to Bethlehem Point Light.

Now I knew the truth. My father was John's personal Sister Thaddeus. Oh, the fabric on God's loom can get so complicated, it's a wonder it just doesn't look like a bunch of knots.

I walked forward, one slow step at a time. "I found out," I said. "About who you really are."

"How?" His pale skin bleached yet more.

"Jude left papers. I found them a couple of years ago."

He rubbed his chin.

"What are you talking about?" John asked.

My father held out his hands palms up and thrust them toward me as if to say, "It's up to you if you want to tell him."

I turned to my son and squeezed his shoulder. "I doubt there's a gentle way to say this, John. But Father Ignatius is your grandfather. He's my father."

John looked at my father, then at me. "You're gonna have to explain this one."

"It'll take awhile to explain and I have a lot of questions myself," I said.

"I'm sure you do," my father said. "Jude never would tell me what you knew."

"How did he figure out it was you?" I asked.

"It was when we were eating crabs together at your wedding. He could see it in us. That's what he said. And we sat on the shore and talked about it and the times and basic circumstances—" He looked up at John. "Perhaps this is a conversation best left for a little later."

I'd been upset with him for so many years, the raping seminarian, but standing here now with this old, old man, I didn't have it in me to humiliate him. We needed a moment of truth and, finally, of reconciliation.

It was Jesus's final prayer before he ascended and who was I to choose with whom I would be unified? Not to mention those pesky verses about caring for the sick and poor, and if anyone was sick, it was my father. His hair had obviously thinned out recently. He had a full, thick head of red hair even in his fifties. And his body seemed to have grayed and loosened at the joints like an old doll.

"All right. I'm here for a good while."

John took one handle on the trunk and I grasped the other. We lifted and walked my father's possessions to the back of the Land Rover.

"Do you have more bags inside?" I asked.

"No. Everything fits right in here."

"How can that be?" I opened the passenger door for him.

"Oh no, I'll sit in the back."

We did the back-and-forth arguing until he pulled rank. So, into the back seat I helped him.

"During my time at the mission on The Block, I saw what possessions and the need to possess do to people. I said once I left there, I'd pare down to just the necessities."

John couldn't seem to talk.

Finally, fifteen achingly quiet minutes down the road, he craned his neck around for a few seconds to look at my father. "Why did you keep it a secret, Father Connelly?"

"Oh, it wasn't up to me to tell. I prayed many years ago that we would be reunited, but I knew, owing to the circumstances of Mary-Margaret's conception, that it was up to the Lord if it was to be. I left it in his hands. I had to."

John looked back onto the road. "Well, I have to say that a lot of things make sense now, but I wish I had known a lot sooner." He honked his horn and waved at a group of school-children walking down the road and hollered, *"Ye-bo!"* They waved and hollered back in kind. Their smiles stretched wide.

My father gripped the back of my seat and leaned forward. "Your son is quite the celebrity around here with all his honking and waving. They call him White Father in siSwati."

John laughed. "Have you ever seen more beautiful children?"

"No," I said. "Well, other than you. Although you were a little pasty."

John's laugh bounced around the vehicle.

"It's that redhead skin," my father said.

"Yes," I agreed.

"Most true," John said.

And I belonged right there in that car, three generations of redheads. All pasty white, all part of a religious order. All with the same blood flowing through their veins.

John tapped the horn at another group of children, waving as he said, "Unfortunately, I didn't get my father's complexion."

"You did get his eyes," I whispered.

"Yes, he did," said my father. "I've always thought that."

How can a heart ache, yearn, and be filled with joy all at once?

So back to Jude and me. This is where it gets sticky.

The first school year ended successfully and my contract was renewed. We'd settled into a life of companionship and tender, procreationless love. But we were both zinging for one another. I could see it in him and he in me. And our kisses told the true tale.

The day after school ended for the summer, we sat on the docks together. "Is life so bad now?" I asked him. I'd taken his hand and set it in my lap.

"No. It's a good life."

"Did you ever think you'd have a life like this?"

"No. Did you?"

I laughed. "What do you think?"

"I'm in a catch-22 now," he said.

"What do you mean?"

"Well"—he scratched underneath his jaw—"if I take the penicillin and live, you'll have to stay with me until I die. And you won't get back to the convent."

"I wasn't a nun, Jude, I was a—"

"You know what I mean. I know that's the life you really wanted. So it would probably just be better for you in the long run if I forgo treatment."

"But—"

He placed a finger over my mouth. "But you want a baby. I know you do." He removed his finger. "Am I right?"

I could only nod.

"But if I take the medicine and give you that baby, I'm part of that bargain, and you may never get back into the order."

"I want you now."

"You mean when I die someday, you're not going back in?"

"I didn't say that. But I'm not wishing you dead, Jude. You have to know that. I want you to be healed."

He sighed. "I know. But I want the best for you. And maybe that's not me."

I touched my wedding ring. "It's a little late for that."

"Maybe." He looked out over the water. "I just don't know."

~~

I could only trust what Jesus said. I knew something had to happen to throw him over the edge, but I would have never guessed what was to come. In fact, I was so mad at Jesus for doing it that way, I didn't see him for months and months. Finally, though, I understood. Jude and his past needed one more sail over the choppy bay together. I could only be there to love him as the storm passed over, raining fire and hail.

It was one of the hottest Julys I could remember when Brister stormed up the steps to our apartment and pounded on the door. We'd just come back from Wednesday night Mass and I was making tea.

"Oh my goodness, Brister!" I said after swinging wide the door. "What's the matter?"

"Where's your husband?"

"In the bedroom sorting the laundry."

He headed in muttering, "Women's work," under his breath. "You ain't going to believe this," he yelled. "She's back.

D--- it, Petra's come back to the island."

The resulting silence roared about me. I'd rather he let out a string of expletives. Grabbing a broom and pretending I was sweeping, I moved closer to the bedroom door to hear the conversation.

Then, "Where is she?"

"At the house. She wants me to take her out to the light."

"Take her. Dump her out in the middle of the bay for all I care."

"You don't want to see her first?"

"No."

"Mary-Margaret?" Brister yelled. "How about you?"

"No, thank you."

I heard the bathroom door shut and the shower begin.

Brister came back into the kitchen, hands on hips. "I never thought I'd see her again."

"How does she look?"

"The same. Just older."

"Are you going to take her back?"

"After what she did to her son?"

"You knew?"

"Not the whole time. After he ran away, I put two and two together. Then I kicked her out, well, kicked her stuff out anyways. Here I'd beat Jude out of jealousy and she was doin' that to him."

I poured a cup of tea and held it out to him.

He took it. "I thought she just left, like she did the lighthouse, and I was a skunk to her, so why wouldn't she have? But she went looking for him. I guess she never could figure out what he'd gotten into. She never would have guessed. She thought that boy was perfect, and around her, he acted that way. Like the perfect son. The man she always thought she needed." He sipped his tea. "Petra wasn't good at picking out men. She picked me and I ain't nothin' to sneeze at."

I would have laughed had it not been so serious.

He drained the cup, the hot liquid seeming to do nothing to his mouth and throat. "Better get her out there. I didn't tell her where Jude is, or about you either. Told her I had to run to the drugstore for some medicated pads. That's going to kill her, to think he's married to somebody."

Good, I thought.

"All right, Brister. Thanks for the warning. But talk to me before you talk to Jude about her again. I'll ask him if he wants to hear anymore about it and if he doesn't, I'll let you know. He has the right to decide that."

"I'm not going to argue with you on that one."

Brister left.

The shower still ran. I took off all my clothes and joined Jude in the shower. He wept, sitting in a ball on the floor, hugging his knees to his chest. I cradled him as best I could, rocking him on the hard tile surface, the steam surrounding us in a heap, until the water went cold and I turned it off. We made our way slowly to the bed and I rubbed his back and neck and shoulders until he fell asleep.

～⌢～

My eyes opened around two a.m. I was facing the alarm clock, its face lit up from the inside by the orange light. Jude was kissing the curve where my shoulder met my neck and his hand caressed my hip and my waist, every stroke widening to include more and more of me.

I turned to face him, wrapping my arms around his neck and pulling his face to mine. *This is it*, I thought.

～⌢～

There were no parlor tricks on Jude's part, he didn't pull fast moves out of a hat. He simply loved me with his body, and I loved him in return with mine. For all his experience, he'd never given himself away, and this he did. I hadn't either, of course, so in that, we were on equal footing.

I forgot about the syphilis.

Later I asked him about that night, if he had forgotten too. He said he did, and for the life of him, he couldn't figure out why; he just saw me there, thought, *This is what love should be. You're a fool if you don't take it,* and reached out. I didn't tell him sometimes miracles are small and, to the naked eye, even a little insane.

~~

The next morning I was scrambling some eggs for our breakfast as he unplugged the percolator and poured our coffee when I realized I held all the cards.

"I've decided what's good for the goose is good for the gander."

"I'm almost scared to ask," he said.

"I'm not going to get the penicillin if you don't."

He set down his cup. "Mary-Margaret, don't be so silly."

"No. I'm serious, Jude." I lifted the pan off the hot burner and set it on a cool one. "If I take the medicine and you don't, I'll be back to sleeping on the floor beside the couch. So I want you with me." I pressed my body against his.

He sighed, cradled my face in his hands, and kissed me softly on the mouth. "I did this to myself, didn't I?"

"Yes. Thank God," I said, dryly.

He placed two pieces of bread in the toaster. "I know you better than to try and talk you out of your plan."

This surprised me. "Are you calling me stubborn?"

"Yep. Think about it, Mary-Margaret. What have you wanted in life that you haven't gotten eventually? You've always done what you wanted. You even convinced me somehow to marry you when I knew marrying you would be the worst thing for you."

If he only knew. He never knew about my talks with Jesus. I never even remotely slipped in letting that out.

It was fine if he thought I was stubborn. People thought worse of me and will continue to. At least he didn't think I had horns! At least he liked my artwork.

"I only did it because I thought I'd be dead in a few years."

"Really, Jude? Really? You know syphilis can take up to twenty years to kill a person."

"I figured mine was worse than that."

"I don't believe you. It was more than that and you know it."

He set our mugs on the table, scratched his temple. "I think the worst thing I could've done was come up to you that day in the schoolyard," he said.

"So you'll get the penicillin too?" I turned off the burner and set the pan of eggs aside.

"You really want to live with me for the rest of my life, Mary-Margaret? Really? What if I go back to heroin, or my old life?"

"Will you?"

He cocked his head in the direction of the lighthouse. "Will you keep her away from me?"

"Yes."

"I've been clean for a long time, Mary-Margaret. I've got good reason to stay that way."

"Why did you marry me, Jude?"

"Because I just couldn't resist anymore. It's as simple as that."

"I wore you down?"

The toast popped up.

"Mary-Margaret, you managed to succeed with me about something I tried to convince you of for years."

I ran a hand down his arm. "You just wanted to sleep with me."

He cocked an eyebrow. "I just didn't know any other way to tell you that I loved you. And really, back then, maybe I just felt it was safer that way."

I took his hand. "That sounds closer to the truth."

He turned his head and looked out the window. "Go ahead and make an appointment with a doctor. Let's finish this business."

~⌣~

The next morning Petra stood at our door and banged and banged, for three hours, yelling, "Judey! Oh, my lovely son!" And other sweet phrases that made my skin crawl. "Let your mommy give you a hug!"

We never did find out who told her where he was. Brister swore up and down it wasn't him.

After she finally left, Jude had me go down to Brister and tell him he wouldn't be coming on the boat for a couple of days. I explained the situation. Brister said that was fine. And it was a good thing, because if he hadn't, I would have just let a thing or two fly out of my mouth and it wouldn't have been pretty.

She kept coming. Jude looked just plain spent, wandering around our apartment, sitting down, standing up, trying to read, doing the cooking, and smoking twice as many cigarettes as usual. At night, he sat up in bed and stared into the darkness until he fell asleep from exhaustion. Thankfully, he'd sleep through Petra's morning barrage.

By the third day I'd had enough.

"This is ridiculous." I slipped on the low-cut nightgown LaBella had bought for me for a wedding present and mussed up my hair. I slapped my cheeks to redden them and pinched my lips until they were red and swollen. By this time, Jude awakened, sat on the bed, whiter than an altar cloth.

I faced him, straddled his legs as he sat on the bed, and

kissed him. "I'll get rid of her for you. Maybe it won't be for good, but hopefully she'll get off our backs sooner or later."

I truly felt in my spirit it was best to keep her from Jude for as long as possible. I wasn't crazy. I figured she'd find her way to him eventually as evil finds its way into our lives no matter how good we are, and I knew he'd have to face her himself, but then, while our love was young and finally growing toward the sunlight, we didn't need to have Petra around shadowing our life.

Should I have reached out to her? Well, sisters, I don't know. Maybe. I'll let you be the judge of that. But I was more worried about Jude's ability to maintain a distant forgiveness than Petra's need for repentance. And while both she and Jude were in God's hands, Jude alone was given to me as my mate, my holy calling. I took my sacramental marriage vows seriously.

I yanked open the door, raised my arm along the door frame, and leaned against the wood, my hip thrust out to the side. "Can I help you?" I said, pretending to arrange my hair. I made my voice sound slightly sleepy and tried to go for a "just made love" tone, but I didn't even know what that was. I think I nailed it, though.

"Mary-Margaret?"

"And you are?"

"Mrs. Keller."

"You mean Petra Purnell? I'm Mrs. Keller."

Let me take a moment to describe Petra. Her hair still jumped around her head in curls, and now behavior I once thought was so carefree I could see for someone acting girlish, someone acting younger than she was, someone trying to get her son's attention.

It made me sick too.

She wore a tight-fitting sheath dress, cut low enough for an inch or so of cleavage to peep over the top of the scooped neckline. Her eyes were lined on top in the Egyptian fashion and she'd painted her lips a cotton candy pink.

Still and all, it couldn't beat my youth or my emerald green, satin nightgown. With my red hair, well, I hate to sound prideful, but I sizzled. LaBella would have been proud.

"I took back my original married name," she said, eyeing my chest. So the larger breasts were finally coming in handy.

"I'd like to kindly ask you to stop beating our door down day in and day out. If *Judey* wanted to see you, he would have opened it by now, don't you think?"

She winced, then her eyes flickered up and focused over my shoulder. Her quick intake of breath told me all I needed to know.

He stood just behind me and I felt his fingers curve over my collarbones and the length of him press itself behind me.

"Mother."

She pouted. "Oh, Judey, I'm your mommy. Why have you been ignoring me like this?"

Jude moved me aside, lightly pressed his mother onto the landing as if he was going to speak to her, and as he shut the door, leaving her alone on the hot iron steps, he said, "I've forgiven you, so leave it at that. If you come here again, I'll hate you for the rest of my life."

He latched the door and leaned against it, staring down at the floor. "I wanted to say, 'I'll kill you,' but I don't think I would. I feel like it sometimes. Some of the dreams I've had." He shook his head.

I approached, placing my arms around him, laying my head against his chest. He was sweaty and yet cold.

Her heels clicked on the metal steps, sending a hollow ring down the length of the staircase and her sickening wails filled the neighborhood. She didn't go back to the lighthouse. In fact, nobody knew what happened to her after that until ten years later when Brister told us a friend of his saw her obituary in the *Baltimore Sun.* She had lived in Dundalk, was survived by a husband, Forrest Blanchette, no children. I thanked God he kept her away.

I JUST FINISHED UP WITH SAMKELA FOR THE DAY. I BROUGHT out the watercolor paints, and he started giggling. I want to take him home with me!

Today I'm going down to Siphewe's house. I'm taking her some laundry soap, a sack of rice, a sack of beans, and other nonperishable items from the little grocery store about a mile away.

Siphewe has a story that made me laugh the first time I heard it, although it isn't at all funny.

She was much like Jude as a young man, I think, only with a violent streak. John had been ministering to her, had invited her to Mass on Sunday at the small chapel on the grounds of the mission. She was dating a young man and they were quite the wild couple and she started bringing him, said she liked the quiet for once during the week, loved the soft chanting of Father Luke (who grew up in the Eastern Rite), and John said she'd sit there with her eyes closed.

During the week she might as well have been a demoniac, she got in such fights with her boyfriend. Fistfights, knife fights, and they'd come back together and do all the things they shouldn't have. She was lucky she didn't get pregnant.

Finally, her boyfriend left her and she was so angry, she

stormed over to his house and hacked at his legs with a machete. I'm telling you, she was a mess!

Now the poor fellow can barely walk. He can't work and to top it all off, a windstorm ripped across the plains about a month ago and Siphewe's house, about fifty years old and not in good shape whatsoever, lost its roof and its western wall. Now she lives in a tent the Red Cross set up.

Of course the priests at the mission have helped her out during this time, bringing her food and caring for the bruises and gashes she sustained during the storm.

Her boyfriend is furious at John and the others and won't come to church anymore. But Siphewe, well, she's changed. She saw love in action, believed, repented, was baptized, and will take her first Communion next week just after she is confirmed. It will be a big day for John, Luke, and Amos. Father Ignatius too.

∼∽

I'm back from Siphewe's. She was thankful for the food and made me a cup of tea and a coarse but delicious corn bread. You don't refuse the offer of food here. I learned that several trips ago. She doesn't speak English, but somehow we understood one another. John doesn't know this yet, but she's taken in three orphans whose mother died, most likely from AIDS, a few days ago. The father has been gone for two years at least. I'll tell him when he's finished looking at patients for the day.

So much to do here. This is a country that crawls along on the backs of its women. But maybe that's another story as well. It's a beautiful evening and the sky would look much better with a colorful kite looping and diving across its expanse.

∼∽

Kites became very important to Jude and me. After we set about the cure for syphilis.

We booked ourselves in a cheap hotel in Salisbury near the hospital for our penicillin treatment, a seven-day round for me, ten for Jude. With each injection, he seemed to change for the better emotionally. Death left him in stages and I gladly watched it go. We took long walks during the day and began to dream about what life could be like with the past truly behind us.

That we would have children was assumed and the sooner the better. Neither of us were teenagers anymore.

We ate ice cream in the evenings and dreamed out loud. "What would you do if you could do anything you like?" he asked me.

"I'd be an artist. Just an artist. I'd do my crazy sculptures again and I'd make them bigger than ever. Outdoor installations. I'd love to try doing a bronze. And I'd like to do something like Brother Joe does, but maybe with runaways or something. What about you? What makes you happy?"

"You're going to think this is crazy, Mary-Margaret. I love to fly kites. I made some great kites when I was a kid. Remember those?"

I used to watch him out of my window at school sometimes, out there on the point, flying his kites. And from off the lighthouse when he was smaller.

"It always made me feel like I was doing something so amazing. Why is that?"

"Because it's attached to you and it's flying and soaring and you're holding on. It's the closest you can get to flying and still be on the ground."

He closed his eyes as we sat on a bench downtown, licking our ice-cream cones.

Finally, I said, "Do you like the beach? The ocean?"

"I do. I almost packed up and went to Ocean City instead of Baltimore. I wish I had, but, anyways, it's water under the bridge now."

"Do you think Brister would lend you some seed money for a business?"

"What do you have in mind?"

"A shop on the boardwalk. A kite shop. People fly kites at the beach all the time, and if they don't they should. And you can make kites too, good kites, not those cheap things you get at the dime store."

"They're such a waste of money."

I pulled a notepad out of my purse along with a pen.

"Get planning."

He began to jot down ideas, supplies, other items we might sell. By the end of the trip, he had it all planned. I'd never seen this side of Jude.

I only knew one thing, people like Jude needed to fly; you just had to help point them in the right direction. It sounded like a good life. And it was.

~~

I put my notice in at the school and they were sad to see me go, but, like most everyone else on Locust Island who were well acquainted with us, thought it was the right move.

The next September, almost a year after our wedding, we rented a furnished efficiency apartment on Wicomico Street and leased a storefront space on the boardwalk between Division and First Street, just down from the Plim Plaza where we honeymooned.

Behind the apartment house, I rigged up my pulleys and chains and prayed that somehow I'd find wood from someplace. We had no truck and it wasn't as if trees were aplenty there on that strip of land between the Atlantic Ocean and the Assawoman Bay.

Jude ordered the materials he needed for kite making: cane and hardwood, stripwood, crepe paper and nylon, glue, twine,

and paints for me to decorate the kites. He ordered manufac-
tured kites to begin selling right away. "I'll make up some kits for
people to assemble themselves. Family projects or what have you.
And we'll sell them for less." I told him that was a fine idea.

We called our business The Kite Shack. I tried to come up
with all sorts of plays on words, High Hopes, The World on a
String, and such, I can't remember them now, but Jude would
have none of it. "Let's just keep it simple, Mary-Margaret, so
folks will remember."

All winter long he worked on his kites and I helped him as
the wood I needed had not yet shown up on our doorstep. I asked
Jesus about it, but he remained silent. So. Kites it was, then. I
painted some beautiful butterflies that winter, dragonflies and
birds, stingrays and colorful, fanciful fish. Peacocks too. I
thought the peacock kites would be best sellers, and they were.

By December I was expecting, happy to think about a September
baby. Good things seemed to happen to me in September. We
both had such hope wrapped up in this child. For me, that
blood connection; for Jude, the chance to break the family's
dark line of abuse.

So while we made kites, God made our baby inside of me,
cells collecting upon one another, forming this human child.
Of course, we didn't have ultrasounds in those days, but both of
us felt the child was a boy. And no, Jesus didn't give me the
scoop ahead of time. But he did tell me one night John had a
specific mission. "He will help save a nation."

Sounded pretty big to me, and I couldn't quite imagine
what he would do.

For twenty years we lived in Ocean City and Jude made and
sold kites and helped found a mission with a Jesuit missionary,
and we both became part of the Jesuit Volunteer Corps. The

Oasis ministered mostly to prostitutes and Jude became a street worker, gentle and loving, but able to say, "I know where you've been. So let's not pretend, okay?"

Oh, we had some crazy meals around our table once we bought a small house on the other side of Ocean Highway, last house on the left, Bayview Avenue. The sunsets we watched over the water of the bay, the sails on the sailboats, turgid silhouettes against the flaming sky, as if someone drew them in India ink. The boats skimmed by, always adding a peaceful benediction to the day. There we'd be, sitting with the rabble of the town, laughing and picking crabs Jude caught in his traps off our dock, then steamed himself, or smelling the aroma of grilled hamburgers and hot dogs. Summer lasted so long there at the beach. Or maybe we just engineered it to be that way.

God allowed my marriage to Jude to last twenty-seven years. I wondered at times if I was sent to Jude, or Jude was sent to me, or we were both given each other to make John. Then again, limiting God like that is never good. Knowing him, he had something up his almighty sleeve for all three of us. He's quite thrifty, you know.

Jesus took to showing up on my birthday, early in the morning before anyone else was up, just to tell me how glad he was that I was born.

When I gave birth to John, I realized this was more than just one human being giving life to another; this was a holy calling, every bit as holy as being a religious sister. Yes, I knew that was the traditional teaching of the Church, but when I held that little boy in my arms for the first time, I knew it in every square inch of my frame.

The birth was grueling, the uterine bleeding so intense a surgeon was called in to perform an emergency hysterectomy. It could have turned into a situation that mirrored my own birth, but we'd chosen to have the baby at the hospital just in case.

Jude gave me a bag of bulbs the day John was baptized. Oh yes! Now I remember, white daffodils, for new beginnings, renewal. Resurrection. "I'll plant them someday, Mary-Margaret." But as happens with some things, they ended up under an old flowerpot in the garage and got pushed back in a corner, then covered with junk, and there they sat until I unearthed them when I moved away from Ocean City. I will plant them as soon as I get back to the island. We all need new life, fresh beginnings, renewal and resurrection. Now is the time. Now is always the time.

There, I just wrote *Plant Bulbs* on my palm again! Let's hope it works this time. I'll keep refreshing it until I'm back in the States.

～

I could tell John was special from the beginning, understanding the importance of our faith from an early age, talking about God in such intimate ways, referring to himself not just as a Christian but God's friend. He began doing that at five and I had no idea from where he heard the term. Perhaps Jesus appears to John too and he's not allowed to tell either! Sometimes I truly have to wonder about that.

Jude never became overly vocal about his faith; he showed it by his actions, however, down at the mission, at the shop where he kept some kites he made out of scraps to give to kids with no pocket change. And Jude could spot them somehow. His ability to discern people was so much keener than mine, as well as his inherent knowing of who was down and out.

No wonder Jesus wanted him for his own.

John came to me one night as I sat out on the dock behind our house at sunset, plopping down next to my lawn chair. He was already almost six feet, all elbows and knees. "I wanted to tell you first, Mom."

"Did you fail your English test?"

"No, I got a C."

"Not bad."

He was definitely more the science/math type.

"I feel like God is calling me to the priesthood."

If the heavens had opened, spilling their light upon us, and if angels themselves had sung the Gloria, the moment wouldn't have felt less holy.

"And . . . I think he wants me to be a missionary."

"So, not a diocesan priest?"

"I don't think so."

"We'll pray God shows you."

As if that was doubtful, but sometimes God does seem to wait until the last minute and that, sisters, can be so utterly frustrating, can't it?

OH MY, I WANTED TO START WRITING ABOUT MY MOTHER yesterday, and don't you know, John came squealing up in the Rover to the mission and jumped out in a cloud of dust. Precious there in the hospital had finally passed away and because no family came to claim her, he volunteered to take the body and bury her here at the mission.

I'd gone into Manzini with John twice a week these past four weeks to feed her, and we even arranged for a woman who attends the Cathedral of the Assumption downtown there to come in once a day to feed her supper. She lay there getting weaker, unable to speak but to say, "Amen," and I read to her from Scripture, particularly the Psalms, as well as from her copy of *The Imitation of Christ*, and a little Thomas Merton always did a soul good. My father provided me with writings that would encourage a dying soul and John did his part too. I was able to bring Communion to her as well.

"She definitely had AIDs, Mom," John said as we drove down the highway, him honking and waving at the kids as usual. "But at least her last few weeks weren't filled with starvation."

"It makes me want to cry how that can happen."

"Don't move over here, then."

Don't worry, I thought. I was more than happy to be with my folk on Locust Island. Although the people in this nation would be lovely to live with.

I wanted to ask him how his view of God has changed since he arrived in this land, but the Spirit stayed me. Perhaps another time. And certainly his faith seemed rock solid. John's stories and thoughts are his own to tell.

So anyway, we brought Precious back, and Luke and Amos built a casket out of spare planking in the shed. I took some leftover room paint and decorated the outside because I had a feeling Precious liked bright colors.

We gave her a Mass of Christian burial and lowered the box by ropes into a hole John and some of the neighbor boys dug together. Women who didn't even know her gathered and cried. They knew her story. They *were* her story. Or would be soon enough.

IT'S LATE NOW. I JUST TUCKED MY FATHER IN AND I SUPPOSE I'll tell you this, because by the time anyone reads this, he'll be dead and so will I. He has AIDS as well. Being a medical worker here, it seemed to be inevitable. Nurses are dying too fast to be adequately replaced. I fear for John, but since it doesn't seem to bother him, I say nothing.

We've had a good time in the past month, my father and I. I simply call him Joe. At our ages, it does seem a little silly to be all starry-eyed and call him Daddy. I've had a Father all my life and he's been wonderful to me. I see that now.

But Jesus told me deep inside of us is a need to know what is true. The truly true, not what we've convinced ourselves is true. And I had done a lot of convincing myself over the years as to who my father was.

So, here's the tale, what truly happened, according to my father, back in 1929. Mary Margaret Fischer (my mother) left Locust Island after high school and graduated with a teaching degree from the College of Notre Dame, according my grandmother. She'd procured a job teaching in South Baltimore and continued to move forward toward her final vows. This was a point of great pride for my grandmother due to the fact that she bore her daughter out of wedlock and that same progeny ended up a college graduate. Who would imagine?

Indeed.

And a religious sister? Even more wonderful.

But my mother never graduated at all. Yes, she wanted to be a teacher, and she planned to be a religious, but she lasted a month having met a fellow who led her down "the wrong path," as people call it.

"It was then she was introduced to opium," he said.

My father and I sat in the chapel at the mission. We'd eaten some of my vegetable stew and a bit of boiled meat over rice, drank a little of the wine, and eaten a square of the Dairy Milk chocolate bar I'd brought from Manzini.

As I write, I'm watching over him as he sleeps. John wanted to head over to Siphewe's house to make sure she has enough supplies now that she's housing three orphans. Only Jesus knows what will happen to that makeshift little family.

Anyway, back to my mother.

My father placed his arm along the back of the pew behind me but did not touch me. He sighed with such sadness, I wondered how any breath was left inside of him. "She went downhill from there, such as is the tale with that substance. The more she smoked or ate opium, the thinner she became. The fellow flew the coop, so she stole, begged on the street, making up stories to finance her habit, becoming more and more dissipated looking. Finally, she ended up at our mission."

"Weren't you still in seminary?"

"Yes. My third year, actually. I'd always taken an interest in rescue work. Sort of the emergency room of social justice I guess you might say."

Outside, the sun had set almost completely, the great clouds still tinged golden, the mountains purpled in the twilight and ready to deflate just a little upon the coming of the darkness.

By this age, my father's voice had hushed itself to just above a whisper, a little early-morning gravelly, but still possessing a throaty bit of warmth at its core, something that said he wasn't going to hurt you. Did my mother feel that way when she entered the mission?

"So she came into the mission on a winter night. Somebody had stolen her coat and her purse, and she was highly inebriated."

"You can say drunk, Joe, I won't mind."

"Oh, I wouldn't want to defame her like that."

He said the words with such sincerity, I knew for certain I was about to hear a new version of this man, one completely unlike what my mother, or my grandmother, or even myself, had concocted.

And yet.

There I sat in all my humanity, having been sired and conceived and then born. So something untoward happened, because I doubt they'd married beforehand.

He cleared his throat, holding his fist up to his mouth. "I want to say this as delicately as possible, Mary-Margaret. You're my daughter—"

"And you *are* a priest," I joked.

"Yes, that too. Your mother had nowhere to go. She was skin and bones, her stare glassy and frightened, darting all around. And jumpy. Yet still beautiful. You've seen pictures?"

I nodded. "We had a couple."

"Then you know. So we set up a cot for her in the women's dormitory and she began to withdraw. Do you know much about opium?"

I shook my head.

"Well, it starts off well. A nice sense of euphoria. But the body soon becomes tolerant of it, causing you to smoke or eat incrementally more to experience the same sensation. So you can imagine the resulting, addictive cycle. The skin develops a rash such that, by the time she came, she had scratched her skin until it bled, sometimes using a metal comb."

"Oh, goodness me!"

"She was in terrible shape. Father Frank, who was in charge of the mission at the time, said she'd have to go to the hospital, but she went crazy at the idea. He was a brusque man and went back to his work, not up to convincing someone who was hell-bent on throwing her life away anyway.

"I felt I only had one option left—to accompany her to a motel somewhere and sit with her, take care of her while she withdrew."

He told me about a little place out Route 40 that looked like a collection of little storybook cottages. "I had a little money from my family, so I checked us in and sat with her. Have you ever been with somebody while they're withdrawing?"

"No. You took care of Jude for me."

"Oh yes. His was one of the worst I'd ever been through."

"Really?"

"Most assuredly. God forgive me of such little faith, but I think I was more surprised than anyone that he kicked it for good. I suppose sometimes it depends on why they started using in the first place. Did he use in high school?"

"No. He rowed out on the bay a lot though."

"Hmm."

The moon broadcast its thin beams through the clear glass of the narrow window, two panes by four, and shone on his slender hands, crabbed a bit, yes, but still lithe and expressive as he moved them for emphasis. I wondered what they would have felt like as they helped me learn how to ride a bike or tie a shoe. I bet he would have been able to do a little girl's hair too.

"Had you known, would you have given up the priesthood for me?"

The words came out before my brain even realized they materialized somewhere in the dark creases of its folds.

"Yes," he said without hesitation. "But until your wedding day, I had no idea you even existed."

"You left so suddenly. Didn't Jude blame it on the crabs?"

"He did."

"You were so pale."

"Well, you can imagine what was going through me at the time."

"I'm sorry."

"No. No, Mary-Margaret. I never want to hear those words come out of your mouth. If anyone suffered in this situation, it was you. You didn't deserve any of it. Honestly, I don't know how you turned out so well. Other than the grace of God," he added quickly.

I laughed. I wasn't about to tell him. But he was right. Maybe my life didn't seem to be one fraught with tension and horrible people, but it was only that way because I was protected. I suppose I could have rebelled against the Divine plan, but honestly, deep in my bones I knew I wouldn't escape, and can I just admit something I've never admitted to anyone? I was afraid to do anything else. I'd lost my mother, had no father, no family. What else could God take from me to put me back on the straight and narrow? My legs? My art? No, I wasn't about to take that kind of chance.

Jesus asked a lot of me, yes, but it all worked out in the end, didn't it? And these days, that's something nobody wants to hear about. But I tell you this, my sisters, because sometimes it takes many decades for it all to become clear. If I had been writing this story just after Jude died, or following my hysterectomy after John was born, the tone would be quite different.

~~

My life wasn't perfect, sisters, but here I am, telling the tale. There's always something to be said for the ability to pass on the details.

But I've rambled. I'm a bit tired after the funeral. And so sad. I haven't cried like that in years. God knit Precious and me together in her listening silence.

My father finished the tale with his confession, one I knew I wasn't the only one to hear. "I stayed with her in that room, cleaning up her vomit and her diarrhea, wiping her forehead when the fever raged. And I loved her. Perhaps it was because I was so weakened and tired from helping her, but the night before we left, she took me in her arms and you were the result. Not that I knew that then." He cleared his throat. "I'd had a past I'd left behind only a few years before. Believe me, it's easier to go back to where you've been than to where you never were."

I nodded. "What happened after that?"

"I was ecstatic! Happy and in love with her and I had so many plans. All that night I lay in bed dreaming of running off, leaving seminary, of course, but I had a little money that would tide us over, and perhaps just get an advanced degree in theology and teach at a seminary somewhere. Of course, those were just rushed thoughts of a person destined to save lives, hers being no exception, and who knows if it would have all worked out that way. I wasn't the only one involved in the matter. Honestly, I didn't have much time to think beyond that."

His voice strengthened a bit and his closed eyes held the memories in tightly.

"What did my mother say about all that?"

"It never came to that, you see. I remember falling asleep at daybreak, I was so excited, you see, and fell into a dead slumber after having been up most of the night, and I was simply exhausted after caring for her." He gripped the pew in front of him. "She was gone, Mary-Margaret. When I woke up, she'd left. And I

tried to find her. People only knew her first name, and in
Maryland . . ."

"It's a pretty Catholic state," I said, my voice dropping.

"It is. Do you know what happened to her after that? Jude
kept mum as you might expect."

I inhaled deeply. "She came back to the island pregnant, but
I don't know how far along she was. Grandmom took care of her
and when she had me, she hemorrhaged and bled to death right
there in the bedroom. My grandmother raised me, but she died
when I was seven and I went to live with the sisters at St. Mary's."

"John did tell me about that when I started as his spiritual
companion. I asked him about his maternal grandfather and he
said both of those grandparents were dead."

"As far as he knew, that was his truth. I just thought it was
easier that way. Too much mystery . . ." I laid my hand atop the
one he'd curled over the top of the pew. "I didn't know what else
to say. And I could have been right. I just didn't know."

"Did your grandmother give you any idea what happened?"

"I don't think she really knew. She had her ideas. My mother
had lied so much to her, as you might imagine."

"Were they even close to the truth? At least about me?"

"All I really knew about you was that you were a seminarian.
She told me my mother was about to say her final vows."

"Oh my," he said.

"She said you raped her."

Though it was dim, I watched as the color drained from his
face.

I reached out and held him as the words sank into both of
us, at the massive injustice the lie had done to both of us. He
was a good man, he'd have been a good father, and here we sat,
seven decades later.

"But here you sit, T—." Jesus sat down on the bench in
front of us.

I hugged my father. "We have a lot to make up for and we're both old."

He kissed me on the forehead and wiped away my tears, then his own.

Who was Mary Margaret the First? I believe that is the saddest part of this tale. My grandmother didn't know her and neither did Aunt Elfi. Perhaps I'll find out someday. And yet, maybe it's time to put the dear soul to rest, someone who'd beg for money, lie to those who loved her, and yet, who gave me life and sacrificed her own in the process.

Yes, rest in peace, Mary Margaret.

And rest in peace, Mary-Margaret, you have found your father and have borne a son, and have grown old with your sisters.

Rest in peace.

I CAN'T BELIEVE I'M COMING TO THE END OF MY TALE AND I think it's only fair I tell you how Jude left us.

In the end, he gave his life for someone like all of us, someone unfaithful and completely undeserving of a sacrifice like that. I suppose, for the faithful follower of Christ, it comes down to that eventually—if not literally, than in some other way. Perhaps we're called to serve a belligerent, selfish spouse, or tend to ungrateful children or parents. Perhaps we serve in a church or parish that expects too much and what we do is immediately criticized. Perhaps our boss gets all the credit for our hard work. I don't know. But as a wise friend of mine, an Orthodox nun, once said, "Dedicated Christian life can be summed up like this: 'Get on that cross and hold still.'"

Not exactly bumper sticker material, that!

But true?

If we heed Saint Paul's words that we are crucified with Christ, then indeed, I'd say my friend is right.

The night Jude died, the off-season was in full swing. Early December in Ocean City would be categorized as bleak by the beachgoer, but for us, it was a time of reflection, building, and renewal. We worked on kites for the coming season and by that time we'd built a studio for me in the backyard. I didn't have the

space or the materials for my larger sculptures, and Morpheus
there in Georgia was cornering the market for intriguing bent
wood designs. So I began sculpting with clay and I found charcoal a most satisfying substance to manipulate on the paper I
began making myself—crude-edged, chunky paper at least an
eighth of an inch thick.

St. Francis's on Locust Island needed new Stations of the
Cross, so I made bronze reliefs that I ended up selling copies of
to several churches. The years were kind for me and my work.
Still no recognition or gallery showings, but Jesus sat with me
quite a bit in my little shed and told me how much he liked what
I was doing.

Jude took care of the kite shop on his own except from
Memorial Day to Labor Day when I joined him there on the
Boardwalk. We anchored kites to deep stakes we drove into the
sand, some of them dipping and diving, others just soaring,
scanning the horizon of the Atlantic. To some he attached
twirling whirligigs; others made flapping sounds and whistles
and screeches.

We didn't realize how many kite enthusiasts flocked to the
beach, and Jude found himself taking special orders that he'd
mostly work on through the off-months. Oh, the shop was
adorable there in a little frame house from 1902. We painted
the shingle siding the blue of the sky and the trim, the porch
spindles, and supports a lime green. I painted a new sign every
year and after about five years it became a tradition for people
to walk the boards, stop in front of our store, and see what that
year's sign looked like. Some were pretty, with birds and flowers, or fish and butterflies. We did Olympic themes and the
Bicentennial year's sign reminded me of something on *Schoolhouse
Rock!* My favorite sign sported a peacock and an owl, birds rep-
resenting Jude and myself, I suppose. Although I don't view the
owl as wisdom, more as something with an ancient outlook.

John continued excelling in science and math, winning state competitions in chemistry and physics during high school. He wasn't popular, as he didn't have an athletic bone in his body, but he was so friendly and laid-back, nobody gave him much trouble. He learned early on that being unflappable was the best way to coast under the radar and get done what he needed. He's been successful at his mission because of this very trait. The day he realized he could be a physician *and* a priest, when he was in seminary, he called me. His voice was infused with relief. "I mean, I knew I wanted to be a priest, Mom, but there was more to it and I just couldn't figure out the other piece. But I met this Jesuit named Father Ignatius today." And he rattled on from there.

John finished his undergraduate degree in two years, utilizing CLEP tests and every summer and micro session. And, well, sisters, you're basically caught up on John, so I won't say any more about that here.

The last summer, though we didn't know it was the last, Jude finally allowed me to do a lighthouse theme for our sign. He finally got over his aversion to them and I told him I'd do the typical conical variety, not the screwpile type that still stands out on Bethlehem Point.

John was in his second year of seminary when it happened. I was fifty-six and Jude fifty-eight. The life of St. Mary's felt so far behind me, except for Angie, who'd join us for her vacations, regaling us with tales of her exciting life all over the world. She never made me feel bad either. Having once been married, sexually active, and, well, Angie's celibacy came hard, she said more than once, "I may have all these battle scars, Mary, but you sleep regularly with the best-looking guy in the state. Let's just be honest."

And I'd laugh.

You see, I did come to love Jude with that sweet married

couple love, and I was blessed not to take him for granted. Sure, he began as a study in holy obedience, but it all turned into something sweet and satisfying. Sort of like a warm donut fresh from the fryer compared to chocolate mousse.

We had tough times like all couples do, life wasn't perfect. Jude never lost his rough edge and I could get "a little nun-nish" as he called it. But we could iron out the wrinkles as they emerged. My goodness, I never knew how marriage could unleash a redheaded woman's temper at times! Jude thought it was hilarious, and that made me even more angry.

The night Jude left, December 12, was quite mild. We'd just come back from a thirty-day spiritual retreat, and it was one of those sorts of days in December along the coast where the wind blows a little warm and the sun shines quite golden in response, it seems. That day was no different. We decided to walk across Ocean Highway and into town to get a beer at one of the few open bars that time of year. The Dutch Mill. Right on the Boardwalk.

Now, it sounds awfully friendly and Jude worked his way around the rougher element quite well, not surprisingly, but The Dutch Mill should have been called "The Bike Lane." The people there all knew him from the mission and they respected him. No one could pull the wool over Jude's eyes and they liked him for it. The bar was filled with locals mostly, bikers—some of whom had been on our deck at times for crabs or ribs (Jude had become fond of grilling ribs)—and some of the working girls who were tying one on to get through the night pounding the sidewalks in their six-inch heels. At least it wasn't going to be quite so cold that night.

Two strangers walked in, dressed in suits and ties, but the fine clothing seemed more like costumage than daily garb. Their atti-tudes were more suited to glitzy, low-cut shirts and tight pants.

Nevertheless, they didn't bother anybody, ordering beers and smoking cigarettes at the bar.

Jude nursed his drink, as did I, and we chatted with a biker couple named Janet and Ron as my husband smoked cigarette after cigarette. He never could break that habit. Honestly, he never really tried.

"After what I did, this is the least of my worries," he always said.

I nagged him about it a little after John was born, but Jesus sat beside me one evening and said, "Let it be, T—. It's not going to matter in the long run."

I didn't realize then, of course, that Jude wouldn't live long enough to develop lung cancer or emphysema. Still, I was glad for the heads-up. It saved us a lot of arguing.

It was important, all through those twenty-seven years, that I be on Jude's side. I can't say it any more simply than that.

So we sat there chatting with our rough-around-the-edges friends, laughing at their crazy stories from the seventies, when one of the working girls got up, stumbled a little as she walked toward the door, teetering into one of the strangers, a guy named Ted.

He turned and grabbed her arm. He'd thrown back at least four beers with a couple of shots. Don't ask me why, it must be the morality meter inside of me, but I count people's drinks. Anybody within eyeshot is going to get a tally in my brain. Isn't that ridiculous? It does wonders for the short-term memory, however.

She cried out. Her name was Barb. I liked her. Had been in Ocean City for about seven years. Runaway. Typical story other than the fact that she was headed for valedictorian and could do long division, and I mean looooooong division, in her head.

Of course, Jude sprang to his feet to try and defuse the situation, and Ted's friend, a man named Dale, did as well. What we didn't know then was that Ted had recently returned from the men's room after taking a hit of PCP.

He reached into his boot and pulled out a knife. He drove it right into Jude's chest and, quicker than you can blink, yanked it out and lodged it into the side of my husband's neck.

Jude went down and Ted scrambled out of the bar.

I saw it all. God help me, I wish I hadn't. The shock in his eyes, the dawning, but not fear. Actually, thinking about it, he looked a little ticked off at first. I don't wish to describe the noises from him and the blood. It's still too much to bear and so you must grant me a little grace in the telling of this.

There we all were, the people who he'd helped at the mission, jumping from our seats and rushing over as he crumbled.

I didn't scream or cry. I just reached under his shoulders as the bartender called the police (and more people quickly left). Even as I held him that day years before on the bay as we sat on the hood of Mrs. Bray's old station wagon and he cried and wailed as life returned to him like blood into a sleeping append-age, I held him as that same life seeped out. He couldn't speak, he just reached for my hand and looked into my eyes. I curved my other hand around his cheek. "Hang on, Jude. It won't be long before the paramedics are here."

He smiled, one corner of his mouth barely lifting. He mouthed the words, "Thank you." And then it was done.

It was done.

～

He'd lost too much blood. The paramedics couldn't save him. I stayed with his body as long as I could, slept little that night, waiting up for John, who came home right away. Together we paced in the coroner's office as the autopsy was done the next day, and rode back to Locust Island, following the hearse that transported Jude's body to the only funeral home in Abbeyville. John and I wept and laughed during the two-hour drive, remem-bering husband and father. I felt a little saddened by the fact that John didn't know just what a transformation had occurred, how God can work so thoroughly, binding a human life to his Own and saying, "It is good."

~⌒

A young couple bought the shop and our house the next year, just after my final season. He'd just inherited enough money to make a go of business but not enough to live on the interest. She did hair and was planning on having a shop on the upper floor where Jude had his workshop. I liked them. They bickered lovingly and liked kites. They didn't want to live a normal life and I told them buying The Kite Shack was a good start.

I contacted the School Sisters of St. Mary's and after several steps and a couple of years, I entered the order, taking my final vows and coming back to the school on Locust Island.

After all those years, I was truly a sister in the place I always wanted to be. Five years later it became the assisted-living village. How's that for irony? But I found out I belonged more to the island than to teaching and was only too glad to stay. Oh, and I'd had so many exciting plans as a young woman, ready to follow Jesus into the darkest places and up to the brightest suns.

It wasn't the same without Jude, though. The place just wasn't the same. And Gerald and Hattie weren't needed to man Bethlehem Point any longer.

Thank goodness Jesus told me I was exactly where I was supposed to be. And Angie returned after a while to pick up where we left off. When the Bray cottage went up for sale a decade ago, I bought it and gave it to the school with the provision that we be allowed to live out our lives there and serve at St. Mary's Village.

Sister Thaddeus, still sharp, and believe it or not, still elegant, thought it was the best idea she'd heard in years.

I think Jude would have agreed.

FEAST OF THE ASCENSION, 2010

I suppose I should tell you what happened to Mary after this because she left this book by accident in Africa with John. When he came home for her funeral seven years later, he gave the book to me and now I'm finally sitting down to tell the rest of the story. So, no. Nobody found it in her underwear drawer. But it was me who cried over each piece of her belongings that we either threw away, kept for posterity, or sent to St. Vincent de Paul's thrift store in Salisbury.

As you can see by what is written here, I'm more of a doer than a teller. I told Mary-Francis that she'd better not expect a memoir from me. And I'm not nearly the upstart Mary says I am.

I miss her more than I can say. She was my life's companion.

Mary-Margaret was extremely busy the last seven years of her life. She brought Father Ignatius back to Mercy House and cared for him for almost two years until his death. Oh, we loved having the old man around and the love they had for each other seemed to have collected over all those years only to be dumped on them all at once. She'd wheel him out to Bethlehem Point and they'd sit and read for hours on end. She also took care of Samkela from afar, ensuring he had school fees, food, and clothing. The rest of us left at Mercy House picked up the torch after she passed away.

Mary continued to teach arts and crafts here at St. Mary's Village, wept beside me the day we buried Sister Thaddeus in Baltimore, and probably the most unusual part of the story happened before her father died.

It tickles me to see Father Joe talking about having "a little money." The man came from an old shipbuilding family and, although he had to give up his inheritance when he took the vow of poverty, he told his brother about Mary-Margaret. Monies were put in trust for her upon his death. You can imagine the interest that accrued.

As life sometimes does, opportunity meets up with resources and Mary found herself the proud owner of a lighthouse. The Coast Guard, making the decision to decommission the structure, and rightly so with the computer navigation ships use these days, was planning on scrapping it.

Mary took her inheritance, bought it for a few thousand dollars, and had it moved to St. Mary's. With the rest of her inheritance the order built another school. The girls give tours for a small fee and it helps keep the school running. She said things needed to be made right about that place. I like the fact that the light is still revolving. What a gift.

Believe it or not, as of this writing, Gerald is still living nearby on that boat and he volunteers on Tuesdays at the lighthouse. People who are privy to his tours of course learn more than they bargained for.

I should tell about Mary's death. We found her upright at the kneeler in her bedroom, a candle burning before her crucifix, her head upright, neck stiff. Her expression was one of such tender joy we hated to close her eyes. But close them we did. Now, after reading this, I know she was looking at her dearest Friend who'd come to collect her as promised. Her final time on this earth was with him. I wish I could write down for you what that was like, for that, truly, was the final chapter to this story.

I miss her. I'd recommend her for sainthood, but she'd yell at me for eternity, so perhaps someone else will have to get that ball rolling. As it stands, though, I finally got her a gallery showing. Mostly drawings of Jude. One of her portfolios was marked My Best Friend and Life's Companion and inside all of the pages were blank. Most mysterious at the time. Now I know.

So, School Sisters of St. Mary's who will follow us old gals,

I don't know what you may take from this little collection of stories and thoughts. But I hope you find peace in the journey and strength for your calling. And when you want to sit in quiet by the lighthouse, there's a bench that Father John donated. Just behind it lays a garden of glorious white daffodils Mary finally planted. If you go there in the spring, close your eyes, and allow the love of God to enfold you as it did the Kellers. Pray for renewal and resurrection. It's always a good time for that.

Glory be to the Father, and to the Son, and to the Holy Spirit. As it was in the beginning, is now, and will be forever, world without end. Amen.

Sister Angie

Acknowledgments, with thanks to God for:

   Sister Ellen Kehoe, who read the manuscript and loves my kids to pieces. Father Walt Bado, SJ, my pastor and spiritual advisor, who encourages me, writer to writer. Father Tom Farrell, also my pastor, who answered a lot of questions by e-mail and in person. Sister Iris Ann Ledden, SSND, whose teaching stories provided so much for the story.

   Ami, Erin, Allen, Natalie, Katie, Jeane, Jennifer, Rachelle, all the fiction gang, sales gang, and marketing gang.

   My agent, Chip MacGregor.

   My family. My friends. My fellow pilgrims. My readers.

   Fellow NFs: Claudia and Alana

   Especially: Will, Ty, Jake, and Gwynnie.

READING GROUP GUIDE

1. Did it surprise you to learn that not all religious sisters wear habits? Did you know that they use such modern technologies as cell phones and computers? Were there other characteristics about being a religious that you found interesting?

2. What did you think about Mary-Margaret's discussions with Jesus? Were they real?

3. Mary-Margaret says she prayed for Jude "without words" (p147). Have you prayed without words?

4. Have you ever felt Jesus calling you to do something that was in complete opposition to what you expected? How did you handle the situation?

5. Mary-Margaret says that her Grandmother "didn't emote much" but she "showed her affection in her sewing" (p147). Are you loved by anyone this way? Do you love anyone this way?

6. When asked if Mary-Margaret could have both Jesus and have a child, she replied, "I don't know. I've never even thought of that as a possibility" (p143). Do you know anybody who feels it's impossible to love Jesus completely and yet be happily married with children? Do you think the two are mutually exclusive?

7. Do you think Mary-Margaret felt she had to become a sister given the way her mother died?

8. Mary-Margaret cannot seem to make the time to plant the bulbs that Jude gave her. Is this a metaphor for something else?

9. What did you think of the author's circular way of storytelling? Why do you suppose she wrote it in this manner?

LISA SAMSON is the award-winning author of twenty-six books including *Quaker Summer*, *Christianity Today's* Novel of 2008, and *Justice in the Burbs*, which she co-wrote with her husband, Will, a professor of Sociology. When not at home in Kentucky with her three children, one cat, and six chickens, she speaks around the country about writing and social justice, encouraging the people of God to "do justice, love mercy, and walk humbly with God." She loves nothing better than sitting around her kitchen table, talking with family and friends, old and new.